Jojo Moyes

NIGHT MUSIC

HODDER &
STOUGHTON

First published in Great Britain in 2008 by Hodder & Stoughton
An Hachette Livre UK company

5

Copyright © Jojo Moyes 2008

The right of Jojo Moyes to be identified as the Author
of the Work has been asserted by her in accordance with the
Copyright, Designs and Patents Act 1988.

A CIP catalogue record for this title is available
from the British Library

Trade paperback ISBN 978 0 340 89595 5
Hardback ISBN 978 0 340 89594 8

Typeset in Plantin Light by Palimpsest Book Production Limited,
Grangemouth, Stirlingshire

Printed and bound by
Clays Ltd, St Ives plc

Hodder and Stoughton's policy is to use papers that are natural,
renewable and recyclable products and made from wood
grown in sustainable forests. The logging and manufacturing
processes are expected to conform to the environmental

To Charles

And to anyone who has ever
considered getting the builders in

It is a dragon that has devoured us all: these obscene, scaly houses, this insatiable struggle and desire to possess, to possess always and in spite of everything, this need to be an owner, lest one be owned.

D. H. Lawrence

We never really belonged in the Spanish House. Technically, I suppose, we owned it, but ownership suggests some level of control and no one who knew us – or the house – could ever have suggested that we had any control over what happened there.

And despite what it said on those bits of paper, it never felt as if it truly belonged to us. It felt too crowded from the start. You could almost feel other people's dreams projected on it, sense the waves of envy, or distrust, or desire that permeated its walls. Its history was not our history. There was nothing – not even our dreams – binding us to it.

When I was little, I thought a house was just a house. A place in which we ate and played and argued and slept, four walls between which we got on with the business of living. I never gave it much thought.

Much later, I learned that a house could be so much more than that – that it could be the culmination of someone's desires, a reflection of how they saw themselves, how they wished to see themselves, that it could make people behave in ways that disgraced or shamed them. I learned that a house – just bricks, mortar, wood, perhaps a little patch of land – could be an obsession.

When I leave home I'm going to rent.

One

Laura McCarthy closed her back door, stepped over the sleeping dog that was dribbling peacefully on to the gravel, and walked briskly across the garden to the back gate. Balancing the laden tray on one arm, she opened it, slid nimbly through the gap, and went into the woods and down to the stream, which, it being late summer, had dried up again.

It took two steps to cross the planks with which Matt had breached the ditch the previous year. Before long it would rain and they would be slippery and treacherous again. Several times, the previous year, she had skidded while crossing, and once the tray's entire contents had ended up in the water, a feast for some unseen creature. Then she was up the other side, the soil damp and sticking to the soles of her shoes, making her way towards the clearing.

Out of the shade the evening sun was still warm, bathing the valley in balmy, pollen-laden light. In the distance she could see a thrush, and hear the peculiar, abrasive chatter of starlings as they rose in a cloud and settled again on a distant copse. She straightened the lid of one of the dishes, inadvertently releasing a rich, tomatoey scent that made her quicken her pace towards the house.

It had not always been so decrepit, so unapologetically grim. Matt's father had told him tales of shooting parties gathered on the lawns, of summer evenings when music floated from white marquees and elegantly dressed couples perched on the limestone walls and drank punch, their laughter muffled by the forest. Matt remembered a time when the stables had been filled with glossy horses, some kept purely for the benefit of weekend guests, and a boat-house on the edge of the lake for those who liked to row. Once, he had told her these stories often; it had been his way of equating it with her family home, of suggesting their future together would match what she had left behind. Perhaps it was a way to imagine what might lie ahead. She loved those stories. She knew exactly how the house would look if she had her way – there wasn't a window she hadn't mentally dressed, an inch of floor she hadn't re-covered. She knew how the lake looked from every east-facing room.

She stopped at the side door and, out of habit, reached into her pocket for a key. Once, it had been locked daily, but there was little point now: everyone around here knew there was nothing to steal. The house sagged, its paint peeled as if it could no longer be bothered even to reflect on its grand past. Downstairs, several missing panes had been covered with odd bits of wood. The gravel was sparse and over-whelmed by nettles, which brushed malevolently at her shins.

'Mr Pottisworth, it's me . . . Laura.'

She waited until she heard a grunt upstairs. It was wise to alert the old man to one's arrival – the lintel was still peppered with shot from the occasions when she had forgotten. Luckily, her husband had remarked, the old bugger had always had a poor eye.

'I've brought you your dinner.'

She listened for the answering grunt, then went upstairs, the wood creaking under her feet.

She was fit, and barely needed to draw breath after several steep flights of stairs. But all the same she stood for a moment before she opened the door to the master bedroom. What might have been a sigh, or a flicker of resignation, passed through her before she placed her hand on the doorknob.

The window was partially open, but the smell of elderly, unwashed male hit her squarely and sourly, with its attendant, underlying odours of dust-filled soft furnishings, camphor and stale beeswax. An old gun was propped beside the bed, and the colour television they had bought him two years ago stood on a small table. Age and neglect could not disguise the room's elegant dimensions, the way the frames of the bay window neatly bisected the sky. But the visitor's attention was never allowed to linger long on its aesthetic qualities.

'You're late,' said the figure in the old carved mahogany bed.

'Only a few minutes,' she said, deliberately bright. She placed the tray on the table beside him and straightened. 'I couldn't get away. I had my mother on the phone.'

'What did she want? Didn't you tell her I was over here, *starving?*'

Laura's smile barely wavered. 'Believe it or not, Mr Pottisworth, you are not always my sole topic of conversation.'

'I bet Matt is, though. What's he been up to now, then? She ring you up to tell you you'd married beneath you, did she?'

Laura turned to the tray. If there was a slight stiffening in her back, Mr Pottisworth failed to see it. 'I've been married eighteen years,' she said. 'I hardly think my choice of husband is breaking news.'

There was a loud sniff. 'What is it? I bet it's cold.'

'Chicken casserole with a baked potato. And it's not remotely cold. It's had a lid on.'

'I bet it's cold. Lunch was cold.'

'Lunch was salad.'

A mottled head, with a scattering of grey hair, emerged from beneath the quilt. Two snake-lidded eyes rested on her and narrowed. 'What you want to wear your trousers so tight for? You trying to show everyone what you've got?'

'They're jeans. It's how everyone wears them.'

'You're trying to get me overheated, that's what. Trying to get me all befuddled with lust so you can kill me with your treacherous feminine ways. Black widow, that's what they call women like you. I *know*.'

She ignored him. 'I've brought you up some brown sauce for the potato. Do you want it on the side of your plate?'

'I can see your nubbles.'

'Or would you prefer grated cheese?'

'Through that top. I can clearly see your nubbles. Are you trying to tempt me?'

'Mr Pottisworth, if you don't stop carrying on, I won't bring you your dinner any more. So stop looking at my . . . my . . . nubbles. Right now.'

'Shouldn't wear saucy little see-through brassières like that, then. Back in my day a respectable woman wore a vest. A good cotton vest.' He raised himself against his pillows, the gnarled hands twitching with remembrance. 'You could still get a good feel, though.'

Laura McCarthy counted to ten, making sure her back was to the old man. She looked down surreptitiously at her T-shirt, trying to work out how much of her brassière he could actually see. Last week he had told her his eyesight was failing.

'You sent that boy of yours up with my lunch. Hardly says a word to me.' The old man had begun to eat. A sound not unlike a blocked drain clearing filled the room.

'Yes, well, teenage boys don't have a lot to say for themselves.'

'Rude, that's what he is. You should tell him.'

'I will,' she said. She moved around the room, clearing glasses and mugs and placing them on the empty tray.

'I get lonely in the day. I've only had Byron in since lunch, and all he wants to talk about is ruddy hedgerows and rabbits.'

'I've told you, you could have someone in from social services. They'd tidy up a bit, have a chat. Every day, if you wanted.'

'Social services.' He grimaced, a thin rivulet of gravy running down his chin. 'I don't need that lot sticking their noses into my business.'

'Suit yourself.'

'You don't know how hard it is, when you're all alone . . .' he began, and Laura's attention drifted. She knew his litany of woes by heart: that no one understood how hard it was to have none of your family left, to be bedridden and helpless, at the mercy of strangers . . . She had heard all the variations on that theme so many times she could have recited it herself.

'. . . course I've only got you and Matt, a poor old man like me. Got no one to hand down my worldly goods to . . . You don't know how it pains a man to be so alone.' His voice diminished, and he was almost tearful.

She softened. 'I've told you you're not alone. Not as long as we're next door.'

'I'll show you my gratitude when I'm gone. You know that, don't you? That furniture in the barn – that's yours after I'm gone.'

'You don't have to talk like that, Mr Pottisworth.'

'That won't be all, I'm a man of my word. And I'm mindful of all you've done for me these years . . .' He peered at the tray. 'That my rice pudding?'

'It's a nice apple crumble.'

The old man put down his knife and fork. 'But it's Tuesday.'

'Well, I've made you apple crumble. I'd run out of pudding rice and I didn't have a chance to get to the supermarket.'

'I don't like apple crumble.'

'You do.'

'I bet you helped yourself to apples out of my orchard.'

Laura took a deep breath.

'I bet you're not half as good as you make out. I bet you'd lie for something you really wanted.'

Her voice emerged through gritted teeth. 'I bought the apples from the supermarket.'

'You said you never had time to get to the supermarket.'

'I bought them three days ago.'

'Don't see why you couldn't have got a bit of pudding rice at the same time. Don't know what your old man must think of you. No doubt you have to keep him happy in other ways . . .' He grinned salaciously, his gums briefly visible under wet lips, then got stuck into the chicken casserole.

Laura had finished the washing-up when he came in, and was stooped over the ironing-board furiously steaming and flattening the collars and cuffs of his shirts into compliance.

'All right, love?' Matt McCarthy bent to kiss her, noting the flushed cheeks, the steely set of her jaw.

'No, I'm not bloody all right. I've had it.'

He removed his work jacket, pockets sagging with tape measures and tools, and threw it over the back of a chair. He was exhausted, and the thought of having to pacify Laura irritated him.

'Mr P's been peeking at her bits,' said Anthony, with a smirk. Their son's feet were resting on the coffee-table as he watched television and his father swept them off with one hand as he passed.

'He did what?' Matt's tone hardened. 'I'll go and have a word with—'

She slammed the iron down. 'Oh, sit down, for goodness' sake. You know what he's like. Anyway, it's not that, it's the way he has me running backwards and forwards like his personal servant. Every single day. I've had it this time. Really.'

When she had realised the old man would not let up, she had returned home and brought him back tinned rice pudding, muttering under her breath as she crossed the wood back to the big house, the bowl covered with a folded tea-towel.

'It's cold,' he had said, dipping in a finger.

'It's not. It was heated only ten minutes ago.'

'It's cold.'

'Well, Mr Pottisworth, it's not easy getting food over from our house without it losing a little heat.'

His mouth had turned down in a *moue* of disapproval. 'Don't want it now. Lost my appetite.'

His eyes flicked back to her, and perhaps he noticed the tic in her cheek. She was wondering, briefly, whether it was possible to kill someone with a kitchen tray and a dessert spoon. 'Stick it down there. I might have it later.' He folded thin arms across his chest. 'When I'm desperate, like.'

'Mum says she's calling social services,' said Anthony. 'She reckons they can deal with him.'

Matt, about to settle on the sofa beside him, felt a stab of alarm. 'Don't be daft. They'll put him in a home.'

'So what? Someone else'll have to put up with him and check his non-existent bed sores, wash his sheets and take him two meals a day. Good!'

Suddenly energised, Matt stood up. 'He's got no bloody money. They'll get him to sign over his house to pay for it, won't they? Use your loaf, woman.'

She faced him. She was a handsome woman, lean and agile in her late thirties, but now her face, flushed and cross, was that of a recalcitrant child. 'I don't care. I'm telling you, Matt, I've had enough.'

He stepped forward swiftly and put his arms round her. 'Come on, love. He's on his last legs.'

'Nine years, Matt,' she said stiffly into his chest. 'Nine years I've been at his beck and call. When we moved in you said he wouldn't last the year.'

'And think of all those lovely acres, the walled garden, the stableyard . . . Think of the beautiful dining room you've planned. Think of us, a happy family, standing in the doorway . . .' He let this vision float in front of her, re-establishing its roots in her imagination. 'Look, the old fool's bedridden. He's falling apart at the seams. He's not going to last much longer, is he? And who's he got, apart from us?' He kissed the top of her head. 'The loans are in place, and I've even got Sven to draw up the plans. I'll show you them later, if you want.'

'There you are, Mum. Put like that, it doesn't hurt to show him your nubbles every now and then, does it?' Anthony chuckled, then yelped as a laundered T-shirt shot out and caught him sharply on his ear.

'Just a bit longer,' said Matt, his voice low and intimate. 'Come on, love. Hang on in there, eh?' He felt her soften and knew he had her.

He squeezed her waist, allowing his fingers to suggest some form of private compensation later that evening. He felt her answering squeeze and wished he had not made that diversion earlier to see the barmaid from the Long Whistle. You'd better die soon, you old bugger, he told Pottisworth silently. I don't know how much longer I can keep this up.

★   ★   ★

A short distance across the valley, in the master bedroom at the big house, the old man chortled at a comedy programme. As the credits rolled, he checked the time and tossed his newspaper to the end of the bed.

Outside an owl hooted and a distant fox barked, perhaps guarding its territory. Animals and humans were no different, he thought wryly, when it came to staking their claim. The fox, with his spraying and fighting, wasn't too far from Laura McCarthy, with her twice-daily dinners and her fussing with clean sheets and whatnot. All marking their patch somehow.

He fancied a bit of chocolate. With an agility that might have surprised his neighbours, he climbed out of bed and padded across the floor to the cupboard where he kept his little treats, the sweets and tasties he paid Byron to fetch when he went to town. He opened the door and ferreted behind books and files until he found the smooth plastic wrapping. His fingers closed round what felt like a KitKat and he pulled it out, anticipating the delight of melted chocolate in his mouth, and wondering whether it was worth putting his teeth back in.

First he closed the cupboard door. No point in Laura knowing anything, he thought. Best if she thought him help-less. Women like her had to feel needed. He grinned to himself, thinking of the way her ears had reddened when he'd mentioned the tightness of her jeans. It was easy to wind her up. High point of his day. He'd start on her about riding horses tomorrow, about how she must do it for the thrill – that always got her riled.

He was still smirking as he walked across the floor and heard the theme tune to another of his favourite shows. He glanced up. Lost in the music, he did not see the bowl of rice pudding on the floor, congealing where he had left it earlier. His bony old foot landed in it heel first and he slid smoothly across the boards.

At least, this was what the coroner pieced together when the final hours of Samuel Pottisworth's life were laid out painstakingly before the court. The thud his head made as it met the floor would have been loud enough to hear some two floors below. Still, as Matt McCarthy pointed out, so deep in the woods where all noise was deadened, things went unnoticed. It was a place where almost anything could happen.

Two

'Say please.'

Theresa glared at him.

Matt shifted. He fixed his eyes on hers. Her mascara had smudged, making her seem rather sluttish. Then again, Theresa was always a bit sluttish, even when she was dressed in her smartest clothes. It was one of the things he liked about her. 'Say please.'

She closed her eyes, locked in some internal struggle. 'Matt—'

'Say. Please.' He lifted himself on to his elbows so that no part of him was touching her, save, perhaps, his feet. 'Go on,' he said quietly. 'You have to ask.'

'Matt, I just—'

'Please.'

Theresa wiggled her hips upwards, in a desperate attempt to meet his, but he moved out of reach. 'Say it.'

'Oh, you—' She gasped as he lowered his head and ran his lips along her neck, her collarbone, his body still raised tantalisingly above her. She was enjoyably easy to fire up, easier than most to keep at a peak. Her eyes closed, and she began to moan. He could taste the sweat, a cool film on her skin. She had been like this for almost three-quarters of an hour. 'Matt . . .'

'Say it.' His lips went to her ear, and his voice became a low rumble as he smelled the perfume of her hair, the muskier scents between them. How easy it would be to let go, to allow himself to give in to the sensation. But it was sweeter to keep some control.

'Say it.'

Theresa's eyes half opened, and he saw that the fight had gone out of them. Her lips parted. 'Please,' she whispered. Then, grasping him, all pretence at decorum gone, 'Oh – *please. Please. Please.*'

Three-quarters of an hour. Matt glanced at his wristwatch. Then, in a fluid movement, he pushed himself backwards off the bed. 'Christ, is that the time already?' He scanned the floor for his jeans. 'Sorry, babe. Got to be somewhere.'

Theresa's hair flopped over her face. 'What? You can't go!'

'Where are my boots? I could have sworn I left them down here.'

She stared at him in disbelief, her skin still flushed. 'Matt! You can't leave me like this!'

'Ah. There they are.' Matt shoved on his work boots, then pecked her on the cheek. 'Gotta go. You can't imagine how rude it would be if I was late.'

'Late? Late for what? Matt!'

He could have stretched it that extra two minutes. It was something few men seemed to understand. But sometimes there was more pleasure in knowing you could have something than actually having it. Matt grinned as he ran lightly down the stairs. He could hear her swearing all the way to the front door.

The funeral of Samuel Frederick Pottisworth took place in the village church on an afternoon so black with glowering rainclouds that night might have come early. He had been the last of the Pottisworths. And as a result, or possibly because he was not the most dearly beloved of men, few people came. The McCarthy family, Mr Pottisworth's doctor, health visitor and solicitor sat in the front pews, spread out a little, perhaps to make the long wooden seats seem busier than they were.

A few rows back, mindful of his traditional position, Byron Firth, his dogs immobile at his feet, ignored the pointed glances and mutterings of the old women in the opposite pew. He was used to it. He had come to accept that there would be wary expressions and whispered asides whenever he had the apparent gall to appear in town, and he had learned long ago to turn to them a face of stone. Besides, he had more urgent matters to consider. As he left home he had overheard his sister on the telephone to her boyfriend, and he had a feeling that she was talking about moving herself and Lily on. He couldn't afford the rent for their house alone, and there weren't many people who were likely to want to share with him and the dogs. More importantly, with the old man gone, it looked like he was out of a job. The estate was paying his wages for now, but that wouldn't last for ever. He flicked through the paper to see if any casual work was going.

A few had come just for the do. Mrs Linnet, the local cleaning lady, made it her business never to miss a good funeral. She could rank them, in terms of turnout, choice of hymns, quality of sausage rolls and joints of ham all the way back to 1955. She had brought with her two of the old women she 'did for'; while they hadn't actually known Mr Pottisworth, they might enjoy the outing, she had told the vicar. Especially as the McCarthys were likely to lay on a good spread, what with Mrs McCarthy knowing how to do things properly. Her kind always did.

And then, at the back, Asad and Henry were pressed close together as they pretended to read from the hymn book.

'Look at them, all dressed up and sitting in the front row like they were family,' said Henry, under his breath.

'Whatever eases their sorrow,' said Asad. A tall man, he had to stoop to ensure that they could both see the words. 'She looks very nice today. I think that coat's new.' In bright red wool, cut in a military style, it glowed in the gloomy confines of the little church.

'They must be expecting to come into some money. She was telling me yesterday he's put down a deposit on one of those flash new four-wheel drives.'

'She deserves it. All those years at the beck and call of that horrible man. I wouldn't have done it.' Asad shook his head. His features, betraying his Somalian heritage, were elegant and a little mournful. He managed in almost all circumstances to resemble a man of dignity, Henry said. Even in his Thomas the Tank Engine pyjamas.

'Which *particular* horrible man are you talking about?' muttered Henry.

The hymn ended. With a shuffle of bottoms on pews, and the soft thud of old hymn books hitting wood, the small congregation settled down for the last part of the service.

'Samuel Pottisworth,' said the vicar, 'was . . . a man . . . who stayed true to himself throughout his life.' He appeared to be stumbling. 'He was one of the most . . . *long-standing* members of our parish.'

'McCarthy's had his eye on that house for years,' said Henry, quietly. 'Look at him standing there with her – like butter wouldn't melt.'

Asad glanced at him quizzically, and then at the couple several rows in front of them.

'You know he was with that Theresa from the pub not half an hour before he got here? Ted Garner came in for some wine gums before I closed the shop. Said he'd seen his van parked outside her cottage.' Henry pulled a face.

'Perhaps she was having some work done,' said Asad, optimistically.

'I've heard she often gets a man in.' Henry adjusted his reading glasses.

'Perhaps she needed her pipes rodded.'

'And he's meant to be very good at banging things in . . .'

The two men began to giggle and battled to straighten their faces as the vicar looked up from his notes, his eyebrows raised in a weary question. Come on, his expression said. Work with me here.

Asad sat up. 'Not that we're ones to gossip,' he murmured.

'Nope. I was just saying so to Mrs Linnet when she came in for some headache pills. That's the second lot the old girl's gone through in three days. No, you won't get gossip in our shop.'

Even though it was a funeral, Matt McCarthy was having trouble ensuring that his face bore the required mournfulness. He wanted to smile. He wanted to sing. Earlier that morning one of the roofers had twice asked him what he was so bloody happy about. 'Lottery numbers come up, have they?' he had said.

'Something like that,' Matt had replied, and disappeared for the fifteenth time, rolled-up plans in hand, to eye the front of the house.

It couldn't have worked out better. Laura had reached the end of her tether with the old goat and, he had to admit, Matt had been worried that last evening. If she had refused to keep seeing to Pottisworth's meals, he would have been done for. In fact, so wonderful had the news been when Laura rang him, her voice tremulous and shocked, that he had made sure he had been with her when the doctor arrived to pronounce the old man dead. Laura had clung to him, believing he had returned because he didn't want her to go through the ordeal alone, but some small part of him – not that he would admit this to anyone – hadn't believed the old bugger could be gone. And that if Matt disappeared too swiftly he might spring up again and announce that he fancied 'a little bit of a roast'.

The service had ended. The little group of mourners went out into the darkening afternoon and clustered together, a few occasionally peering about to gauge what might happen next. It was plain that no one was going to accompany the old man to the graveyard.

'I thought it was very civil of you and Mrs McCarthy to arrange Mr Pottisworth's funeral.' Mrs Linnet laid a feather-light hand on Matt's arm.

'Least we could do,' he said. 'Mr P was like family to us. Especially my wife. I'm sure she's going to miss him.'

'Not many could expect such generosity of spirit from their neighbours in their later years,' said Mrs Linnet.

'And who can say what prompts such acts? He was truly a lucky man.'

Asad Suleyman was beside him, one of the few men in the locality who could make Matt feel short. Among other things. Matt looked up sharply at his words, but Asad's face, as ever, was unreadable. 'Well, you know Laura,' he said. 'Her side of the family likes to see things done properly. Very big on form, my wife.'

'We were just wondering . . . Mr McCarthy . . . whether you were likely to be commiserating Mr Pottisworth's life in any other way today . . .' said Mrs Linnet, from under the brim of her felt hat. Behind her two other old women waited expectantly, handbags clutched to their chests.

'Commis—? Of course. You're all welcome, ladies. We want to give dear old Mr P a proper send-off, don't we?'

'What about you, Mr Suleyman? Will you have to get back to the shop?'

'Oh, no.' Henry Ross had appeared beside him. 'Early closing on Wednesdays. You couldn't have planned it better for us, Mr McCarthy. We'd love to – ah – commiserate.'

'We're all yours.' Asad beamed.

Nothing was going to spoil Matt's day. 'Wonderful,' he said. 'Well, all back to ours, and we can toast him. I'll just go and tell the vicar. Ladies, if you wait by my car, I'll give you a lift down.'

The house that Matt McCarthy had built – or renovated, with his wife's money – had once been the much-smaller coach house, sited on the edge of the woods, before the driveway had been split from that of the Spanish House. From the outside, it was in keeping with the architecture of the area, with its neo-Georgian façade, long, elegant windows and flinted frontage. Inside, however, it was more modern, with downlighting, a large, open-plan sitting room with laminate flooring and a games room in which Matt and his son had last played pool several years before.

It gave on to open countryside, and the two houses were shielded from each other by woods. They were a mile and a half from the village of Little Barton with its pub, school and shop. But the long, winding driveway, which had once allowed easy passage from the nearest main road, was now an overgrown track, rutted and pitted with neglect, so Matt and his wife required sturdy four-wheel drives to leave their house without fear for the undersides of their vehicles. Occasionally Matt would drive the quarter-mile worst part of the track to pick up visitors; twice it had ripped exhausts from elegant, low-slung cars and Matt, who was no fool when it came to business relationships, did not like to start any meeting on an apologetic footing.

Several times he had been tempted to fill in the drive with hardcore, but Laura had persuaded him it was tempting fate. 'Do what you want when the house is ours,' she had said. 'There's no point in spending all that money for someone else's benefit.'

Now the drinks table was loaded with fine wine – far too much, considering the number of people who had shown up, but Matt McCarthy would not have it said that he was a mean host. And a little lubrication smoothed business contacts. He knew that as well as anyone.

'See the old man buried, did you?'

'Someone had to make sure he wasn't going to get back up.' He handed Mike Todd, the local estate agent, a large glass of red wine.

'Is Derek here yet? I imagine he'll want to talk to me about putting it on the market once probate's sorted out. Got to tell you, the plot might be fantastic but it's going to take deep pockets to sort out the old wreck. Last time I was in there was . . . four years ago? And it was falling apart then.'

'It's not in great shape, no.'

'What's it say over the gate? *Cave*? Take care, is it? Sounds about right to me.'

Matt leaned in to him. 'I wouldn't hold your breath, Mike.'

'You know something I don't?'

'Let's just say you might be marketing this property before you look at that one.'

Mike nodded. 'I'd suspected as much. Well . . . I can't say I wouldn't find yours an easier commission to earn. Think there's a few more in the market for a house like this. Did you know our area's been named in one of the Sundays as the next property hot spot?'

'You're going to be busy, then. But you'll do me a good rate?'

'I'll always look after you, Matt, you know that. In fact, let's have a chat later. There's a woman put an offer in on that barn conversion behind the church. She's going to need an awful lot of work doing and I told her I might know just the man. Thought we could both make it worth our while.' He took a long slug of his drink, and smacked his lips. 'Besides, if you're after doing up that old wreck, you'll need all the money you can get.'

It was surprising how many more people turned up to the funeral tea than had for the service, Laura mused. Out of the window the sky had cleared and she could almost smell the musty scent of the woods. She had walked the dog there earlier, and even in September you could detect the subtle change in the air that heralded the approach of autumn. She hauled her attention back to the fruit cake, which sat on a tray in front of her on the work surface, ready to go into the front room. If their guests settled in, as they seemed to be threatening, she would be playing hostess until well past dusk. That was the thing with small communities. They all led such isolated lives that they tended to leap on any event and milk it for all it was worth. At this rate she'd have to get the Cousins to reopen the village shop for her.

'All right, beautiful?'

Matt's arms were round her waist. He had been lovely this past week, cheerful, relaxed, attentive. Much as she felt guilty to admit it, Mr P's death had been a blessing.

'Just wondering how long before chucking-out time,' he murmured.

'The old ladies may need taking home soon. Mrs Linnet's gone all silly on her third gin and Mrs Bellamy's snoring on a pile of coats upstairs.'

'They'll be making passes at the Cousins, next.'

She smiled and put a cake knife on to the tray. Then she turned so that she was facing him. He was as handsome as the day she had met him. The weathering of his face, the lines that spread from the corners of his eyes, only made him more attractive. Sometimes she winced at that; today, filled with wine and relief, she just felt glad of it. 'Everything's going to change now, isn't it?' she said.

'Oh, yes.' He bent to kiss her, and she let her hands slide round him, feeling his familiar shape against her, the taut-ness of muscles primed by hard work. She thought she had probably never held him close without feeling an echo of desire. She kissed him back, feeling a brief, reassuring sense of possession in the pressure of his lips on hers. These were the moments that made it all worthwhile, that made her feel as if he was restored to her. That everything in the past had been an aberration.

'Not interrupting anything, am I?'

Matt lifted his head. 'If you don't know by now, Anthony, we wasted all that money on your biology lessons.'

Laura slid from her husband's grasp and picked up the tray with the cake. 'Your father and I were talking about the future,' she said, 'how good it's looking.'

There were times, thought Matt McCarthy, adjusting himself surreptitiously, when he was pretty pleased to be married to his wife. He watched her as she went into the drawing room, totting up her attributes: waist still narrow, legs shapely, something classy informing her walk. Not a bad old stick, all told.

'You not going out?' he asked his son. 'Thought you'd be

long gone by now.' It took him some moments to grasp that Anthony was not wearing his usual complicit grin.

'Shane gave me a lift back from football.'

'Nice for you.'

'I saw your van outside Theresa Dillon's.'

Matt hesitated. 'So?'

'So – I'm not stupid, you know. And neither is Mum, even though you act like she is.'

Matt's convivial mood evaporated. He fought to keep his voice light. 'I've no idea what you're talking about.'

'Right.'

'Are you accusing me of something?'

'You told Mum you were coming straight from the builders' merchants. That's fourteen miles the other side of the church.'

So this is it, Matt thought. His anger was partially offset by pride that his son wasn't a fool and that he wasn't afraid of his father. That he had grown some balls. 'Listen, Inspector bloody Clouseau, I stopped off because Theresa rang and asked me to give her an urgent quote for putting in some new windows, not that it's any of your business.'

The boy said nothing, just stared at him in a way that told Matt he was disbelieved. He was wearing that ridiculous woollen hat, low over his brow.

'After she rang me I worked out there was nothing I needed from the builders' merchants that I couldn't get tomorrow,' he added.

Anthony looked at his feet.

'You really think I'd treat your mother like that? After everything she's been doing for this family – and that old man?' He might have had him then – he saw uncertainty in his eyes. Matt's response was instinctive – never admit, never explain – and had got him out of God only knew how many holes.

'I don't know, do I?'

'No, you don't. So next time use your brain before you open your mouth.' He had him now. 'You've spent too much time in the village. I told your mother we should have brought you up somewhere busier.' He tapped his head. 'People round here have got nothing going on in their lives, so they like to make up stories, let their imaginations run riot. Bloody hell – listen to you! You're as bad as those old women out there.'

'I saw her with you before, remember?' Anthony said, angrily.

'So I'm not allowed to flirt with anyone now, right? Talk to a pretty woman? Shall I look at the ground as I walk so I don't catch anyone's eye? Perhaps we can ask Mrs Linnet to knit me a burka.'

Anthony shook his head.

'Listen, son, you might be sixteen, but you've still got a bit of growing up to do. If you think your mother would prefer me to be some kind of poodle, you don't understand very much about human nature. Now, why don't you go and find yourself something more useful to do than playing Miss Marple? And get a bloody haircut.'

As he slammed the kitchen door, Anthony's back was bent with defeat.

The afternoon slid into dusk and then darkness, the densely woven blanket of night creeping down until the house, with the trees and fields, was smothered in the immutable black of deep country. Behind the glowing windows of the McCarthy house, the mourners had shown little sign of leaving. In fact, they had shown little sign of mourning. As the drink had slipped down, the stories of Samuel Pottisworth had become steadily less reverential, until the greyed woollen long johns he had worn even into summer, and his rather fruity suggestions to the pretty young health visitor had become conversational currency.

No one was quite sure whose idea it had been for the party to transfer to the big house. But somehow, fuelled by increased merriment, and an explosive burst of laughter, the french windows had been opened. Laura was trailing after her husband when she saw where the straggling group was going.

Outside the air was unusually warm and still thick with the calls of wild creatures and the swinging beams of the torches; the woods were alive with feet slithering down banks, the rustle of the first leaves of autumn underfoot, and the squeals of the older ladies as they tried to negotiate their way in the gloom.

'And he wasn't beyond making a pass at my wife,' said Matt. 'Filthy old bugger. Mind yourself on these planks, girls.'

'Matt,' said Laura, as she passed him, 'don't.'

'Oh, come on, love. You're not going to tell everyone he was an angel.' He winked at Mike Todd, who was holding his glass aloft as if afraid he might spill his wine. 'Everyone here knows what he was like, don't they, Mike?'

'I don't think it's right,' she said.

'To speak ill of the dead? I'm only telling the truth. Aren't we, everyone? It's said with affection, right?'

'Still . . .'

The house loomed before them, illuminated by moonlight that bounced palely from the still water of the lake. In the blue glow, the building seemed spectral, less solid than in daylight, the mist rising from the earth so that it could almost have been floating. The red-brick slab of its eastern wall gave way to Gothic windows, the later additions to north and south dressed in a more traditional Norfolk flint. Above the huge bay window that marked the master bedroom, two sets of battlements looked out over the lake. It was grand but unlovely, a strange, contrary building, not unlike its previous owner. But it had potential. Laura found herself suppressing an involuntary shiver. The Big House. The one she would re-create, where she would spend the rest of her life. The one that would show her parents, everyone, she had been right to marry Matt.

'Look at it,' came Matt's voice. 'He would have let it fall to bits around him.'

'I remember when his parents had it,' said Mrs Linnet, who was clutching Asad's arm. 'Beautiful, they kept it. There were stone peacocks here and here, and boats on the lake, and all along that border they had the most beautiful roses. Proper scented ones, not like you get nowadays.'

'It must have been quite something,' said Asad.

'Beautiful, this house could be again, in the right hands.'

'I wouldn't like it. Not out here in the middle of all these woods.'

Laura looked at her husband, who was standing a little apart from the group, lost in thought, head tilted back. There was something rested about his face, she thought. As if long-held tension was melting away. She wondered briefly whether that expression was replicated on her own features, and decided it probably wasn't.

'Actually, Matt.' It was Derek Wendell, the solicitor, his voice quiet. 'Can I have a quick word?'

'Did I tell you about the time he was going to sell the thirty-acre field? The one by the old barn?' Mike Todd was beside him, his voice booming theatrically in the dark. 'Got offered a good price, well above what he'd asked. Everything was set to go through and then he met the buyer at the solicitor's office.' He paused for dramatic effect. 'Di*sa*ster.'

'Go on, Mike.' Laura was giggly. She had been drinking

all afternoon, which was rare for her. Usually she limited herself – it was no fun to wake up with a hangover.

'He discovered the buyer came from France. Or, at least, his parents had – poor man had lived here twenty years. And that was it. "I'm not selling my land to a bloody appeaser. No Frog's getting his clammy hands on my ancestral home . . ." The irony was that no Pottisworth had ever served in the bloody war. They all managed to get themselves invalided out, or into the ruddy Payroll Corps.'

'I don't think I ever heard him speak well of anyone,' said Matt, staring up at the house.

'Mrs McCarthy, surely. After everything she did for him . . .'

'Nope,' said Matt. 'Not even Laura. Not to my knowledge.' He had sat down on one of the long, low walls that surrounded the house, broken by steps that led into what had been the driveway. He sat with an air of relaxed ownership, as someone would if they were about to have their picture taken.

'Matt.' Derek Wendell was at his shoulder now. 'I really need a word.'

Laura noticed the look on his face before Matt did. Even in her hazy, drunken state, she recognised something in it that sobered her.

'The will, is it? Can't we talk details later?' Matt clapped him on the back. 'Do you never go off duty, Derek?'

'I haven't been in this house for thirty years,' Mrs Linnet announced, from behind them. 'Last time was the old man's funeral. Two black horses they had, pulling the coffin – I went to stroke one and it bit me.' She held out her hand, squinting at it. 'Look, I've still got the scar.'

People were talking over each other now, more interested in telling than listening.

'I remember that funeral,' said Matt. 'I was standing at the top of the drive with my old man. He wouldn't go inside the gates, just stood there as the cortège went past. I remember he wept, even after everything that had gone on. Ten years after they'd chucked him out, left him with no home, nothing, he still wept for that old man.'

Laura was standing still, just watching. Derek, too close to Matt, trying to get his attention, turned briefly to her and she suddenly knew what he was trying to tell her husband. The world fell away from her, like the segments of an orange. She blinked hard, trying to convince herself that what she had seen was the result of poor light or her own tipsiness. But then Derek leaned in and whispered something in Matt's ear, and from her husband's hardened features, and the 'What? *What?*' that broke into the scented evening, she knew that the old man had indeed remained true to himself, as the vicar had said. Even in death.

Three

It was difficult to play the violin when she was crying. The angle of her head meant that the tears pooled briefly in the small hollow between tear duct and nose, then trickled down her face or, worse, on to the violin, where they had to be swiftly removed if they were not to stain or even warp the wood.

Isabel broke off to grab the large white handkerchief and wipe the tiny droplets from the burnished surface. Crying and playing. One should separate one from the other. But it was only when she was playing that she could express how she felt. It was the only time she didn't have to put on a brave face, be Mummy, daughter-in-law, efficient employer or, God forbid, 'stoic young widow'.

'Mum.' Kitty had been calling her for several minutes. She had tried to block out her daughter's voice, unwilling to relinquish the last few bars of Mahler's Fifth, not quite ready to go down and rejoin real life. But Kitty's summons was gathering in strength and urgency. 'Mum!'

She couldn't play properly if she couldn't concentrate. She took the violin from under her chin, wiped her eyes, and shouted down, trying to inject lightness into her voice, 'What is it?'

'Mr Cartwright's here.'

Cartwright . . . Cartwright . . . She laid her instrument in its case, then opened the door of the attic room and went slowly downstairs. She didn't remember the name, although it was possible she knew him. She had never had to know so many people's names before Laurent died. 'Just coming,' she said.

Cartwright. *Mr* Cartwright. A businesslike name. Not one of the neighbours. Not one of Laurent's friends, who still called occasionally, shocked if they had only just heard and who had to be comforted, there on her sofa, as if she were the one who now had to take care of everyone's feelings.

Not one of her friends, few of whom had kept in touch since she had had to leave the orchestra.

Cartwright. She peered into the living room and saw, with vague relief, that the man on the sofa in a dark grey suit and a tie was familiar. He had been at the funeral. She tried to gather her thoughts, and glanced to the kitchen, where Kitty was making tea. 'Can't Mary do that?'

'It's her afternoon off. I told you earlier.'

'Oh.' She was always forgetting things now. Her daughter carried the tea to Mr Cartwright, who was struggling to climb out of the low sofa and stand, right hand extended. In his polished shoes, with his stiff demeanour, he was out of place amid the room's gentle chaos. She saw it suddenly through a visitor's eyes. There were piles of books and magazines on the tables. On the arm of the sofa, someone had left a Hallowe'en mask and a tumbled heap of washing. A pair of her knickers was working its way down the back towards the cushions. Thierry was sitting watching television oblivious to the mess around him.

'Mrs Delancey, I hope I haven't come at an inconvenient time . . .'

'No, no.' She waved in a conciliatory manner. 'How lovely to see you. I was just . . . upstairs.'

Kitty sat in the red damask chair and curled her legs under her. The seat fabric had become so frayed that the grey stuffing was leaking out – and she watched Kitty attempt to push some back in surreptitiously.

'Mr Cartwright has come to talk about money,' she said. 'Your tea's on the side, Mum.'

'Of course. Thank you.' Accountant? Financial adviser? Solicitor? Laurent had always dealt with such people. 'Is there something you need me to sign?'

Mr Cartwright leaned forward, which wasn't easy because his rear was a good six inches lower than his knees. 'Not quite. In fact . . . it might be a good idea to have this conversation . . . somewhere else.' He glanced meaningfully at Thierry, then at Kitty.

Thierry turned off the television resentfully.

'You can watch the set in Mary's room, darling. I'm sure she wouldn't mind.'

'The remote control's broken,' said Kitty.

'Well . . . perhaps . . .'

But Thierry had gone.

'I'll stay here,' said Kitty, calmly. 'Sometimes it's easier to remember stuff if there are two of you.'

'My daughter is . . . very efficient for her age.'

Mr Cartwright seemed uncomfortable, but evidently realised he was stuck with this arrangement. 'I have tried to reach you for several weeks now,' he began. 'I thought you really should have a full picture of your financial situation now that the . . . ah . . . dust has settled.' He blushed at his choice of words. His briefcase was on his knees and, having flipped open its lid in a way that suggested this might be the most pleasurable moment of his working day, he pulled out sheaves of paper, lining them up in neat rectangles on the coffee-table. He ceased when he got to the Pile.

'Mum doesn't do post,' said Kitty, in explanation. 'We're waiting until the heap becomes big enough to do her an injury.'

'I *will* sort out the post, Kitty. I've just . . . got a little behind.' Isabel smiled awkwardly at Mr Cartwright, who was unable to conceal his horror at the sight of the teetering pile of unopened envelopes.

'That's probably why we didn't reply to you,' Kitty added.

'It might be . . . wise to take a look at them,' he said carefully. 'There may be bills.'

'Oh, it's all right,' said Kitty. 'I open anything red, fill in the cheques and Mum signs them.'

Isabel registered his disapproval. She had noticed it on other mothers' faces when she said that the nanny did the cooking, or that she didn't know her children's schoolfriends' names. It had been apparent on the faces of those who had visited since Laurent's death when they took in the shambles of the house. Occasionally she had even spotted it in Mary when Isabel had lain in bed and howled instead of helping to get the children to school. That stage, the one at which she had felt half demented, had seen him in passing faces, raged at God for taking him, had passed. But the path out of grief wasn't any easier.

Mr Cartwright took up a pen and closed his briefcase. 'What I have to say will not come as good news.'

Isabel half wanted to laugh. My husband is dead, she thought. My son is still in shock and won't speak. My daughter has aged twenty years in nine months and refuses to admit that anything is wrong at all. I have had to give up the one thing I love doing, the one thing I swore I would never do, and you think you can give me bad news?

'Now that some time has passed and the – ah – legal side of things has been sorted out, I have had a comprehensive look at Laurent's financial affairs, and it seems he was not quite as . . . solid as he may have appeared.'

'Solid?'

'I'm afraid he has not left you as well provided for as you might have expected.'

That's not a disaster, she wanted to say. Money has never been important to me. 'But we have the house. And his life insurance. It can't be that bad.'

Mr Cartwright was reviewing the piece of paper in his hand. 'Here is a summary,' he said. 'On the top left are his assets, and on the other side a list of what Mr Delancey owed when he . . . passed over.'

'He died,' she corrected. 'I hate that expression,' she muttered, catching Kitty's reproachful eye. 'He – he died. My husband died.' There was no dressing it up. It should sound as bald, as hard, as it was.

Mr Cartwright sat in silence as Isabel swallowed the lump in her throat.

Blushing, she picked up the piece of paper. 'I'm sorry,' she said distractedly. 'I don't really do figures. Could you possibly explain them to me?'

'Put simply, Mrs Delancey, your husband had borrowed heavily against this house to maintain your lifestyle. He was relying on the value of your property continuing to increase. Now that may happen, in which case your situation might not be so bad. But the biggest problem is that when he extended the mortgage, he did not increase his life insurance to cover the new sum. In fact, he cashed in one of his policies.'

'The new job,' she said vaguely. 'He said the new job would bring in big bonuses. I didn't really understand . . . I never really understood what he did.' She smiled apologetically. 'Something about . . . emerging markets?'

He was looking at her as if everything should be self-explanatory.

'I don't . . . Could you tell me what it all means for us?'

'The house is not paid for. The level of life-insurance payout means that less than half of the sum owing will be covered, leaving significant mortgage repayments outstanding, repayments that I'm not sure you'll be able to meet. Until now, the remaining money in your joint and savings accounts has been covering them, but I'm afraid there is little left. You will receive a proportion of your husband's pension, and perhaps there are some benefits, but you must find some other way of meeting your remaining mortgage payments if you want to keep your house.'

It was like a crow cawing, an ugly, invasive noise. At some point she had ceased to hear his words and simply heard jargon. Insurance. Payments. Financial decisions. All the things she felt least capable of. She thought she might be getting a headache.

She took a deep breath. 'In that case, Mr Cartwright, what can I do?'

'Do?'

'His investments? His savings? There must be something I can sell to pay off the mortgage.' She was not sure she had ever used that word before. I never pretended to understand any of this, she railed at Laurent. It was meant to be your job.

'I have to tell you, Mrs Delancey, that in the months before his death Mr Delancey spent heavily. He all but emptied several accounts. As well as using the proceeds of the life-insurance policy, any monies remaining will have to settle his credit-card debts and his – ah – back payments due on the alimony to his ex-wife. As you know, you as his spouse will have no inheritance tax to pay on his estate, but I suggest that in the meantime you reduce your outgoings to a minimum.'

'What did he spend it on?' said Kitty.

'I'm afraid you'd have to go through his card statements to get any idea. Most of the cheque stubs are blank.'

Isabel tried to remember what they had done in those last months. But, as had happened in the first weeks after his death, time had blurred her memory. Her years with Laurent had become an amorphous, shifting bank of recollection. They had had a lovely life, she thought wistfully. Long holidays in the south of France, meals out in restaurants several times a week. She had never questioned where the money had come from.

'Does that mean no school fees? No nanny?'

She had almost forgotten Kitty was there. Now she saw that her daughter had been taking notes.

Mr Cartwright turned to Kitty with relief, as if she was speaking his language. 'That would be advisable, yes.'

'And you're basically saying we're going to lose the house.'

'I understand that your . . . Mrs Delancey no longer has a . . . regular income. You may find it easier to cope if you move to a cheaper area, reduce your household expenses.'

'Leave this house?' Isabel asked, stunned. 'But it was Laurent's. It's where we brought up our children. He's in every room. We can't leave it.'

Kitty was wearing the determined expression she had adopted as a small child when she had hurt herself and was trying hard not to cry.

'Kitty darling, go upstairs. Don't worry. I'll sort this out.'

Kitty hesitated only briefly, then left the room, her shoulders suspiciously fixed. Mr Cartwright watched her go, looking awkward, as if he were responsible for inflicting her pain.

Isabel waited until the door closed. 'There must be something we can do,' she said urgently. 'You know about money. There must be something I can do to keep the children near their father. They loved him. They probably saw more of him than they did of me because I was away working so much. I can't do this to them, Mr Cartwright.'

He had gone pink. He stared at the papers, and shuffled them a little.

'Are you sure he didn't have any assets in France?' she asked.

'I'm afraid he has only debts there. He appears to have stopped paying his ex-wife almost a year before his death. I'm pretty sure that what we have here is an accurate picture.'

She remembered Laurent complaining about the alimony. They'd had no children, he would grumble. He did not understand why *that woman* could not support herself.

'Look, Mrs Delancey, I really can't see any way of reorganising your debts. Even if you let the nanny go and take your children out of private school you'll be left with significant mortgage repayments.'

'I'll sell something,' she said. 'Perhaps he had some good art. There might be a few first editions in the bookcase.' Her eyes rested on the haphazard arrangements of tatty paperbacks and she conceded privately that this was unlikely. 'I can't put them through this. They've suffered enough as it is.'

'You wouldn't want to return to work?'

You have no idea, she thought. 'I think for now the children need . . . one parent . . .' she cleared her throat '. . . to be here. And what I earn with the orchestra has never been enough to cover our household expenses.'

Mr Cartwright murmured something to himself, flicking backwards and forwards between the pages. 'There is one possibility,' he said.

'I knew you'd think of something,' she said eagerly.

He ran his finger down his list. 'I'm afraid there's nothing financial you can cash in. But to the best of my

information, the most valuable asset you hold outside
your house is . . . your violin.'

'What?'

He had reached for his calculator now, was nimbly totting
up figures. 'I understand it is a Guarneri? You have it insured
for a six-figure sum. If you sell it for something like that
amount, it won't cover the school fees, but you should be
able to keep your house.' He held out the calculator to her.
'I'm figuring with commission, but you should still be able
to clear your mortage with a little over. It would be a wise
course of action.'

'Sell my violin?'

'It's a lot of money. At a time when you're in need of it.'

After he had gone, Isabel went upstairs and lay on her bed.
She stared at the ceiling, remembering all those nights she
had felt Laurent's weight on top of her, the evenings spent
reading and chatting about nothing much, unaware that such
domestic mundanity could be a luxury, the nights they had
flanked the sleeping bodies of their newborn babies, gazing
at them and at each other, in wonder.

She let her hand run over the silk coverlet. Such sensual
pleasure seemed pointless now. The coverlet itself, its rich
reds and ornate embroidery, was overtly sexual, as if it
mocked her solitary state. She wrapped her arms round
herself, trying to blot out the encroaching grief, the sense
of amputation that hit her every time she was alone in the
vast bed.

Through the wall, she could hear the muffled sound of the
television, and imagined her son slumped in front of it, probably lost in a computer game. For a while she had hoped that
one of her children might be interested in music but, like
their father, they had little talent, and even less inclination.

Perhaps it's just as well, she observed. Perhaps there's only room for one person to follow their dream in this family. Laurent spoiled me. He allowed me to be the lucky one.

She heard Mary arriving home, and a brief conversation between her and Kitty. Then, knowing she could no longer afford the indulgence of lying there, she got up, straightened the bedclothes, and went slowly downstairs. She found Kitty sitting cross-legged at the coffee-table. In front of her the Pile was divided into separate smaller heaps of brown or handwritten envelopes, subdivided into addressees.

'Mary's gone to the supermarket.' Her daughter put down another envelope. 'I thought we should probably open some of these.'

'I'll do it. You don't have to help me, darling.' Isabel stooped to stroke her daughter's hair.

'Easier if it's both of us.'

There was no rancour in her voice, just the practicality that made Isabel feel a combination of gratitude and guilt. Laurent had called Kitty his '*vieille femme*'. Now, Isabel realised, at the tender age of fifteen, her daughter had naturally assumed that role.

'Then I'll make us some tea,' she said.

Mary had been with them since Kitty was a baby. Sometimes Isabel thought the nanny knew her children better than she did. Mary's air of calm efficiency had held them together these past few months, her stability stitching a thread of normality through what had become surreal. Isabel did not know how she would cope without her. The thought of cooking and ironing, changing bedlinen and the myriad other things Mary did every day filled her with despair.

I must be strong, she told herself. Worse things happen than this. In a year, perhaps, we will be laughing again.

When she returned with the two mugs, she kissed her

daughter's head, filled with gratitude for her presence. Kitty smiled vaguely, then flapped something at her. 'We need to pay this quickly.' She handed Isabel an overdue gas bill. 'They're threatening to cut us off. But it says at the bottom we can pay it by phone if you have a card.'

The credit-card statement Isabel had just opened informed her that she had failed to make the minimum payment for the past two months, and had added what she considered a grotesque sum to the already oversized total owing. Isabel shoved it to the bottom of the pile. There was no money. Mr Cartwright had said so. 'I'll sort it out,' she assured her daughter. She would pay the bills. Find the money. It would be all right. What am I supposed to do? she asked herself. If I do one thing, I may break their hearts. If I do the other, I'll certainly break my own.

'I don't recognise this one.' Kitty threw a thick white envelope at her, with pointed, elegant handwriting on the front.

'Put those to one side, darling. Probably one of the French relations who's just heard.'

'No, it's addressed to Dad. And it's marked "personal".'

'Put it with those, then, the typed ones. Anything that needs urgent attention throw at me. Anything else, leave it for now. I don't have the energy today.' She was so tired. She seemed to be tired all the time. She imagined the relief of sinking into the sofa's exhausted cushions and closing her eyes.

'We will be all right, Mum, won't we?'

Isabel sprang upright. 'Oh, we'll be fine.' She could sound convincing when she wanted to. She was forcing her facial muscles into an encouraging smile when she was arrested by the piece of paper in front of her, Laurent's signature at the bottom. An image of him signing floated before her eyes, the dismissive inky flourish, the way that he rarely looked at the paper while he wrote. I will never see his hands again, she thought. Those squared fingers, the seashell-coloured nails. I will never feel them on me. Holding me. Nine months on, she knew these moments: loss hit her with no delicacy, no warning. There was nothing gentle about grief. It launched itself at you like a rogue wave on the seafront, flooding you, threatening to pull you under. How could those hands simply cease to exist?

'Mum, you need to see this.'

It took all her reserves of strength to focus on Kitty. Her head felt strange, as if she couldn't work her face into anything resembling neutrality.

'Just put any bills to one side, lovey.' *Laurent*, she was screaming inside, *how could you leave us?* 'I tell you what, why don't we finish this tomorrow? I think . . . I need a glass of wine.' She heard the tremor in her voice.

'No. You've got to look at this.' Kitty waved another letter in front of her.

More official things to sign, decide. How am I meant to make this choice? Why do we have to sacrifice everything? 'Not now, Kitty.' With an effort she kept her voice under control.

'But look. Here.' The typewritten letter was thrust into her hands. 'I don't know if this is some kind of joke but it says someone's left you a house.'

'Isn't all this . . . a bit dramatic?'

Fionnuala was taking a break from rehearsals at the City Symphonia. They were sitting in the bistro where they had had hundreds of lunches, close enough to the auditorium to hear a double bass being tuned and retuned, a few experimental scales from an oboe. Alternately Isabel felt blissfully at home and an acute sense of loss, this time of her old life, her old self. A year ago I was an innocent, she thought, untouched by real pain. She was uncomfortably envious now of her friend, who was chatting away, unaware of the depth into which Isabel had sunk. It should be me sitting there, moaning about the conductor, with half my brain still stuck in the Adagio, she thought.

'Don't you think you're in danger of throwing out the baby with the bathwater?' Fionnuala sipped her wine. 'God, that's good.'

Isabel shook her head. 'It'll be better for the children. Lovely country house, good state schools, a small village. You know how awful London parks are – Mary always said she had to spend half an hour picking up bits of broken glass before they could play.'

'I just wonder whether you shouldn't go and see this place first, take your time.'

'We don't *have* time, Fi. We don't have any money. And, anyway, I've seen it, years ago when I was a child. I remember my parents taking me there for a garden party. It was a glorious place, as I remember.' She had almost convinced herself.

'But Norfolk? It's not even the nice bit by the beach. And it's such a huge step to take. You won't know anyone there. You've never liked the country very much. You're hardly green-welly material, are you?' She lit a cigarette. 'Please don't take this the wrong way, but you can be a bit . . . impulsive, Isabel. You should come back to work and see if you can scrape by. I'm sure people would find you extra engagements. You're lead violinist, for God's sake. Or you could do some teaching.'

Isabel raised an eyebrow.

'Okay, so maybe teaching was never your strong point.

But it does seem an awfully extreme thing to do . . . What do the kids think?'

'They're fine,' she said automatically.

'But this is our house. This is *Daddy*'s house,' Kitty had said. 'You told me you'd sort it out.'

Isabel wondered at her own composure. Laurent would forgive me, she told herself. He wouldn't have asked me to part with my violin, which he gave me, not on top of everything else. 'How come you get to make all the decisions? There's three of us left in this family, you know.' Kitty's face was pink with perceived injustice. 'Why can't we sell the new house? It must be worth loads.'

'Because . . . even after I've paid the inheritance tax on it there would be too many debts, okay? It's worth a lot less than our home and, besides, anything we make from this house is ours, not the taxman's.' She softened her voice. 'I don't expect you to understand, Kitty, but your father . . . left us with no money. Less than no money. And we need to sell this house to survive. It won't be that bad. You can still come back and see your friends. And the new house is big – they can come and stay with us. All school holidays, if you want.'

Thierry's face had revealed nothing of what he was thinking.

'There just isn't the money, my loves,' she had said, trying to bring them back to her. 'We have to move.'

'I still think you're making a mistake,' Fionnuala said now, dipping a piece of bread into olive oil, then wiping it round her empty plate. You're still shaken and now is not the time to make life-altering decisions.'

Mary's face had suggested she thought the same thing. But Isabel had to do this now. If she didn't, she might crumple. The house offered her a pragmatic solution. It was the only possible way she had of salvaging something of her life, of ceasing to be haunted by the lack of his. In her more fanciful moments she had told herself that Laurent had sent the new house to her, that he had done it to atone for his debts. And children were adaptable, she told herself daily. Think of those whose parents were refugees, diplomats or in the armed forces. They moved all the time. Anyway, it might be easier for her two to be away from reminders of their old life. It might even be easier for her.

'I understand the house is in need of modernisation,' the solicitor had said.

She had gone to see him in person, unable to believe it might not be some trick. 'My great-uncle was living in it so it can't be that bad,' she had replied.

'I'm afraid I know nothing more than the details on the deeds,' he had said, 'but congratulations. I understand it's one of the more important houses in the area.' She was his only surviving relative, and she had been bequeathed a house through the invisible thread of intestacy.

'It's taken you for ever to make lead violin. And you're bloody good,' said Fionnuala. 'Plus you'll never meet anyone stuck out in the middle of nowhere.'

'What makes you think I want to?'

'Not yet, of course. But eventually— Look, I didn't mean—'

'No,' said Isabel, firmly. 'There was only Laurent for me. There could never be anyone who would . . .' Her voice faded. Then, 'It's a new start,' she told Fionnuala firmly. 'This house is a new beginning.'

'Well, I suppose that's important,' Fionnuala said. She put a hand on Isabel's and squeezed. 'Oh, bugger, I'm due back. Sorry, Isabel, but Burton's conducting, and you know what a miserable git he is when you're late.'

As Isabel reached for her purse, Fionnuala said, 'No, no, my treat. I'm feeling flush because we're doing a film score tomorrow. Four hours' sitting around for forty minutes' playing. I worked out the rate per note the other day – bloody marvellous.' She thrust some money on top of the bill. 'You can do me a roast when I visit. Go shoot yourself a partridge. Astonish me with your new-found country skills.' She reached across the table to hug her friend. Then pulled back and studied Isabel's face. 'When do you think you might play again?'

'I don't know,' said Isabel. 'When the children are . . . happy again. But it's only a couple of hours by train. Not exactly the Outer Hebrides.'

'Well, make sure you hurry. We miss you. I miss you. The man who has taken your place is hopeless. Leads with his head down and expects us to follow. We all gawp at him as if he's showing us what he's about to do by sign language.'

She threw her arms round Isabel again. 'Oh, Isabel, I'm sure it'll be all right, your new house and everything. Sorry if I was unsupportive earlier. I'm sure you're doing the right thing.'

I am, Isabel thought, as her friend disappeared through the double doors, her violin case tucked under her arm.

Best for everyone.

Sometimes she even believed it.

Four

Henry nudged Asad from behind the counter, pointing to his watch. Mrs Linnet had taken almost twenty-three minutes to buy a box of teabags. It was a new personal best. 'Do you need any help, Mrs Linnet?' he asked.

She broke off from her soliloquy. It had involved, in no particular order, CCTV, granite kitchen surfaces, her neighbour's gammy leg and a woman she had once worked with whose infertility she ascribed to the wearing of tights in bed. 'I don't know about these hard-water teabags. Do you have to have hard water to use them? I know we've got limestone. It's all round my kettle.'

'Limestone? That must be a trial,' said Asad.

'Good for the upper arms, though,' said Henry, trying not to laugh.

The dull thrum of rain on the roof increased in volume, and all three started as thunder rumbled overhead.

'I was just about to make a cup – one for you too, Mrs Linnet, so you can judge our anti-limestone teabags for yourself.' Henry winked at Asad and headed to the back of the shop. 'If you're not in too much of a hurry, that is.'

It had been a slow afternoon. The torrential rain and school half-term had conspired to keep all but the most desperate customers away. Other local shopkeepers grumbled about the trickling custom, at former regulars now lured away by supermarket offers and the promise of home delivery. But the proprietors of Suleyman and Ross, unencumbered by debt and cushioned by pensions built up during their years working in the City, viewed such afternoons as an opportunity for a more leisurely exchange with their customers. They had not taken over the shop with the aim of making money, but the low prices, unconventional stock choices and personal attention they offered had kept them assured of people's loyalty. And, perhaps, protected them from the prejudices of those who might initially have been less welcoming to the men now known diplomatically – and against all evidence – as the Cousins.

The shop window had misted, obscuring the relentless sheets of rain. Asad turned on the radio and melodic jazz flowed round them. Mrs Linnet gave a yelp of pleasure and fluttered her fingers. 'Ooh!' she exclaimed. 'I love a bit of Dizzy, but my Kenneth can't abide modern jazz.' She lowered her voice conspiratorially. 'He finds it too . . . isotonic. But, then, you lot are made for it, aren't you?'

Asad was too polite to let his silence stretch for more than an instant. 'My lot?'

She nodded. 'Dark people,' she faltered. 'You . . . you've got rhythm. It's – you know – in the genetics.'

Asad considered this. 'That would explain, Mrs Linnet, why on a day like this I'm barely able to contain myself.'

It was with visible relief that Deirdre Linnet turned to the door.

A familiar voice instructed dogs to stay, and Byron Firth brushed raindrops from his hair as he came in. 'Good afternoon, Byron.' Asad smiled.

'I need a card,' the newcomer told him.

'They're in that corner,' Asad replied. 'Was it for anyone in particular?'

'Lily,' he said quietly. 'My niece. It's her birthday.' He

seemed too large a presence for the shop, even though he was not as tall as Asad, and uncomfortable with himself, as if he were trying perpetually to make himself invisible. Perhaps that was why he worked in the woods, Asad thought. Permanently obscured from view.

'Afternoon, Mr Firth,' said Henry, bearing the tea into the shop and letting his eyes run over Byron's dripping oilskins, his muddy boots. 'I see you've been communing with Nature. And I believe we can announce that Nature, today, is the victor.'

'Where are the handmade cards, Henry?' Asad was scanning the shelves. 'We did have some, didn't we?'

'We don't stock the ones with ages any more,' said Henry. 'All the fours and fives would go and you'd be left with a ton of elevens.'

'Ah. Here.' Asad held out a pink card, decorated with sequins. 'There was a woman who made these on the other side of town. That's the last one and the envelope is a little bent so I can give you fifty pence off, if you would like it.'

'Thanks.' Byron handed over his money, and waited as Asad put the card into a brown-paper bag. With a nod to the shop's proprietors, he tucked it inside his jacket and left. Through the steamy window it was just possible to see the elation of the dogs as their master stooped down to greet them.

Mrs Linnet had been studying labels with unusual intensity. 'Is that man gone?' she asked unnecessarily.

'Mr Firth has left the building, yes,' said Henry.

'I don't think you should be serving the likes of him. Gives me the willies, that man.'

'You wish,' murmured Henry.

'I don't believe Mr Firth's distant past has any bearing on whether we should sell him a birthday card for his niece,' said Asad. 'He has always seemed pleasant to us, if a little uncommunicative. Mrs Linnet, as a good Christian woman, I'm sure you're familiar with the notion of penitence, and forgiveness.'

'He's the thin edge of the wedge, as far as I'm concerned. Word will get out,' she said mysteriously, tapping her nose. 'We'll become a magnet for all sorts of undesirables. It'll be paediatricians next.'

Henry's eyes widened. 'Heaven forbid.'

The little bell heralded the opening of the shop door again. A girl came in, a teenager, no more than fifteen or sixteen. She was wet, but she wore no coat and wasn't carrying an umbrella. She was somewhat crumpled, as if she had been on a long journey. 'Sorry to bother you,' she said, pushing her hair out of her eyes, 'but you wouldn't happen to know where . . .' she consulted a piece of paper '. . . the Spanish House is, would you?'

There was a brief silence.

'I would indeed, dear,' said Mrs Linnet. 'You're not far at all.' She had clearly forgotten her previous trials. 'Might I ask who you're hoping to find there?'

The girl looked blank.

'Old Mr Pottisworth died recently,' Mrs Linnet explained. 'There's nobody living there now. If you're here for the funeral I'm afraid you're too late.'

'Oh, I know,' said the girl. 'We're moving in.'

'In where?' Henry was in the doorway to the back room.

'The Spanish House. This young lady's moving into the Spanish House.' Mrs Linnet could barely contain herself, given the portentousness of the news. She thrust out a hand. 'In that case we'll almost be neighbours, dear. I'm Deirdre Linnet . . .' She peered out of the steamed-up window. 'I take it you're not here on your own?'

'My mum's outside in the car with my brother. Actually, I'd better go because the removal van's waiting for us. Erm . . . where did you say it was?'

Asad gestured towards the road. 'Turn left opposite the signs for the pig farm, right at the crossroads, and then follow the track all the way down until you get to the sign marked "*Cave!*"'

'"Take Care,"' Henry and Mrs Linnet added helpfully in unison.

'We'll be open till five,' said Asad, 'if you need anything. And go carefully on the track. It's a bit . . . unfinished.'

The girl was scribbling on her bit of paper. 'Left pig farm, right crossroads, follow track. Thanks,' she said.

'See you again,' said Henry, handing a mug of tea to Mrs Linnet.

They watched as she disappeared into the road. Then, after a brief, barely decent delay, they scrambled to the window and wiped a viewing hole in the steam. Through it they watched the girl climb back into the passenger seat of a large, battered old Citroën. Behind it the removals van was almost blocking the lane, its windscreen wipers periodically revealing three burly men inside.

'Well, how about that?' said Henry. 'Young people in the big house.'

'She might be young,' said Mrs Linnet, reprovingly, 'but that's no excuse for the state of those shoes.'

'Shoes may be the least of her worries,' said Henry. 'I wonder what kind of welcome they'll get from the neighbours.'

Kitty sat in silence as her mother attempted to negotiate her way down the dirt track. Every now and then she would check her rear-view mirror for the removals lorry swaying precariously behind them and mutter a plea under her breath.

'Are you sure they said it was this way?' she asked Kitty, for the fourth time. 'I don't remember this track.'

'Right at the crossroads. I even wrote it down.'

The car jolted and crunched on to its front bumper as it came through another water-filled rut. Kitty heard the wheels spin briefly without purchase, the engine whining in protest, before they moved forward again. Around them the pine trees towered, blocking what remained of the afternoon light.

'I can't believe it's down here. We'll need a tractor to get out.'

Kitty was secretly glad that the track was so awful. Perhaps it might make her mother see sense about this stupid move. For weeks she had hung on to the vain hope that Isabel would admit it had been a mistake, and decide that somehow she could juggle their finances to keep them in their home. But no. She had made Kitty say goodbye to her school, to her friends, in the middle of the spring term, and head off to God only knew where. And it didn't matter what Mum said about everyone keeping in touch – she knew that once she was no longer there, swapping texts and gossiping, she would no longer exist for them. Even if she went back to visit every couple of weeks she would only ever be on the periphery, missing all the in-jokes, behind on the moment's trend.

The windscreen wipers swung back and forth with a delay and a slight creak, as if every move was an effort. A year ago today, I was happy, she thought. She had kept last year's diary, and checked everything she had done so she knew this was true. Sometimes she tortured herself with it: 'Dad picked me up from school. After dinner we played chess and I won. *Neighbours* was really good.' Sometimes she wondered where she would be exactly a year on. It was hard to believe they might be back in London. Harder to believe they might be happy.

Thierry, in the back, raised his earphones briefly. 'Almost there, T,' she said.

'Oh, come *on*, Dolores, you know you can do it.'

Kitty winced. It was so embarrassing that Mum called the car by name. Suddenly they drove out of the trees into a large clearing. 'There's a sign.' Kitty pointed.

'"*Cave!*"' read Isabel. 'Mmm . . . "Take care."'

'That's it,' said Kitty, relief in her voice. 'That's what they said in the shop.'

Isabel peered through the streaming windscreen. There was an orderly two-storey flint house on the left, which looked nothing like the photograph. The car crawled forward, round a tree-lined bend, and then it was before them. A red-brick house, three storeys high, its walls half covered with ivy, the roof lined with incongruous battlements. Tall windows gave out over a front garden so overgrown that only the box hedge showed where it had once ended and the wilderness began. The house was a hotch-potch of designs, as if whoever had started it had got bored, or seen a picture of something else they liked and adapted it accordingly. A flint wall led to the battlements; Georgian windows nestled against Gothic arches.

The Citroën swept into the drive and pulled up outside the front door. 'Well,' said Isabel, 'this is it, kids.'

It looked cold and damp and unwelcoming to Kitty. She thought wistfully of their Maida Vale house, with its cosy rooms, its smells of cooking, spices and perfume, the comforting mumble of the television. It's derelict, she almost said, but stopped herself. She didn't want to hurt her mother's feelings. 'Doesn't look very Spanish.'

'If I remember right, it was meant to be Moorish. And

there's the lake. I didn't remember it as big as that. Look!'
Isabel had tugged a large envelope out of the glove compartment. She rummaged around in it and took out a key with
a sheaf of paper. Beside the car a huge magnolia had burst
into early life, its pale flowers glowing like white lanterns in
the dim light.

'Now, according to the solicitor, we sold off sixty acres
to pay the death duties, and twenty to put some money
into our bank account. But that still leaves us seven acres
to the left there . . .' The sky was darkening so it was hard
to make out much beyond the trees. '. . . and to the front
of the house. So we've got the whole view, the woods and
the lake. Imagine that! We own almost as much land as we
can see.'

Great, thought Kitty. A muddy pond with a scary forest.
Haven't you seen any horror movies lately?

'You know, if Granny was still alive it would have gone to
her. He was her brother. Can you imagine her living in a
house like this? After her tiny flat?'

Kitty thought she couldn't see anyone living in a house
like this.

'That water. Oh . . . it's magical. Daddy would have loved
the lake – he could have gone fishing . . .' Isabel trailed off.

'Mum, he never went fishing in his whole life,' Kitty said,
gathering up the rubbish bag by her feet. 'We'd better get
out. The removals men are here.'

Thierry pointed towards the trees.

'Good idea, darling. You have a scout round outside.' Kitty
could tell her mother was glad that Thierry had shown any
interest at all. 'What about you, lovey? Do you want to explore
too?'

'I'll help you get organised,' said Kitty. 'Thierry, put your
coat on, and don't get lost in the woods.' The slam of the

car doors echoed round the little valley as they tramped across the wet gravel to the front door.

The smell hit them first, the cold, musty odour of long neglect; subtle hints of hidden mould, exposed damp and wet rot mingled with the fresher air of outside. A holdall slung over her shoulder, Kitty let the stench seep into her nostrils with a mixture of appalled fascination and disbelief.

This was worse than she could possibly have imagined. The hallway was floored in cracked lino, patches of which had worn away to reveal an indeterminate surface underneath. Through an open door she could make out a front room, whose walls were covered with a print that looked as if it dated from the Victorian era, and a rickety painted sideboard of the sort found in a 1950s kitchen. Two windows appeared to have been broken and boarded up, half blocking out the daylight. From the ceiling a wire hung without a fitting, let alone a bulb.

It didn't look like a house one could reasonably live in. It didn't look like a house that had ever been lived in. Now she'll see, Kitty thought. She'll have to take us home. There's no way we can stay here.

But Isabel gestured to her daughter. 'Let's have a look upstairs,' she said. 'Then we'll find the kitchen and make a cup of tea.'

The two upper floors were barely more reassuring. Several bedrooms appeared to have been shut off for years. The air held the chill of disuse, and in places the wallpaper was peeling away in strips. Only two seemed remotely habitable: the master bedroom, nicotine-yellow, which still contained a bed, a television and two cupboards of tobacco-scented clothes, and a smaller room beside it, which had been decorated in the 1970s, perhaps two or three decades more recently than everywhere else. The bathroom suite was cracked and limescaled, and brackish liquid sputtered from the taps. The landing creaked underfoot, and trails of droppings suggested the presence of mice.

She's *got* to see, thought Kitty, as she and her mother confronted each new horror. She's got to see that this is impossible. But Isabel apparently didn't. Every now and then she would mutter something like 'A few nice rugs . . .' as if she was talking to herself.

Kitty counted perhaps three rusting radiators in the whole house. And on the top landing, a piece of the ceiling was missing, revealing a skeletal structure of struts and plaster through which a slow but constant drip made puddles in the bottom of a strategically placed tin bath.

But it was the kitchen that made Kitty want to weep. If a kitchen was supposedly the heart of a home, this one said the house was unwanted, unloved. It was a long, rectangular room with filthy windows along one side, set a few stone steps down from the ground floor. It was dark and infused with the smell of stale fat. An old range cooker stood beside the sink, its lids dulled, grey and sticky with some unidentified collusion of substances. To the other side of the room there was a free-standing electric stove, not quite as filthy but bearing the same signs of abandonment. There were a few 1950s-style units, but the shelves that lined the walls held a random assortment of cooking implements and packets of food, sprinkled with dust, mouse droppings and the occasional petrified corpse of a woodlouse.

'This is lovely,' said Isabel, running her fingers along the old pine table in the centre of the room. 'We've never had a decent-sized kitchen table, have we, darling?'

Above them the removals men thumped and heaved some unidentified piece of furniture. Kitty stared at her mother as if she were mad. The house was like something out of a war zone, Kitty thought, yet her mother was wittering on about pine tables.

'And look,' Isabel said, from beside the sink, as a tap coughed into life. 'The cold water's running clear. I bet it tastes fabulous. Isn't water meant to be better in the country? I'm sure I read that somewhere.'

Kitty was too upset to hear the faint note of hysteria in her voice.

'Mrs Delancey?' The largest of the removal men had joined them. 'We've unloaded the first of the items into the front room, but it's pretty damp. I thought I'd better check with you before we go any further.'

Isabel looked at him blankly. 'Check what?'

The man stuck his hands into his pockets. 'Well, it's . . . it's not in the best . . . I didn't know whether you might want to put your stuff into storage. Stay somewhere else. Till you're sorted out a bit.'

Kitty could have hugged him. Someone, finally, had seen sense.

'The damp's not too good for all those antiques.'

'Oh, they've survived a few hundred years. They'll cope with a bit of damp,' said Isabel, dismissively. 'There's nothing here we can't sort out. A few blow-heaters will warm the place up.'

The man glanced at Kitty. She detected a hint of pity in his eyes. 'As you wish,' he said.

Kitty imagined him and the others marvelling at the madwoman who would have her family living in a leaking wreck while she eulogised a pine table. She thought of their homes: snug, centrally heated, with well-stuffed sofas and huge plasma-screen televisions. 'Well, where's the kitchen stuff? I suppose we'd better start cleaning,' she said.

'Kitchen stuff?'

'Household cleaners. And food. I put two boxes by the front door before we left so we'd be ready.'

There was a short silence.

'Those were for us?'

Slowly Kitty faced her.

'Oh, hell – I thought you'd put them out as rubbish. I left them by the bins.'

What were they going to eat? Kitty wanted to yell. How would they get through today now? Did she ever think about anything but bloody *music*?

Why do I have to deal with this? Kitty turned away so that her mother couldn't see how much she hated her at that moment. Her eyes had filled with tears of frustration, but she fought the urge to dab them away. She didn't want her mother to see them. She wished she had the kind of mother who came prepared and bustled about getting things to work. Why couldn't her mother be just the littlest bit practical? A rush of grief assailed her for her father, for Mary, who would have seen this house for what it was – a massive, ridiculous mistake – and told Isabel that there was simply no question. They would have to go home.

But now there were no grown-ups. Just her.

'I'll go and get some stuff from that shop,' she said. 'I'll take the car.'

She half waited for her mother to protest that there was no way she would allow her to drive. Perhaps even to ask how she thought she could. But Isabel was lost in thought, and Kitty, one palm wiping her eyes now, left.

Isabel turned as her daughter stalked out of the room, making her displeasure plain in every footstep. She heard the door

slam and the sound of the car ignition. Then she turned to
the window and closed her eyes for a long time.

It had stopped raining, but the sky was still low and forbid-
ding, as if it had not yet decided whether to offer a reprieve.
It took Kitty almost twenty minutes to make her way to the
top of the track; her father had only ever allowed her to drive
short distances on holiday, in friends' fields or up a private
road to a beach. Now the car skidded and growled over the
ruts as she hung on to the steering-wheel, praying that the
wheels wouldn't get stuck while she was alone in these horrible
woods. She kept remembering the horror films she had seen,
and saw herself running through the trees pursued by
shadowy monsters.

Once she made the top of the lane, she abandoned the
car and walked the last five minutes down the road into the
village.

'Hello again.' The tall black man smiled as she opened the
door. 'Did you find it all right?'

'Oh, we found it.' Kitty couldn't keep the resignation from
her voice. She picked up a wire basket and made her way
round the little shop, grateful for the warmth, and the smell
of bread and fruit that suffused the air.

'Not what you expected, perhaps?'

She didn't know whether she was irritated by his enquiry,
the assumption that he had known better, but there was
something so gentle about him that she replied honestly. 'It's
awful,' she said miserably. 'So awful. I can't believe anyone
was actually living there.'

He nodded sympathetically. 'Things always look worse on
days like this. You might find it's better in a good light. Most
of us are. Here.' He took her basket from her. 'Sit down. I'll
get Henry to make you a cup of tea.'

'Oh, no, thanks.' Suddenly she was picturing newspaper headlines of vanished girls and wondering about his motives. She knew nothing about these people. She wouldn't have dreamed of accepting food or drink from any London shop-keeper. 'I'd – I'd better—'

'Hello again.' The other man, Henry, emerged from the back of the shop. 'How are you getting on? Anything we can help with? We can order stuff in, you know, if you can't see it on the shelves. Anything. Waders, waterproofs . . . I've heard you might need them where you are.' He spoke kindly and lowered his voice, even though there were only the three of them in the shop. 'We've got some really good mousetraps. They don't actually kill the little beggars, just trap them. You can take them for a drive a few miles down the road and let them out into the wild.' He wrinkled his nose. 'Like a little touring holiday for them, I like to think. Saga for rodents.'

Kitty looked up at the first man, who had started to fill her basket with candles and matches. She thought of the drive home down that track. She thought of her father's hand reaching across to straighten the steering-wheel. Several times on the way up she'd thought she might burst into tears.

'The first basket's on us,' said Henry. 'A housewarming present, isn't it, Asad? But if you accept it you agree to a legal obligation to come in and tell us everything at least three times a week . . .' He winked.

His friend, Asad, looked over his shoulder. 'And listen to Henry when he tells you what passes for news around here.'

'You're so cruel.'

Kitty sat down and raised a wan smile, possibly for the first time that day. 'Actually, I'd love a cup of tea,' she said.

'It's all very romantic,' said Henry, as they were closing the shop. 'Dead husband, poverty, violins . . . a bit more interesting than the last lot who moved into the village, the Allensons.'

'Everyone needs loss adjusters, Henry.'

'Oh, I know.' Henry double-turned the key, then checked the handle to make sure he'd secured the door. 'But you can't help wondering what'll happen to them down there. Especially with McCarthy's nose so severely out of joint.'

'You're not suggesting . . .'

'Oh, I don't think he'd do anything, just that they might find themselves a bit isolated. It's a big old house in the middle of nowhere.'

'It makes me very glad for our cottage.'

'And central heating.'

'And you.'

They peered up at the hilltop where a bowed line of scraggy pines trooped across the horizon, leading to the wood, into which Kitty had disappeared. Asad held out his arm, and Henry took it. As the two streetlamps of Little Barton flickered into life, they walked up the road to their home.

At certain points of the year, when the deciduous trees had lost their leaves and only the pines remained clad, it was just possible to see the Spanish House from the McCarthys'. Matt nursed a tumbler of whisky and gazed at the light that shone from one of the upper windows.

'Come to bed.'

Laura admired her husband's muscular back, the exquisite machinery of his shoulder muscles as he lifted the glass to his lips. Matt never aged; he still wore some of the clothes he had owned when they'd first got together. Occasionally, faced with her own stretchmarks, the gravitational descent of her bosom, she had resented it: Now she felt a faint flicker of anticipation, a brief sense of her own good luck. 'Come on, you've been standing there for ages.' She pulled the strap of her nightdress off one shoulder so that it fell seductively towards her breast.

It had been several weeks now. She always became a little anxious if it went that long. 'Matt?'

'What are they going to do with it?' he was murmuring, almost to himself.

His dark mood had resolutely failed to lift, and she felt a mix of despair and irritation at his apparent determination to let the house colour their lives. 'You shouldn't let it bother you like this. Anything could still happen.'

'Anything has happened,' said Matt, sourly. 'The old bugger left it to strangers. They're not even from round here, for God's sake.'

'Matt, I'm as cross about it as you are. After all, I'm the one who put in all the work. But I'm not going to let it depress me for the rest of my days.'

'He tricked us. He had us running around after him for years. He's probably laughing at us from up there, or wherever he is. Just like old Pottisworth bloody laughed at Dad.'

'Oh, not this again.' The seductive urge evaporated. If he carried on much longer she'd be too cross to make love.

Matt didn't seem to have heard. 'He must have known for months what he was going to do – years. He and the new people probably cooked it up between them.'

'He didn't know. Nobody did. He was stupid enough not to write a will so they got it as his last surviving relatives. That's all there is to it.'

'He must have told them years ago. They've been sitting there, doing nothing, waiting for him to drop dead. Maybe he even told them about the idiots next door who were fetching and carrying for him. They'll have been laughing.'

There was such a fine line between desire and anger. As

if the nerve endings were primed for anything. 'Do you know something?' she said angrily. 'He's probably up there laughing at you, wasting your time in front of the window like a sulky child. If you're that unhappy about it, why don't we go round tomorrow and find out what they're planning to do?'

'I don't want to see them,' he said, mulishly.

'Don't be ridiculous. We'll have to at some point. They're our nearest neighbours.'

He said nothing.

Keep him close, Laura told herself. You cannot afford to give him an excuse. 'Look,' she said, 'you might find they don't even want it now they've seen all the work it needs. They sold the farmland – if you made them an offer . . . Well, my parents would lend us some more money.' She threw back the duvet on his side. 'Come on, love . . . We've got most of the land and the buildings at a good price. Let's look on the bright side. That's something, isn't it?'

Matt put his glass down. He made his way heavily into the bathroom, pausing only to yell over his shoulder, 'What bloody use is the land without the house?'

Five

Isabel was freezing. She couldn't remember ever having been so cold. Somehow the chill of the house had penetrated her bones so that no matter what she did, however many extra layers she put on, warmth eluded her. Finally, shivering in the darkness, she had got up and pulled on her day clothes over her pyjamas. Then she had laid her long wool coat over the bed, along with whatever she could find of the children's clothes, and topped it with a candlewick bedspread they had found in a cupboard. The three had ended up in the one bed. Exhausted after unloading their things, and working out which rooms were habitable, Isabel had forgotten to put on the heater in the master bedroom so that when they'd headed upstairs shortly after ten, they were met not with blissful rest but draughts from unseen cavities, damp sheets and the inter-mittent drip of rainwater hitting the tin tub on the landing.

Piling in together had seemed the best way to keep warm. At least, that was what they had told each other. Isabel, with the sleeping figures of her children at either side of her, had known they needed basic maternal comfort, one of the few things she could capably offer just by existing. What have I done she asked herself? She listened to the panes rattle in the windows, the unfamiliar creaks and groans of the house, the noisy scurryings of unidentified creatures in the roof. Outside it was unnaturally quiet, without the reassuring punctuation of cars passing, or footsteps on the pavement. The expanse of water and the trees muffled any sound. The dark was oppressive, unrelieved by any neighbouring buildings or sodium light. It felt primeval, and she was glad that her children were close. Tenderly she stroked their faces, conscious of the extra liberty that their sleep afforded her. Then reached over Thierry's head to check that her violin case was beside her.

'What have I done?' she whispered. Her voice sounded unnatural, disembodied. She tried to picture Laurent, to hear his words of reassurance, and when he refused to come she cursed herself for moving here, and wept.

Just as she had been told, in the morning things seemed better. She woke to find herself alone in the bed. The day was bright, with the kind of early-spring light that induces beauty even in the most jaded scenery, and outside sparrows squabbled noisily in the hedgerows, occasionally breaking off to fly above the window, then settling again. Downstairs, she could hear the radio, and a buzzing, which told her that Thierry was racing a remote-control vehicle around the echoing floors. Her first lucid thought was, This house is like us. It has been bereft, abandoned. Now it will look after us, and we will bring it back to life.

The idea propelled her out of bed, through the trials of a cold-water wash because neither she nor Kitty had mastered the antique and labyrinthine hot-water system, and back into the same clothes as she had worn that night and the previous day – she had been unable to locate which cardboard box contained her wardrobe. She walked slowly down the stairs, observing the countless problems of their new home, which she had failed to notice the previous evening: cracked plaster, rotting window frames, the occasional missing floorboard . . . On it went. One thing at a time, she told herself, when it threatened to overwhelm her. We are here, and we are together.

That is what is important. A few bars of music had crept into her head: Dvořák's opening from the New World Symphony. It seemed appropriate, a good sign.

The music stopped when she reached the kitchen. 'Kitty!' she exclaimed.

Her daughter had been at work for some time. The shelves were cleared, and while the surfaces were still cracked and tired, they gleamed, free of dust and detritus. The floor was several shades lighter than it had been, and the garden was visible through translucent windows. In the sink, full of hot suds, a large pile of cooking implements was soaking, while a pan of water was coming to the boil on the electric stove. Kitty was putting what food they had on the shelves. The radio muttered on the work surface, and a mug of tea stood on the table. Isabel was filled with pleasure at the sight of the renewed room, yet appalled and guilty that her daughter had had to be responsible for it.

'This room is for cold storage,' Kitty said, pointing to a side door. 'I thought we could keep the stuff that needs refrigerating there until we can get a power point put in for the fridge.'

'Shouldn't it just plug in?'

'Of course, but there isn't a socket – as I said. I've looked everywhere. Oh, and I've put a mousetrap down there. It won't kill them, and once we've caught a few we have to take them for a drive.'

Isabel shuddered.

'Unless Thierry wants to keep them as pets,' Kitty offered.

Her brother looked up hopefully.

'No,' said Isabel.

'I can't get the grill to work, but there's cereal and we have bread and butter. The two men who work in the village shop make the bread themselves. It's quite good.'

'Homemade bread. How lovely.' A lump rose in Isabel's throat. Laurent, you would be so proud of her, she thought.

'There's only jam to go on it, though.'

'Jam is perfect,' said Isabel. 'Kitty, you've made that range look wonderful. Perhaps today we'll be able to get it going. I think they're meant to heat the whole house.' The idea of warmth provoked a kind of hunger in her.

'Thierry had a go at it earlier,' said Kitty, 'but he got through a whole box of matches and nothing. Oh, and the telephone's on. We had a wrong number.'

Isabel surveyed her new kitchen. 'A telephone! Kitty, you're a wonder.'

'It's only a telephone. Don't get too excited.' Kitty shrank away from her mother's embrace, but she was smiling.

Two hours later, the mood in the house was less optimistic. The boiler resolutely refused to start, leaving them with the prospect of another day without heating and hot water. The range would not light, and the yellowed instructions that they had found in the knife drawer were incomprehensible, as if the diagrams had been drawn for another system altogether. Thierry had gone out to fetch wood for a fire, but had laid the grate with damp logs, which smoked, filling the drawing room with soot. 'Perhaps the chimney's blocked.' Kitty coughed – and a decomposing pigeon fell on to the wood. They all shrieked and Kitty burst into tears.

'You should have checked the fireplace, stupid,' she yelled at Thierry.

'I think it was already dead,' said Isabel.

'You don't know that. He might have killed it.'

Thierry stuck two fingers up at his sister.

'How could you be so stupid as to use damp wood?' she snapped. 'And you've trodden mud all through the house.'

Thierry regarded his trainers, which were caked with claggy soil.

'I don't think it really—' Isabel began.

'You'd never have done that if Mary was here,' Kitty interrupted.

Thierry stormed out, ignoring Isabel's outstretched hand. She called after him, but was met with the slam of the front door. 'Darling, did you have to be quite so mean?' Isabel said. *If Mary was here* . . . The words smouldered inside her.

'Oh, this place is bloody hopeless. Everything's hopeless,' said Kitty, and stamped past her mother to the kitchen. The cheerful home-maker had disappeared.

Isabel stood in the middle of the smoky room, and lifted her hands to her face. She had not had to deal with squabbles in her old life. Mary had had all sorts of ways by which she could divert them, or persuade them to behave nicely towards each other. Did they argue more now that it was just her? Or was it that she had been shielded from the bickering and name-calling of everyday life?

'Thierry? Kitty?' She stood out in the main hallway, calling them. She hadn't a clue what she would say to them if they came.

Some time later, when she went back tentatively into the kitchen, she found Kitty hunched over the table, a magazine and a mug of tea in front of her. She looked up, guilt and defiance in her eyes. There was a soot mark on her cheek. 'I didn't mean to get at him,' she said.

'I know, lovey.'

'He's still upset about Dad and everything.'

'We all are. Thierry has . . . his own way of showing it.'

'It's just this place is impossible, Mum. You've got to see

it. There's no water, no nothing. We can't keep ourselves warm and clean. Thierry's got to start at his new school on Monday – how are you going to wash his clothes?'

Isabel tried to look as if she'd already considered this. 'We'll go to the launderette. Just till we get the machine plumbed in.'

'Launderette? Mum, did you *see* the village?'

Isabel sat down heavily. 'Well, I'll just have to drive to the next town. There must be a launderette somewhere.'

'People don't go to launderettes any more. They have washing-machines.'

'I'll wash his things by hand, then, and dry them with a hairdryer.'

'Can't we go home?' Kitty pleaded. 'We can find the money somehow. I'll take a year off school and work. I'm sure I can do something. We'll manage.'

Isabel felt the claw of inadequacy.

'I'll be really, really helpful. And Thierry will. Even being poor at home would be better than this place. It's awful. It's – it's like something a tramp would live in.'

'I'm sorry, darling. It's not possible. Maida Vale is sold. And the sooner you start to see this as our new home, the easier it'll be for everyone. Look past the problems to the beauty of it all. Imagine what it could be like. Look,' she said, her voice conciliatory, 'everyone has teething troubles when they move in somewhere new. Tell you what – I'll call a plumber and we'll get the hot-water system sorted. And then we'll ring a chimney sweep. Before you know it we'll forget we were ever this miserable.' It was a plan. 'The phone's working so I'll do it now.'

With an encouraging smile, Isabel walked briskly out of the kitchen, unsure whether she was rushing to make a start or escaping the crushing disappointment in her daughter's face.

★ ★ ★

Her mother's quilted Oriental jacket glowed out of place in the sad, shabby house. Kitty put down her magazine, rested her head in her hands and checked strands of her hair for split ends. When that grew boring she wondered what else she could attack in the kitchen. Mum had gone over the top about how wonderful and practical and clever she was. She didn't know that Kitty kept busy because it was the only thing that stopped her wanting to cry. While she was working, she could pretend this was an adventure. She could see the difference she had made to their surroundings. She could, in the words of the school counsellor, take control. But the moment she stopped, she was thinking about Dad, or about their house in London, or Mary, who had hugged them and wept when she left, as if they were her own children. And all of that made her want to shout at Mum, because she was the only person left whom she could shout at. Except they couldn't shout at her because she was still grieving. And she was fragile, a little like a child herself, Mary had said. 'You often find that with people who have a talent,' she had told Kitty one evening. 'They never have to grow up. All their energy goes towards doing the thing they love.' Kitty had never been able to decide whether or not she had meant this as a criticism.

But Mary had been right, and when Kitty had been small she had resented the Guarneri so much that she had frequently hidden it, and watched with guilty fascination her mother tear through the house, white with anxiety, trying to find it. Their lives had been governed by that instrument. They had not been allowed to disturb Mum while she was practising, or have the television on too loud, or make Mum feel guilty about the times she had to go away on concert trips. She had not been allowed to mind that Mum never played outdoor games or helped her to make things with glue and ripped-up boxes because she had to protect her hands. Kitty's most abiding memory of her childhood had been of sitting outside the study door, listening to her mother play, as if that might bring her closer.

She knew she had almost been an only child because Mum wasn't sure that she could balance the needs of two children with her musical career. And even after Thierry arrived, unexpectedly, she had still never been at school evenings or netball matches, because she had had to play. They would understand when they were older, her father had said, if they were lucky enough to find the one thing they were really good at.

Mary had been to so many events with him that most people assumed they were married.

Kitty felt a surge of childish resentment. I hate this house, she thought. I hate it because Dad and Mary aren't here, and because I can't even be myself.

The plumber had promised to come the following morning, but had warned that his attendance would be charged as an emergency call-out. He had sighed heavily when she told him she wasn't sure what the problem was and explained that the house had not been occupied for some time. 'No guarantees,' he kept saying, 'not with them old systems. It might have seized up.' She had been apologetic, then furious with herself for it.

The chimney sweep had been friendlier, had whistled when she told him the address and remarked that the last time he had swept those chimneys had been almost fifteen years ago. 'The old man was a tightwad,' he said. 'Lived in one room for years, far as I know. Let the rest of the house fall down round him.'

It was a little . . . tired, Isabel had agreed. She thanked him profusely when he said that he would come round later that afternoon. 'Bring you a bag or two of logs, if you like. I do a lot of the houses round here.'

The prospect of a fire had lifted Isabel's spirits. She put down the telephone, wondering at how small and sparse her pieces of furniture seemed in this house, even with so many rooms closed. A fire will improve everybody's mood, she thought.

She tried to think of ways to cheer the melancholy drawing room. The fire would help, of course, but they should have one room that felt homely, even if it involved leaving others empty. The southern end of the house seemed marginally less damp and uninhabitable. She began to fetch things, a rug, two pictures, a small table and a vase, and arranged them in the room, trying to make it warmer and livelier. The rugs did not cover the floorboards, but they broke up their dusty expanse, and covered the worst of the knotholes. The pictures obscured chips in the walls, and a strategically placed armchair put paid to the view of rising damp above the skirting-board. She shook the curtains and coughed at the dust that billowed out. Then she assessed her efforts. It was not quite Maida Vale, but it was a start.

Outside, Thierry, a small, disconsolate figure, his green jumper bright against the grey and brown of the landscape, was walking out of the trees by the lake. He held a large stick with which he swung at plants periodically. His head was down, his breath emerging in small, cloudy bursts. As she watched he rubbed his sleeve several times against his eyes.

Her small victories felt suddenly cheap and unimportant. She remembered something a cellist had told her when she was pregnant with Kitty: as long as one of your children was unhappy, you couldn't be happy. I must try harder, Isabel told herself. I have to make this into a home, a place that is not dominated by what is missing. I am all they've got.

The sweep, Mr Granger, came when he had said he would, sucked his teeth only briefly and swept three chimneys, with the minimum fuss and mess, considering the amount of soot he brought down. He told Thierry with a wink that chimneys were 'like nostrils. They need a regular clean-out,' emphasising this with a blow into his handkerchief and a display of the blackened results – a demonstration that made Kitty wince and Thierry smile.

Later that afternoon, as the premature evening crept in and the children were engaged with Mr Granger, who was teaching them how to lay what he called 'a proper fire', Isabel wandered upstairs. The previous evening she had noticed that a door led from the top landing out on to the flat roof that ended in the battlements and had brought with her the vast ring of keys that hung downstairs in the kitchen to open it.

She had planned to step out there just for a few moments, to enjoy the view from her elevated position, the iced blue and warm peach of the early-spring sunset reflected in the lake. The outside of the house was less sad and more compelling than the interior.

She had been out there for only a few seconds when she realised what she needed. She slipped back inside, took her violin from its case, and brought it outside. Standing close to the battlements, she tucked it under her chin, not knowing until she started what she was going to play. She found herself in the first movement of Elgar's Concerto in B Minor.

Once she had hated this piece, had found it overly

sentimental. They had agreed at the Symphonia that it was hopelessly long and old-fashioned, but now, unexpectedly, it spoke to her, demanded to be played. And she lost herself in it. It is almost exactly a year since you died, she told Laurent. I will come up here and play for you. A requiem to the things we have both lost.

The notes took on a life of their own, became deep and impassioned, and she heard them echo across the chilly countryside, carried on the soft, still air, on the wings of the waterfowl. She made few errors, and did not care about those she did. She needed no score, no instruction: the concerto, which she had not played for years, reached her fingers by some strange osmosis. By the time she was playing the devastating third movement, she was lost, oblivious to everything but her feelings, vibrating down the bow and into the strings. *Laurent.* She heard his voice in the melodic themes, lost herself in the sheer technical challenge. *Laurent.* This time there were no tears, all emotion contained in her, the grief, anger and frustration translated into sound, redeemed and comforted by it.

The sky grew darker, the air cooler. The notes lifted skyward, spread out and flew, like birds, like hopes, like memories. *Laurent,* she told him. *Laurent. Laurent* . . . Until speech and even thought itself became drowned out by sound.

Asad lugged the crate of fruit through the door, and Henry hurried out from behind the till to hold it back for him. 'Mrs Linnet was on the phone,' he said. 'She told me that the new woman has her music on full blast and that you can hear it half-way down the valley. She said it drowned out her *Wartime Favourites* on the radio, sounded like a bagful of strangled cats, and that if she was going to do it every night she'd report her to the Elemental Health.' He grinned. 'Not a happy bunny.'

Asad put the crate down by the fruit shelf. 'It's not a recording. She stopped twice. I was listening while they unloaded the fruit. If you step outside you'll hear it.'

'She still going?'

Asad motioned him forward. 'You can just hear it.'

The two men went outside. The sky was darkening, and the village street was empty but for the two of them. The windows of the cottages that lined the sides of the road cast out long rectangles of light. Here and there curtains shimmied as they were drawn.

Henry shook his head. 'Nope,' he said.

'Wait,' said Asad. 'Perhaps the wind's changed direction. There . . .' His eyes were fixed on Henry's. 'You hear?'

Henry stood very still, as if that were a requirement for improved hearing. Then slowly, as the distant strains of a violin became audible, a smile spread across his face. The two men enjoyed the pleasure to be gleaned from the unexpected in a place where it was rare.

A small smile played on Asad's lips, as he was transported, perhaps, to some place far away from the chill of an English village.

'Do you think she knows the theme tune from *Cats*?' Henry said, when the music died away. 'I'd love it if she'd play it to me. We could ask if she does parties.'

The bin bags huddled under an ash tree, incongruous against the just-budding greenery, the dewy freshness of the life around them. Spying them half-way down the dirt track, Matt slowed the van and switched off the ignition, cursing the fly-tippers. He climbed out of the cab, walked over to the bags and swung them into the back. Things were getting worse round here, he thought sourly, when people would rather divert half a mile down a woodland track than drive to the tip to get rid of some rubbish. It seemed a fitting end to his day, which had included problems on both of the sites he was overseeing. A carpenter had almost severed his thumb and was likely to be out of action for weeks, and a long, whining phone call from Theresa, who had complained that it was almost six weeks since they had spent any 'quality' time together. She was slow to get the message, that one. She might turn into a liability.

He had stopped to wipe his hands on a rag when he heard it: a long-drawn-out note that called across the valley, not unlike the sound of a wild animal or bird, if none from round here. He stood still, his ears straining to confirm what they'd heard, and then the music became distinct. Classical stuff.

Matt was in too foul a mood to be moved. Loud music from the big house. 'That's all I bloody need,' he muttered, climbing back into the cab. He reached for the ignition key and glared at the distant outline of the house, just visible beyond the treetops, feeling the familiar resentment that its silhouette now provoked.

But instead of firing the engine, he sat there. And listened.

'There's your wick, see? That's what you want to get lit. You open that little window there and tilt a match . . . That's how mine works, anyhow. Yours don't look no different.'

Mr Granger was peering into the innards of the range when they heard the knock. Isabel, who had stopped playing when the children told her what he was doing, was annoyed to be interrupted just as the secrets of the beast were to be revealed.

'You expecting guests?'

Isabel wiped her hands on her trousers. 'I don't know

anyone.' She called upstairs: 'Kitty? Thierry? Can you answer the door? Mr Granger, could you tell me that bit again about what it means when the flame burns yellow?'

There was thumping upstairs, and Isabel heard the front door open, then feet coming down the creaking stairs.

'Nothing wrong with the flue,' said Mr Granger. 'I stuck me head up there, and you can practically see daylight. You shouldn't have no problem with it.'

The kitchen door opened and a man in workman's clothes, with several pens sticking out of the pocket of a faded khaki jacket, came in. Her children appeared behind him.

'All right there, Matt?' said Mr Granger. Not like you to be finished before dark. Come to sort out our new neighbour, have you? Reckon you'll have your work cut out here, mate.'

There was a brief delay before the man smiled and thrust out his hand. Isabel took it, struck by the roughness of his palm. 'Hello,' she said, a little disarmed. 'Isabel Delancey. These are my children, Kitty and Thierry.'

'Matt McCarthy,' he said. Clealy he knew that he was attractive. The phrase 'alpha male' popped into her head. She couldn't think where she had heard it.

'I've been teaching them to make a grand fire, I have.'

'We're going to lay another in the bedroom now,' said Kitty, cheerfully.

'Oh, let's have one in every room, darling.' Isabel tossed her a box of matches. 'Let's really warm the house up.'

'Hold on. You want to make sure you've got enough logs. Rate you're going you'll be through the lot by this evening.' Mr Granger chuckled. 'More used to central heating, you see, Matt. Reckon I've created a pair of little firebugs.'

'Not from round here, then?'

Matt McCarthy was studying her intently and Isabel

wondered if there was soot on her face. She fought the urge to rub it. 'No,' she said, smiling to hide her self-consciousness. 'We've moved from London. We're a bit hopeless at things like proper fires. Mr Granger's been sorting us out.'

'Just looking at this old range,' said Mr Granger. 'She wants to get it working. I heard there's going to be a late frost day after tomorrow. They'll freeze in this draughty old place.'

'That range hasn't been used in years,' said Matt McCarthy. There was a faint note of assertion in his tone.

'Don't look like there's nothing wrong with her, though.'

'Have you filled up with oil?'

'Oil?' Isabel queried.

'Oil?' Matt McCarthy repeated. 'Fuel?'

'It needs oil?'

Mr Granger laughed. 'You didn't tell me you hadn't filled the old girl up. There you go. What did you think she ran on? Fresh air?'

'I don't know. I've never had one before. Logs? Coal? I hadn't thought about it,' Isabel confessed.

Mr Granger clapped her on the back, making her flinch. 'You'll need to order some. Crittendens'll be your quickest – tell 'em it's an emergency. They'll fill you up in a day or two. The others'll make you wait a week.'

'What do I fill?' she said, wishing she didn't sound quite so clueless.

'The tank.' It was the first time Matt McCarthy had smiled properly. But there was something not quite friendly in it. She was just registering this when he spoke again, more warmly now. 'It's at the back near the barn. You want to get your husband to check it for holes, though – it's a bit rusty.'

'Thank you,' she said, a little stiffly. 'But it's just us.'

'Don't like to see a lady and her children without hot water.

It ain't right. Still, at least you'll have your fire tonight.' Mr Granger wiped his hands and put on his hat, ready to leave.

'I'm very grateful,' Isabel said, scrabbling in her bag for her purse.

'Oh, don't worry about that now. See me at the end of the week once you've got yourself straight,' Mr Granger said. 'I'll be down this way so I'll call in Friday morning. See how you're getting on. And I'll bring you a trailer of logs, if I can get them down your drive. More warmth you can put into this place, the better – dry it out a bit.' He gestured out of the window towards the trees. 'Reckon you'll be all right for next year, eh? Matt.' He nodded, then made his way up the stairs, followed by Kitty and Thierry.

Once he had gone the room seemed inordinately quiet. Conscious of the sorry state of the kitchen and her own dishevelment Isabel felt awkward, as she often did with men now. It was as if Laurent had taken with him a layer of her skin. 'So, we're neighbours,' she said, trying to recover her composure. 'Yours must be the house we passed on our way in. Would you like a cup of tea? I'd offer you something stronger but I'm afraid we're at sixes and sevens.'

Matt McCarthy shook his head.

'It's a bit of a mess.' Isabel was talking too fast, as she often did with people who seemed possessed of unusual self-assurance. 'We'll have to sort it out bit by bit. As you can probably tell, we're not the most practical of families . . . I'm sure I have a lot to learn.' She pushed a strand of long hair off her face. She had heard a hint of desperation in her voice.

He looked at her steadily. 'Sure you'll be all right,' he said.

Laura had just finished sorting out the freezer in the garage. She wiped her hands on her jeans and went over to the van.

As Matt got out, he surprised her with a kiss full on the lips. 'Hello,' she said. 'Good day, was it?'

'Not really,' he said. 'But it's improving.'

God, it was lovely to see him smile. Laura grabbed his belt and pulled him to her. 'Maybe I can improve it further,' she said, and then, 'Steak for tea. With my special pepper sauce.'

His appreciation came in the form of a low, rumbling murmur, which vibrated pleasantly against her skin.

He closed the van door, put an arm round her shoulders and walked with her to the back door. She took his hand, letting it rest against her collarbone, keen to prolong the moment. 'You've had two cheques in from the Pinkerton job. I've banked them. Did you hear that music earlier? Anthony thought it was a fox caught in a trap.'

'I heard. In fact, I went to see our new neighbours.' Laura tripped over the old dog, who uttered a whimper of protest. 'Oh, Bernie . . . You went over there?'

'Thought it wouldn't hurt to say hello. We are neighbours, after all.'

She waited for the barbed comment, the bitter curl of his lip. But none came. Even the mention of the big house hadn't bothered him. Oh, please let things turn round, Laura prayed. Please let him have come to terms with it. Please let him cheer up again.

'Well, that was a good thing to do. I'll pop over later in the week.' She tried to keep her fears from her face. 'I've got to tell you, Matt. It's lovely to see you smiling again. Really lovely.'

Her husband stooped and kissed her nose. His lips were cold against her skin. 'I've been thinking,' he said.

Six

There were not many people of her generation who could say they had married the first man they fell in love with, but the moment Isabel Hayden met Laurent Antoine Delancey she knew she would look no further. This conclusion, which popped into her head half-way through a performance of Bruch's Romance for Violin and Orchestra, came as a surprise to her: she had never felt the slightest twinge of romantic interest in the pale, earnest youths who had surrounded her at music college. She had already decided that she probably wouldn't marry, it being too much of a distraction from music. But as she fought her way through the solo she thought about the serious, rumpled man who had taken her out to dinner in Les Halles the previous evening – a proper restaurant, not a café. He had told her he had never been so moved by music as he had when she had been busking outside Clignancourt station, and she realised that the mythical One, about whom her girlfriends wittered, might actually exist, and that he might appear at the strangest moment and in the most unexpected way.

There had been obstacles, of course – all the best love stories had them: a former wife, a 'neurotic' actress, from whom he had not yet been tidily divorced; her parents' objected – she was, at twenty, too young, too impulsive – and so did her music teachers, who suspected she would throw away a perfectly good talent on domestic minutiae. Even the vicar had said that the twelve-year age difference and the cultural gap between the French and the English – he had hinted to her about the possibilities of mistresses and the importance of deodorant – might cause the marriage to fail.

But Laurent had met all of this with a Gallic shrug and his passion for the girl with the burnished tangle of long hair, while Isabel found, unlike many of her peers, that marriage did not lead to disappointment, cynicism or compromise. Laurent loved her. He loved her if she fell asleep into her breakfast because she had been up all night trying to perfect the last bars of some sonata; he loved her when, yet again, the meal she had prepared for him was both burned and bland. He loved her when they strolled arm in arm on Primrose Hill and she tried to sing to him pieces of music she loved, filling in with wild arm movements for bass drum and tuba. He loved her when she woke him up at three a.m., desperate to have him inside her, the taste of him on her lips. He bought her the Guarneri, leaving it on the pillow of the hotel where they had lost themselves one weekend, and laughing when she was shocked into breathlessness by it. He loved her.

She had been shocked to find herself pregnant after their honeymoon, not sure if she was ready for another person to break into their romantic idyll. But Laurent had confessed he had wanted children throughout his first marriage and, still overwhelmed by the passion she felt for him, she decided to give him this gift.

It had been an easy pregnancy and, stunned by the depth of love she felt for Kitty after she arrived, she had tried to devote herself solely to motherhood. It seemed no less than the baby deserved. But she had been hopeless at it, had never managed to establish the mysterious 'routines' that the health visitor went on about, was never quite on top of the piles of soiled vests or able to throw herself into the soft-play events that other mothers adapted to so easily. It was the only time that she and Laurent had fallen out. She had been tetchy and martyred, as if she had sacrificed too much of herself, and found herself blaming him for it.

'You know, I would like my wife back now,' he had said, with Parisian pomposity, one evening after she had railed at him about the unwashed dishes, her lack of freedom, her exhaustion, her disinterest in sex. She had thrown the baby monitor at his head. The next morning, confronted by the chip in the wall, she had known something had to change.

Laurent had held her. 'I won't think any less of you if you need your music. It was one of the things I loved you for in the first place.' And after she had checked several times that he meant it, that he wouldn't resent her for it, they had found Mary. Isabel had justified leaving her beautiful child by telling herself that everyone was happier.

Besides, Kitty had been such a good baby. If she had been unhappy with Mary, or unsuited to being with someone other than her mother, wouldn't she have been less smiley? Less placid? There was a price to pay; one of the things she learned fastest about motherhood was that there always was. It was the way Kitty would run first to Mary if hurt, even if Isabel was in the room, and the way that Laurent could talk to the child knowledgeably about her friends, or discuss the special school assembly they had attended. It was, also, in the racking guilt she endured at being in a hotel room several hundred miles from a child she knew to be sick, or in the plaintive notes she found in her suitcase: 'Mummy I love you I miss you when you are gone.' She missed her family too, and ached with remorse. But Laurent and Mary afforded her the freedom to be herself, to pursue the thing she loved to do. And the older she grew, the more mothers she met, Isabel recognised that she was one of the lucky few who were not deprived by marriage and motherhood of their creativity. Or, more importantly, their passion.

It was not always easy. Laurent still loved her impulsiveness, indulged her wilder moments – the time she had taken the children out of school to go on a balloon ride, or when she threw away the plates because the colour irritated her and forgot to buy new ones – but he could be bad-tempered if he felt he was not foremost in her mind. She came to know the danger signs when he considered she was too immersed in her music. He would be irritable, announcing that he might appreciate his wife's presence occasionally. He could tell when she was mentally rehearsing, even as she pretended to chat about what Kitty had done that day. She was wise enough always to give him what he needed, and ask what passed for pertinent questions about his job at the investment bank, even when she didn't fully comprehend the answers. Laurent's job was a mystery to her. She understood only that he earned enough to pay for everything, and occasionally to take them on holiday, when she would leave the violin behind and for two or three weeks devote herself to her family.

The greatest crisis had come when she had found herself pregnant with Thierry. Six years after Kitty's birth, she had stared at the blue dot, which, despite the evidence, she had not expected to see, and panicked at what lay ahead. She couldn't have a baby now: she had just secured her position as lead violinist in the City Symphonia; she had tours of Vienna and Florence lined up for the spring. She had proven herself ill-suited to full-time parenthood, even with a child as amenable as Kitty.

Several times she had considered not telling Laurent.

He had reacted, as she had suspected he would, with delight, then horror when she told him what she was considering.

'But why?' he demanded. 'You have me and Mary to help. Kitty would love a brother or sister – she has begged us for one so many times.'

'We agreed, Laurent,' she said. 'We agreed no more children. I couldn't cope with two.'

'You don't have to cope with one,' he had retorted, 'and I have never minded. But you can't deprive me – deprive us – of this child because it doesn't fit in with your schedule.' His face told her she must concede. He asked for so little.

She never confessed her dark thoughts as she passed each pregnancy milestone, as birth became an impending date in her diary. And he had been right: when Thierry arrived, his arms out thrust in protest against his delivery, perhaps against his unwanted nascence, she had loved him with the same instinctive passion as she loved Kitty. And felt a deep relief when, three months later, she had been able to return to work.

Isabel pulled her scarf round her neck, and strode down the path to the woods, the moisture-laden cow parsley and long grass catching at her boots. It was the first time she had been on her own for weeks. She had seen the children off to school two hours earlier, Thierry ducking away from her kiss, shuffling off with his uniform stiff on his shoulders, Kitty setting out with her customary determination.

She had looked forward to being alone again – God knew she had longed for some time to herself. But she missed them. Without the noise and bustle of the children, the house had seemed too sad, too overwhelming, and within an hour she had realised that if she didn't do something, she would sink into melancholy. She could not face unpacking the remaining boxes, did not feel robust enough to start the Sisyphean exercise which would be cleaning the place, so she had gone for a walk. After all, there was nothing a walk couldn't put right, Mary had told her often enough.

She had decided to cut through the woods to the village shop. The simple act of buying milk and something for supper would give her a focus. She would make a stew or roast a chicken for the children to come home to.

Somehow, it was less upsetting to think about Laurent when she was outside. A year on, she found that there were times now when she could think of him in relation to the things she had loved, rather than what she had lost. The sadness never went away, she had been told, but it would became easier to cope with.

She thrust her hands into her pockets, breathing in the tang of new growth, observing the shoots of bulbs beneath the trees or hinting at where a flowerbed might once have been. Perhaps I'll make him a garden, she thought. But she knew it was unlikely: digging, forking and cutting with shears would be too hard on her hands. Gardening had long been on the unofficial list of things violinists couldn't do.

She had reached the edge of the woods, and walked their length, the lake to her left, trying to remember where she had noticed a gap. She found it and ducked through. On the other side the ground was even less contained than it was around the house. Briefly, she turned back: its dark-red expanse and haphazard windows stared back at her without warmth or welcome. Not yet hers. Not yet a home.

You mustn't think like that, she scolded herself. It will be our home if we make it so. They now had hot water, albeit at an exorbitant price, and a vague metallic-scented warmth in some rooms. The plumber had told her the radiators needed bleeding, but he had been so patronising that she hadn't asked him what that meant. As there was a huge crack

in the bath, they had to wash in a tin tub, a state of affairs
Kitty protested about bitterly every morning.

She stopped to examine some oversized fungi fanning
from a rotten tree-trunk then peered up at the overcast sky,
visible in filigree patterns through the twigs and branches.
The air was damp and she blew into her scarf, enjoying the
warmth that bounced back on to her skin. The woodland
smelled of moss, damp wood and healthy decay, so unlike
the sinister damp of the house, where she often found herself
wondering what might be rotting away around them.

A twig snapped and she stood very still, her city-bred mind
fluttering with images of mad axemen. She held her breath
and revolved slowly towards where the sound had come from.

Some twenty feet away, a huge stag was staring at her, its
head lifted, its licheny antlers resembling the unclad branches
behind it. Thin streams of vapour puffed from its nostrils,
and it blinked several times.

Isabel was too entranced to be afraid. She stared at it,
marvelling that such creatures could still exist in the wild,
that in their built-up, overcrowded little country there was
still room for such a beast to roam free. 'Oh.' Perhaps that
small sound broke the spell, because the stag bounded into
the open field and away.

Isabel watched it go. A snatch of music entered her head:
The Transformation of Acteon into a Stag. The animal slowed
and hesitated, its head swinging round as her mind filled
with the fanfare of arpeggios that opened the symphony,
a symbol of the young men who had come hunting, the
gentle flute Adagio that spoke of murmuring streams and
breezes.

Suddenly the silence was broken by a gunshot. The stag
took off, stumbling across the claggy soil. Another shot rang
out and Isabel, who had initially leaped behind a tree, now

raced out into the open after the animal, trying to work out where the shooting was coming from.

'Stop it!' she yelled, her scarf falling away from her mouth. 'Whoever you are! Stop shooting!' Her heart was racing. She tried to run, but the earth had stuck in huge clods to her feet.

'Stop!' she shrieked, hoping the unseen hunter could hear her. She tried to push the mud off one boot with the toe of the other. The stag appeared to have got away, but her heart still thumped as she waited for the next shot.

It was then that she saw the man striding across the field towards her, apparently unhampered by the mud. She saw his rifle, now cocked downwards towards the ground, resting in the crook of his arm.

She pulled at her scarf, so that her mouth was free.

'What on earth do you think you're doing?' Shock had made her louder than she had intended.

The man slowed as he reached her, his own face flushed as if he had not expected to be interrupted. He was probably not much older than her, but his height gave him authority and his dark hair was brutally shorn. His face had the winter colour of one who spent his time outdoors. contours whipped by the wind into precise planes.

'I'm shooting. What do you think I'm doing?' He seemed shocked to find her there.

Isabel had managed to free her feet, but adrenalin still washed through her. 'How dare you? What are you – a poacher?'

'Poacher? Hah!'

'I'll call the police.'

'And tell them what? That I was trying to scare away the deer from the new crops?'

'I'll tell them you're trespassing on my land.'

'This isn't your land.' His voice held a faint burr.

'What makes you think that?'

'It belongs to Matt McCarthy. All the way up to those trees. And I have his permission to clear it of anything I want.'

As he spoke, it seemed to Isabel that he looked meaningfully at his gun. 'Are you threatening me?' she said.

He followed her gaze, then glanced up at her, eyebrows raised. '*Threatening* you?'

'I don't want guns so close to my house.'

'I wasn't pointing it anywhere near your house.'

'My son comes out here. You could have hit him.'

The man opened his mouth, then shook his head, turned on his heel and walked back across the field, shoulders hunched. His parting words floated to her: 'Then you're going to have to teach him where the boundaries are, aren't you?'

It was as she watched him go that she remembered the last part of the von Dittersdorf symphony. The stag was in fact a young prince, who had been transformed into an animal when he had strayed into the wrong part of the woods, then been torn to pieces by his own dogs.

Asad was checking the eggs, removing one or two from each box and using them to fill others. The organic eggs from the farm down the road were all very well, but they tended to be covered with . . . organic matter, which did not always go down well with ladies of a sensitive disposition. He was cradling the dirty ones in his hands, about to clean them, when the woman came in.

She stood in the doorway for a moment, casting around her as if she were looking for something. She was wearing a long blue velvet coat, whose hem was splashed liberally with mud. Family resemblance told Asad who she was.

'Mrs Delancey? Would you excuse me while I put these down?'

Her eyes widened when she heard her name.

'Not too many casual passers-by around here,' he explained, wiping his hands as he returned to her. 'And you're very like your daughter.'

'Oh. Kitty. Of course.'

He hesitated. 'Are you all right? You seem a little . . . startled.'

She lifted a hand to her face. Beautiful pale hands, he observed. Long white fingers. She was trembling. 'Tell me,' she said, 'do many people around here own a gun?'

'A gun?'

'I've just been threatened . . . well, perhaps not threatened, but confronted by a gun-wielding man on what I thought was private land.'

'That would be startling . . . yes.'

'I feel a bit shaken. I'm not used to meeting people with guns. In fact, I don't think I've even *seen* a gun up close before.'

'What did he look like?'

She described him.

'Sounds like Byron, Mr Pottisworth's land manager. He's doing some work for Matt now. But I believe he only uses an air rifle.'

'Matt McCarthy.' The woman appeared to mull this over, then deflated.

'I was about to put the kettle on,' he said. 'I believe a cup of hot sweet tea is very good for shock. Let me introduce myself. My name is Asad Suleyman.'

She bestowed on him a sad, sweet smile that expressed all manner of gratitude for his offer. She was not conventionally good-looking, thought Asad, but she was undoubtedly beautiful. And her hair, when most people's was neatly cut and coloured, was extraordinary.

'I suppose it must have been him, which is reassuring. But I hate the thought of someone with guns roaming so close to us. And it's difficult,' she said. 'I don't know where my land ends and Mr McCarthy's begins.'

Darjeeling. She looked like a Darjeeling woman. Asad put a mug into her hands, and cocked his head to one side. 'Have you not thought of asking your solicitor for the deeds?'

'Would they show me?'

'I believe so, yes.'

'Thank you so much. I'm pretty hopeless at judging these things. I haven't had much experience of . . . land.'

They sat in companionable silence, sipping their tea. Asad stole surreptitious glances at her, trying to register the details that Henry would demand from him later. Rather exotically dressed – in the muted browns and greens favoured here-abouts. The pale, slender hands. He could easily imagine them on some magical instrument. The long, rather unkempt tangle of dark blonde hair tied back chaotically – the antithesis of her daughter's glossy bob. Eyes that strayed off to the side, their downturned corners perhaps betraying her recent sadness.

'This isn't what I expected,' she observed.

'No?'

'Your shop. It's beautiful. You have things I'd want to eat. Parma ham! Sweet potatoes . . . I thought village shops were all crates of apples and synthetic cheese slices, run by fat, middle-aged women. Not tall . . .' She was suddenly discomfited.

'Black men,' he finished. 'Actually I'm Somali.'

'How did you end up here?' She blushed, perhaps conscious that her question might be considered intrusive. 'Sorry. I haven't had much in the way of conversation lately.'

'Not at all. I came here in the 1960s. I met Henry, my partner, and when we could afford to we decided to escape the city. It's a quiet life here . . . better for my health. Asthmatic,' he explained.

'It's certainly quiet.'

'And are you surviving, Mrs Delancey? In the big house?' He reached under the counter and lifted out a tin of biscuits, which he opened and offered to her. She took one.

'Isabel. We're getting there. Slowly. Hot water and heat are a luxury. We'll have to get lots of work done. I have a little put away, but I didn't realise the scale of what we were taking on. What *I* was taking on,' she corrected herself. 'It was very different the last time I visited.'

He wanted to say something then, to warn her that her presence might have upset people other than a land manager, that it might not only be men bearing guns she should beware of. But she seemed so vulnerable that he hadn't the heart to add to her troubles. After all, there was nothing he could say with any certainty.

'You will always be welcome here, Mrs Delancey – Isabel,' he said. 'Any time you want to stop by, I'll be glad to have a cup of tea with you. You and your family. We want you to feel welcome.'

'You haven't noticed.'

Matt lifted his eyes from his pint to meet Theresa's slanting green ones. She was so close that he could smell her perfume, even over the pub food and beer. 'Noticed what?'

'That there's something different about me.' She leaned back, keeping her hands on the bar, her painted fingernails outspread before him. Behind her, two young men in track-suits were exclaiming over the fruit machine.

'You got your nails done?'

Her eyes flashed. 'No!'

She was wearing that bra with the purple lace. He caught glimpses of it peeping over her low neckline as she moved. 'Try again,' she commanded.

He let his gaze wander across her body, as she had known it would. 'You shouldn't have to look *that* carefully,' she said, mock-offended.

'What if I like to?' he said quietly.

'Keep trying,' she said, with an edge, but he knew he had unbalanced her. Theresa was easy to read, always had been.

'You've lost weight.'

'Flatterer.'

'New lipstick?'

'Nope.'

He gulped his drink. 'I don't know. I'm no good at games.'

Their eyes locked. Oh, no? hers said, and he remembered what she had felt like the previous week, writhing beneath him in the bedroom at her low-beamed cottage. He felt his groin tighten, and glanced at his watch. He had told Laura to expect him home at seven thirty.

'Matt.'

He spun round to find Byron climbing on to the stool beside him. 'All right there? Pint, is it?'

Byron nodded, and Matt gestured towards Theresa. 'Stella, please,' he said.

'Do you give up?' She pouted.

'Can't a man enjoy a pint in peace?' Matt had turned to Byron. 'All right. I give up. I've forgotten what the question was.'

'My hair,' she explained, one hand lifted from the pump. 'I've had highlights. Two colours. Look.' She dipped her head as she passed the glass over the counter, fanning out fronds to show them.

'Lovely,' said Matt, dismissively, and then as she stalked off, he rolled his eyes at Byron, as if they were complicit in the incomprehensible ways of women. 'Everything all right?'

Byron drank some of his lager. 'Not bad. I've sprayed the low paddocks. I wasn't sure about the soil quality but it doesn't look too bad. Maybe lying fallow all that time has done it good.'

'Great. Means nothing to me, mate, but Laura will be pleased.'

'There's deer in the hollow between the bridleway and the small copse. I saw a stag today, and a few does yesterday. I've scared them off for now with a few shots, but they'll be back.'

'That's all we need. They'll eat their way through the seedlings. Keep an eye on them.'

'Your new neighbour came out shouting at me for scaring the animals.'

'She did, did she?'

'Virtually accused me of shooting at her.' Byron seemed uncomfortable. 'I don't know if she's going to make anything of it. I should have told her it was just an air rifle.'

A bellow of laughter escaped Matt. 'Ah, blessed townies! Wants to rescue all the little Bambis, does she? Oh, that's marvellous.'

Theresa was edging her way back round the bar.

'Next time you see her,' Matt went on, 'say we'll set her up a little nature reserve. She can have all the bunnies and deer she wants off that land. We'll even throw in some birds – a few crows and starlings, say – for her to feed. She can be a regular Snow White.'

Byron smiled uneasily, as though mockery did not come naturally to him.

'Tell you what, we'll have a chat later, about you working

for me on a more permanent basis . . . I reckon Pottisworth's land'll need a fair bit doing over the next year and I could use an extra pair of hands. You're twice the size of my son. I know it's not much in the way of forestry, but what do you reckon?'

Byron coloured, and Matt guessed that the younger man had been more concerned about his lack of a job than he had let on. That, and his history, could work in Matt's favour – he wasn't likely to ask too high a wage. Pottisworth could only have paid him a pittance.

'That . . . would be good,' he replied.

Matt caught Theresa's eye, and winked recklessly. He would ring Laura and tell her he was running late. It would be a shame to waste the evening. After all, he was in a very good humour.

Seven

'As you can see, it's in need of decorative repair, but you're really paying for the potential. This area, as you know, is becoming quite desirable.' Nicholas Trent smiled encouragingly at the young woman beside him as she contemplated the crack running up from the corner of the window frame, like a bolt of lightning. 'It may be new plaster,' he said, following her gaze. 'You get a fair amount of shrinkage with it. Nothing a decorator can't fix.'

She peered down at the details and muttered something to her partner. Then she said, 'Where's the third bedroom? We've only seen two.'

'The third bedroom.' Nicholas pulled open a door and fumbled for the light switch.

'That's a bedroom?' the man asked, incredulous. 'It's got no windows.'

There was nothing Nicholas could say to this. In former days, it would have been described as a large cupboard.

'It's very small,' said the woman.

'It *is* on the economical side,' he agreed. The baldly illuminated little space couldn't have been more than six feet by four. 'But to be fair, Miss Bloom, there are very few examples of this type of property with a third room. Most are only two-bedroom. I believe those lucky enough to have a third tend to use it as a study or computer room, where natural light isn't such an issue. Now, shall we view the kitchen?'

It took twenty minutes to show them the rest of the little flat, despite its limited size. And for each of those twenty minutes Nicholas Trent heard himself praising its limited advantages, and his inner voice contradicting what he was saying. This is a revolting flat, he wanted to tell them. It's right next to a main road, sits above a tube line underneath a flight path in a street that has a crack-den at both ends. Quite possibly it has subsidence, the rooms that don't have Anaglypta wallpaper have rising damp, and there isn't an original feature left in it. It is ugly, badly designed, poorly adapted and not worth a third of the asking price.

And yet there was little point. He knew that by the end of the day the couple would have put in an offer, and that in all probability it would not be so far below the asking price that negotiation was impossible. That was the way it was at the moment. Properties that would have gone for peanuts five years ago were being snapped up by people happy to sign themselves into debts that made him giddy.

Don't you remember that last crash? he wanted to ask. Don't you know what mortgaging yourself to a property like this could do to you? Can't you see you're about to ruin your lives?

'Have you got many more people to show round?' The young man had moved closer to him.

'Two this afternoon,' he said smoothly. It was the stock response.

'We'll be in touch.' The young man held out his hand.

Nicholas took it with rare gratitude. There weren't many people who shook hands, these days, especially not with estate agents. 'Don't worry,' he said. 'If this one goes, I'm sure we can find you something better.' He could see the young man

disbelieved him. He saw the brief furrowing of his brow as
he tried to work out whether this was part of some sales
pitch, some secret agenda. That's what the property business does to you, thought Nicholas, sadly. Turns us all into
suspicious fools. 'I mean . . . the decision is entirely yours,
of course.'

'We'll be in touch,' the young man said again, and Nicholas
held open the door of the little flat and watched them go,
their heads down as they pictured their new life in it.

'Your wife rang,' said Charlotte, her mouth full of something
that might have been muesli. 'Sorry, ex-wife,' she said cheerfully, thrusting a piece of paper at him. 'Don't like to say
that. It sounds wrong somehow.'

It did sound wrong. It wasn't the kind of word one expected
to apply to oneself. Ex-husband. Failed husband. Failed
human being. Nicholas took it and thrust it into his trouser
pocket.

The office was humming with activity. Derek, the residential manager, was leaning over his desk, one hand in the air
as he talked into his telephone. Paul, the other residential
agent, was drawing up some new instruction on their sales
board. A middle-aged woman was talking with the lettings
agent, sniffing occasionally into a handkerchief. The glass
door closed behind him, muting the growl of the high-street
traffic.

'Oh, and Mike somebody called – wanted to invite you
over for dinner. Said you and he went back a long way. I
told him about your wife because he didn't know and he
said he was ever so sorry.'

Nicholas sat down at his desk. 'Please ring Mrs Barr,' said
a Post-it note. 'Not happy about new survey.'

'Mike somebody.'

'He said he lives in Norfolk. It's nice round there.'
'Norfolk where?'
'I don't know. Most of it, I suppose.'

*Buyers have pulled out of Drew House at point of exchange.
Pls ring Mr Hennessy urgently.*

He closed his eyes.

*Kevin Tyrrell wants to reschedule viewing for 46 Arbour
Row. Says he doesn't want people interrupting the football
match.*

He'd have to ring all four buyers he'd scheduled for that
evening. All of them would be put out. But we couldn't interrupt Kevin's football, could we?

'He said he was at your wedding. Sounds ever so grand,
Nick. You never told us you got married at Doddington
Manor.'

'Nicholas,' he said. 'My name is Nicholas.'

'Nicholas. I didn't know your wife's family were so wealthy.
Sorry, ex-wife. You're a dark horse. You'll be telling us you
live in Eaton Square next.' Her cackle was interrupted by
the telephone.

Eaton Square. He had once considered buying a property
there back in the early 1980s, before the last property boom,
when London was still full of rackety places worn thin through
decades of rental. Places ripe for modernisation, for empire-
building. He still remembered it, out of all the flats he had
ever looked at for development, because it had had its own
ballroom. An apartment in Eaton Square with its own ballroom. And he had turned it down, judging that the returns
would not be great enough.

He was haunted by the houses he had not bought, teetering
profits he had not been brave enough to secure.

He sighed. Time to ring Mrs Barr. *Not a happy bunny.*
'Nick.'

Derek was leaning over his desk so he put the receiver back in its cradle. No sense of personal space, that man. He leaned so close to you that you could detect not only his last meal on his breath but the brand of soap powder he used. Nicholas forced his face into an expression of blank amenability. 'Derek.'

'That was Head Office. We're not meeting targets. We're two hundred and eighty K behind Palmers Green on commission. Not good.'

Nicholas waited.

'We need to move higher in the table. Even Tottenham East is catching us up.'

'With respect, Derek, I've agreed sales on four properties since the beginning of this week.' Nicholas tried to sound measured. 'I'd say that was pretty good by anybody's standards.'

'A blind one-legged deaf-mute could have agreed sales on those properties with the market as it is. Property's flying, Nick. It's got legs. We need to be reaching out more, selling better properties, pushing up our margins. And we should be selling harder. You're meant to be the big dealer round here. When are you going to start acting like it?'

'Derek, you know as well as I do that more than forty per cent of the properties in our area are ex-local authority. They don't produce the same prices or the same margins.'

'So who's getting the remaining sixty per cent? Jacksons. Tredwell Morrison. HomeSearch. That's who. We should be eating into their market share, Nick, grabbing those properties for ourselves. We want to see Harrington Estates boards all over this town like a bloody fungus.'

Derek stretched his arms behind his head, revealing two

damp patches. He strolled round the office, arms still raised. Like a combative baboon, Nicholas thought. Then he turned back to rest both palms on his desk. 'What appointments have you got for this afternoon?'

Nicholas flipped open his desk diary. 'Well, I've got a few calls to sort out, but my Arbour Row viewing has been post-poned.'

'Yeah. Charlotte said. You know what, Nick? You should get out there on the streets, rustle up a bit of business.'

'I don't understand.'

Derek reached behind him and picked up a pile of glossy papers. 'Go and drop some flyers for us this afternoon. Down the better streets. Laurel Avenue, Arnold Road, and by the school, that end. I had these printed this morning. Let's see if we can pull some of that business our way.' He slapped them on to Nicholas's desk.

Out of the corner of his eye Nicholas saw Paul smirking into his phone. 'You want me to push flyers through people's doors.'

'Well, Paul and Gary are chocka. And you said you've got no appointments. No point us paying some youth-training-scheme git to do it when he's likely to dump half of them in the bin and bugger off down the snooker hall. No, Nick,' he slapped the older man on the back, 'you're thorough. I can rely on you to do a job properly.'

He walked back to his desk, arms once again raised over his head, as if in victory. 'Besides, do you good to walk a few pounds off. You never know, you might be thanking me later.'

If it hadn't been for the leafleting, Nicholas thought after-wards, there was little chance he would have accepted Mike Todd's invitation to dinner that Saturday. His social life had dwindled almost to nothing since Diana left, partly because fewer invitations came his way – she had always been the more sociable one – but mostly because he did not want to have to explain his new circumstances to people he had known in his previous life. He had come to recognise that look of appalled pity when they grasped how far he had fallen. In the women's eyes a kind of sympathy, a glance at his thinning hairline; in the men's discomfort, barely hidden impatience to move on, as if what had happened to him might be catching.

Four years after the crash, he knew he looked different; they remembered the Savile Row suit, the top-of-the-range Audi, the easy charm. The steel. Now they saw a middle-aged man, hair greyed with stress, complexion no longer burnished by trips to Geneva and the Maldives, working as a negotiator in a bottom-rung estate agent in a run-down part of London.

'You going to this dinner, then?' said Charlotte, as he got off the phone. 'Be nice for you to get out a bit.' She had chocolate on the side of her chin. He decided not to mention it.

So here he was, about to put himself through it again. Dinner would give him no chance to elude questions about his life, no music, no moving screen in which he could pretend to be absorbed. Half-way up the M11 he was wondering why on earth he had agreed to come.

Then he remembered Thursday afternoon, spent tramping rubbish-strewn streets, the desolate clatter of letterboxes, the suspicious twitch of greying net curtains, the distant barking of furious dogs as he pushed each leaflet through. The rain that steadily permeated his once-handsome wool suit. The bleak realisation that, at forty-nine, this was what his life had become. An uninterrupted, lonely vista of disappointment and humiliation.

Mike was a good sort. He had never been so successful that he was likely to be a painful reminder of what Nicholas had lost. And he had only met Diana once. That was always a help. Nicholas crunched the gears on the old Volkswagen, trying not to remember the seamless change of his old automatic, and swung the car back into the middle lane.

It had taken some doing, his accountant had said afterwards, to crash so spectacularly when the rest of the market was going up. His complicated empire of mortgages, developments and rental property had fallen like a house of cards. He had bought an eight-bedroomed detached house in Highgate, putting down a non-refundable deposit to secure the property against the other developers who had been circling it. Then the sale of his finished house in Chelsea had fallen through, and he had been forced to borrow the remainder of the deposit. Two other deals had collapsed, just when he had to complete on the Highgate house, and he had been forced to borrow against two properties he had owned outright. He could still remember the nights he had spent in his office, calculating and recalculating, juggling interest-only mortgages against bank loans. It had all begun to collapse inward, equity lost in rising interest costs. And so incredibly swiftly what had felt like an impermeable fortress of property interests had become so much financial rubble.

It had cost them their own home. Diana had just finished decorating the nursery for the children they had not had. He remembered how her gilded head had lifted as he explained the depth of their problems, and her beautiful cutglass voice saying, 'I did not sign up to this, Nicholas. I did not sign up to bankruptcy.' If he had listened hard enough he would have heard the farewell in her voice back then.

He had done pretty well, all things considered. He had

avoided bankruptcy by the skin of his teeth, and, four years on, had finally paid off the last of the big debts. On some days he could tell himself he was on the way up again. It had been a surprise to receive a bank statement with a black column on the right, rather than a red one. But he had lost the trappings: the houses, the cars, the lifestyle. The respect. He had lost Diana. Yet people recovered from worse. He told himself this all the time.

The traffic had thinned, signalling the shift from commuting territory to true country. Nicholas turned up the radio, ignoring the interference that stemmed from the broken aerial.

He was close enough now for the village's name to appear on signs. He had not been to Mike Todd's home for years. He remembered a weekend spent somewhere large and beamy, a yeoman's house, Mike had said proudly. Higher ceilings. It hadn't stopped Nicholas banging his forehead several times.

He had just passed the first sign for Little Barton when the nagging discomfort became urgent. He needed a service station, but the country was wild now, and he wasn't sure there was even a pub. He drove another two miles, then knew he could hold on no longer. He took a left turn down a single-track lane. If he couldn't have a proper loo, at least he could find privacy.

He regretted this decision almost as soon as he'd made it. He couldn't risk stopping in case someone came through, and there was no passing place. He was forced to continue, lurching over potholes, until finally he found somewhere to pull over, deep in woodland. He leaped out of the car, leaving the engine running.

There was nothing like relieving yourself after an interminable wait. Nicholas stepped back from the tree-trunk and checked that he had not splashed his shoes, then climbed back into the car. He'd have to continue down the track as there was no obvious place to turn round. He swore and drove on, trying to protect the car's suspension against the worst of the bumps, telling himself that it had to end soon. All tracks had to end somewhere.

The car made an ominous grinding sound as the chassis hit a rut. Next time, he told himself, I'll forget decorum and become one of those white-van men who please themselves. 'I'll pee on the verge,' he said aloud, then wondered if this was a sign of new liberation, or simply that he had crossed a line and started talking to himself.

The track split, swung to the left, and he could just see the outline of a white-fronted coach house. Then, as his car lurched to the right, he glimpsed through the trees two misaligned sets of battlements and a curiously majestic flint and red-brick façade. He hit the brakes, his engine idling, and stared for a minute, not just at the house, which, he observed immediately, was architecturally flawed. Probably some late-nineteenth-century folly, some ill-thought-out piece of grandeur that had been swiftly reconciled to an architectural dustbin. But the setting! Flanked by woodland, the house looked out over water. The overgrown lawns and unkempt hedging were unable to disguise what must have been the aesthetically compelling vista of that landscape, the grandeur of its classical setting.

The lake was eerily still, the soft grey skies reflected in it, the gentle curves of its banks providing a narrow green margin before the woodland. Beautiful, ancient woodland of oak and pine, the tops of the trees touching the far horizon of the distant valley, the colours fading to an impressionistic haze. It managed to be both grand and intimate, wild, yet with a hint of formality, far enough from the road to offer complete seclusion, yet with a decent driveway . . .

He turned off the engine and climbed out, listening to the

distant flapping of Canada geese, the low murmur of the wind in the trees. This was the most spectacular setting he had seen for years. And the house had been untouched for decades. It was unlikely to have been listed, he thought. There was no symmetry, no clear references to a historical past. It was a mishmash of styles, an Anglo-Moorish bastard, its age showing only in its visible air of disrepair. It was the kind of building one never saw any more; virtually untouched, yet full of potential.

He walked a little closer, his car forgotten, half expecting the angry bark of a dog or the shout of an outraged inhabitant. But the house was deserted, his approach unnoticed, except by the sparrows and crows. No car in the driveway suggested an occupant, so he peered through a window. The lack of furniture suggested long absence. Only the fields showed human activity; they had been carefully drilled, and the hedges were neatly topped.

Afterwards he wasn't sure what had made him do it. These last few years he had been cautious, not prone to risk-taking. But he tried the door, and when it opened obligingly, Nicholas Trent did not obey the rules of common sense. He did not even call out. He walked into the main hallway. The light fittings there were characteristic of the 1930s, the bureau visible through a door a decade later. He went into what must have been a drawing room, which had been inhabited recently – there was an Ikea armchair – but overall his impression was of neglect. The pleasing dimensions of the rooms were flawed by holes in the plaster, missing skirting, the pervasive smell of damp. The high ceilings were marred by sepia patches that spread across their once-white surfaces. The windows were spoilt by missing panes and rotting frames. Where would you start? Nicholas wondered, and almost laughed at the ridiculousness of the question. Because there were no houses like this any more. They had been demolished or converted years ago by speculators like himself. He moved quietly up the stairs, and headed to an open door. It led into the master bedroom, a generous room, overlooking the lake, with a vast bay window whose view seemed to encompass the entire grounds. He stepped closer to it and let out a long, slow breath of pleasure. He tried to ignore the faint smell of cigarette smoke.

Nicholas Trent was not a fanciful man; he had lost any penchant for wistfulness when he had lost his wife. But he stood now, staring at the lake and the forest, hearing the unexpected silence of the house, and could not ignore the idea that he might have been sent there for a reason.

It was then that he saw the suitcase, clothes spilling out chaotically. A paperback book and a hairbrush. Someone was staying here. Those small domestic items broke the spell. *I am in someone's bedroom,* he thought. Feeling suddenly like an intruder Nicholas turned and walked swiftly out of the room, ran down the stairs and was out of the house in seconds. He did not turn until he reached his car, and at that point he paused and stood for a moment, regarding it at a distance and trying to imprint it on his memory.

Because Nicholas Trent didn't see a semi-derelict house. He saw a development of twelve five-bedroom executive homes of exceptional quality, discreetly arranged at the edge of the water. He saw an apartment block of award-winning modernistic design, a country retreat for the middle classes, marketed in *Country Life*. For the first time in five years, Nicholas Trent saw his future.

'Tell me about the Spanish House.' It had been hard to sound casual, but he had no choice. No one was more likely to know what was going on with that property than Mike Todd: he had sold houses in the Bartons for almost thirty years.

Mike handed him a glass of brandy. They were seated in front of the fire, their legs stretched in front of them. Mike's wife, an unusually contented sort who insisted the 'menfolk' relax while she sorted out the kitchen, had disappeared. Nicholas had been unable to contain himself any longer.

Mike looked at him speculatively. 'The Spanish House, eh? What do you want with it?'

'I took a wrong turn this afternoon and ended up on that godawful track. I was wondering who owned it. Strange-looking place.'

'Eyesore, you mean. It's a wreck.' Mike took a deep swig of his brandy, then swirled it round his glass.

He affected to know about alcohol, and had spent much of the meal lost in appreciation of the wines, none of which Nicholas had found remarkable. Nicholas worried that he was now going to lecture him about cognac. He had forgotten Mike could be a bit of a bore. 'Listed?'

'That heap? No. It was missed when they listed everything else round here as it's so deep in the woods. But very little's been done to it in years.' He sniffed. 'Actually, interesting tale, that place. It was owned by the Pottisworths for God knows how long. They were an important family round here, but more interested in the outside than the in – huntin', shootin', fishin' types. And old Samuel Pottisworth did nothing to it for fifty years. He had promised it to Matt McCarthy, an old friend of mine. He and his wife looked after the old boy for years. But it went to his last surviving relative. A widow, apparently.'

'Pensioner?' If she was elderly, Nicholas thought hopefully, she might not want the bother of a house like that.

'Oh, no. In her thirties, I believe. Two children. They moved in a couple of months ago.'

'Someone's *living* there?'

Mike chuckled. 'God knows how – the place is falling apart at the seams. Put Matt's nose out of joint, though. I think he wanted to do it up for himself. His dad had worked there for years. There was bad blood between his family and the Pottisworths. I think it was his way of settling a score. You know, some *Upstairs Downstairs* thing.'

'So . . . what's she planning to do with it?'

'Who knows? She's not the villagey type. I hear she's a little . . .' he dropped his voice, as if he might be overheard '. . . *eccentric*. Musical. You know the sort.'

Nicholas nodded, although he didn't.

'Up from London too – talk about a baptism of fire.'

Mike lifted his balloon glass to the light. What he saw appeared to satisfy him. 'Yes, that house is the definition of a money pit. You could drop a hundred K into it and not touch the sides. Still, poor old Matt was bitterly disappointed when it went elsewhere. Fatal, getting too emotionally involved with a property. He made the mistake of taking it all personally. I told him, estate agent's advice: "There's always another property." You know that better than most, eh, Nicholas? How is the London market, anyway?'

'You're absolutely right. There's always another property,' echoed Nicholas, his elegant hands closing round his glass. But his head was full of the Spanish House.

Eight

The mingling of eight different perfumes in her centrally heated living room was nauseating. Laura opened a window a fraction, even though the temperature outside was still far from spring-like. Around her seven other women sat or perched on chairs, some with their stockinged feet tucked under them, others balancing coffee cups on their laps.

'I can't believe she was the only one who didn't know. It was practically common knowledge at the pre-school.'

'He was hardly discreet, was he? Geraldine saw him kissing her in the staff car park. And it's a church school – she's hardly an advertisement for the sixth commandment.' Annette Timothy's angular neck lengthened as her voice rose.

'I think you mean the seventh.' Michelle Jones always liked to stir it a little. 'The sixth is murder.'

'If a head teacher of a church school can't set an example, I don't know who can,' Annette continued. 'Anyway, God only knows what's going to happen to poor old Bridget. She's a wreck. Although, frankly, if she'd put the odd bit of lipstick on occasionally he might not have strayed . . .'

'She did put on an awful lot of weight after her last pregnancy.'

Laura tuned out. An acute moral sense – and perhaps a dash of self-interest – meant that she rarely participated in such conversations, or the round-up of local scandal that passed for conversation in the Bartons. She ran a practised

eye over her immaculate room, taking her habitual quiet satisfaction from a room properly arranged. The peonies were
beautiful in the Chinese vase. It had come from her parents'
library, where she could still picture it on the mantelpiece.
She had decided against lilies: their scent would have been
overpowering.

Matt never noticed things like that, only when she had
failed to do something – her moments of mutiny, as she
privately called them. When he came home late three times
in a row, she made sure he had no clean socks. Or she didn't
record his favourite television programme. Enough to get
him shaking his head and muttering as he went off the
following morning that he didn't know what the world was
coming to. This is how it would be if you were without me,
she would tell him silently. Your world as you know and like
it would collapse.

'What time did you tell her to come, Laura?'

Laura dragged herself back to the room. Hazel's coffee
was nearly finished, she saw, and got up to make more. 'Ten
to ten thirty.'

'It's nearly eleven now,' Annette expostulated.

'Perhaps she got lost.' Michelle grinned.

'Across the lane? I don't think so.' Annette let her tone
reflect exactly what she was thinking. 'Not very polite, is it?'

Laura hadn't been sure she would come anyway.

'A coffee morning?' Isabel Delancey had said, as Laura
stood on her doorstep two days previously.

'It's just a few neighbours. Quite a few have children. It's
our way of saying hello.'

It had been strange to see someone else in Mr Pottisworth's
house, *their* house, but Laura had been unable to take her
eyes off the woman's dressing-gown. It was almost half past
nine on a weekday morning and Mrs Delancey was wearing

a man's yellow silk robe, her hair wild round her face as if it had not seen a brush in several weeks. It was possible she had been crying, or perhaps her eyes were puffy from sleep.

'Thank you,' she said, after a minute. 'That's – that's very kind. What do I do?'

Behind her, Laura could see a clothes-airer draped with damp, crumpled clothing. All the items were pinkish, as if they had been infected by a rogue red sock. 'Do?'

'At the coffee morning. You want me to play?'

Laura blinked. 'Play? No, you just turn up. It's all very relaxed, very informal. It's a way for us to introduce ourselves. We're quite isolated out here, after all.'

The woman looked at the derelict outbuildings beside the house, the empty lake, and Laura suspected suddenly that this was how she liked it. 'Thank you,' she said eventually. 'It's kind of you to think of me.'

Laura hadn't wanted to invite her. Although she hid her feelings from Matt – she believed it was pointless to carp about things you couldn't change – she resented the new owner of the house almost as much as he did. That the woman was from London and seemingly had no knowledge of or interest in the area or the land had made it worse. But Matt had suddenly become keen that the two women make friends. 'Get her out and about a bit. Get close to her,' he urged.

'But we might not even like each other. The Cousins say she's a bit . . . different.'

'She seems all right. She has kids. You've got that in common. What happened to *noblesse oblige*?'

'I don't understand, Matt,' she had protested. 'You were completely against her until last week, and now you want us to be best friends.'

'Trust me, Laura,' he had said. When he smiled down

at her, she could see amusement in his eyes. 'It'll all work
out.'

Trust me, she thought, refilling the coffee filter. How many
times had she heard that?

'Do you think she has any idea what she's taking on?
Michelle, pass me one of those lovely biscuits. No, the chocolate ones. Thank you.'

'It's in an awful state. Well, Laura would know – Laura,
you said it was in an awful state, didn't you?'

'I did,' said Laura, putting a tray down on the coffee-table
and picking up an empty cup.

'I'm not even sure what you'd do with it. It's such an *odd*
place. And so isolated all the way out there in the woods. At
least you can almost see the road from yours, Laura.'

'Perhaps she's got money. I suppose the advantage of taking
on somewhere like that is that there's almost nothing worth
saving. You could just go mad. Build a glass extension or
something.'

'I'd knock the outbuildings down first. They're about to
fall down anyway. Can't be safe with children around.'

Laura knew what was coming before Polly Keyes spoke.
'Don't you mind, Laura? All that work you put in with that
awful old man, and then not getting the house. You're very
generous to invite her here.'

She had braced herself for this. 'Oh, no,' she lied. 'I was
never particularly keen on it. It was Matt who had big ideas.
You know him and his projects. He saw it as a blank canvas.
Sugar, anyone?'

Annette put her cup on its saucer. 'You are good. When
I lost the rectory I howled for a week. I knew every inch of
that house. I'd been waiting years for it. It went to sealed
bids, and the agents told us the old owners went with the
Durfords even though we offered more. What could we do?

Of course, we're very happy in our house now. Especially now the extension's finished.'

Polly sniffed. 'I think Mr Pottisworth was very mean not to leave you anything. You were so good to him.'

Laura wished they'd change the subject. 'Oh, he left us some bits and bobs, some furniture. He told us ages ago it should be ours. It's still in the garage. I think Matt wants to treat it for worm before we do anything with it.' She thought of the shoddy old bureau, now diplomatically covered with a blanket. Matt hadn't wanted it, and she had thought it ugly, but he'd said he was damned if that woman was going to get a single thing she wasn't entitled to.

'Matt's going over there later to help her assess what needs doing. He knows the house better than anyone, after all.'

'Well, you're both very generous befriending her in the circumstances. Oh – oh, shush! Was that the doorbell?' Polly said excitedly.

'Try not to talk too much about your husbands, girls. The Cousins say she's quite recently widowed . . .' Annette told them. Then a thought struck her. 'You could talk about yours, Nancy. You're never nice about him.'

Isabel Delancey walked into the overheated room and felt the weight of eight pairs of eyes settle heavily upon her. In them, she saw that they knew she was a widow, thought her clothes eccentric, and disapproved of her lateness. She was amazed at how judged one could feel in a split-second silence. Then the eyes dropped to her feet. Her dark red suede boots were covered with a thick crust of mud.

'Oh!' she exclaimed, noticing the footprints behind her. 'I'm so sorry.' She stooped and made as if to pull them off, but a chorus of voices leaped in.

'Oh, please don't worry.'

'It's what vacuum-cleaners are for.'

'You should see what my children tread in.'

Persuaded not to remove her footwear, even though most of the other women had taken off theirs, Isabel was led to an empty seat and invited to sit. She smiled waveringly, already knowing this had been a mistake and wishing she had pleaded a prior engagement.

'Coffee?' Laura McCarthy was smiling.

'Thank you,' she said quietly. 'Black, please. No sugar.'

'We were wondering if you were going to come.' A tall, prematurely grey woman with a long neck had spoken. It sounded a little like an accusation.

'I was practising. I'm afraid I often lose track of time. Forgive me,' she said to Laura.

'Practising?' The long-necked woman leaned forward.

'Violin.'

'How lovely. My Sarah is very much enjoying learning it. Her teacher says we should think about putting her in for exams. Have you been learning long, Mrs Delancey?'

'I . . . Actually, I do it for a living.'

'Oh. Lovely,' said a shorter woman. 'Deborah's desperate for lessons. Perhaps you can give me your number?'

'I don't do lessons. I was with the City Symphonia.'

The idea that she might have had a professional life appeared to dumbfound the women.

'And you have children?'

'Two.' God, it was hot. 'A girl and a boy.'

'And your husband?' Two women glared at the questioner.

'He died last year. In a car crash.'

'I'm so sorry,' said the woman. 'How awful for you.' There were murmurs of commiseration from around the room.

'You're very brave, starting afresh all the way out here.'

'It's a lovely area for children,' someone said reassuringly. 'The school is very good.'

'And how are they finding the move? It's a big place for you to be rattling around in, with so much work to do . . . and without . . .'

This was the point at which they were expecting her to crumble a little. If she confided how awful and decrepit the house was, how miserable her children, that she was haunted not just by the absence of her husband but by the recklessness of her own actions, those brittle glances might soften. The women would sympathise and reassure her. But something in Isabel wouldn't let her do this.

'They're fine,' she said. 'We're settling in well.' Her tone suggested this was not a topic she wanted to pursue.

There was a brief silence.

'Yes,' said the grey-haired woman. 'Good. Anyway, welcome to the village.'

As Isabel raised her cup to her lips, she noticed something odd in Laura McCarthy's expression. It vanished, and she met Isabel's smile with a broader one.

Byron Firth lifted the metal sheath and brought it down hard, with both hands, against the fence post, the impact juddering through him as the wood sank into place. He had done twenty-two so far, ready for the wire that would mark out Matt McCarthy's boundary. A machine could have sunk the posts in a tenth of the time, but Matt was reluctant to hire one. He was paying Byron a weekly wage, and couldn't see the point in spending more. Byron would continue until the task was completed. But in the hard earth you could still feel the chill of winter, and Byron knew his shoulders would be knotted and sore that evening, and that with his sister's boyfriend a permanent guest at their house, he was unlikely to get a bath.

She was leaving in four weeks, she had told him. She and Lily were moving into Jason's house on the other side of the village. 'You knew we couldn't stay for ever,' she said apologetically. 'Especially with Lily's chest and these damp walls. And at least you're working again. You'll find somewhere else to rent.'

'Don't worry, I'll be fine,' he had told her. What he did not say was that the rent of every cottage he had seen so far was more than twice what Matt paid him. At the one flat he might have been able to afford dogs were not allowed and Meg was due to whelp any day. The man at the housing department had almost laughed when he had tried to sign on there. Apparently they worked on a points system, and as an able-bodied single man not on benefits, that would have been of no more value to him than flicking through the property section of *Country Life*.

'I'd say come with us. But I think Jason would like us to make a start by ourselves . . .'

'Don't fuss, Jan. He's right. You should try to be a family.' He put an arm round his sister's shoulders. He didn't like to think how much he would miss his niece, the casual chaos of their life together. 'It'll be good for Lily to have a dad around.'

'And you're all right now . . . aren't you? Now that everything's . . . well, you've got a clean slate.'

He sighed. 'It's fine. I can look after myself.'

'I know you can. I guess I just feel . . . responsible.'

'You were never responsible.' He met her gaze, but neither of them said what hung in the air between them.

'Well, come for Sunday lunch. I'll do us a proper roast every week. Okay?'

Whumph! He brought the metal cylinder down again, driving the post into the earth, squinting against the sun. He had thought about moving to a new area, somewhere the rents weren't going up so fast. But the classified ads in the farming magazines wanted qualified land managers, people who'd been to agricultural college. He had no chance against people like that, especially with his history. Besides, he understood the land here, still had a few contacts. And a job with Matt McCarthy was better than none.

Byron lifted the metal cylinder, and as he prepared to bring it down on the post, he saw, out of the corner of his eye, a movement to his right. A boy was standing by the hedge. The sight distracted him and Byron caught his thumb between the cylinder and the post. As the pain shot through his hand he let out an expletive. The dogs jumped up, whining, and when Byron, his thumb shoved painfully between his knees, looked up, the boy was gone.

Isabel habitually walked with her head held high, her almost exaggeratedly erect posture her way of compensating for years of crooking her neck round her violin. But today her head was down as she strode through the mossy undergrowth on her way back down the woodland path to her house. What had possessed her to go to such an event? Why had she pretended that she and those women might have anything to say to each other? The rest of the morning had been spent in painfully stilted conversation. Laura had asked more about Isabel's children, but when she confessed how much she missed their nanny, and then that she couldn't cook and, no, she didn't have any domestic skills, they had seemed disappointed. And Isabel, instead of being cowed and silenced, had felt increasingly mutinous. She remarked, a little tactlessly, that she found caring for a house unfulfilling, and watched their jaws drop as if she had said her signature dish was human flesh. 'Oh, well,' said one woman, placing a hand on her arm, 'at least now you've stopped working, you'll really get to *know* your children.'

Isabel wrenched open the door, which she had forgotten to lock. She ran upstairs and pulled out her violin. Then she returned to the kitchen, the only room that retained any warmth, and flicked open a book of music. Eyes on the notes in front of her, she began to play, the notes harsh and angry, the bow scraping gracelessly across the strings. She forgot the damp kitchen, the washing hanging from the dryer, the dirty breakfast things. She forgot the women across the lane and their barely concealed distaste, Laura McCarthy's unreadable face. She focused only on the music, until she had lost herself, stretching out the notes until her body eased. Finally, several pages in, Isabel relaxed.

After some unknown length of time, she stopped. She pushed her shoulders back and let her neck roll first to the left and then to the right, lengthening the tendons, letting out a long, slow breath. When someone clapped behind her she jumped and spun round.

Matt McCarthy stepped forward. 'Sorry,' he said. 'You left the door open, and I didn't like to disturb you.'

Isabel felt exposed, as if she'd been caught doing something she shouldn't. Her spare hand went to her neck. 'Mr McCarthy.'

'Matt.' He nodded towards her instrument. 'You really do get stuck into that, don't you?'

She put it carefully on a chair. 'It's just . . . what I do,' she said.

'I've got those figures you asked for. Thought we could go over them if you've got five minutes.'

It was still cold outside, and chilly enough within for Isabel to have kept her coat on, but Matt McCarthy was wearing only a grey cotton T-shirt. Everything about his demeanour suggested that he was impervious to temperature. The solid outline of his upper body made her think of Laurent, and she was briefly disoriented. 'I'll make some tea,' she said.

'Not got your fridge working yet?' He pulled out a chair at the kitchen table, and nodded towards the appliance, which still sat, unplugged and redundant, at the end of the room.

'There are no power points.'

She pulled up the sash window and took in one of the bottles of milk that stood on the windowsill.

'Yeah. I don't think this room has been updated since the 1930s.'

While she made tea, Matt got out a notepad and calculator, humming to himself as he ran through a series of figures with the stub of a pencil. When she sat down, he pushed the pad towards her. 'Okay – these are your initial works, as I see them. You should fix the roof. It really needs a complete overhaul, but until then you must make the place waterproof. With materials, patching it up will cost in the region of that . . .' He tapped the pad. 'Internally it gets a bit more complicated. You need a damp-proof course throughout. The drawing-room and dining-room floors have to come up because there may be dry rot underneath. At least eight windows want replacing, and the rest should have the rotten wood dug out and made good. And there's your electrics. To be on the safe side, you're looking at a complete rewiring job.'

Isabel stared at the figures.

'You've got a few structural problems too. It's possible there's some movement at the back of the house. If that's so it'll need underpinning, although we can take out some of the trees near the back wall and leave it a few months to see if it settles. That'll cost you . . .' He sucked his teeth. Then he smiled reassuringly. 'Tell you what, let's not talk about it just yet.'

Matt's voice had begun to recede. This couldn't be right.

'Up to you,' he said, tapping his pen on the table. 'I'll cut costs where I can.'

He spent another twenty minutes going round the house, wielding his tape measure, making notes. Isabel tried to go on practising in the kitchen but his presence made concentration impossible. The sound of his footsteps and his whistling made her oddly self-conscious, her playing halting and erratic. In the end, she went up the steps to the ground floor and found him peering up the dining-room chimney.

'I'll need to get up a ladder and have a look at that,' he said. 'Think one of the pots may have collapsed on itself. It's okay,' he added, 'it's not a big job. We can just cap it off. I won't charge you for that.'

'How very kind. Thank you,' said Isabel.

'Right,' he said. 'I'd better be off and pick up some of the materials.' He nodded towards the window. 'How'd you get on at ours this morning?'

Isabel had forgotten that Laura was Matt's wife. 'Oh . . .' she said, twisting her hands behind her back. 'Oh . . . it was very kind of Laura to invite me.' She realised, too late, that she had failed to imbue her voice with any enthusiasm.

'Trial by housewife, eh?'

Isabel blushed. 'It . . . I don't think I was what they were expecting.'

'Don't let that lot worry you. Got nothing better to do than natter about each other's soft furnishings. Bunch of curtain-twitchers. I tell Laura she spends too much time with them.' He had reached the door. 'Don't worry about all of this. I'll be back first thing tomorrow. If you can clear your stuff out of the dining room we'll start with the floorboards in there. See what's going on underneath.'

'Thank you,' said Isabel. She felt unaccountably grateful.

She had found his presence a little nerve-racking at first. Now she was reassured by it.

'Hey,' he said, saluting as he went down the steps, 'what are neighbours for?'

There was no place on earth lonelier than an empty double bed. The moonlight slanted through the window on to the ceiling as Isabel listened to the panes rumble peacefully in their frames, the distant calls of wild creatures. They did not frighten her now, but neither did they alleviate her sense that she was the only person awake in the whole world.

Earlier that evening, when she had first climbed into bed, she had heard weeping. She had got up again, pulled on her dressing-gown and hurried to Thierry's room. The covers were over his head and he wouldn't come out, despite her pleading. 'Talk to me, darling,' she had whispered. 'Please talk to me.' But he wouldn't. But, then, he didn't have to. She had laid a hand on him, feeling the muffled shudder of his crying, until his tears became her own. In the end, she had lain next to him and curled her body round his. When, at last, he slept, she had peeled the covers off his face, kissed his cheek, and almost reluctantly padded back up the rickety stairs to her own room.

She stood barefoot in it now, the rough boards against her soles, gazing at the curiously illuminated landscape. The trees in the distance had become a deep purple abyss. The shadows, the walls and pillars round the house shifted in the half-light. Something dark and swift ran across a path and disappeared into the black. She saw him suddenly, walking towards her from the trees, his jacket slung over his shoulder. But then he was gone, a spectral trick of her imagination.

'Laurent,' she whispered, pulling her robe round her as she climbed into the cold bed. 'Come back to me.'

She tried to picture him getting in beside her, his weight depressing the mattress, the creak of the springs, the comforting heaviness of his arm draped over her waist. Her own hands on the silk of her robe were too small, too fine. There was no weight, no meaning behind her touch. She felt the empty expanse of linen beside her, the unwarmed pillow. She heard the silence of a room with no one else breathing. She imagined Matt, across the lane, his strong body enclosing his wife's, his arms wrapped round her, Laura smiling in her half-sleep. She saw all the couples out there breathing, murmuring to each other, their hands entwined, skin meeting skin. No one will ever touch mine again, she thought. No one will ever take pleasure in me like he did. And a wave of longing so powerful swept over her that she thought she would choke.

'Laurent,' she whispered into the darkness, tears leaking from her closed eyes, and began to move against the silk. 'Laurent,' she cried, her hands trying to conjure music from a body that refused to listen.

Somewhere below, Byron called Elsie, his terrier, to heel, hearing her excited scurryings in the undergrowth. He lifted his torch, swinging its beam in front of his feet, watching the shadows move as creatures fled into the dark woodland. The lads in the pub had told him poachers had been laying traps up this end of the woods, and while he knew his little dog was too smart to get caught in one, he wanted to lift them before anything else did. You didn't forget your first sight of a fox or a badger that had been stuck in one for a few days, gnawing at its limb to free itself. And besides, being out with the dogs was better than sitting in an empty cottage brooding about his future.

His phone rang, and he retrieved it from his pocket,

whistling Elsie back as he did so. She sat down, half on his boot.

'Byron.'

'Yes?' Matt didn't bother to introduce himself now. It was as if he thought he owned him, even at this hour.

'You finish sinking those posts?'

Byron adjusted his neck. 'Yes.'

'Good. Tomorrow I need you to help me pull up the floorboards in the dining room at the Spanish House.'

Byron thought for a minute. 'The dining room? Surely that's the only good room in the house.' It had been a joke among the locals – Pottisworth's only sound room was the one he hadn't used for decades.

There was a brief silence. 'Who says it is?'

'Well, whenever I've been in—'

'Who's the builder here, Byron? You or me? Know much about wet and dry rot, do you? Learn that while you were inside?'

'No.'

'I'll meet you there at eight thirty. And the next time I want your opinion on building work, I'll ask for it.'

The space in front of the narrow beam of his torch was pitch black, the terrain unreadable. 'You're the boss,' Byron said.

He flipped his telephone shut, thrust it deep into his pocket and tramped wearily on into the wilderness.

Nine

Kitty sat in the tin tub, drew her knees up to her chest and laid her neck on the hand-towel she had folded and placed behind her. The towel got sopping wet, but it was the only way you could relax in a tin bath without severing your head. That, and tucking your knees up so your calves didn't have to hang over the top, cutting off your circulation. She had the electric heater on nearby so that when the water cooled, as it did really quickly, she didn't shiver for a full twenty minutes when it was time to get out. Her mum swore Kitty was going to electrocute herself but, given the state of the house, she thought she'd take her chances here as well as anywhere else.

She heard a vehicle outside, and decided it was time to begin the laborious process of emptying the bath, which she had, of course, overfilled. She thought she would never again take a plughole for granted: the sheer backbreaking tedium of endlessly lowering a bucket into the bath until it was empty enough to lift made it not worth filling in the first place. She heard Matt's voice downstairs as she wrapped herself in her towel. He was saying something about breakfast, telling Mum to put the coffee on, laughing at some joke she hadn't heard.

Most people complained about having builders in. Kitty remembered the mothers at her old school exclaiming about the dust and dirt, the cost and upheaval. They talked as if it were an ordeal that had to be endured. Like surgery.

It had been almost ten days now, and despite the chaos, the fact that she couldn't walk in a straight line downstairs without watching for missing floorboards or hold a conversation without being interrupted by the tearing sound of planks being wrenched from joists or hammering, she was enjoying it. It was nice to have other people around, and not just her and Mum, who always had her mind somewhere else, and Thierry, who never said anything any more anyway.

Matt McCarthy always chatted to her as if she was older than she was, and she recognised his son from school. She found it difficult to go into a room when Anthony was there because somehow his presence made her blush and go a bit tongue-tied. She wished one of her friends was around so they could tell her whether he was actually lush, or whether she was imagining it.

When Matt and his son had turned up that first morning she had been embarrassed that Anthony had seen their house looking as it did, that he must think this was how they had always lived. She wanted to say, 'We used to live in a normal house, you know. With a fridge.' Mum had begun to put the stuff that had to be kept cold in little baskets that she hung from the masonry outside the kitchen windows where foxes couldn't get it, and their fruit in orange nets, protection from the mice, and half of Kitty loved that because from outside it made their home look a bit like a gingerbread house, or something out of a fairytale, but the other half was humiliated. Who else had to leave their food hanging outside? She was terrified that Anthony would say something at school and everyone would laugh at her, but so far he hadn't.

Once, last week, when Matt had found out they were at the same school, he had said, 'Why don't you take Kitty out one night, boy? You could go into town, show her the sights.' Just like that. Like it was nothing. Anthony had sort of shrugged as if he might, but she wasn't sure if he'd done it because he wanted to, or if he was trying to keep his dad happy. 'I bet you're finding life out here a bit slow after London,' Matt said, when she brought them a mug of tea – as if she'd always been out clubbing and stuff like that. She could have sworn Anthony had raised his eyebrows, which had made her blush again.

Byron, who had only come for the first two days and then gone back to working outside, hardly said anything. He had seemed awkward in the house, as if he were built for outdoors. He was taller than Matt, and quite handsome, but he never met anyone's eye. 'Byron's our great conversationalist, aren't you, mate?' Matt would joke, but Byron smiled as if he didn't find it funny.

Mum was a bit stressed most of the time. She didn't like the builders' radio always being on. She didn't get pop music and Dad had always said that having it burbling on in the background was just another form of pollution, but she didn't seem able to ask them to turn it off. She had been forced to move out of the master bedroom, as it needed too much structural work, and into the box room, so she went on to the battlements to practise – the only place, she said, that she could find silence. When Kitty went outside and heard the violin up top and Matt McCarthy's radio down below it sounded like a competition.

Thierry seemed not to notice. He spent most of the time he wasn't at school in the woods, and Mum said to let him be. Kitty had collared him to ask him what he did out there, but he had just shrugged. For the first time Kitty could see why Mum and Dad had found shrugging irritating.

On the floor above Kitty, Matt McCarthy unrolled the architectural plans Sven had drawn up eighteen months previously, and held them to the light from the landing window, trying to decide which parts of their carefully thought-out renovations he could legitimately use. Some things, such as the extension at the rear, were not possible yet, but others, such as the resited bathroom, the master bedroom and the new windows in the upper floors, could be considered part of any straightforward repair work. There was little point in trying to do anything in the kitchen until he knew whether planning consent would be forthcoming for the extension, but there was plenty of basic structural work to be taken care of before then. In fact, thought Matt, it was fair to say there were months of remedial works to do. At significant expense.

He breathed in the familiar scents of the old house, grateful suddenly for this turn of events. It was a pleasure to be working here. Within the walls of the old place, he felt he had been given back control of his life and of something that had been snatched away from him.

He rolled up the plans, and placed them carefully in the cardboard tube, put on the lid and slipped it back into his holdall as Byron emerged at the top of the stairwell. For a man of his size he moved quietly – too quietly for Matt's liking.

'Right,' said Byron. 'Where do we start today?'

'Good question. And there are a million possible answers.'

'How's the house coming along?' Asad was polishing apples, his long, dark fingers working the soft cloth. Kitty sat on the crate by the freezer and sipped her tea. 'I see Mr McCarthy's there most days.'

'And his son. And Byron, but he doesn't come every day.'

'Are things improving? Are you more comfortable?'

'I wouldn't say that exactly.' Kitty inhaled – Henry had been making olive bread and it smelled delicious. She was half hoping they might offer her some. 'They've ripped lots of stuff out, though.'

'I've heard there's not much worth saving.' Henry appeared and put two loaves carefully in the bread basket. 'Does it have any original features?'

Kitty grimaced. 'I don't know. I think spiders are the main one. I found one in my sock drawer last night. It was so big I thought it was looking for some to wear.'

Asad tilted his head to one side. 'And how is your mother?' He said it as if there might be something wrong with her.

'She's okay. She's worried about how much it's all costing. She says it's a lot more expensive than she thought it would be.'

'I don't suppose Matt McCarthy comes cheap,' said Henry, and sniffed.

'Oh, Mum says he seems to be doing half of it out of the goodness of his heart.'

Henry and Asad exchanged a glance. 'Matt McCarthy?'

'She says we're lucky to have such good neighbours and if this had happened in London we'd be in terrible trouble. He's doing everything he can to keep costs down.' She stood a little closer to the bread. It was ages since breakfast.

'Would you like one? You can pay when you next come in if you like.' Asad gestured to the loaf.

'Really? I'll bring the money tomorrow. I can't face walking all the way back to get my purse now. And Mum's stopped me using the car.'

Asad shook his head, as if it were of no consequence. 'Tell me, Kitty, has Matt . . . mentioned anything about the history of the house?'

Kitty was too busy sticking her thumb into the bread to notice the way Henry looked at his friend. 'No,' she said absently. Why were people so obsessed with history around here?

'Of course not,' said Asad. 'Let me get you a bag for that.'

Byron had been coppicing the wood for almost half an hour when he discovered what Elsie had been looking at. She had been unsettled since Meg, his collie bitch, had whelped the previous week and he had put down her constant whining to that, but as he brought the axe down on the ash sapling, then hauled the fallen trunk into a pile with the others, he caught a flash of blue and saw what the dog had been watching.

The boy had been following him for several days. When Byron tended the pheasant chicks, fixed the electric fencing, or now when he was thinning out the wood that stood between Matt's place and the Spanish House, he had discovered he had a small, pale shadow. The boy would watch for fifteen, twenty minutes at a time, half obscured by trees or bushes, then disappear when Byron gave even a hint that he might move towards him.

He had realised pretty quickly who he must be. Now he turned back to the stump and drilled a few holes into it with his cordless electric screwdriver, preparing to poison the roots. These ash saplings were buggers for coming back. 'You fancy giving me a hand?' he said quietly, without turning.

There was silence.

Byron drilled six more holes. He could feel the boy's eyes on him. ''S all right. I don't feel like talking much of the time, either.'

He still didn't turn, but after a moment he heard light footsteps behind him. 'Don't pet the dog. She'll come to you when she's ready. And if you want to help, grab some of those smaller branches. Careful, now,' he said, as the boy bent and gathered an armful.

Byron dragged three of the young trees out into the field. He had planned to collect them later and cut up the larger ones to season for firewood. But there was no point in chopping logs if he didn't know where he would be living.

He thought of the pile of floorboards they had removed from the Spanish House and stacked by the big barn. Most were dry, as far as he could see, but he had learned better than to question Matt.

'Just leave it there,' he said, pointing to the pile. The boy heaved a sapling through the grass at the edge of the field and, with a grunt, dropped it.

'What to help some more?' The boy's eyes, beneath dark lashes, were solemn. He nodded.

'What's your name?' The boy looked at his feet. Elsie sniffed at his trainers, and he glanced up at Byron, as if he was checking that it was okay, then bent down to rub her head. Elsie rolled on to her back, shamelessly exposing a pink stomach. 'Thierry,' he said, so quietly that Byron barely heard him.

'You like dogs, Thierry?' He kept his voice low, casual.

The boy nodded shyly. Elsie grinned at him upside-down, her tongue lolling out of her mouth.

Byron had seen him in the house a couple of times, a shadow even in his home, stuck in front of a computer game. He wasn't sure why he had spoken. He was a man who preferred his own company.

'You help me with a few more of these and when I'm done we'll ask your mum if you can come to see our new pups. Would you like that?'

The child's smile caught him unexpectedly, and he returned to the fallen trees, already unsure what he had agreed to. Unsure whether he wanted to be responsible for so much of someone's happiness.

★　★　★

'Bright as the new, new day.' Those had been Thierry's last fluent words. His voice had rung out, confident and piercing, closing in a smile with the last line of his poem. He had won a prize for it, read it out to the parents in his class perform-ance, and Isabel, freed for once from the demands of the orchestra, had sat and clapped madly in her moulded plastic chair, wondering now and then why the one beside her had remained empty. Laurent had sworn he would make it in time. She had not been irritated by his absence, like the other women whose husbands had not appeared, but had instead felt vaguely superior that for once she had been the parent to get there.

'He was very good, wasn't he?' muttered Mary, on her other side. A mother in front of her turned and grinned.

'Perfect,' said Isabel, beaming. 'Absolutely perfect.'

She had caught Thierry's eye as he walked off-stage, and he had given her a little wave, trying not to let the pride on his face shine through. She had wondered whether to get up and meet him behind the curtain to tell him how proud she was, but respectful of the other performers – and well versed in what an intrusion it could be when people randomly nego-tiated their way out of an audience – she had stayed in her seat. She had regretted that decision. She had wished so often that she had reached him before the police arrived back-stage, so that she had heard him, just once more, repeat the poem he had rehearsed a thousand times. His beautiful, care-free eight-year-old voice, full of schoolboy gripes and *Star Wars* and demands for sweets and counting the days till his best friend came for a sleepover. Telling her he loved her, surreptitiously, so that his friends couldn't hear. 'Bright as the new, new day.' That voice. Instead of those few, crushing words from the sombre policeman. *Yes,* she had said, clutch-ing Thierry's shoulder, her physical self somehow already grasping what her mind could not. *Yes, she was Mrs Isabel Delancey. What did he mean, an accident?*

'Sorry – I didn't catch that.' Isabel stood in the middle of the kitchen with the man who had brought Thierry home, his hands green, his jumper studded with tree bark. She repeated what he'd said. 'You want my son to go to your house to see some puppies?'

'My bitch had a litter last week. Thierry thought he'd like to see them.' He pronounced it 'Terry'.

'Your puppies.'

Byron's face darkened as he heard the underlying question in what she'd said. 'My sister and her daughter will be there,' he said stiffly.

Isabel blushed. 'I didn't mean—'

'The boy's been helping me. I thought he'd like to meet my niece and the pups.' His voice hardened.

'Hello, Byron. You finished?' Matt appeared behind her, making her jump. He was one of those men who radiated something far beyond the confines of their physical selves.

Byron's jaw had clenched. 'I've taken out about forty saplings, ash mainly. I'd like you to have a look before I take any more.' He gestured to his dog, which left the kitchen. 'I was just telling Mrs Delancey that her son was welcome to see our new litter. But perhaps it's best left.'

She could see he was furious. They had barely spoken during the two days he had worked at the house. He had nodded a greeting and she, remembering their exchange over the gun, had felt too awkward to raise the matter again.

Thierry looked pleadingly at his mother.

'Well, it's fine by me,' she said uncertainly. She stepped aside to allow Matt into the kitchen.

'Your boy will be all right with Byron. Going to see someone's puppies means something different in the city.'

He let out a bark of laughter. 'You'll have to be careful how you word that in future, Byron.'

'I didn't think for a minute—' Isabel's hand was at her throat. 'Byron, I didn't mean to imply—'

'Don't worry about it,' said Byron, head down as he left. 'Best leave the pups for now. I've got to get on. I'll see you tomorrow, Matt.'

Thierry tugged at his mother's sleeve, but Byron was gone. He stared at the space where the man had been, then shot his mother a look of furious disappointment and ran out of the kitchen. She heard his footsteps all the way to the door, which slammed emphatically.

'Don't listen too much to what's said about Byron,' said Matt, his eyes twinkling. 'He's a good man.'

Isabel had barely time to consider this as she rushed past him, took the steps two at a time, and tore out of the front door in time to see Byron stalking towards the far hedge. 'Byron!' she yelled. And when he didn't turn, she shouted again: 'Please! Please wait!'

She was out of breath by the time she caught him. 'I'm sorry,' she said, her heels sinking into the wet clay. 'Really. I'm so sorry if I offended you.'

His expression, she saw, was of resignation rather than anger. 'Please let Thierry come.' She dropped her hands to her sides. 'He's had a difficult time . . . He doesn't speak very much. At all, really. But I know he'd love to see your dogs.'

Byron's terrier had run to the edge of the garden and was waiting expectantly for him.

'I'll get him,' she said, taking his silence as acquiescence. 'I'm sure I can find him if you'll wait five minutes. There are just a few places he tends to go.'

'No need.' Byron nodded towards the far hedge, where a

blue sweater could be seen through the yew. 'He was following me home anyway.'

Laura McCarthy painted the sixth tester colour on to a strip of her bedroom wall and stood back. It didn't matter what combination of lights she used, it didn't look right. None of the colours had worked. None of the fabric swatches she had brought home for new curtains, none of her classic combinations. She had decided to freshen up her and Matt's bedroom to take her mind off the loss of the Spanish House. But somehow the joy had gone out of the task. The walls were just their old walls, and the curtains would not adorn the huge bay windows of the master bedroom at the Spanish House, with its view of the water.

She had wanted that house. She hadn't said so to Matt, not wanting to aggravate his own sense of grievance, but she felt as if it had been stolen from her, as if a squatter had moved into her family home. She was not prone to melodrama, but it was almost like the loss of a child. And trying to pretend it didn't matter in front of the other women had required superhuman effort. She had made plans for every inch of it, could see so clearly the best way forward for each room. It would have been beautiful. But it was not so much the house that she mourned. It was the prospect of what it might have been, what they might have become as a family within it.

Laura sighed and put the lid back on the little tin, her eyes on the patchwork-painted wall as she listened to the distant sounds of hammering that signified Matt's working day. He had been upbeat for several weeks but a little detached, as if his mind was permanently on other things. That morning he had handed her a cheque from the Delancey woman. 'Better pay it in soon before they start bouncing,' he said, cheerfully. She hoped that it was the prospect of this, and not some other preoccupation, that had brought about his cheeriness.

The woman was so odd, so vulnerable. She plainly didn't have a clue about living in the country or renovating a house. She wasn't even very good at talking to people. She had stood in Laura's front room in those odd clothes like a fish out of water, and while Laura found herself relaxing as she saw the depth of the other woman's mistake, she could not help imagining what it must be like to be her, with two children to bring up alone in that house. She had seemed lost, but oddly fierce too, as if she might have turned on them for the slightest reason. The Cousins said she was a breath of fresh air, but they were nice about everyone, even if she suspected they didn't always mean it. Whenever she went into the shop Asad's hooded brown eyes would settle on her in a way that suggested he knew about Matt, which made her uncomfortable. He would smile in a way that managed to be both kindly and pitying. Perhaps he saw her as she had found herself regarding Isabel Delancey at the coffee morning. Matt had urged her to visit, but had stopped now. Perhaps he had picked up on how reluctant she felt. Laura had found it easier to keep her distance. She was not deceitful by nature. If Mrs Delancey had asked her her true opinion of the house, what on earth would she have said?

From the Spanish House she heard a creak and a muffled crash and wondered what Matt was doing. He says it will be ours in the end, she thought. That's all I have to keep in mind. That woman is not suited to living there. And all is fair in love, war and property.

Laura McCarthy straightened a curtain. She had a heap of ironing to finish and Ruby, the cleaner, could never do creases in Matt's shirts the way he liked them.

Ten

As spring morphed into early summer, Isabel's day had settled into something like a routine – not one she had ever expected, but little of her life now resembled anything she might have foreseen. Each morning she would send the children up the track to the school bus. Then, after a restorative cup of coffee, she would make the beds, scrabble under them for stray socks, haul a basket down to the new washing-machine in the kitchen and then, if the weather was good enough, peg the laundry on the line. She would clear the breakfast things, answer the mail, try to work out what to cook the children for supper, then sweep or vacuum the endless trail of foot-prints that led in and out of the house.

She would make Matt and whichever of the men he brought with him the first of their many mugs of tea, then try to work out the answers to a dozen questions she had not until that point considered: where did she want the new light switches? What kind of light fittings? How far across did she want this opening? She thought she had never been more bored in her life, or more conscious of the efforts Mary had made while she had been lost in her music. And all the time she hung on impatiently for some quiet hour in which to practise, some time in which she could clear her mind and remember that she was more than the domestic servant she had become.

She suspected that her children were enjoying this new parent. She could cook several dishes tolerably well now, had customised the east side of the house so that the rooms that were not sheathed in plastic and scaffolding had an air of homeliness. She helped, as far as possible, with homework. She was there, all the time.

What they did not know was that she chafed at the never-endingness of it. No sooner had she cleaned one surface than it was dirty again. Clothes, even those barely worn, found themselves in crumpled heaps in linen baskets so that she yelled at Kitty and Thierry, hating her shrewish voice. Once, bored to within an inch of her sanity by the act of hanging out yet another lineful, she had simply turned, dropped the basket and walked straight into the lake, pausing only to remove her shoes. The water had been so shockingly cold that it had knocked the breath from her chest, and left her laughing for the sheer joy of feeling something. Matt had been on the scaffolding with his son, both staring at her in astonishment.

'Is this your way of saying you want me to get on with the bathroom?' he had joked, and she had nodded, teeth chattering.

Sometimes she wondered what Laurent would say if he saw her scrubbing in industrial rubber gloves at whatever pan she had burned. Or when he saw her swearing and pushing the rusting old lawnmower in a vain attempt to impose order on the gardens. Occasionally she pictured him seated on some piece of furniture with an amused smile. '*Alors, chérie! Mais qu'est-ce que c'est?*' But all of this was as nothing compared with the growing list of problems that arose from Matt's work. It seemed as if every time she came across him he was prodding at a piece of rotting wood with the end of his ballpoint pen, or rubbing some rusting residue between his thumb and forefinger. The house was in an even worse condition than she had thought.

Each day brought some nasty surprise: woodworm in joists, leaking pipework, an area of roof that needed replacing. Matt would outline the problem reluctantly, then add reassuringly:

'Don't worry. We'll find a way round it.' He made every problem seem surmountable, and had an air of calm capability that was magnetic. There was little, he told her comfortingly, that he hadn't seen before, even less that couldn't be rectified. So far she had handed over nearly half her savings for materials. The wood, electric cable, insulating boards and slates sat in neat piles in the outbuildings, next to overflowing skips, as if the house was a builders' merchant.

He had warned her that they would be there for months. 'We'll try to keep out of your way,' he said. After a week she had known that that wasn't going to be possible. Plaster dust was everywhere, permeating not just every surface but every crevice of their bodies. Kitty's eyes were red and Isabel sneezed incessantly. All food had to be covered, and periodically Isabel would enter a room to find the floor missing, or a door off its hinges. 'At least it means something's happening, Mum,' said Kitty, who was surprisingly untroubled by the chaos, 'and it will be a proper home at the end of it.'

Isabel tried to keep this thought in mind when she surveyed the rubble-strewn site they inhabited. She tried not to wonder whether the money would run out long before that happened.

Isabel sat on the sofa, her legs folded under her, with a huge box of receipts and bank statements. Occasionally she would frown, and hold up two pieces of paper, as if she were comparing them, then throw them down in despair. Kitty, struggling with her homework, tried to ignore her. Thierry sat on the easy chair, hooked up to a computer game, only his thumbs moving. Mr Granger was downstairs, relining one of the flues. Above, Matt, Byron and Anthony were doing something momentous – or Kitty assumed it was: the drilling made the rest of the house shake, and puffs of plaster dust kept floating down the stairs, like the sinister breath of some demonic creature. And all the while it rained, which kept the skies low and grey and cast another layer of depression over the already gloomy house. The water dripped into buckets in the hallway and a bedroom, with a melancholic irregular beat.

'Oh!' Isabel exclaimed, shoving the box away from her. 'I cannot look at another row of figures! How your father managed this day in and day out is beyond me.'

'I wish he could help me with this maths,' said Kitty, sadly. 'I don't understand any of it.'

Isabel stretched and went to peer over her shoulder. 'Oh, lovey, I'm sorry but I haven't a clue. Your daddy really was the clever one.'

As they considered this, Thierry slid off his chair and went to the window. He began to hit the heavy drapes with his fist, so that clouds of dust billowed out.

'Don't do that, T,' said Kitty, irritably.

Thierry hit it harder, deliberately sending great powdery gusts into the air.

Kitty scowled. 'Mum!' she protested.

And then, when Isabel did nothing, 'Mum! Look at him!'

Her mother walked over to him and stroked his head with a pale hand and said, looking up at the red velvet: 'They are awful, aren't they? Perhaps I should give them a good shake. Get the worst of it out.'

'Oh, not now—' Kitty began, but it was too late. Her mother was shaking the curtains vigorously so that great clouds of dust flew into the room, making Thierry cough.

'Don't worry,' Isabel said, as she swung them back and forth. 'I'll vacuum afterwards.'

'I can't believe you—' Kitty gasped as the heavy curtain pole fell out of the plaster and landed on the floor, a good portion of the wall still attached to it. Her mother's hands covered her head as chunks of plaster rained down and the curtains settled, billowing around her. After an appalled silence, during which Kitty contemplated the great holes above the window, through which you could see the bricks, Isabel giggled.

'Oh, Mum . . . what have you done?' Kitty came across to inspect the damage.

Isabel shook plaster dust from her hair. 'They were horrible.'

'Yes, but at least they were curtains. Now we don't have any.' Her mother could be infuriating. She was going to the CD player now. 'I don't care, Kitty. In the grand scheme of things, they're just curtains. I've spent all day bogged down in bloody curtains and bills and domestic stuff. I've had enough. Let's have some music.'

Above, the banging had stopped. Oh, no, Kitty muttered silently. Please not now. Not while Anthony's here. 'Mum, I need to do my homework.'

'And you also need some fun. I'll try to help you with the homework afterwards. Come on, Thierry, unhook me a curtain. I know what we can use them for.'

Her mother stepped away from the stereo and Kitty heard the first bars of Bizet's *Carmen*. Oh, no, she thought. No, you can't. But Isabel was crouched near Thierry, pulling one of the curtains round her waist.

'Mum, please . . .' Kitty said. But a few bars in her mother was lost in the music, swirling round in her new red outfit, swishing it round her shoulders as the aria reached its heady heights. Thierry picked up the other and mimicked her, his mouth shaping words he no longer said aloud. Exasperated, Kitty walked across the room to turn off the music, but caught her mother's smile at the sight of Thierry dancing, and saw that she was trapped. She stood, her arms folded, while they sashayed round each other, miming to the opera, and prayed it wouldn't last too long and that nobody would come downstairs.

So, of course, Anthony arrived. Byron came first, carrying

a shoulderload of waste wood to the stairs. But Anthony paused in the doorway, his woollen hat pulled low on his head, and peered round, a hammer in his hand. Kitty caught his eye and fought the urge to bury herself under the sofa. It was pretty well the most embarrassing thing that had ever happened to her. Until her mother saw him, and, with a cry of 'Hey! Anthony!' hurled a curtain at him. 'Bullfight!' she yelled, and Thierry raised his fingers to his head.

Kitty decided she actually wanted to die. Bullfight was the game they had played with their father, him waving towels around, she and Thierry attempting to charge him as he nipped out of the way. Her mother couldn't do Bullfight. It wasn't right. And Anthony would tell everyone at school that they were mad.

But he caught the curtain, dropped his hammer and, in a second, was waving it for Thierry to charge through. Perhaps galvanised by the presence of another boy, Thierry's performance was increasingly bullish. As the music grew in pitch and fervour, he barrelled round the living room, sending rugs and coffee-tables flying, causing Anthony several times to collapse on to the sofa. Her mother stood in the corner by the stereo, helpless with laughter. Thierry was bellowing, his foot pawing the ground. And Anthony was grinning, sweeping aside his curtain with a flourish. '*Olé!*' he shouted, and suddenly Kitty was shouting too. And for the first time in ages, with the noise and the shouting and everyone laughing, she was happy – really happy. Her mother had grabbed the other curtain again, and was swirling it around in time with the music, and Kitty made to grab it from her, and tussling over that piece of rotten scarlet fabric was funny. And then a crash from upstairs, heavy enough to make the floor beneath them tremble, stopped everything. The CD jammed on repeat, and Isabel crossed the room to turn it off. 'What the hell was that?' she said, and there came another, lesser crash, followed by a muffled exclamation.

The curtain was settling around Kitty's feet as everyone bolted for the stairs, then stopped on the landing. There, clouds of plaster dust emanated from the doorway of the master bedroom, and Matt appeared, coughing and wiping his eyes. 'Christ. That was close,' he said. 'A few minutes earlier and it might have landed on Anthony.'

Anthony stared into the room. He, too, was shocked and grey – either because he had blanched at the sight or because he was covered with dust. Isabel put a hand over her mouth and nose and went in, ignoring Matt's warning. Kitty followed.

The ceiling had gone. Where once there had been a smoothly plastered surface, there was now a skeletal gap, through which it was possible to make out the ceiling of the empty attic room above. A great pile of timber and plaster lay at the centre of the room, the struts sticking upwards. Mum's bed was there, thought Kitty. All of that could have landed on her.

'I was removing the light fitting to check the electrics,' said Matt, 'and the whole lot went *whoosh*, joists and all. Could have killed us. Could have killed anyone.'

Mr Granger's face was pink from running. 'Thank the Lord you're all right,' he said. 'Thought the whole house were coming down. My old ticker's still pounding.'

'Are we safe?' Isabel asked.

'What?' said Matt.

'Is that it – only rotten joists? Nothing else is likely to fall down?' Her eyes burned into his.

Matt said nothing.

'Never seen a floor joist come down like that before,' said the old man.

'But that's it, isn't it?' Isabel insisted. 'Everything else is okay. It was just that room.' Kitty saw she was holding her violin. She must have picked it up when she thought the house was falling down.

There was a brief silence. Say something, she willed Matt. Say it now.

'It should be fine,' said Anthony, from behind her. 'I don't understand it. All the other floors upstairs are good. I've checked them myself. It was just this one.'

'Yes, Anthony, but you don't have the experience to know that for sure,' Matt said.

'But I'm sure—'

'You're going to start issuing guarantees, are you, son? You can be absolutely sure that this building's rock solid?' He was staring at his son as if he was daring him to say something different.

'What do you mean, Matt?'

There was a brief silence.

'I can't promise anything, Isabel.' He shook his head. 'I've told you what I think of this house. I can't reassure you.'

Kitty was about to go back downstairs when she heard the explosion. A loud bang ricocheted round the walls.

'What the bloody hell—' Isabel broke off.

It was as if all the air had been sucked out of the house. Matt, his hair white with plaster dust, bolted for the stairs, Kitty, with her mother, behind him. Oh, God, she thought. This house is going to kill us all.

She ran into Matt at the door. In the middle of the kitchen Byron held a gun to his shoulder. Several feet away, just outside the back door, lay a dead rat.

'Bloody hell, mate,' said Matt, stepping into the kitchen. 'What have you been up to?'

The rat's innards, a vivid red, spilled on to the cracked step. Byron seemed shocked too. 'I just came in to pick up the keys to the van and it was sitting there, bold as brass.'

'Yuk,' breathed Thierry, suddenly animated.

Kitty stared at the creature, feeling both repulsed by it and sorry for it. Her mother's hand tightened on her arm. She drew herself up to her full height. 'What the *hell* do you think you're doing, bringing a gun into my house? Are you some kind of madman?' Her voice was hoarse.

'I didn't bring it,' said Byron. 'It's Pottisworth's.'

Isabel did a double-take. 'What?'

'He kept it at the top of that cupboard. Had done for years.' Byron gestured above the pantry. 'I thought you knew.'

'But why were you shooting it?'

'It's a rat. What were you going to do – ask it nicely to leave? You can't have rats in your kitchen.'

'You're a maniac!' said Isabel, pushing past Kitty and shoving at him. 'Get out of my house!'

'Mum!' Kitty grabbed her. Her mother was trembling.

'Steady on, Isabel,' Matt said. 'Let's all calm down now.'

'Tell him,' she demanded. 'He works for you. Tell him you cannot fire a gun in someone's house!'

Matt's hand lay on her shoulder. 'Strictly speaking, it wasn't quite inside. But, yes, you're right. Byron, mate, that was a little extreme.'

Byron was rubbing the back of his head. 'I'm sorry. I didn't think it was safe, with young kids around. This house has never had rats. Never. I thought if I got it quickly . . .'

'It was safer to let a gun off in my kitchen?'

'It wasn't in your kitchen,' said Byron. 'It was in the doorway.'

Isabel stared at the dead creature, the colour drained from her face.

'Don't fret, missus. No harm done,' Mr Granger said soothingly. 'I'll clear it up for you. Here, boy, you hand me that bit of newspaper. Come on now, Mrs Delancey, sit down and have a cup of tea. You've had a bit of a shock. Never a dull moment in this house, eh?'

'Collapsing floors, rats, guns? What is this place?' Isabel

said, as if to no one. 'What on earth have I done?' And then as Kitty stood, still breathing hard from the dancing, her mother turned and walked slowly from the kitchen, as if none of them was there, her violin clutched to her chest.

That evening, the music that echoed across the water was frenzied. It held none of its usual melancholic beauty, but hit the air in furious, jagged notes.

Kitty lay on her bed, knowing she should go up and talk to her mother, but she couldn't get too worked up about Byron or his stupid rat. She kept thinking about Anthony with his red curtain, the way he had grinned at her, as if he didn't think her family was mad. For the first time, Kitty was almost glad to be there.

Henry and Asad, walking home, paused as the last note drew to an angry close.

'PMT,' said Henry, knowledgeably.

'I thought she said she was with the CSO,' said Asad.

Across the lane, Laura McCarthy was finishing the washing-up. 'That noise,' she said, drying her hands on a tea-towel, 'is going to drive me insane. I don't understand why the woods don't swallow the sound, like they do everything else.'

'Should have heard it earlier,' said Matt, who had been cheerful all evening, even when she'd told him her car needed two new tyres. 'Never seen anything like it. Have you, Ant?'

Anthony, eyes on the television, made a noncommittal sound.

'What do you mean?' said Laura.

Matt flicked open a can of beer. 'Mad as a March hare, that one. We'll be in by Christmas, Laura. Mark my words. Christmas at the latest.'

Eleven

There were few sights more beautiful than the Norfolk countryside in early summer, Nicholas observed, as he drove the last few miles to Little Barton, passing the flint cottages, the skeletal rows of pines whose only greenery teetered at the pinnacle of spindly trunks.

Admittedly when one had left the unlovely environs of north-east London, almost anywhere seemed green and picturesque in comparison. But today, as the reservoirs, industrial parks and weary rows of pylons that marked the outskirts of the city melted away, the lush growth of the hedgerows and fresh-minted green of the verges had an almost unbearable piquancy. The symbolism was not lost on Nicholas Trent.

The bank had pronounced itself happy to back him to a certain level, and wanted to see detailed plans. 'Good to see you,' Richard Winters had said, clapping him on the back. 'Can't keep a good man down, eh?'

He had tried to tell himself many times that the woman might not want to sell. That there were plenty of other sites that could equally well accommodate his plans. But when he closed his eyes, he saw the Spanish House and its grounds. He saw the fabulous valley, surrounded by scenery so perfect it was hard to believe that it was not straight out of a picture book.

And even though he had known he would have a more straightforward journey back to business with a smaller-scale development on some brownfield site in the city, he had still headed out of London towards Little Barton for the third time in a month. So that, once again, he could accidentally find himself in the place that preoccupied him, that showed itself in the glorious technicolour property brochures of his dreams.

At work he had told them nothing. Every day he turned up at the agents' offices, punctual and polite, and subjected himself to the same stressed customers, the same unfathomable changes of mind, the same collapsing deals and unmet targets. Derek had become increasingly snappy – he had been passed over for the area-manager promotion – and Nicholas knew that the leaflet dropping and coffee runs were his way of taking it out on someone. But he no longer minded. In fact, he relished the opportunity to be out of the office, with its petty irritations and fervid jealousies, so that he could lose himself in his thoughts. His brain hummed with ideas.

'What have *you* got to be so cheerful about?' Charlotte would ask, as if his happiness somehow caused her offence.

Twelve energy-renewable homes with solar panels and thermal heating, he wanted to answer. Five executive houses with an acre of grounds each. A top-of-the-range apartment block, each high-spec unit with glass frontage, offering spectacular views of the lake. So many possibilities, so much potential, all dependent on one thing: persuading the widow to sell.

I used to have the gift of the gab, Nicholas reminded himself, slowing down as he saw the sign for Little Barton. Once I could have sold ice cubes to Eskimos. There's no reason why I shouldn't pull this off. I just have to pitch it right. Ask someone too eagerly and they became convinced they had a potential goldmine on their hands. Offer too low and they'd be so offended they wouldn't sell to you at any price.

There was no point in pinning all his hopes on one property, he thought, no matter how good an opportunity it represented. Better than anyone, he knew that that was the way to ruin. He pulled up in the village, arguing with himself, trying to put a brake on his own enthusiasm. He wouldn't visit the house today. He'd try to find out a little more about it, perhaps drive around, look in a few agents' windows. It was an up-and-coming area, after all. Rackety old barns were being knocked into habitable shape, workmen's cottages reconfigured to meet rising demand. He would investigate all the other possibilities, and not let his heart rule his head. He didn't want to raise his hopes, then cope with the aftermath when they were dashed.

But it was so hard.

Nicholas Trent sat in the quiet street for a few minutes. Finally he climbed out of his car.

'What that man is doing is immoral.'

'You can't say that, Asad. You have no proof.'

'Proof.' Asad snorted as he stacked peppers on the vegetable display. Red, yellow, green, in meticulous order. 'It is plain to see that he is pulling that house apart from the inside. You only have to mention his work to Mrs McCarthy for her to turn the colour of *this.*' He held aloft a red pepper. 'She is well aware of what he is doing. This is probably something they have cooked up between them.'

'Mrs McCarthy being embarrassed is no proof of anything. She may still feel awkward about the house because of all the hard work she put in with the old gentleman for no reward.' Henry shook his head. 'In fact, there are all sorts of reasons Laura McCarthy might feel awkward when she talks to people about her husband, and you know as well as I do what those might be.'

'I know what I know. And you know it too. That man is as good as stealing from Mrs Delancey. And he is doing it with a smile on his face, pretending to be a good Samaritan.'

The sun streamed through the windows of the little shop,

lighting up the buckets of flowers, which swayed cheerfully in the breeze, harbingers of warmer months ahead. But the peonies and freesias, visible through the pristine glass, and the pots of hyacinths that decorated the windowsills were at odds with the air of foreboding inside. Henry watched Asad as he straightened, listening for wheezing. The hay-fever season was approaching, and Asad's asthma always took a downturn at this time of year. 'I think,' he said, 'it would be a good idea if you didn't get yourself too worked up about this.'

'I think,' said Asad, pointedly, 'that it is about time someone stood up to Matt McCarthy.'

The door opened, and a man entered the shop to the tinkling of the bell. Middle-aged, middle class, good suit, thought Henry. A traveller on a through route. 'Can I help you?' he said.

'Er . . . not just yet, thank you.' He went to the delicatessen counter. 'I wanted some lunch.'

'We can certainly help you there,' Henry assured him. 'Let me know when you're ready.' He left the man and went back to Asad who, having perfected the vegetable display, was now rearranging the shelves.

'The canned fish,' whispered Henry, 'really doesn't need to be in alphabetical order.'

Asad made sure his voice was low when he spoke. 'This troubles me, Henry. It really troubles me.'

'It's none of our business. And white crabmeat should be next to sardines.'

'Kitty comes in here every day saying he has knocked down this wall or that ceiling has collapsed. Mrs Delancey comes in white with worry about her finances.'

'Anyone who's had building work knows it's disruptive and expensive. You remember what it was like when we had our kitchen done.'

'That house existed for fifty years with no work at all.'

'Exactly,' muttered Henry. 'That's why it probably needs knocking around now.'

'She knows nothing about building. She knows nothing about anything except music. She is still preoccupied with her dead husband. He is taking advantage.' His voice had lifted with frustration.

'But we don't know anything about what's wrong with the house. As you said, nobody's looked at it for fifty years. Who's to say what Matt McCarthy's found?'

Asad gritted his teeth. 'Any other builder, Henry, anybody but that man, and I would be content to believe that the house needed so much work.' He put a can of pilchards on the shelf.

The customer was examining the bread basket.

'But you tell me something from your heart. Tell me you don't think Matt McCarthy is doing this so that he can have the house. You tell me this is not some kind of revenge.'

Henry stared at his feet.

'Well?'

'I can't say that. I don't trust him any more than you do, but it's none of our business. And getting involved will only lead to grief.'

They stopped talking abruptly as the customer appeared at Asad's elbow. He gave them a courteous smile. 'I'm so sorry to interrupt, but could I possibly have one of the wholemeal rolls with some of that goat's cheese?'

Henry scooted back behind the counter. 'Certainly. Shall I throw in a couple of the vine tomatoes? They're ever so good at the moment.'

Nicholas Trent walked out of the little shop with a brown-paper bag. Despite his earlier appetite he was no longer hungry. He threw the bag on to the passenger seat and headed off down the road, brain humming, stomach taut with excitement, searching for the overgrown lane beside the piggery that marked the way to the Spanish House.

'A Spring Chorus.' An attractive mixture of freesias, narcissi and hyacinths, available in white, mauve or pale blue. Available as a bouquet, a hand-tied arrangement or, for a little extra, arranged in a glass vase. Prices started at a little over thirty pounds, not including delivery. Laura had looked it up on the Internet. Flowers to gladden your heart in late spring. Flowers to say thank you. Or I'm thinking of you. Or even I love you.

Flowers she had not received.

Flowers that had been charged to Matt's credit card the previous month.

Of course, she hadn't seen the statement – Matt had long been too canny to leave credit-card statements around, and she knew he used his work card for anything he didn't want her to see. But she had been going through his pockets before she washed his work jeans, and the crumpled receipt had fallen out with some self-tapping screws and a handful of loose change. She knew it was his card number, just as she knew everything there was to know about him.

What she did not know was who had received the flowers.

Laura McCarthy walked up the lane, the dog running in front of her, and let the tears fall down her cheeks. She couldn't believe he had done it again. After everything he had said to her, after everything he had promised. She had thought they were past this. She had lost the anxious, nervy feeling that she was not quite enough for him, that her lack of something indefinable meant she should always be on her guard. She had stopped viewing any woman she came across as a potential threat.

Fool.

Laura blew her nose, failing to notice the glory of the budding hedgerows, the narcissi and bluebells pushing through the earth. Her stomach was a mass of knots, her head a whirling din of rage and accusation. She could see only Matt's face, leering into that of some other woman's . . . No! She had long known that was the way to madness. She could hear her mother warning her when she had made such an 'unsuitable' match that she would have only herself to blame when it went wrong. She could see herself, politely turning a blind eye to her husband's infidelities until he was too old to commit them. 'Bugger you, Matt,' she yelled into the breeze, feeling faintly stupid that her upbringing and manners forbade the use of earthier language.

What should she do? What *could* she do, when he knew he held all the cards? How could he do this to her when she loved him so much, had done nothing but love him their whole life together?

In her heart she had guessed something was up. He had been too cheerful, too removed from her. He had not wanted to make love for almost three weeks, and with Matt there was little doubt as to what that meant, despite his protestations of exhaustion, or his staying up at night to watch 'unmissable' films.

'Oh, God . . .' Laura sat down on a tree stump and let the sobs rack her. She was made of stern stuff, but today she was beaten into submission by that tiny scrap of paper. Her marriage was a sham. It didn't matter what he said – that it was nothing to do with her, that it was just the way he was made. It didn't matter that he denied it. She loved him, and it was no use.

'I'm sorry. Are you all right?'

Laura's head shot up. A man in a suit stood fifty yards away, his car some distance back, the engine idling and the driver's door open. He leaned sideways, as if to see her better, without coming too near. Bernie, her dog, was sitting at his feet as if Laura was nothing to do with him.

Laura, mortified, wiped frantically at her face with her hands. 'Oh. Goodness.' She got up quickly, cheeks flooding with colour. 'I'll get out of your way.' She was appalled that someone had seen her in this state. So few people came into the woods that she had never considered she might not be alone.

As she rummaged in her pockets, she heard him approaching. He held out a handkerchief to her. 'Here,' he said. 'Please take this.'

She reached out reluctantly, and pressed it to her face. Nobody used linen handkerchiefs any more, she thought absently. She felt vaguely reassured, as if there could be no malice in someone who kept one on his person. 'I'm so sorry,' she said, trying to stop shuddering. 'You've caught me at a bad moment.'

'Is there . . . anything I can do?'

She half laughed. The idea of it, as if there were anything that could help this now. 'Oh . . . No,' she said.

He waited while she dried her face. Crying was so alien to her.

'I wasn't sure if you could hear me. I didn't know if you were wearing one of those things . . .' He mimed earphones. 'Dog-walkers often do, you know.'

'No . . .' She glanced around for Bernie, then made to give back the handkerchief, and realised how wet it was. 'I'm sorry. I don't think you're going to want it like this.'

'Oh, that . . .' He waved a hand, as if it were of no importance.

She got the dog by the collar and stood for a moment, head bowed, not knowing what to say.

'I'll leave you in peace, then,' he said, seemingly unwilling to move, 'if you're sure you're okay.'

'I'm fine. Thank you.'

Suddenly she remembered where they were. 'You do know this is a private road? Were you looking for somebody?'

It was his turn to look awkward.

'Ah,' he said. 'A private road. I must have taken a wrong turning. Surprisingly easy to get lost in woods.'

'This is a dead end. Where are you after?'

He seemed reticent. He pointed to his car. 'Just somewhere nice to eat my lunch, I suppose. I live in the city, so anywhere seems pretty to me.' His smile was so apologetic, so genuine, that Laura relaxed.

She took in the good, if tired suit, the sad, kind eyes. A kind of quiet recklessness overtook her. Why should she care? What did any of it matter, given Matt's behaviour?

'I know somewhere nice you can eat it on the other side of the lake,' she said. 'If you pull your car on to the verge, I'll show you. It's only a few minutes' walk through the trees.'

A short distance away, in the stultifying confines of her history lesson, Kitty was mulling over her discovery. She had tried to be fair, as Mary had taught her, but however she looked at it, the message came with only one explanation.

'Hello, Mrs Delancey. It's Mr Cartwright here. I wondered if you'd thought any more about our discussion. I've had another call from Mr Frobisher, who is still interested in seeing your Ge– Guar– your instrument. I don't know if you got my previous messages, but I do think it's worth considering. As we discussed, the amount he's suggesting would change your financial situation considerably. It's more than double what your husband paid for it . . .'

Change your financial situation considerably. Kitty remembered Cartwright, with his big shiny briefcase, and his embarrassment at the laundry pile teetering beside him. Mum had sent her away, even though she couldn't cope with what the man was saying. And now Kitty had an idea why. She hadn't wanted Kitty to know that there had been a choice. In spite of everything, that stupid violin was more important to her even than her family's happiness.

Thierry was no help.

'Did you hear any of these messages?' she had said to him in his room the previous evening, as he sat in front of his computer game, his thumbs beating out some apocalyptic tattoo. 'Did you know Mum could have sold her violin?'

He had gazed at the screen blankly as if he didn't want to know anything.

'Don't you get it? If she knew she could have sold the violin, Thierry, we didn't have to move to this hole. We might have been able to keep our house.'

Thierry stared fixedly in front of him.

'Do you hear me? Doesn't it even bother you that Mum lied to us?'

He had shut his eyes then, as if he were determined not to even look at her while she was talking. So she had told him he was a freak, an attention-seeking idiot, and gone off to her room to brood.

Mum had known something was up. She had kept asking Kitty questions over dinner, whether school was all right, whether she was okay. Kitty was so mad she could hardly look at her. All she could think was, we could still be in our Maida Vale house. We could be in our old road, with the neighbours we knew, and our old school and maybe even Mary, if the violin was worth enough.

Her mother had gone on about how she had decided to do some teaching to bring in more money. She had put a notice in the Cousins' shop. She said, 'It won't be so bad,' so many times that Kitty knew she was dreading it. But still she couldn't feel grateful or sympathetic. Because her mum talking about lessons made her think about violins again.

'Do you love us?' she had said pointedly.

Her mother had been shocked. 'How can you ask that? Of course I love you!' Even Kitty had felt guilty about how upset she had been. 'Why?' Isabel had asked. 'Why are you even asking?'

'More than anything?'

'More than anything you can imagine,' her mother said, all fierce and emotional. She had hugged her after they had eaten, as if to reassure her, but Kitty could not hug her back, as she normally would. Because they were just words, weren't they? It was obvious what she loved most. If that stupid violin hadn't been their only hope of anything, Kitty would have thrown it out of the upstairs window.

That afternoon she walked home with Anthony. She had missed the school bus, and Anthony had too, and it was only when she got home that she realised he might have done so deliberately. They walked together quite a lot now, and Kitty was definitely less shy with him. He was quite nice to talk to, and she felt safe walking through the wooded bit if he was there. When she was by herself she was always imagining someone watching her from behind the trees.

'What would you do if your parents lied to you?' she said, as they kicked their way down the path. They walked quite slowly in the afternoons, as if neither was in a hurry to get home.

'About what?' Anthony held out a stick of chewing-gum. She took it and unwrapped it as they walked.

Kitty wasn't sure she wanted to tell him. 'Something big,' she said eventually. 'Something that affected the whole family.'

Anthony snorted. 'My dad lies the whole time.'

'Don't you ever say anything?'

He tutted. 'The thing about parents,' he said, 'is that there's one rule for you and another for them.'

'My dad wasn't like that,' said Kitty. She stepped on to a fallen tree-trunk and walked its length. 'He talked to me like I was the same as him. Even if he told you off it felt like . . . like he was just explaining something.' She couldn't say any more about him, or tears would well in her eyes.

They moved back as a car came up the lane, slowing almost to a halt as it edged past them. The driver, a man in a suit, lifted a hand as he passed.

Anthony watched him go, then moved back into the middle, shrugging his schoolbag on to his shoulder. 'My dad lies to everyone, and he always gets away with it,' he said bitterly. Then he changed the subject. 'Saturday,' he said. 'Me and a few others are going to the pictures. You can come if you want. If you fancy it.'

The violin was briefly forgotten.

Kitty glanced at him from under her fringe.

He was looking straight down the lane, as if there was something really important down there that he had to focus on. 'It's nothing special. Just a few of us having a laugh.'

The lump had disappeared from Kitty's throat. 'All right,' she said.

Nicholas Trent blinked in the bright sunlight as he left the wood, drove to the top of the lane, and signalled right to head back on to the main road. Given the amount of time it had taken to get there, and his unexpectedly long lunch break, he should have headed off to the estate agents', as planned. But, distracted, he drove back towards the motorway. His head was too full, his mind spinning too hard for clarity.

And this time it was nothing to do with houses.

Twelve

The boy lay on his back, giggling as the puppies crawled over him, their fat stomachs and oversized paws scrabbling for purchase on his sweater. Boys that age were like puppies themselves, Byron thought, taping round another cardboard box. The child had spent much of the morning tearing round the small garden, racing the terrier, who yapped excitedly at his heels. He was different here, away from his mother. He was keen to learn – how to mend fencing, how to rear the young pheasants, which mushrooms were safe to eat, and unleashing such a torrent of affection on the dogs that both bitches had expanded their previously exclusive loyalties to include him as well. It was not as if he'd said much – it was hard enough to get a simple 'yes' or 'no' out of him – but he'd let his guard down a little.

It didn't seem right on a boy his age, the way he was. When Byron compared him with his niece, Lily, and her noisy chatter, her uncomplicated demands on everybody's time and affection, he felt sad. They said it was understand-able, in a boy who had just lost his father, that all kids reacted in different ways to such a trauma. He had overheard the widow on the phone to the school, fighting off psychiatrists and suchlike that some teacher had wanted to press on her. 'I've talked to him about it, and he doesn't want to go. I'm happy to let my son deal with things in his own way for now,' she had said. He had noticed that while her voice was calm her knuckles, gripping the drawer handle, were white. 'No – I'm well aware of that. I will certainly let you know if I feel he needs specialist help.' He had silently applauded her: he had an instinctive need for privacy, for freedom from interference and supervision. But it was hard not to wonder what on earth was locked behind the boy's closed-off little face.

He leaned over the half-door of the kitchen. 'You all right down here for a minute, Thierry? I've got to get a couple more bits down from upstairs.'

The boy nodded, hardly seeing him, and Byron ducked out of habit as he made his way up the narrow staircase to his bedroom. Two suitcases, four large cardboard boxes and a trailer-load of bits and pieces, plus a bootfull of puppies. Not a lot to show for a life, not a lot to find a home for. He sat down heavily on his bed, hearing the yaps downstairs. It wasn't the smartest or most luxurious bedroom, but he had been happy these last few years, with his sister and Lily. He had not brought women here – on the few occasions he had felt the need of female company he had made sure he went to theirs – and consequently, without any feminine input, it had the blank, utilitarian appearance of a hotel room. His sister had insisted on making matching curtains and quilt covers – an attempt, he knew, to make him feel like he was part of a home again. He had told her not to bother. He spent most of his time outdoors anyway. Still, it had been home, and he realised that he was sad to leave it.

Landlords did not want tenants with dogs. The only one who had said he would be happy to accept Byron's dogs had demanded six months' rent as a deposit, 'in case the animals cause damage'. It was a laughable figure. The other possible landlord had not wanted the dogs indoors. Byron had explained that once the puppies were gone his dogs would be happy to sleep in his car, but the landlord wasn't buying it. 'How do I know you're not going to let them in as soon as my back's turned?'

The weeks had ticked by, his sister had left, and it was now a matter of days until the tenancy formally ended. He had considered asking Matt for a loan, but even if he had agreed, something in Byron balked at the idea of being even further beholden to him.

'What we going to do, then, old girl?' He rubbed the collie's head. 'I'm thirty-two years old, I have no family, a job that pays less than the minimum wage, and I'm about to be made homeless.'

The dog looked mournful, as if she, too, had grasped the uncertainty of their future. Byron smiled, and made himself stand up, trying not to think of what he had just said, or of how oppressively quiet the house already felt now that he was alone. He tried not to let the voice that spoke of despair drown his determination. He knew from another time how easy it was to let such thoughts overwhelm you.

Life wasn't fair, and that was that. Young Thierry downstairs knew it, and he had had to learn a harder lesson than Byron at a painfully young age.

Byron made his way downstairs. It was nearly time to get the boy home. The local newspaper was out this afternoon. He hoped something would turn up in it. He watched the child, registered his joy, suddenly grateful for the distraction.

'Come on, you,' he said to Thierry, making himself sound more cheerful than he felt. 'If you're good we'll ask your mum if you can sit in Steve's digger when we clear that bottom field.'

Isabel heard the low whistle as she came down the stairs, and found her hand creeping across her chest to pull the two sides of her shirt collar together. Matt was on the other side of the hallway, feeding electrical cable into a gaping cavity, his leather tool-belt slung low round his hips. He was flanked by two other young men she had seen a couple of times before. He was smiling at her. 'You're very smart, Mrs D. Going anywhere nice?'

Isabel blushed, and cursed herself for it. 'Oh . . . no,' she stuttered. 'It's just an old shirt I dug out.'

'Suits you,' said Matt. 'You should wear that colour more often.' He went back to the electric cable as one of the men muttered to him. He began to sing quietly to himself. Eventually she recognised the tune. 'Hey there, lonely girl . . . lonely girl . . .'

She fought the urge to turn round and instead walked into the drawing room, her hand still at her throat. This was the third time Matt had commented on her appearance in a week, but she found it hard to believe that her shirt was worthy of note. It was navy blue linen, and so old as to be worn paper-soft. Laurent had given it to her many years ago during a trip to Paris – it was one of a number of old garments that had recently begun to fit her again. In truth, a large proportion of her wardrobe now hung off her. She hadn't had much appetite since Laurent had died. Sometimes she felt that if it hadn't been for the children she would have lived on biscuits and fruit. And there was nobody to talk to about the children, about Kitty's foul temper, her son's continuing silence. She probably spoke to Matt more than any other living being.

'This bathroom,' he said, appearing in the doorway. 'Have you made a decision about moving it? It would be much better in the third bedroom.'

She tried to remember their previous discussion. 'Didn't you say that would cost more money?' she said.

'Well, a little more, but you could divide it up then into a dressing room and en-suite for your room and it wouldn't be that hard to reroute the plumbing. It would be much better than stuck away in that corner.'

She considered this, then shook her head. Since the ceiling collapse she had found it hard not to glance upwards during every conversation. 'I can't do it, Matt. I think we should stick to putting in a working bath.'

'I'm telling you, Isabel, it really would work much better. It would add value, a decent-sized bathroom and dressing room.'

There was something so persuasive about him, and it was clear from his tone that he usually got his own way.

'I know you've given it a lot of thought,' she said, 'but not this time. Actually, the thing I really wanted to talk to you about was a power point in the kitchen. I must be able to plug in the fridge before it gets too warm.'

'Oh. Yes, the power point. It's not as straightforward as it sounds because of the way the cabling is laid out in there.' He grinned. 'I'll work something out. Don't worry. Hair looks good, by the way.'

She caught a flash of her reflection in the wall mirror, and tried to work out whether there was anything different about her appearance that day. He had commented twice now. Then she turned away, fearful that he would catch her examining herself. There were days when he seemed omnipresent, popping out of a room she was about to enter, humming when she practised her violin, taking his coffee break in the kitchen when she was cooking, and passing comment on the day's newspapers. Sometimes she didn't mind.

'I have to warn you. I found a few more rat droppings when I was lifting the skirting. They might have been disturbed by the building work.'

She shuddered. She had barely been able to sleep since the rat. 'Should I call out the pest-control people?'

'No point. There's too many places for them to hide while the floorboards are up. They could be coming in from outside. Leave it till we've finished.'

Isabel closed her eyes to visions of rats scampering into the house at dead of night. She sighed heavily, then reached for her keys and wallet. 'Matt, I'm going to the shop. I'll be back soon,' she called. She was not sure why she had to keep him abreast of her movements. If he needed to come and go he used the key that lived under the back doormat. It had been he who had revealed it several weeks previously. She had been shocked to discover that she and the children had slept for months in a house that everyone else knew how to enter.

'Matt?'

He didn't hear her. As she closed the front door she could hear him somewhere above, whistling.

It had taken her almost ten minutes to reach the front of the queue for the cashpoint, largely because the elderly man in front of her had insisted on reading aloud every option offered him by the flickering screen. 'Ten pounds, Twenty pounds, Fifty pounds, Other . . .' he had muttered. 'Now, how much do I want?'

Isabel had not tutted, like the woman behind her, even though it was raining and she had forgotten to bring an umbrella. She knew from recent experience how easy it was to feel daunted by tasks that seemed simple to other people. Instead she had tapped him on the shoulder when he left his money in the machine and accepted his gratitude with a smile.

Thinking about the old man, and how easy it was to be

distracted, meant that when she had typed in her own pin number and a request for money, it was some seconds before she noticed the message that flashed up on the screen. 'Insufficient funds to complete transaction,' it read. 'Please contact your local branch.'

She left the queue and entered the bank. The woman behind the counter had examined the card, typed something, then confirmed what the machine had told Isabel. 'You don't have enough cleared funds in your current account,' she said.

'Can you tell me what I do have?' Isabel asked quietly.

The woman tapped her keyboard, then scribbled a figure on a piece of paper and pushed it towards her. 'You're overdrawn. If you go any further than that,' she scribbled another figure, 'then you'll have to pay charges as the overdraft automatically becomes unauthorised.'

Isabel tried desperately to remember what she had paid for recently and came up with the unexpected order of roof tiles, the new soil pipe, the light fittings that had cost twice what she'd expected.

'Could you transfer some money from my savings account, please? There should be some in there. Just to get me out of the red.'

The woman carried out her request with impersonal efficiency, and handed Isabel another piece of paper, on which her savings had been totalled. The figure was much reduced from the one Isabel had imagined, but the woman, turning the screen towards her as if bestowing some kind of unusual gift, pointed out all the transactions that had taken place over the previous month.

'Oh . . . I'm having building work done,' said Isabel, shakily.

The woman smiled at her, as if in commiseration. 'Painful, isn't it?' she said.

Isabel drove home, deflated, with potatoes and baked beans

instead of the roasting chicken and salad she had intended. To cheer herself up she put on an old tape of Handel that had been lurking in the glove compartment. She had never considered the cost of things like food before, but now, faced with her rapidly dwindling cache of savings, she understood that she had to economise. By cutting meat and fish from their diet she could save almost twenty pounds from the grocery bill, and squash was significantly cheaper than pure juice. She had spent the previous evening darning Thierry's socks when once she would have thrown them away and bought replacements. There had been something almost meditatively pleasing about sitting in front of the fire with her handiwork as evidence of domestic efficiency.

She was almost a quarter of a mile down the lane when Dolores, with impeccable timing, decided to squash any remnant of optimism. The engine, which had struggled to turn over in previous days – a fact which Isabel had chosen to ignore – finally spluttered into silence as the car's under-carriage lurched over a large puddle in the middle of the track. Isabel sat there, the wipers splayed across the wind-screen, the music blaring. She turned it down and tried the ignition to no avail.

'Oh, *bugger* you!' she yelled. She climbed out of the car, cursing as her foot sank into cold muddy water, then squelched to the bonnet and fumbled it open. Half sheltered from the rain, she stared at the ticking engine with no idea of what she was looking for.

'Why?' she said aloud. 'Why now? Why couldn't you have got me home?' She kicked the wheel arch, then reached for the dip stick – the only item in the engine she knew. But once she had checked it she couldn't think of anything else to do. Rain continued to plummet from the slate-grey sky, and she fought the urge to rail at the elements.

She didn't even know if she wanted to return to the house. Some days she felt eaten by it, as if her whole self was enslaved to it, her energy devoted to its interminable upkeep. Her once-free thoughts were filled with an endless series of decisions – where should this power point go, what quality of wood should be used here, which height of skirting?

She tried not to think what would have happened if Laurent had been alive. It was the small things that felled her, rather than her loss: the car that wouldn't start, the bank statement she couldn't understand, the school report she couldn't discuss with anyone, the rat in the kitchen. 'I don't care,' she wanted to shout, when the workmen approached her for the fifteenth time. 'I just want a house that works, one that I don't have to think about. I want to be thinking about adagios, not insulation.'

'And I want a car that goes to the shop and back!' she yelled. 'Is that too much to ask?' She kicked the front wheel, almost relishing the pain that sparked in her foot. 'I don't want to deal with any of this! I want my old life back!'

She climbed back into the car, her hair dripping on to her shoulders. She screwed her eyes shut, took a few deep breaths. She tried to work out whether it would take longer to walk back to the shop to call for a recovery vehicle, or carry on down the lane to the house. She had given Kitty her own mobile telephone that morning in an attempt to raise her daughter's foul mood, and she calculated that it would be a fifteen-minute walk in the rain whichever way she went. Isabel closed her eyes and let the music remind her that this, too, would pass, that she had another way of being.

When she opened them, she could just make out, through the watery channels on the windscreen, a red shape lurching up the lane towards her. It was Matt's van.

'Car trouble?' He got out a few feet in front of her.

'It just stopped.' She was unable to contain her relief at his presence. 'I don't know what the matter is.'

He walked over, lifted the bonnet and peered inside. The music rang out of the open driver's door. 'You never stop, do you?' he said. He stuck his hand inside, feeling deftly around the engine, then removed it. 'Start her up.'

She sat in the car and tried the engine.

He listened, then motioned at her to turn the music down so that he could hear better. 'Again,' he commanded. And then, 'Hold on a moment.'

'What can you hear?' she said, intrigued. 'What can you hear that I can't?'

She got out of the car. It seemed wrong to sit in the dry when he was doing the work. When he saw her, he took off his jacket and signalled that she should shelter under it, then went back to his van, leaned in and brought out a rag. He came back, pulled out a piece of rubber and wiped it meticulously. He then cleaned several small plugs. By the time he had finished, his grey T-shirt was wet through and his hair glistened.

'Now try,' he said. Isabel climbed back into her seat and fired the engine, her wet fingers slipping on the key. It turned over obediently. 'Oh!' she exclaimed, delighted. She jumped as Matt's face appeared at the window, his skin gleaming in the rain.

'Distributor cap,' he said, squinting against the water trickling down his face. 'They get soaked on a low-slung car like this, what with all these puddles. You want to stick some WD-40 in there. Tell you what, I'll come with you and get the boys to turn at the top and follow us back to the house. Make sure you get back okay.'

Before she could protest, he had climbed into the passenger seat and motioned at her to edge the car past his van. She felt the eyes of the men on her as she passed, acutely aware of her wet shirt, the proximity of the man beside her.

'You can have your music back on now,' he said. She turned it up a little, letting the triumphant sound of the harpsichord wash over her. 'Handel,' she said, when she saw him looking at the tape box.

'Don't tell me—'

She giggled. 'Yes. Yes, it is. His *Water Music*.' And heard his great answering guffaw of a laugh in response.

She was not sure afterwards whether it was relief about the car, despair over her finances or merely some long-repressed emotion seeking an outlet, but as her unreliable old car bounced back up the lane towards her lonely, leaking, costly house, Isabel's giggle escalated and she laughed so hard that tears sprang to her eyes and she was afraid that hilarity would spill into something else.

She pulled up in the drive, turned off the engine and stopped laughing. With the absence of either motion or music the silence within the confines of the car felt suddenly significant.

She stared at her hands, at the darkened fabric where the rain had soaked through her long skirt, the clear outline of her breasts against her damp shirt. She felt, rather than saw, him looking at her, and tried to straighten her face.

'It's nice to see you smile,' said Matt, quietly. His eyes met hers, intense and blue, and appeared to lose their habitual knowingness. He laid a hand on her shoulder.

Something jolted through her, but he opened the car door and got out. He walked through the rain to his waiting van, as Isabel's hand reached up to the warmth his had left.

There was nothing – even for someone earning twice what he took home. Nothing for a man who wanted to live within a reasonable distance of the place he had spent most of his life. Byron sat in his car, the rain beating on the windscreen, the puppies whining and growling at each other in the back, as he searched the local newspapers for the few lines that might offer him a home. There were executive homes, two-bedroom flats, workmen's cottages that no longer housed workmen. But there was nothing for a man on a low income with little in the way of savings.

When he considered the brutal truth of his situation, Byron couldn't quite believe it. It was the kind of thing you imagined happening to someone else. Then again, several years ago he had found himself living in circumstances that he could never have envisaged. What was that saying about making God laugh? Telling Him your plans?

Byron no longer had plans, other than to find some temporary place to stay. In desperation he had thought of taking the puppies to an animal shelter so that he could more easily find somewhere for himself. But they were so young that it would have meant leaving the bitch with them, and he couldn't bear to lose either Meg or Elsie. They were pretty much all he had.

He could have asked his sister if he could sleep on her sofa for a few weeks, but it didn't seem fair. She had started a new life and he was too proud to sabotage her first few weeks as a proper family. He had friends in the village, but none close enough to ask such a favour. He had discovered that a whole stratum of people were in a similar position; none would have labelled themselves homeless, but they were somehow between homes, sleeping on friends' sofas, in temporarily unoccupied beds, mobile homes, calling in favours to ensure another week with a roof over their heads. He might, he supposed, have driven the two hundred miles to his parents' retirement bungalow on the coast, but what would that solve?

He would have no job, and their house, with its immaculate, carpeted floors and endless knick-knacks, was not somewhere he or the dogs could reasonably fit in. He would not ask them for money, knowing how little they survived on.

Besides, the thought of confessing how far he had fallen – of disappointing them a second time – was untenable. No one wanted to describe themselves as homeless; he did not want others to see him as that word would label him. Byron's face set in a mask of despair. He thought until the sky darkened and the dogs whined with frustration at their confinement.

Finally he started the car, and began to drive.

It was dark by the time he parked his old Land Rover in the clearing by the pheasant enclosure. He had chosen this spot because it was on Matt's land; the presence of his car would elicit no comment, no curiosity. It was almost eight o'clock. He loaded the puppies into a cardboard box, and then, hoisting a bag over his shoulder, his two adult dogs at his heels, he set off.

Byron knew the land so well that he did not need a torch. He had walked it almost daily for many years, had grown up in the neighbourhood, so he could traverse every rut, every fallen branch with the unthinking surefootedness of a mountain goat. He moved through the thick darkness, under the canopy of the trees, accompanied by the distant hooting of owls, the desperate shriek of a rabbit pinned by some predator, but he heard nothing except the whisper of the rain, the relentless tread of his soil-clagged feet.

Finally he saw the lights. He stopped at the edge of the field, wondering, briefly, whether he could really do this. And as he looked up at the window from that distance, the woman stepped forward, her silhouette fluid against the light of the room, to draw the long curtains, slowly removing herself from view. Afterwards, he realised, that had been the nadir: as he had watched that one domestic task, he had never felt more shut out, more alone.

The puppies were wriggling in the damp cardboard box. It won't be for long, he told himself, wiping his face with his free hand. Just till this lot are weaned and I can sell them. Just till I get myself on my feet. He hoisted the box under his arm and, instructing his dogs to be silent, walked round the black edge of the field until he saw the door he had been aiming for, a brick-and-weatherboard lean-to, jutting out from the main body of the house.

The lock had been broken for as long as he could remember, the wood around it rotten, barely able to support the cast-iron catch. Silently, he opened it, hearing the distant sound of a violin, the briefly raised voice of a child. He slipped in through the gap and went down the stone steps. It smelled oily and vaguely sulphurous under the house, but at least it was dry, and several degrees warmer than the night air outside, which still held the chill of winter. In the distance he heard the dull roar of the boiler but only when the door was closed behind him did he feel brave enough to turn on his torch.

It was as he remembered it: the L shape of the boiler room under the house, the dilapidated contraption in the far corner, the old woodpile by the door, large enough to shield him from casual view. The dirty old sink, for tradesmen, and the door that led up to the kitchen via the back stairs, which was padlocked shut. There was no risk that one of the children would pass this way, no reason for anyone to come down here. It was entirely possible that the widow didn't know the room was here.

Byron placed the box on the floor and unrolled his sleeping-bag. Meg lay down and, with an air of contented exhaustion, began to suckle her pups. He would fetch the rest of his belongings tomorrow. He put out food for her and Elsie, filled a bowl with water, and attempted to wash in the little sink. Then, finally, he turned off his torch and sat in the corner, beside a grille that revealed a patch of the night sky, listening to the dogs, and trying not to think about his surroundings. He tried not to think about anything. It was a knack he had learned long ago.

He was about to climb into his sleeping-bag when he caught the glint of metal. Bright, new metal, not like the rusting, tarnished catches and fastenings that characterised the old house. Byron reached for his torch and switched it on, pointing the beam to where he had seen it. A pet-carrier stood in the corner on the ground by the door to the kitchen. A new pet-carrier, made of wire but with a solid tray at the bottom, the kind you might use for a small cat.

As Byron picked it up, he noticed droppings in the corner. The carrier had not been used for a cat.

The lock to the kitchen corridor was broken.

Byron sat down, his predicament briefly forgotten. He was thinking of an unexpected visitor to the kitchen above him.

Thirteen

She had been told that a house so large, so dilapidated, so isolated, would be testing in the winter months. That the endless chill, the leaks and draughts would penetrate what remained of the roof, and damp would seep along the ground from the lake. But now that summer was here, she had found that warmer weather brought its own brand of insurgence to her home. It was as if Nature knew that the last Pottisworth had died, that a usurper was in his place, and had decided to reclaim the Spanish House for its own, brick by brick, inch by inch. Bluebells, tulips and hyacinths, their bulbs bunched and replicated, had sprung up, and between the flagstones that surrounded the house weeds revealed themselves briefly as green shoots before towering into unfriendly thistles, rosettes of poisonous ragwort or rampant chickweed. The weeks of rain left mossy outcrops on the rendering, while the hedgerows swelled, woven with brambles and ivy. The grass, a sparse, threadbare carpet, became lush and long, flecked with dandelions and buttercups, obliterating pathways and gravel. A couple of aged fruit trees simply fell over and lay prostrate, a mute accusation of her inability to manage the garden. As if in answer to Nature's call, rabbits dug networks of warrens, the ankle-twisting holes hidden by the grass, while moles left piles of freshly dug earth dotted at intervals, great full-stops of organic subversiveness.

Inside, things were little better. Matt and his accomplices

came and went daily, knocking holes in walls and apparently filling them in again. In some places she could see improvement: the roof was now secure, and the chimney no longer leaned precariously to one side. She had a soil pipe that transferred bathroom waste without the risk of typhoid, some new flooring and a decent sink in the kitchen. There were several new windows, intermittent hot water and a partially installed heating system, which promised warmth next winter but for now leaked water into the new floorboards.

But she had no working bathroom, no power point for the fridge, despite her repeated requests. And, more importantly, she had a pile of bank statements that detailed the spiralling costs, and a book in which she wrote down the works Matt McCarthy had told her needed doing, with the amounts he had quoted scribbled opposite. The multi-zero totals shocked her daily.

She sat at the kitchen table all morning, putting her statements in order, seeing in print the reality of her financial situation. What she saw made her feel almost unsteady, as if she were balanced precariously on the edge of a cliff. There's only this left, she thought. And there's only me. I'm responsible for everything. The children depend on me. They hadn't seemed to consider the possibility that she might not be up to the task.

At that moment Matt walked into the kitchen with a bag of croissants from the baker. He sat down in front of her. 'Go on,' he said, holding one to her lips. 'Delicious. Take a bite.' She felt oddly self-conscious, aware that he was watching her mouth as she opened it. He grinned. 'Good, aren't they?' He had large, square-fingered hands, the skin scuffed and dry, roughened by years of hard work. And as she nodded, chewing, he smiled again, as if asserting something to himself. He often brought her things now: real coffee, so that she could make it for him, eggs they had been given on a previous job, chocolate muffins and teacakes when one of his crew disappeared to the town. She never knew whether to feel glad of his presence, as it meant she was not alone with the possibility of rats, leaks or a failing range, or to dread it, as he always seemed more in control of her home than she was. He had charisma, which somehow persuaded her to agree with his course of action, even if she had originally intended the opposite.

'Look at your hands,' he exclaimed, as she picked up the croissant again. Byron stood in the doorway. 'Look at them, Byron. Ever seen fingers like that?' She blushed as he took one.

'They've been protected,' she said. 'They've never done much, except play the violin.'

'Not a mark on them. So smooth. They're like . . .' He turned to Byron. 'Like the hands of a statue, aren't they?'

Byron muttered agreement, making her feel ridiculous. Matt finished his coffee and got to his feet. 'Don't eat them all at once,' he called back as he left the kitchen.

Isabel gazed at her thinned cheque book and the crumpled paper bag next to it. She didn't think even the delights of a croissant would make this day any better. Her statements had told her the incontrovertible truth. She swept them into a pile. Outside she could see Matt supervising the man driving the digger. They were laying a secondary pipe to the outside supply.

It had to stop, she told herself. It didn't matter how bad the house was, there was almost nothing left.

Isabel was trudging across the grass from the house. She was wearing a full skirt and a bulky woollen cardigan. Her hair fell loosely round her shoulders, stray fronds whipped about her face by the stiff breeze. Matt went to the digger and put Sven's plans inside it.

'I've brought you both some tea,' she said, holding out two mugs.

Matt grinned at Byron. 'Mrs D here knows how to look after us. Not like some, eh, Byron?'

'Thank you.' He watched Byron take the mug from her, his fingers still black with earth.

'We were just saying, there used to be a kitchen garden over there before that wall fell down.' Matt pointed at an area enclosed on two sides by soft red brick. He could still picture it, remembering espaliered apple trees, with names like Gascoyne's Scarlet, D'Arcy Spice and Enneth's Early. 'There's still a few fruit trees. You should get some nice produce off them this autumn.' *If you're still here, he thought suddenly.*

Byron lowered his mug. 'There's a few raised beds at the back. What used to be the vegetable patch. Thierry might like to sow a few bits and pieces. My niece likes to grow things.'

It was one of the longest speeches Matt had ever heard him make unprompted.

'I'll show him how, if you like,' he went on. 'Sweet-peas are easy enough.'

'He might like that,' said Isabel, pushing her hair back from her face. 'Thank you.'

Byron stepped forward, shuffling his boots, which were thick with mud. 'Also, I wanted to say I'm sorry about the business with the rat. I've put the gun in your loft where no one can get at it.'

'Thank you,' she said again.

'I don't suppose you'll be bothered by rats again.'

'You can't say that for sure,' Matt interjected.

'I think I can,' said Byron, firmly, his eyes on a patch of

ground just in front of Matt's feet. 'I think I can safely say that it was a one-off.'

'Well . . . that's a relief,' Isabel conceded. 'I've had nightmares about that rat. I couldn't sleep for nights . . . Actually,' she turned to Matt, 'can I have a word? I need to talk to you about the work.'

Wordlessly, Byron began to busy himself with the digger.

Isabel opened her mouth to speak, then closed it again. Finally she looked up at Matt, one hand keeping her hair off her face, her expression apologetic and slightly defiant. 'I have to bring this to a halt.'

Matt raised an eyebrow.

'The building work,' she said. 'What you've done so far has been wonderful, but I can't do any more. Not for now, anyway.'

'You can't just stop,' he said. 'We're in the middle of all sorts of jobs. You can't leave them half finished.'

'Well, that's the way it has to be. I've been over the figures and it doesn't make sense for us, for me to continue, not just now. I do appreciate what you've done, Matt, really, but I have to think about what's sensible.' She blushed as she spoke.

'But it's not sensible to stop right now.' He gestured at the digger. 'The works we're doing are mostly essentials. You're not going to get far without a new mains feed. And we've only half finished putting in that bathroom. I guess you can do without the heating in the top rooms over the next few months, but my advice would be to finish it – you'll never get anyone out when we're heading towards winter, and once I leave you I'll be booked solid.' He noticed suddenly how pale she was.

'You don't understand, Matt.'

'So tell me.' She smelled vaguely of citrus.

'Okay. It has come to a lot more than I expected, and we

can't afford for you to continue. I can't pay you for any more work.'

She was on the verge of tears. The lashes at the outer edges of her eyes glistened, little black points of stars. 'I see,' he said, shifting slightly. Piles of earth lay around the newly dug trench, with pipework still to lay. The new bathroom suite sat in its packaging against the back porch. He had picked it out several months ago, an antique cast-iron Victorian bath with claw feet and an oversized basin. It was just what Laura had wanted. Quite often, these days, he forgot it was Isabel's house.

'Believe me,' she said quietly, 'if I could afford to carry on, I would.'

'That bad, is it?' he said.

'Yes.' She did not meet his eye.

They listened to the crows cawing in the distance.

'You all right, Isabel?'

She nodded, biting her lip.

'Well, let's not worry too much for now. I'll get the boys to finish off the jobs we're doing and then we'll leave it.' She made to interrupt but he held up a hand. 'Don't worry about it. You don't have to pay me for everything right away. We'll come to some arrangement.'

Afterwards he decided he had not chosen his words care-fully. In fact, he had barely thought about what he had said. Because although he had anticipated this moment for months – almost since he had grasped the unworldliness of the house's new owner – Matt could take no pleasure in it. He had been distracted by Byron – by the younger man's tone when he had mentioned the rat. By the way he had looked at Isabel when he had taken the mug of tea from her.

Matt McCarthy felt unbalanced.

As Isabel walked away, head down, shoulders hunched

against the wind, he strolled over to the other man. 'A word,' he said casually.

Byron looked up.

'The widow,' he said. 'Don't get too involved.'

To his surprise, Byron didn't protest. He didn't even try to pretend that he didn't understand what he was saying. He stood up straight, so that he was a good half a head taller than Matt and their eyes met, for longer than Matt had expected. Byron's were unreadable.

'You're warning me off,' he said, low and even. Then walked away, but his expression had said clearly what he had failed to say aloud: *Even you can only warn someone off what is actually yours.*

In the late afternoon the wind picked up, and Matt and the men, spattered with rain, and struggling with the increasingly claggy ground, left early. The digger sat immobile on the lawn in a swelling sea of mud. Now and again Isabel would look at it, then away, reminded by its glaring yellow presence of their financial position. In an attempt to lift her mood she had made some biscuits, but it was impossible to tell when they were ready in the range and, diverted by a Schubert symphony, she had forgotten them. By the time the children came home they were the colour of burnished leather, with an aroma not dissimilar.

Thierry hurled his schoolbag over a kitchen chair, picked one up from the wire tray, sniffed it and put it back. Kitty merely looked at them and raised her eyebrows.

'Good day, lovey?' said Isabel.

Thierry shrugged. Kitty was rummaging through her bag.

'Kitty? Did you have a good day?'

'Just the same as any other,' she said offhandedly.

Isabel frowned. 'What does that mean?'

Kitty's sharp little face spun round. 'It means that stuck in a new school where I don't have any friends, in a house I hate, in an area I don't know, one day is as crap as any other. Okay?'

Isabel felt as if she had been kicked in the stomach. Kitty had never spoken to her like that before. 'What's the matter?' she said. 'Kitty, what on earth's got into you?'

Kitty's eyes showed contempt. 'Don't pretend you don't know,' she said.

'But I *don't* know.' Isabel's voice rose. She could not cope with this today, not on top of everything else.

'Liar!'

Isabel grabbed a chair and sat down opposite her daughter. She saw that Thierry's wide, dark eyes were darting from his sister to herself, his mouth clamped shut. 'Kitty, tell me what you're so angry about. I can't help if I don't know what's going on.'

'You!' said Kitty, venomously. 'You go on and on about how much you love us, and when it comes down to it you don't love us at all. Even now Dad's dead, we're still second to that bloody violin.'

'How can you say that? I gave up my career to be with you. I'm here every morning, every evening, waiting for you to come home. I haven't worked since we got here.'

'That's not the point!'

'It *is* the point! You and Thierry come first in everything!' You don't know how much it costs me to be here, to have sacrificed my career, she wanted to add, but she couldn't cast that burden on to her daughter.

'I *know*!' Kitty yelled. 'I know about Mr Cartwright. I know you could have sold the Guarneri and we could have stayed in our home!'

Isabel blanched. She had almost forgotten about that, so thoroughly had she immersed herself in the Spanish House.

'You lied to us! You told me we couldn't afford to stay in our house, the house we loved, with all our friends and Mary. You said we had to move here – and all the time you could have sold that violin and we could have stayed at home with the people we loved. You lied!' She drew breath, then hit Isabel with the killer blow. 'Dad wouldn't have lied to us!'

Thierry pushed back his chair and sprinted out.

'Thierry – Kitty – I'm not even sure that if I had—'

'Don't! I heard what Mr Cartwright said!'

'But I—'

'This isn't a bloody home to you! It never was! It was just a way for you to keep your precious violin!'

'Kitty, that's—'

'Oh, leave me alone!'

Kitty flung her schoolbag on to the table and stalked off, rubbing her face with her sleeve. Isabel wanted to follow her children, try to explain, but she saw it was pointless. Because Kitty was right. And there was little she could say to defend herself.

Supper was a subdued affair. Thierry said nothing, but ate the macaroni cheese, refused an apple, then disappeared to his room. Kitty kept her head down, and answered Isabel's questions monosyllabically.

'I'm sorry,' Isabel said. 'Really, Kitty. I'm so sorry. But you have to know that nothing is more important to me than you and your brother.'

'Whatever.' Kitty pushed her plate away.

She and Thierry went to bed without protest, which was disturbing in itself, and Isabel was alone in the drawing room, with the lights flickering and the wind whistling through the undergrowth outside.

She built up the log fire, drank half a bottle of red wine too quickly, and found that even the roaring flames offered little comfort. She noticed with relief that there was a comedy programme on television. But as the opening credits rose, there was a sudden *clunk*. The pixellated picture shrank into a white dot and disappeared. Simultaneously the lights went out, leaving her cloaked in silence and darkness. It felt almost like an insult, as if the house itself was laughing at her. Isabel sat immobile on the sofa, illuminated by the embers of the fire. Then her face crumpled and she was sobbing.

'Bloody house!' she yelled. 'Bloody stupid house!' She stood up and fumbled for matches, then searched for the candles she had not thought to put in a particular place, still swearing, her voice muffled by the wind outside, and by despair.

Matt had spent the evening at the Long Whistle. He had been avoiding Theresa who, picking up on his lack of interest with finely tuned antennae, had become irritable and petulant, flouncing around behind the bar and casting meaningful looks in his direction. He had met her flashing eyes and attempts at intimacy with indifference. There was nothing he liked less than a desperate woman who couldn't get the message.

Besides, his mind was on other things.

He had come to the pub, rather than going home, because he knew that, while she chose to ignore much, Laura could not ignore his obvious and growing disquiet. He felt uncharacteristically at odds with himself. Whenever he closed his eyes, he saw Byron's face as he looked at Isabel. He had caught in it something raw and unguarded, and slowly it had dawned on him that it had reflected something in himself. When he closed his eyes he saw not Theresa or his wife but the pale expanse of Isabel Delancey's collarbone, the scattering of freckles where her chest had been exposed to sunlight.

He saw her smiling and swaying up to him, her hips undulating, her self-consciousness lost in sensuous appreciation of her music.

Byron's response had been right. She did not belong to anyone. She was not tethered, as he was. The thought of Byron going near her made his beer taste sour. The thought of anyone else with her in that house, the house that held his imprint on every board, made his jaw set in a determined line.

'Going to be a wild one tonight,' said the landlord, his eyes on his crossword.

'Yup.' Matt downed his drink and put his glass on the bar. 'You might be right.'

He ignored Theresa's frantic attempts to get his attention. He was not sure what excuse he was going to use to explain how late he was. But driven by something he did not entirely understand, fifteen minutes before closing time, Matt found himself in his van, heading towards Little Barton.

Down in the boiler room, Byron settled the dogs, turned off his radio, and prepared to read his book by the light of the candles he had bought that morning. It was odd how quickly you could adapt to your surroundings, as long as you had the barest of home comforts. To his new home under the house he had now brought a chair, his battery-powered radio, the dogs' baskets and a camp stove. Having washed in a cleaned sink, eaten proper food and drunk a mug of tea he was feeling, if far from cheerful, at least more even about his fate. It was only three weeks until the puppies could be weaned. One of the farmers on the other side of the church had already offered to pay him a couple of hundred for the boldest. If all of them fetched that much he'd be well on his way to a deposit.

When he was more stable financially, he would set about finding a job somewhere else. He was increasingly uncomfortable about Matt's involvement with this house. There was nothing he could put his finger on but he had felt in his gut that all was not right, that Matt had not given up on owning the Spanish House. It would blow up at some point, or Mrs Delancey would be forced to move on, and Byron did not want to be around when either took place.

It was almost ten to eleven when he heard the boiler click off. He glanced at his watch, puzzled. The timer was set for eleven thirty. He climbed out of his sleeping-bag, ignoring the hopeful glances of his dogs, and went to the door. Every light was off.

A few minutes later he heard sobbing. 'Bloody house,' she was yelling. 'Bloody stupid house.'

The power was down. He froze. It might be a fuse, but she might not know where the fuse box was. He could turn it back on for her, but then he would have to explain how he had come to be so close to her house.

Byron stood still, and Meg whined, picking up on his discomfort. He shushed her.

He listened in the dark to Isabel Delancey tramping up and down and felt a deep disquiet. None of this was right, yet he was powerless to do anything about it. He heard her violin start up and her misery transferred itself to the strings. He was no connoisseur of music, but even he thought he had never heard anything so sad. He recalled her earlier that day, approaching Matt McCarthy with her well-thumbed book of figures, her sleep-deprived face. So, even those who appeared wealthy could be teetering on the edge of debt. In some respects, she was no better off than he was.

It was this that drove him from the boiler room – that and the observation that it might have been his sister and Lily in Isabel's place. He could hear her, preoccupied by her instrument on the other side of the door, playing her melancholic song in the dark. He would walk to the front of the house, see if the coach-house lights were on, and knock on the door. He would say he was just passing. He would feel better knowing that she and the children had light.

He was just closing the door when he heard the crunch of tyres on the gravel. Without his own car there, he had no convincing explanation for his presence. He could certainly not afford to be seen. He reopened the door silently, and withdrew back into the space under the house. Then he sat in the dark, waiting.

There were no lights on at the house, and for a moment he suspected she and the children had gone out and felt something like disappointment. Then, as the wind dropped momentarily, he heard her violin, and guessed that the electricity was down. Perhaps because he had downed several drinks, or because the last few months had endowed him with some appreciation of this kind of music, Matt McCarthy remained where he was and listened. His window open, the cool wind on his skin, he let the music match the anguished, riven mood of the weather whistling around him. He sat outside the house that should have been his and let himself feel something alien to him.

The lights stayed out.

He didn't know what finally drew him in. Later he thought it might have been the desire to help, perhaps to check the fuse box. Or it might have been the music. In neither instance was he being honest with himself. The front door, as was common, was unlocked. He walked in and closed it softly behind him, and stood for a moment as the house creaked gently around him, like an old ship on high seas. He wondered whether to call out, but part of him sensed that this would halt the music, and he found, to his surprise, that he did not want it to stop. So, he walked stealthily along the hallway, then down the staircase to the kitchen corridor, and there, in the doorway, he saw her. She was playing, tears rolling down her cheeks, her eyes closed.

He looked at her, and something in him short-circuited. Her mouth was slightly open, her head tilted forward, shoulders back. She was lost in something he could not own. She bit her lower lip, wincing as the music reached a crescendo, as if the sound caused her pain. He could not tear his eyes from her. He felt like a boy again, as if he were watching something he was not supposed to see, something beyond him, something he could not have for himself, and his throat caught. And as he stood, frozen, her eyes opened, and widened slightly as she saw him through the gloom.

He made as if to speak, but she carried on playing without a break. She was watching him now, her eyes fixed on his, her arm working as if she was incapable of halting the flow.

'You have no power,' he said, as the music quieted briefly.

She nodded.

His eyes were locked on hers. He moved closer to her, drawn to the rise and fall of her chest, the juddering movement of her body. Her utter self-containment, set against what he suddenly saw in her eyes – something raw with need, with physical loss.

She dropped her hands to her sides before he reached her and made a faint sound, as if in surrender. He had his arms round her waist, half folding her body backwards, crushing her to him, pushing her through the door into the kitchen. She scrambled to place her violin on the table, and then her pale, cold hands were in his hair, her mouth open against his. He heard her gasp, felt them against his skin, the shocking warmth of her thighs as he pushed his hands up her skirt, the sweet, gratifying melding of her body against his. Something inside Matt McCarthy sang, loud and piercing, became deafening, as she pulsed against him, and something low and gutteral escaped his chest.

They slid inelegantly to the floor and he had her beneath him, where he needed her, where he had needed her to be since he first saw her. And he knew he wanted ownership – not just of the house but of this woman. He bit her neck, made her submit, felt her surprisingly strong fingers clutching at his skin, and his last thought as the wind rumbled against the windows, as the house groaned like a living thing around them, a faint surprise that her eyes were tight shut when his own were open, wide open, as if he were seeing a whole universe for the first time.

He was not sure how long he had been asleep, possibly hours, possibly minutes. When he opened his eyes, his exposed skin protesting at the cold of the flagstone floor, there was a quilt half over him, scattered items of clothing beneath his head, and the deep black of the small hours cloaking the windows. He tried to work out where he was, what he was doing there, and then he saw her, her clothing intact, as if nothing had happened, seated on a chair, watching him, her silhouette black against the dim light.

He raised himself, smelling the faint scent of her on his skin, and the answering echo of his immediate arousal. His mind was flooded with images, the sensation of her on him, around him, her cries in his ears. And he lifted a hand. 'Come here,' he murmured, 'where I can see your face.'

'It's nearly two,' she said. 'You need to go home.'

Home. Oh, Christ, this would take some explaining.

Matt stood up, letting the quilt slide to the floor. He

refastened his jeans and belt. The air was cold, but he hardly felt it. Something astonishing was moving through him, as if his own blood had been washed, renewed. He walked up to her, still unable to see her face clearly. But he touched the hair that he had grasped earlier.

Everything had changed. And he was strangely glad, accepting this.

'Thank you,' he said. He wanted to tell her what it meant. How it had altered him. And then he realised, as he drew his thumb across her cheekbone, that it was wet with tears – and he knew suddenly that he could remedy this. 'Don't be sad,' he said softly. 'It'll be all right, you know.' She did not reply.

'Look,' he said, wanting her to smile, wanting to lift her unhappiness, 'about the money. Forget the next instalment. We'll work something out.' For an insane moment, he thought he might confess to her how things might change. But even he was not disoriented enough for that. 'Isabel?'

He felt, rather than heard, the new quality of the silence. She had stiffened, drawn back from his touch.

'I have never done this before,' she said, and her voice was cold.

'Done what?' he said, trying to see her face.

'I'll pay you everything I owe you.'

He was dumbfounded, as the true nature of their exchange struck him. 'Look – I didn't come here tonight because . . . I . . . Christ.' He was half laughing, unable to believe what he had heard. 'I wasn't suggesting—' He had been wrong-footed. 'I've never . . . paid for it in my life.'

'And I've never offered it.' Her tone was icy now. 'I'd like you to go.'

Matt found himself outside in the chill, walking towards his van, head spinning. He had to make her understand. He couldn't believe she had thought that that was about money. But even as his feet crunched back across the gravel he heard the heavy, unanswerable sound of a door being bolted.

On the other side, Isabel sank to the floor with a silent howl of despair and self-loathing. She let her head drop to her knees, her bruised lips fall against the soft fabric of her skirt, hiding her face from her own betrayal.

Her whole body ached with loneliness, the loss of her husband, the rough communion with a man who wasn't him. She was sober and she was empty. Emptier than she had ever been.

Laurent! she cried. *What have you brought me to? What have I become?* The house met her with a silence that was deafening.

Fourteen

There was a train every two hours that shuttled between her new home and London, and Isabel had calculated that even if this one arrived on time, she'd be lucky to get back before the school bus. She sat, resigned, as the man opposite worked his way methodically through his newspaper and the two back-packers to her right chatted in some language that sounded harsh and northern European, letting the dull monotony of the wheels on the track lull her mind into nothingness.

She thought of Mary, who had met her for coffee, and who had commiserated about the tyranny of the school run. 'Just be glad you're not doing it in London,' she had said cheerfully. 'I spend half my life in the car.'

It had been good to see her, a reminder that Isabel had once been part of another life. Mary asked eagerly after Kitty and Thierry, told Isabel she looked a lot better (a diplomatic fib, Isabel guessed) and promised to visit soon. But it was clear that she belonged elsewhere now, that she was already at the hub of another family. She had brought one of her new charges with her, a doe-eyed baby whom she dandled on her knee with the calm confidence she had shown in dealing with Isabel's children.

'Not been shopping, then?'

Isabel glanced down the carriage and saw a woman she recognised. She took in the neat pastel mackintosh, the inappropriate hat, and the woman smiled.

'Linnet. Deirdre Linnet. You know me from the Cousins' shop. You live at the Spanish House.' She told Isabel this as if she were offering information. She gestured at Isabel's legs. 'I thought you might have gone to London for a bit of shopping but you've no bags.'

'Bags,' said Isabel.

'Of shopping.'

'No,' she said. 'Not today.'

'I've gone a bit mad. I only go up twice a year and I like to have a splurge. My little treat.' She patted the plastic carriers that flanked her seat, each bearing some brand name that announced to the world the avenues Mrs Linnet's savings had taken. 'My little treat,' she repeated to herself.

'I'm in a mess,' Isabel had told Mary. 'I've got it all wrong. The children are desperately unhappy and it's all my fault.' Mary had listened to almost the whole story (there was one part Isabel had deliberately omitted) and then laughed easily, as if none of this were particularly worrisome. 'She's a teenage girl,' she had said. 'It's her job to be unhappy. You've actually got off lightly so far. Thierry . . . Well, he'll find his voice in time. But they're doing okay at school. They're coming home every day. They're eating. Strikes me they're doing fine, considering. It's you who's the unhappy one.'

'Work, was it?'

'I'm sorry?'

'Work. Your trip to London.'

Isabel smiled wanly. Her eyes felt gritty with tiredness. She had spent most of the previous night awake, and the missing hours of sleep were gaining on her. 'Something like that.'

'You're a musician, aren't you? Asad told me. He's not one to gossip, him or Henry, not really, but you've probably worked out there's not a lot happens in our village that doesn't go through the shop.'

Isabel wondered dully how long it would be before last night became conversational currency.

'I saw your advert for violin lessons. I used to sing, you know. I could have done it professionally, my husband always said. But I got caught up with the children . . .' She sighed. 'You know how it is.'

Isabel turned to the window. 'Yes, I do.'

'You need to work,' Mary had said. She had paid for the coffee, which Isabel had found almost unbearably humiliating. 'You need to do a bit with your orchestra again, bring a few pounds in, restore your peace of mind. You can leave them for a day. Kitty's old enough now to look after her brother.' She had hugged Isabel, then walked off, pushing the pram, back to ease the path of some other family.

They had passed the last stop before Long Barton. She watched Mrs Linnet gather up her bags, clutching them to her, poised to disembark the train some time before that might be necessary. She noted the now familiar landmarks of church and houses, the glimpse of the high street through trees, the verges and hedgerows green with new growth and wondered what it took for any place to feel like home.

It was only when the train drew into Long Barton station that Isabel stood up and did what she had sworn she wouldn't. She reached out and found her hand closing on the handle of a violin case that was no longer there.

When she returned they were in front of the television, Kitty with her stockinged feet up on a table in front of the sofa, eating a packet of crisps, Thierry lying across an old easy chair, his school tie rolled into a ball on the floor.

'You weren't here when we got in,' said Kitty, accusingly. 'Even Matt wasn't. We had to use the key under the back-door mat.'

Isabel dropped her shoulder bag on a side table. 'Thierry, did you eat your lunch today?'

Her son nodded, his eyes not leaving the television.

'All of the sandwich?'

His eyes flicked towards her and he nodded again. The room was unusually peaceful and she realised it was because the builders were absent. Even when they were not banging or crashing about, their presence added a vibration to the air. Or was that just Matt McCarthy? Isabel rubbed at her eyes. 'I'm going to make a cup of tea,' she said.

'Where have you been?'

Kitty's natural curiosity must have swamped her desire not to talk to her mother. She saw her daughter register her tiredness, and felt herself flush, as if the reason for her exhaustion might be apparent.

'London,' she said. 'I'll explain in a minute.'

When she came back with her tea, the television was off and they were sitting upright. They sprang apart, as if there had been some muttered conversation to which she had not been privy. Except it would have been one-sided, she thought. Because her son did not speak.

Isabel met their eyes, and told them. 'We can go back to London,' she said.

Afterwards she was not sure what she had expected, perhaps not tumultuous applause but some excitement, maybe smiles, a little bounce of joy. But they sat and stared at her.

'What does that mean?' said Kitty, a little aggressive still.

'What I said,' said Isabel. 'We can go back to London. We'll pay to have this place smartened up, get it to a point where it's saleable, and then, hopefully, we'll have enough to find ourselves somewhere near our old house. And your friends,' she added.

Still they stared at her.

'It probably won't be as big as our old house, but I'm sure we'll find something we like.'

'But . . . how can we afford it?' Kitty was frowning, one finger looped unconsciously round a lock of hair.

'That needn't concern you,' Isabel said. 'I just thought you'd like to know.'

Kitty was staring at her suspiciously. 'I don't understand,' she said. 'You told me we had no money. You said the building work was costing everything we had. What happened?'

'I've . . . reorganised our finances. That was why I was in London.'

'You don't know anything about finances. I know our finances and we don't have any.'

Suddenly it hit her. Her eyes cast around the room, to the table, the bureau. 'Oh, my God,' she said quietly.

Isabel had rehearsed a calm, serene smile. A smile that told her children nothing of what it had cost her, of the anguish she had experienced when she had handed her instrument to the dealer. It had felt as if she was parting with one of her children.

'You didn't sell it.'

Isabel nodded.

Kitty broke into hysterical sobs. 'Oh, no!' she cried. 'Oh, no! I made you do it.'

Isabel's smile vanished.

'I didn't mean you actually to sell it. I know what it meant to you. And now you're going to be really miserable and hate me for ever. Oh, Mum, I'm really sorry.'

Isabel sat down heavily and pulled Kitty to her. 'No,' she said, stroking her hair. 'You were right. That instrument was an extravagance we couldn't afford. And, besides, Mr Frobisher has found me a replacement – much cheaper but with a very nice sound. He's fixing it up and he's going to send it next week.'

'You'll hate it.' Kitty's voice was muffled.

'No, I won't,' said Isabel, although she knew that her daughter was right. 'Kitty, I made a big mistake, and I'm going to put it right,' she said. 'Music is going to take a back seat. The sooner we can raise the cash to get this house into shape, the sooner we can go home.'

It was then that she noticed Thierry's expression. He didn't look delighted at all. 'You still want to go back, don't you, Thierry? Back to London?'

There was a short silence. Then, slowly, her son shook his head. Isabel stared at him, then at Kitty. 'Thierry?' she said again.

His voice, when it came, was small but definite. 'No,' he said.

Isabel looked at Kitty, who seemed incapable now of meeting her eye.

'Actually,' said Kitty, 'I . . . don't mind it here.' She glanced behind her at her brother. '. . . I mean, I don't mind staying for a bit . . . if that's what Thierry wants.'

Isabel wondered if she would ever truly understand her two awkward, mercurial children. She took a deep breath. 'Okay,' she said. 'We'll pay Mr McCarthy what we owe him, and see how we go. But at least we have some options. And now,' she said, 'I'm going to sort out some of this paperwork.'

The sun was setting through the drawing-room window, and the children turned on the television. Isabel sat at the table and began to open the letters she had ignored and to write lists of things to be done. She felt almost physically bereft at the loss of the object she had cherished for so long, daunted by the months ahead of her but, curiously, better than she had in months.

He said no, she told herself, eyeing her son as she opened another envelope. That had to be better than nothing.

'She looked terrible,' Mrs Linnet said, with relish. 'Pale as a ghost, with big, dark shadows under her eyes. She hardly said a word to me the last two stops.'

Asad and Henry exchanged a glance. It was possible that Mrs Linnet's conversation might not exert the same pull on everyone she met.

'That house will give her a nervous breakdown. You know one of the ceilings fell in not two weeks ago? Anything could have happened. Her children might have been underneath.'

'But they weren't,' said Henry. 'So all is well.'

'I don't know what Matt McCarthy's thinking of. A man of his experience . . . You'd think the first thing he'd do is make sure it was safe. Especially with the children.'

'You would think,' said Asad, who was counting notes in the till.

'I'm sure it was a one-off,' Henry put in.

'I wouldn't be surprised if it was the ghost of Samuel Pottisworth come to haunt them.' Mrs Linnet gave a theatrical shiver.

'Oh, Mrs L, you don't believe in ghosts,' Henry chided her.

'But we do believe in evil spirits, don't we, Henry?' Asad snapped a rubber band round the notes.

'I like to have proof before I believe in anything, Asad.' Henry glared pointedly at his partner.

'Oh, some entities are far too clever for that.'

'And some people see things where there are none.'

Mrs Linnet had been distracted from the thread of her own conversation and was staring at them.

Asad closed the till. 'It's one of your more endearing

character traits that you see good everywhere, Henry, but sometimes it blinds you to what's really around you.'

'I know exactly what's going on, but I also believe in protecting oneself.'

'"For evil to survive, all that is necessary is for good people to stand by and do nothing."'

'But you have no *proof*.'

Mrs Linnet put down her bag. 'Have I missed something here?' she said.

At that moment the door swung open, and all three fell silent as Anthony McCarthy entered. He was talking to someone on his mobile telephone, so did not see the glances that shot between them, or the way that the two men behind the counter began to busy themselves. Mrs Linnet remembered she had to buy some jam, and set off to search the shelves at the far end.

The boy ended his conversation and shut his phone. His woollen hat was pulled low over his long hair, and his clothes hung off him, as if he had bought them several sizes too large.

'Good afternoon, Anthony.' Asad smiled. 'Can I help you?'

'Oh. Yeah.' He squatted in front of the cold counter, biting his lip. 'My mum asked me to bring home olives, smoked turkey and something else.' He grinned. 'But I can't remember what the something else was.'

'You men,' said Mrs Linnet. 'You're all the same.'

'Cheese?' suggested Asad.

'Fruit?' Henry held out a basket. 'We've got some lovely grapes.'

'Bread?'

The boy was so much like his mother, Henry thought. Same nose, same pleasant but reserved manner. Same curious mixture of defensiveness and pride, as if being related to Matt was cause for both celebration and shame.

'She'll kill me,' he said cheerfully.

'I'll get the olives and turkey together,' said Asad. 'That might jog your memory.'

'Is it definitely something to eat?' said Mrs Linnet, who enjoyed a challenge.

'Fruit cake? She likes that.' Henry held some aloft.

Anthony shook his head.

'Milk,' said Mrs Linnet. 'I always forget milk. And loo roll.'

'Why don't you ring her?'

'I just did. That was the answer-machine. She must have gone out. It'll come to me when I'm back in the van.'

Asad placed the two paper-wrapped parcels in a bag, and handed them over the counter. 'Are you still helping your father up at the big house?' he asked, as Anthony held out a note.

'Sometimes.'

'How is the work progressing?' Asad chose to ignore Henry's frown.

'She's asked us to stop for now,' said Anthony. 'I think it's all okay. Mind you, I wouldn't know. I just do what Dad says.'

'I'm sure,' said Asad. He counted out the change into Anthony's hand. 'And how is young Kitty?'

The boy flushed. 'She's . . . all right. As far as I know,' he muttered into his collar.

Now Henry was suppressing a smile.

'It's nice that she's got a few friends,' said Mrs Linnet. 'It must be ever so lonely for a young girl in that big house. I was just saying, her mother looks terrible—'

Anthony caught Henry's eye as the door opened again and Matt came in. 'What's taking you so long? We were meant to be at Mr Nixon's house fifteen minutes ago.'

'I forgot what Mum wanted,' Anthony said.

'Well, son,' Matt grinned, 'what women want is one of life's eternal mysteries, eh?' Suddenly he seemed to realise whom he was addressing, and the grin faded. 'Anyway, best get on the road.'

Asad smiled. 'Mr McCarthy, I was just going to tell Anthony – I watched a very interesting programme last night about builders.'

'Oh, yes?' Matt was glancing at the door, as if he was in a hurry to leave.

'It showed what happens when builders overcharge innocent householders, or invent jobs that don't need doing. An appalling thing to do, wouldn't you agree, Mr McCarthy?'

There was a sudden silence. Henry closed his eyes.

Matt came back in and shut the door behind him. 'I'm not sure I know what you mean, Asad.'

Asad's smile was steady. 'Oh, I think you're a more worldly man than you give yourself credit for, Mr McCarthy.'

Matt moved closer to his son. 'It's good of you to say so, Asad, but you'll find nothing of that nature goes on in this village. Round here we trade on our reputations, as you know. Builders and shopkeepers.'

'Indeed. We're familiar with people's reputations in this shop. But I'm glad you have such a positive view of things. Because you must agree that anyone who knew of such an act would feel obliged to speak out about it.'

Matt's smile was steely now. 'Asad, mate, if I had a clue what you were on about, I'm sure I'd agree with you. Come on, Anthony. We must go.' The door closed with slightly more emphasis than usual, making the bell jangle for several seconds.

*   *   *

Matt's ears glowed as he crossed the pavement. As he climbed into the van he was unable to keep his feelings in check. 'Bloody cheek! Did you hear him, Ant? Did you hear what he was insinuating?' Fear that his night with Isabel might be discovered made him more aggressive than he had intended. 'Sanctimonious prick. I could do him for slander, talking like that. Bloody holier-than-thou – he's always got on my nerves.'

The white noise in Matt's head was so loud that he didn't hear his phone until his son pulled it from the dashboard and answered it. 'It's Theresa,' he said, baldly, and he too turned away from his father.

It was shortly before seven the following morning when Isabel spotted the dogs. It was Saturday, so there was no compulsory early start, but she slept only fitfully now, and had decided that the only way to clear her head was to get up.

How to explain the plans she had found in the yellow digger? They clearly related to the Spanish House, were some sort of template for the work Matt had been doing. They showed the bathroom in the space he had suggested, back to back with a new dressing room. Yet he had never mentioned architects or plans. They were too recent to have belonged to Samuel Pottisworth – and she found it hard to believe that her great-uncle would have wanted to embark on major building work, having neglected the house for decades.

But if Matt had paid an architect to draw them up for her, surely she should have had a say in what was suggested? The thought of discussing any of this with him made her feel unhappy again.

And then there was the money. She had never thought about it before Laurent's death. It had been his domain, an

abstract that existed to facilitate life's pleasures. Family holidays, new clothes, meals out. Their casual profligacy shocked
her now.

Isabel knew exactly how much money she held in both
purse and bank account. Once she had paid Matt's latest
invoice, she and her family could survive on what was left
for three months without any further income. Teaching three
or four violin lessons a week would make it last longer. If
they could get at least one room straight and a decent bathroom, they could let it, which would bring in up to forty
pounds a week. But it was a big *if.* They were still washing
in the kitchen sink and using the downstairs cloakroom. 'I
can't see many tenants being keen on a tin bath,' Kitty had
remarked.

Isabel had been standing, half-awake, at her window,
watching the ducks and geese rise into the air, honking at
some unseen predator, when she saw dogs on the other side
of the water, chasing each other in joyous circles.

Almost on impulse she pulled on her dressing-gown and
ran down to the front door. She put on her wellingtons and
half walked, half ran across the lawn to the lake, her arms
wrapped round her against the morning air.

She stopped where the dogs had been, wet weeds brushing
against her bare calves, her ears filled with birdsong. The
dogs had vanished.

'Byron?' she called, her voice echoing across the lake.

He had already gone. He must have been on his way to
work. And then, a short distance away, a head broke the
water. A sleek dark head, and rising up from the liquid
surface, a torso, bare to the waist.

He had his back to her so for a couple of seconds Isabel
was free to watch him unnoticed. She was struck by the
unexpected magnificence of him, the broad, taut shoulders

that slid into the narrowed waist. He wiped water off his face, and she was flooded with conflicting emotions, awe at his physical beauty, then shame at the remembrance of the last male body to be close to her, and loss – of uncomplicated physicality, a hard male body against a yielding female one, pleasures she suspected she would never enjoy again.

He jolted as he caught sight of her, and she spun away, embarrassed to be caught staring.

'I'm sorry,' she said, her hair falling over her face. 'I . . . didn't realise you were there . . .'

He waded to the edge of the lake, seeming almost as uncomfortable as she was. 'I often come here in the mornings to swim,' he said. His clothes lay in a heap near a laurel bush. 'I hope you don't mind.'

'No . . . Of course not. You're very brave,' she said. 'It must be freezing.'

'You get used to it,' he said. There was a short silence, during which the dogs raced past, tongues lolling. Then he smiled. 'Erm . . . Isabel . . . I need to get out . . .'

She realised immediately what he meant, and turned away, cheeks flaming. How long did he think she'd been standing there? In her dressing-gown, of all things. Suddenly she saw herself as someone else might. Had Matt told him about the other night? Should she even be here at all? Isabel felt suddenly crushed. She pulled her gown around her. 'Look,' she said, 'I'll talk to you another time. I've got to get back.'

'Isabel, you don't have—'

'No. I do. I'm really—'

It was then that she saw her son. He came out of the trees, holding up the edge of his sweatshirt, which was filled with mushrooms. 'Thierry?' she said, perplexed. 'I thought you were in bed.'

'I thought you knew,' Byron said, behind her. 'He's been coming out with me every Saturday morning.'

She hadn't had any idea. But Mary would have known if Thierry had been out in the wilds shortly after dawn. Isabel felt cold. Her silk dressing-gown was no protection against the damp air.

'I'm sorry,' said Byron, still waist deep in the water. 'I wouldn't have let him come if I'd known.'

'It's fine. If it makes him happy . . .' she said, in a small voice. Thierry stepped forward and offered her the mushrooms, from which a pungent, earthy smell arose.

'They're safe,' said Byron, 'just chanterelles. I've been picking them for years. They're off Matt's land, but he won't mind.'

At that name Isabel let her hair fall further over her face and stooped to take the mushrooms from Thierry. She made sure she had her back to Byron and heard splashing as he emerged from the water. To have him naked in such close proximity made her feel acutely self-conscious, so she muttered something inconsequential to Thierry, who was rifling through his haul with expert fingers.

'Actually I needed to ask you a favour,' she said to Byron, her back still to him.

He waited.

'I need to use our land – live off it as far as I can. You said you could teach Thierry how to grow vegetables – well, perhaps you could show me what I can do for myself. I know you're employed by Matt, and you're probably very busy, but I'd be grateful for anything you can tell me . . . There isn't anyone else I can ask.'

She tried to gauge his reaction, then blustered on, 'I don't want cows or pigs or anything, and I'm not going to be ploughing fields. But there must be something we can do to help ourselves.'

'You'll be getting your hands dirty.'

She turned round to find him in a T-shirt and jeans, his skin still visibly damp. Then she looked down at her fingers, protected for thirty years from the wear and tear of the everyday, already flecked with soil from the fungi. 'They'll get used to it,' she said.

Byron rubbed a towel over his head, and surveyed the land around him. 'Well, there's your breakfast for a start,' he said, then, pointing at the mushrooms. 'You can pick those until autumn. And, if you're not squeamish, you could probably feed your family for months.'

She waited.

A small smile played around his lips. When he smiled he looked like a different person. 'Erm,' he said eventually, and gestured at her dressing-gown. 'You'll not get far in that.'

'Oh!' she exclaimed, suddenly laughing. 'Oh. Five minutes. Give me five minutes.'

There was food everywhere, should you choose to see it, Isabel discovered during her morning with Byron. While Kitty stayed at home, chatting on the telephone, she and Thierry followed him round the garden and lake, Isabel trying to commit to memory everything he told her about the potential of her land, which felt now like a place of provision rather than a soul-destroying drain on her resources. 'The easiest things for you to grow will be potatoes, tomatoes, perhaps onions and some beans. They're all pretty foolproof in this soil. This whole corner you can use for rhubarb – it used to do well here.'

Thierry grimaced.

'You'll like it in a crumble.' Byron nudged him.

I must make one, thought Isabel, but she had never asked Mary for the recipe.

'Out by the stables there's the old greenhouse. If you start your seedlings under glass, protect them a bit, you can put them out after the frosts. Cheapest to grow everything from seed, although this year you've probably left it too late. If we tidy this up,' he pulled at some weeds near the red-brick wall, 'you might even find a few raspberry canes . . . There they are. Cut those back to about here,' he indicated with his thumbs, 'and you should get a good crop. All these brambles you may as well leave for the blackberries.'

He strode along, increasingly voluble. Here, in his element, his watchful demeanour lifted, the odd smile drifting across his face. His voice was soft and low, as if unwilling to disturb his environment.

'You've got all different varieties of apple along here. They'll be ready in the autumn. You need to get yourself a freezer so you can keep what you don't eat, then they'll last you the winter. Stew as many as you can. The rest you wrap individually in newspaper,' here he mimed polishing one, 'and leave them in one of the outbuildings somewhere cold – somewhere the mice won't get at them,' he added.

'And you've got Victoria plums, pears, crab apples, damsons . . .' He waved at the fruit trees. She couldn't tell them apart. 'Greengages here. Gooseberries on this bush. Mind the thorns when you pick them, Thierry. You can make jam, chutney, maybe sell it even. There's a lot of people sell stuff at the roadside.'

'Who would come all the way down here to buy jam?' said Isabel.

'If it's good enough you could ask the Cousins to sell it for you as organic. No spray's been used here, as far as I can remember.' He paused. 'Only things you'll have trouble with are lettuce and carrots.'

'The rabbits,' said Isabel.

'Yup. But we can rig something up to keep them off. And there'd be rabbit stew every night if you fancied it.'

'You mean *kill* them?'

'Like shooting fish in a barrel round here.'

She shuddered at his choice of words.

'It's not hard to skin a rabbit. Thierry's done it.'

She was astounded, but Byron seemed suddenly ill-at-ease. 'I was careful. I watched him with the knife.' It wasn't the discovery that her son had been handling blades that had stunned Isabel: it was the expression on his face of quiet pride as he glanced shyly at Byron, apparently basking in his approval.

'He's good at it, aren't you, T? Bit of a natural, your boy.'

'Did you enjoy doing it, Thierry?' Watching him now, with Byron, she thought briefly that he might answer. But he just nodded. She caught Byron's eye and saw reflected in it an acknowledgement of what she had hoped for. But he continued to talk quietly, as if he had noted none of it.

'And there's pheasant, deer. A couple of sides of venison will keep you in meat for most of the winter. You can hang it in one of the outbuildings. It's good. Very lean.'

'I don't think I could quite manage that,' she said, and smiled.

They stood for a minute as Thierry ran off with one of the dogs, weaving in and out of the trees.

'You'd be surprised what you can do,' Byron said, 'if you have to.'

They walked along the path round the lake and back towards the house, the sun warming the earth so that a few bees flew around them. Isabel's mind hummed with possibilities. Her provisions hung outside from brackets, unconventional hanging-baskets, piled with onions, fruit, a clear plastic tub of milk. She pictured them overflowing with her own produce, herself suddenly capable, peeling, skinning, cooking.

'And you'd teach me?' she said. 'To shoot?'

Now he seemed properly uncomfortable. 'An air rifle, yes. I shouldn't have used that shotgun. No licence. I know someone who'll give you lessons, if you want.'

'I can't afford it,' she said.

'You can shoot rabbits with an air rifle,' he said. 'You don't need a licence for that. You can borrow mine, if you want. I'll show you how to use it.'

In twenty-four hours, Isabel reflected, she had gone from a lead violinist to a gun-toting market gardener.

She sat on the rickety garden bench by the back porch, Byron's .22 in her hands, a row of cans lined up on the wall before the open field so she could not injure anything accidentally. He had told her to keep practising. She lifted the gun to her shoulder, found the can in her sights. You had to get them in the head, he had told her. A straight kill. It's cruel to wound them.

They're not cute fluffy bunnies, she told herself. They're food for my children. Money saved for this house. Our future.

Pow! The shot rang out over the countryside and, with a satisfying clang, the pellet met the can. She heard her son step forward, felt his touch on her shoulder. She turned and he beamed at her. She motioned to him to step away again.

This is it, Laurent, she said silently, her slim white finger closing again round the trigger. It's time to move on.

Fifteen

They thought Anthony couldn't hear. Shut behind the office door, they seemed to believe their voices wouldn't carry round the house, ricochet off the walls like bullets.

'I really don't think it's a lot to ask, Matt. I just want some idea of when you'll be home.'

'I've told you I don't know. You know I can never tell from one day to the next.'

'You used to give me *some* idea. And now you turn your phone off so half the time I don't know where you are.'

'And why the hell should I have to tell you where I am every minute of the day? I'm not a child. You want the Spanish House, don't you? Well, let me earn the bloody money to get it.'

In the living room, Anthony slumped on the chair, and wondered whether to put on his earphones.

'I don't know why you're being so aggressive about it. All I'm asking is that you let me know roughly what time you'll be home.'

'And I'm telling you, as I've told you a hundred times already, that I can't do that. I could be working at the big house and hit a problem. I could be called by someone on the other side of town with an emergency. You know as well as I do that I have to be flexible. Where's my bloody VAT book?'

Drawers being opened and shut.

'In the blue folder where it always is. There.' A pause. 'Look, I understand that, Matt, but why can't you ring me and give me some idea? That way I can plan my evening too. And supper.'

'Just stick my dinner in the oven, woman. If I'm not worried about eating it lukewarm, why are you making such a fuss?'

'Because you're being evasive.'

'No, you're being controlling. Like you want to control everything – this house, that house, the finances, Anthony, and now me. "You need to do this, you need to do that", harping on all the time!'

'How can you say that?'

'Because it's true. And it's getting on my nerves.'

'It seems to me, Matt, that pretty well everything I do is guaranteed to get on your nerves.'

It was the third time this week. His dad had been antsy and bad-tempered for almost ten days. For some reason he hadn't told Anthony's mother they had stopped work at the Spanish House, and he wondered privately whether this was because Kitty's mum had run out of money. Kitty was always saying her mum hadn't any. It was possible his dad was trying to work out what to do about it before he told Mum.

Whatever, something was going on. Usually when Matt headed off to a job, he would take Anthony with him after school, supposedly training him, steering him towards the day when he would take over. That's what he always said, even when Anthony suspected he wanted an extra pair of hands he didn't have to pay for. But he hadn't asked him to come lately. Byron was out working on the land, so he wasn't taking him either. Anthony didn't even know where his father was working – Theresa's house probably, not that you could call that *working*. In fact, it didn't bother him – it meant he could head down to Kitty's and hang out with her. It was easier than having to listen to this. He pulled his mobile phone from his pocket. 'Do u think social services would take my parents into care?' he typed, then sent the message to Kitty.

'I don't want to argue with you, Matt—'

'You surprise me. You pick fights whenever you can.'

'That's not fair. I just want to feel as if I'm not married to a – a vacuum. Because that's how it feels. Even when you're here you're not really with us.'

Anthony's phone beeped. He looked down. 'No use asking me. Mine has taken to waving a gun around – K XX.'

'You're doing my head in. I'm going.'

'Matt, don't—'

'I don't have time for this.'

'But you've got time for *her.*'

A long silence. Anthony flipped the phone shut, then sat up in his chair, listening, as if to the slow fizz of blue touchpaper.

'What are you talking about?'

His mother, tearful now: 'I'm not stupid, Matt. I know. And I'm not going to put up with it again.'

His father, dismissive, cold: 'I don't know what you're talking about.'

'Who is it this time, Matt? Some shopgirl? Barmaid? A grateful client? Hell – the woman across the lane, perhaps? You spend enough time over there.'

His father exploded. 'Who told me to go over there? Who wanted me to do the work? Who's spent the last nine years going on and on about how much she wanted that bloody house? Don't start bitching at me when I'm doing the one thing you said you wanted!'

'Stop twisting my words! You wanted that house as much as I did!'

'I'm not listening to any more of this,' his father spat. 'I'm going to work.'

Anthony scrambled to put on his earphones as the office door opened and his father strode out. 'I'll be back when I'm back. All right? Anthony, you should be at school, not sitting there earwigging like some old woman.'

'Don't treat me like a fool, Matt.' His mother was crying now. 'I'm not going to stand by while you screw your way half-way around the county. Matt! Matt?'

His father's van disappeared out of the driveway in a spray of gravel, and Anthony removed his earphones as his mother came in. She started when she saw him, and wiped her eyes, trying to recover her composure. 'I didn't know you were still here, darling. Are you waiting for a lift?'

'Free period. I'm not due in till ten.' He fiddled with his phone so that she could straighten her hair. It was always perfect, and it made her look vulnerable when it was all messed up as it was now. 'Just wanted to make sure you were okay.'

Her eyes were red-rimmed and her skin blotchy. 'I'm fine. Really. You know what your dad's like . . . just a bit difficult sometimes.' Then she said, apparently casually, 'I don't suppose he mentioned where he was working?'

'No.' He added, 'But he's not at the big house for now. Kitty says he hasn't been there all week.'

'Really?'

'She'd know.'

His mother sighed, as if she wasn't sure whether she was disappointed or relieved by this information. 'So he's not there,' she said, almost to herself. 'Anthony, can I ask you something? Do you think he's . . . involved with Mrs Delancey?'

Anthony was glad he didn't have to lie. 'No. Not her. She's . . . different from us.' He had been about to say she wasn't his father's type.

'He's been so . . .' Laura mustered the kind of smile she wore when she was trying to convince Anthony that everything was okay. 'I'm sorry. I shouldn't involve you in all this. I suppose you think I'm a fool.'

He realised he wanted to hit his dad – really, really hit him. The words came even before he knew what he was going to say. 'We could leave him.'

His mother's eyes widened.

'I mean, don't stay because of me. I wouldn't be devastated or anything if we went.'

'But, Anthony, he's your father.'

The boy shrugged and grabbed his schoolbag from beside the sofa, already realising that anything he said would make no difference. 'Doesn't make him a good person, though, does it?'

At first she had thought it was the Cousins. She couldn't think who else would leave two boxes of fresh eggs outside her door – where she had almost trodden on them. She had picked one up, opened it and examined the speckled, irregularly sized eggs, some still bearing dirty straw or a feather. When she had broken one into a pan it had sat almost upright instead of spreading. Like a silicon breast implant, Kitty had suggested. 'The Cousins say that means it's really fresh.'

She had gone into the shop that lunchtime, and thanked them for their unexpected delivery. 'They were absolutely delicious,' she said. 'Almost meaty in flavour. I never expected eggs to taste like that. And the colour! So vivid!'

Henry had looked at her blankly. 'Darling, I'd love to think we were adding to your egg count but we don't do deliveries. Even to our nicest customers.'

Then, several days later, firewood appeared. It had a note attached to it: 'Needs seasoning for at least a year. Have put rest in barn by orchard.'

She had gone out and found a neatly stacked pile of freshly cut wood, some still leaking sap. She had breathed in its scent, running her hand over the bark. There was something elementally satisfying about a woodpile, the knowledge of warmth to come.

Two days later, crouching blank-eyed and furious in a rusting wire crate, six hens arrived. 'These are point of lay (eggs coming soon),' the note read. 'Will need corn or layers' mash, regular supply of grit and water. Old coop by greenhouse. Shut them in at night. Colin of Dorneys Farm will be round to take the old pallets at back of garage in payment.'

She and Thierry had strung up a ramshackle run out of old bits of chicken wire and posts, and watched the birds peck their way round the garden. Thierry had enjoyed this, busy with stakes and wire, brushing off his hands with satisfaction afterwards. The first time he had found an egg, he had rushed to hold it at her cheek so that she could feel the residual warmth. She had prayed that this might be a turning point for him.

And then there had been the rabbits. She had been upstairs, brushing her teeth in the unfinished bathroom, when she'd heard Kitty shriek. She had run down in her dressing-gown, mouth still full of toothpaste, to find her daughter hugging herself beside the back door. Her face was pale with shock. 'Oh, my God, someone really hates us!'

'What?' Isabel had cried. 'What's the matter?'

'Look!'

Isabel had opened the back door, Thierry at her side. There, on the steps, lay three dead rabbits, their hind paws tied together with baling twine, a small bloody patch on each head signifying where they had come from. 'It's like *Deliverance*.'

'Byron,' said Thierry, happily.

'What did you say?' asked Isabel. But he was silent again. He picked up the rabbits and brought them inside to the kitchen table, laying them down gently.

'Eurgh! Don't put them there! They're dead!' Kitty shrieked, huddled against the wall as if the rabbits might suddenly revive and leap up at her.

'It's okay, darling,' Isabel soothed her. 'We've been left them as a present. Thierry will prepare them for us.'

'Someone left us *roadkill*?'

'They're not roadkill. People used to eat rabbit all the time.'

'Yes, and they used to send children up chimneys. It doesn't make it right.' Kitty was clearly appalled by the idea. 'If you think I'm eating dead rabbit you're out of your minds. Ugh! You're both disgusting!' She flounced out of the kitchen.

Thierry was grinning.

'Show me, darling,' Isabel said. 'Show me what Byron showed you and we'll do it together.'

It had been like this for almost two weeks. Early potatoes, tentative shoots emerging from their rumpled skins, envelopes of seeds, clearly labelled with instructions, two sacks of manure. Isabel had tried to find Byron to thank him, but he was never around. In fact, the house was deserted, apart from her and the children. Matt had not returned. The digger and his tools were scattered about the house and its grounds like landlocked relics of the *Mary Celeste*.

Thierry laid a plastic bag on the table, and put a rabbit on its back, its head facing him. He took the small kitchen knife and placed it on the left of the soft white belly, pulled a pinch of fur between his fingers and began to cut. Isabel fought the inclination to steer him away from sharp implements, but his fingers were as precise as hers were on strings, and his whole self seemed absorbed in his task. And as Isabel watched, marvelling at how tenderly he did it, her son put down the knife and peeled away the rabbit's pelt, almost as if he were removing its clothing, to reveal the raw pink flesh beneath.

She didn't know what she would say to Matt about that night. She couldn't explain her actions, let alone his, and although drink might have played a part, she knew it wasn't enough to blame the wine. If she were honest, some part of her had felt indebted to him – although the ugly truth in his offer had turned her blood to ice.

She had been at her lowest when he had suddenly appeared, a strong man who always took charge . . . and there, in the dark, lost in the music and her loneliness, she had persuaded herself he was not some near-stranger. That somehow she had called up Laurent in the dark and the wind. Some spectral version of him.

She could not plead unwillingness. She had wanted it.

Her son had removed the head. As Isabel tried not to wince, he cut through the animal's groin and upwards, tugging at the innards. He chewed his lower lip with concentration. His hands, she thought absently, looked as they had when he had been a toddler, finger painting with red and brown.

She had been shamefully glad to feel Matt's hands on her, his breath, his embrace – to hand herself over to him. To feel raw desire reciprocated. She could still remember the piercing physical joy of having him inside her.

And then the spell had been broken. Some minutes before it might comfortably have done so. He was not her husband. He was not someone she wanted, against her, inside her. But it had gone too far for her to stop so she had closed her eyes, tried to separate herself from what was happening as her body, which had betrayed her initially, remembered who he was and shut down, turning her into someone cold, unfeeling and ashamed. Then, the worst of it, he had been so pleased, so affectionate afterwards. He seemed to believe she might want to prolong it, or even to do it again.

And now, on top of everything, this crushing guilt – not just for his wife, but that she, a woman who had spent little more than a year mourning her husband and still carried him in every thought, had offered herself up so casually to another man. She had betrayed what she and Laurent had had. She felt as though Matt's presence had erased everything that had gone before.

Isabel jumped as, with a snap, Thierry broke off the rabbit's legs. There was no fur now, no head, no paws, just a lump of raw flesh. Painful, and exposed. Thierry washed it under the tap, standing on tiptoe, then held it out proudly to her. There was nothing left inside it, just a clean cavity where its heart had been.

Isabel suppressed a shudder. 'Wonderful, lovey. Well done.' His hands were still spattered with blood and fur, when he pulled the next rabbit on to the plastic bag.

Isabel put the prepared carcass into salted water, as Byron had told her. Apparently this would make it more palatable.

She saw the car before she saw him, glimpsing it through the trees on the far side of the lake. It was the spot she had shown him on the day they had met. Since then she had returned to it more than once, on the days when Matt had been especially awful. Her son's words still rang in her ears.

'We're married,' she had told him. 'Believe it or not, that means something. It means not walking away when the going gets tough. It means we work through our problems.'

'If you say so,' Anthony had muttered.

'What's that supposed to mean?'

'Well, I'm never getting married if it means being like you

two. Look at you both,' he had said. 'You're not friends. You never have a laugh together. You never actually *talk* to each other about anything.'

'That's not fair.'

'You're like some 1950s sitcom. He upsets you. You forgive him. He makes a mess. You clear it up. You're like some kind of crummy deal.'

His car was parked a little way back, just off the lane, and as she walked past it she glanced in at the map, the scattered bits of paper, already knowing there could be only one reason why he had returned. Laura straightened her lapels, glad that she had taken the trouble to repair her makeup.

He was sitting on the tree stump and scrambled up at her approach, a smile breaking across his face. She smiled back. It had been a while since anyone without fur or hoofs had been so pleased to see her.

'It *is* you!' he exclaimed. 'I'd been hoping it was.'

He had a lovely voice, low, gentle and slightly clipped. A little like her father's. She was suddenly shy. 'Enjoying the view?' she asked feebly.

He reached down to pat Bernie, who had no hesitation in welcoming him. 'It's a fabulous spot. I dreamed of this view every night after . . . our last chat.'

The house was just visible on the far side, partially obscured by trees and hedging, partially mirrored in the glassy water. There had been times when she had sat here and let her imagination drift, picturing herself arm in arm with her husband, strolling down the stone steps towards the lake. The parties they would have on the lawns. The elegant drapes they would hang at the windows. There had been other, more recent times, when she had been unable to walk round this side of the land, when she couldn't see the house without being eaten up by envy and frustration that, after everything, it was not hers.

Today, for the first time, that wasn't important. The object neither of frustration nor desire, it was just a shabby old house, gazing placidly out across the water.

There was a brief silence, broken by ducks fighting in the reeds. Nicholas was fondling the dog's ears. She recalled the things she had told him the last time they had met. Perhaps it really was easier to tell your secrets to a stranger.

'You look . . . lovely,' he said.

She lifted a hand involuntarily to her hair. 'Better than last time.'

'You looked wonderful last time.' He stood up. 'Would you like some coffee? I was just having some. I – I brought a spare cup.' The implication of his last statement made them laugh.

Laura sat on the tree stump. 'I'd love some,' she said.

She didn't know who it was, she told him, some time later. She knew her husband was sleeping with someone, but she did not know who. 'It makes life in a village impossible.' She was careful not to look at him as she said this, knowing she could continue only if she pretended he wasn't there. 'Everywhere I go I'm wondering, Is it you? Or you? It could be almost anyone. The girl at the supermarket. The woman in the fabrics shop. The waitress at the restaurant he takes me to. He's always been attractive to women.'

Nicholas said nothing. He sat next to her, listening.

'I can't talk to anyone about it. Not my friends or neighbours – I know of at least one he's slept with, although she'd deny it. There's no point in asking him. He could tell you black was white and you'd believe him. He's done it to me enough times. Even now he won't admit to anything. He makes me feel that I'm the stupid one for suspecting him.'

He turned now to study her face. She knew what he must be thinking. *Fool.* But his expression didn't say so.

'Last time he had to admit it. He sent me a text message instead of her. He must have got muddled. "Meet me at the Tailors' Arms," it said. "Got two hours before curfew." I've never forgotten it. *Curfew.* As if I was some kind of gaoler.'

'What did you do?'

She laughed humourlessly. 'I turned up at the pub. He went absolutely white when he saw me.'

Nicholas smiled sympathetically.

Laura fiddled with a cuff. 'He admitted everything and said he was sorry. We'd been trying for a baby, you see. I thought it would bring us together, but he said it had made him feel pressured and this woman – this *girl* – was the result. That was three years ago.'

'And now?'

'I don't know. I talk to the shopgirls and the hairdresser, my female friends and neighbours and . . . I have no idea which of them is sleeping with my husband.' She fought to control her voice. 'That's the hardest thing, you see. That she could be there looking at me, laughing at me. One of these pretty young girls with their firm bodies and perfect skin. That's what I see in my head. The two of them, laughing at me.' She clenched her jaw.

'I'm sorry,' she said, after a moment. 'You just wanted a cup of coffee and to enjoy the view and I'm rambling on about my marriage. You must forgive me.' Don't be nice, she told him silently, or I'll fall apart.

But as she stared fixedly at the house in the distance a hand closed over hers. A hand that was warm, firm and unfamiliar. And the voice that spoke to her was unexpectedly tough.

'The man's a fool,' it said.

It was another two hours before he checked his watch. 'That's some lunch break,' she had said, when he exclaimed at the time. He had smiled and nodded, creases at the corners of his eyes. 'Wasn't much of a lunch, though, was it?'

They had looked down at the chocolate wrapper.

They had not discussed Matt further. He had chivalrously changed the subject, telling her of a place he had known as a boy, not dissimilar to this, where he and his siblings had spent hours roaming and making camps. Then they had talked about childhood pets, elderly parents, steering clear of relationships, of why they might be sitting alone at the edge of a wood. And then she had glanced at her watch to discover that two hours had passed.

'Perhaps you'll let me make up for it some time,' he said. 'An improved culinary offering.'

She had understood what he was saying. And her smile had faded. A proper lunch. It was one thing to bump into someone while she was walking the dog, even to sit down and share a conversation with them, but lunch was premeditated. It spoke of intention.

It was the kind of thing Matt would do with his conquests.

Her thoughts must have been transparent, and she saw disappointment in his face. 'I'm sorry,' he said. 'I realise . . . things are complicated.'

'It's not you . . .'

He winced.

'You're . . . very good company.'

'And so are you, Laura.' He got up and offered her a hand. 'Really. I've enjoyed this afternoon more than I can say.'

'The ramblings of a whining housewife . . .' She straightened her shirt.

'No,' he said. 'Just an honest one. I'm flattered.' He was still holding her hand. 'I've been on my own for a long time, partly because I've wanted to be, but it's been good simply to talk to someone – someone intelligent and kind and—'

'I'd better go,' she said.

He released her hand. 'Of course.'

'Perhaps we'll bump into each other again,' she said. She couldn't ask. She couldn't admit to herself that she might want to.

He reached into his pocket, took out a pen and scribbled on a piece of paper. 'In case you ever fancy that lunch,' he said. And as she walked towards the path, the paper radio-active in her pocket, she heard him call, 'Three courses or a bar of chocolate. I really don't mind.'

He watched her go down the path, something a little self-conscious in her gait, as if she knew his eyes were on her. She wouldn't look back, even if she wanted to, he thought. Everything about her spoke of delicacy, of a way of doing things he rarely encountered these days. Even the way she had held her cup was elegant. He could have watched her for hours more. He had made himself look across the lake at the house lest his intensity alarm her. But he had felt her beside him acutely, his nerve endings sharpening when the breeze carried a hint of her scent to him. His breath had caught in his throat when she had lifted those sad grey eyes to his. Now, freed from restraint, he let his eyes rest on her until she was swallowed by the trees, her blonde hair briefly dappled in the sunlight.

He suspected he understood her, this beautiful, gentle woman whom he hardly knew. He had not wanted someone so completely, so unhesitatingly, since his wife had left, and he wasn't sure that he had ever wanted her in the same way.

Walking towards his car, he told himself not to hope. Like the house, this was likely to be a waiting game. He might not have had the self-awareness to recognise it, but despite his recent past, Nicholas Trent was still, at heart, a dealmaker. And his knowledge of a rival, no matter how invisible, how unknown, how potent, only sharpened his desire.

That evening Byron finally appeared. There was a knock at the kitchen door, and as Isabel could see through the glass who it was she opened it. He stood, filling the frame, just a worn blue T-shirt to keep out the evening chill.

'Hi,' he said, and his smile was so unexpected that she smiled back. 'Hope you don't mind,' he said, 'but I wondered if I could have a word.'

'Do you want to come in?' she said, gesturing into the kitchen. Thierry, who had been doing his homework, was already out of his chair.

'No, no,' said Byron. 'Probably best out here.' He nodded towards the garden, and Isabel stepped out, closing the door behind her.

Oh, God, she thought. He's going to want money for all the things he's left. 'Is everything all right?' she asked.

'It's Thierry,' he said quietly.

'What?' she said, anxious now.

'Nothing's wrong,' he said hastily. 'It's just I've sold most of my pups — well, reserved them for people — and before I get rid of the last two, I was wondering whether you'd want one. Thierry's grown fond of them, you see.'

She saw that two black and white puppies were wrestling in a box on the ground nearby.

'They're nearly ready to go,' he went on, 'and I just thought . . . well, he seems to get a lot from being around animals.' He hesitated, as if he was afraid he might say too much. 'I make him shout for them.'

'Shout for them?'

'I tell him he has to call them so that he can train them. I get him to do it in the woods.'

'And he does?'

Byron nodded. 'Gets quite loud sometimes.'

A huge lump came into Isabel's throat at the thought of her silent son's voice ringing out. 'What does he say?'

'Nothing much. Just shouts their names and "Here", "Sit", that kind of thing. I thought it was good to have him making some sound. I think he finds it easier in the woods.'

They stood facing each other, silent.

'How much have you been selling them for?' Isabel asked.

'Oh, a couple of hundred each.' And then, as he saw Isabel's face, he added, 'But not for you. For Thierry. I wasn't planning on . . .'

'On what?'

'Charging you.'

Isabel coloured. 'I'll pay what everyone else pays.'

'But that's not what I—'

'It's better if I pay. Then we're square.' Her arms folded across her chest.

'Look, I didn't come to sell you a puppy. I came to ask if Thierry would like one. A gift. But I had to check with you first that it was okay.'

Why would you give us something for free? Isabel wanted to ask, but the question stalled on her lips.

'It's the runt of the litter,' he added, pointing to the darker of the two.

She suspected this wasn't true but she couldn't challenge him. She bent down and lifted it from the box. It squirmed against her, trying to lick her neck. 'You've given us an awful lot already,' she said, sombrely.

'Not really. Round here most people help each other out.'

'All that stuff,' she said. 'The firewood, the hens –'

'– weren't really from me. I told Colin you'd be happy to swap those wooden pallets for some layers. Really. It's nothing to get worked up about.' He picked up the other puppy. 'Be good to see that little chap go to a good home.'

She looked at him, this unreadable man whose discomfort mirrored her own. She realised he was younger than she had thought, that his size, his strength, his containment masked something like vulnerability. And she did what she could to unbend. 'Then thank you,' she said, with a smile. 'I think – I know he'd love to have a puppy of his own.'

'He's—'

Byron broke off as a van emerged from the trees. Isabel flushed when she recognised the distinctive sound of its diesel engine. Some childish part of her wanted to run inside and wait for it to go away.

But, of course, it didn't. Matt jumped down from the cab and strolled casually to the back door, then saw them. Isabel noticed distantly that Byron took a couple of steps away from her as the older man approached.

'Byron, did you pick up that insulation?' he asked.

'Yes.'

'And have you finished clearing the drainage?'

Byron nodded.

His questions answered, Matt half turned from him, as if he was of no more interest. Byron, Isabel saw, had retreated into himself, as if his body were a shell. His face was blank.

'Sorry I haven't been round.' Matt stood directly in front of Isabel. 'Been caught up on a job in Long Barton.'

'That's fine,' said Isabel. 'Really.'

'But I wanted you to know I'll be back tomorrow. As usual.' He was looking at her intently, as if there were some extra meaning in what he had said.

Isabel held the puppy closer to her chest, grateful for the excuse to focus elsewhere than on his eyes. 'Okay,' she said.

He didn't move. She met his eyes, straightening her

shoulders. He held them slightly longer than necessary but, apparently unable to read anything in them, at last looked away.

'Whose is the pup?' he said.

'Mine,' Byron told him.

'Bit young to be out, isn't he?'

Byron took the puppy from Isabel and put it back in the box. 'I'm taking them home now,' he said.

Matt did not seem to want to go. His gaze flickered from one to the other, until he turned to Byron. 'I forgot to mention – from tomorrow I'll want you on the Dawson job. All right? They've some land needs clearing. Oh, and I've got something for you.' He brought out an envelope, and began to count out bank notes ostentatiously. '. . . and twenty. There's your wages.' He grinned. 'Don't spend them all at once.'

Byron took the money stiffly. His eyes burned.

'So, Byron, we don't want to be bothering Mrs Delancey all evening. Do you want a lift back into the village?'

'No,' said Byron. 'I'm parked the other side of the lake.' At the sound of his whistle, his two dogs appeared and bounded after him as he strode down the path. Isabel fought the urge to call him back.

Matt watched him go, then turned to her. His swagger had diminished. 'Isabel,' he said quietly, 'I wanted to talk—'

The kitchen door opened and Kitty appeared, a strand of hair in the corner of her mouth. 'Are you going to help me with supper?' she said, briefly removing it. 'You've been ages out here.'

With relief, Isabel turned back to him. 'Sorry. I can't talk now.'

Kitty held out a colander. 'Most of the potatoes have got bits growing out of them.'

'Look –' she said abruptly, 'we have . . . I have enough to

cover the other works you suggested.' She registered his sudden look of pleasure and realised he might think she had some other reason for keeping him there. 'The pipework, the heating and the bathroom. We really need the bathroom.'

'I'll be back tomorrow,' he said.

'Fine.' She slipped through the kitchen door and closed it thankfully behind her.

Sixteen

Byron Firth was a man of few expectations, but even he had to admit that the house on Appleby Lane was not what he had imagined. He had predicted it would be small, semi-detached, perhaps a little like the house he and his sister had left, or in a 1970s cul-de-sac with a small, boxy garden front and back.

Two bedrooms, his sister had said, and he had suspected it might even be a maisonette or a council flat. But this was a thatched cottage set on a quiet lane in a third of an acre, almost a parody of an olde-English idyll, with heavy beams and flowerbeds.

'D'you want anything else, Byron?'

He leaned back in the plush comfort of the sofa. 'No, thanks. It was delicious.'

'Jason's just putting the kettle on. He wants to show you some plans we have for the garden. Hedging and stuff. Maybe you can give him some advice.'

Byron knew that Jason would want to do no such thing. The two men had never really warmed to each other. Byron regarded Jan's boyfriends – any potential stepfather to Lily – with suspicion. But he understood what she was trying to do and, mindful of their hospitality, he was content to play along.

'Sure. Just say when,' he said.

Summer had arrived abruptly in this small corner of

England. In the woods this meant a riot of activity, with green shoots firing upwards from coppiced trunks, and a carpet of flowers at the east side that had lasted weeks.

As his sister went back to the immaculate kitchen, Byron allowed his head to sink on to the cushions and closed his eyes. The roast beef had been delicious. But the sofa . . . He had not imagined how luxurious a sofa could feel until he had spent several weeks sleeping on a concrete floor. He was physically tough, but now he wondered how he would get through another night in the boiler room.

It was taking longer than he'd hoped. The old man at Catton's End had not yet paid for the smaller bitch, and Mrs Dorney from the garden centre wanted her puppy after she had moved house.

He had found a tied cottage three miles away, on a huge dairy farm. They didn't mind the dogs, and might even put the odd bit of work his way, but until all of the puppies were gone, he couldn't raise the full deposit. Even the proceeds of their sale would not add up to the amount the landlord was asking. He would have to take all the overtime Matt could offer.

'Can you help me put this chair together?' Lily climbed on to his lap and handed him the pieces of the dolls'-house furniture he had brought with him. She had shown him her room, and the dolls' house 'Uncle Jason' had given her. It was almost three feet tall, with a thatched roof of straw.

'He wanted her to feel welcome,' Jan had said. 'He made it himself. It's a copy of this cottage.'

He had been surprised by the monosyllabic Jason, and not for the first time that day. Nothing in the man's demeanour had hinted that he might be capable of creating something like that. 'Pass me the glue, Lily.' He leaned forward, careful not to let the little tube drip.

'Can you do the kitchen stuff next?'

'Sure.'

She eyed him with a mischievous smile.

'Mum's friend Sarah fancies you. Mum told her she could have you as long as she took your laundry too.'

She had said as much to him when he'd handed his clothes over. 'Jeez, Byron. How long since you did this lot?' She had held the laundry bag away from her. 'This isn't like you.'

'My mate's machine's broken down. I got a bit behind.' He pretended to be diverted by the garden. It was the worst thing about where he was staying. The nearest launderette was sixteen miles away, which would cost him valuable pounds in diesel. If he rinsed things in the lake, they still looked dirty and took several days to dry. Sometimes, as he sat listening to Isabel's music, he pictured himself sneaking into the laundry room and secretly using her machine. But that would feel furtive and wrong. What if she found a stray sock?

Now he listened comfortably to the distant spin of his sister's machine. A full stomach, a soft place to sit and the prospect of clean clothes. He handed Lily the fixed dolls' chair. It took little in life to make a person happy, when you thought about it.

'She's quite pretty,' said Lily. 'She's got long hair.'

'Byron.' Jason came in and sat in one of the easy chairs.

Byron pushed himself a little more upright on the sofa. It would be so easy to fall asleep. 'Nice place,' he said. 'Everything. It's . . . really nice.'

'I did most of the building work with my dad a few years back.'

'It's better than our old house.' Lily was applying stickers to the wooden furniture. 'Although I did like it.'

Byron smiled at her as he remarked to Jason, 'You'll be giving Matt McCarthy a run for his money.'

'No offence, mate, but I wouldn't have that man in my house. Not with all the stories you hear about him.'

What stories? Byron wanted to ask.

Lily was humming tunelessly as she arranged and rearranged the dolls' furniture. Eventually Jason said, 'Lily, sweetheart, can you go and ask your mum if she wants me to get some more biscuits?'

Lily scrambled up and went to the kitchen, drawn by the magic word. When she was out of earshot Jason muttered, 'Look, Byron, I know you haven't been that happy about me and your sister—'

Byron tried to interrupt, but Jason held up a hand. 'No, let me finish. She told me what happened to you. Prison and stuff. And I want you to know something.'

His gaze was piercing and sincere. 'I will never lay a finger on your sister or Lily. I'm not . . . that kind of man. I wanted you to know that. And I wanted you to know that if I'd been you I'd probably have done the same.'

Byron swallowed – hard. 'I didn't mean . . .'

'Yeah?'

'He fell badly,' he said eventually. 'It was a long time ago.'

'Yeah. She said.'

The 'but' hung in the air. Through the door, Byron could hear the kettle boiling, the clatter of cups being pulled out of cupboards.

'Anyway, just so you know, I'll probably ask her to marry me, when they're settled in and that.'

Byron allowed his head to sink back on to the cushions, trying to digest this latest twist, the new version of a man he had been predisposed to dislike. He was different in his own home. Perhaps most people were.

Several long minutes passed.

'I'll see what's going on with the tea,' Jason said. 'White no sugar, isn't it?'

'Thanks,' said Byron.

Then his sister popped out of the kitchen with a tray. 'I don't know why you're going on about biscuits,' she said, nudging Jason as she sat down beside him. 'You know we finished off the last of the digestives this morning.'

She poured a mug and handed it to her brother. 'You still haven't told me – even though you landed me with half a ton of washing. Who is this mate you're staying with?'

For three days Thierry was sure he had heard it. He had been passing by the barns on the far side of the house and there it was, a growling, whimpering noise, but muffled, a bit like it was underground. 'Probably fox cubs,' Byron had said, when he motioned to him. 'They'll be in an earth some-where. Come on, we've got pheasants to feed.' Byron had told him you should never disturb wild animals without a reason, especially the young. If you picked up a baby, or disturbed a nest, the parents might get scared and never come back.

But Byron wasn't here today. Thierry stood in the sun, very still, tilting his head to gauge where the sound was coming from. Upstairs he could hear music in Kitty's room, where she and Mum were painting. Mum had said Kitty could have anything she liked on her walls. He was going to ask if he could have the planets. He liked the thought of having the solar system outside his window and inside too.

Around him he could hear the whisper of the Scots pines, their scent wafting towards him on the warm breeze. There it was again. Thierry took his hands out of his pockets and began to walk round the side of the house. He stopped when he got to the rotten old door. Byron had shown him about tracks, and now, looking at the ground, he could see that this door had been opened recently.

He frowned. How could a fox open a door – especially a heavy one like this? He walked forward, put his fingers round the edge and tugged. He stepped inside and let his eyes adjust to the dark. The whimpering had stopped.

Thierry could just make out the L shape of the room. As he closed the door behind him and went down the steps the whining and growling started again and he followed it to a familiar sight. He stooped and took one of Byron's puppies out of the box, holding it firmly. He must have put them here to be safe while he was working.

Thierry sat on the concrete floor, letting the puppies jump up on him and lick his face, which his sister always said was revolting.

It was only when they calmed down and were sniffing around that he noticed they weren't the only things in the room. There was a folding chair in the corner, a sleeping-bag on a tarpaulin, a rucksack and a couple of bags. Nearby, he saw the dogs' bowls. A cup with a toothbrush and toothpaste was balanced on the side of a small sink. Thierry squeezed a worm of tooth-paste into his mouth. Why would Byron be camping here?

'Thierry!' his mother called, from above. 'Lunchtime! Thierry!'

He put the toothpaste carefully back where he had found it. 'Ssh,' he told the dogs, and held a finger to his lips. 'Ssh.'

Thierry knew all about secrets, why some things were best kept close, and he didn't want Byron to feel that his nest had been disturbed.

A hand remembers music long after it has ceased to play. In the same way Isabel's hand recalled the feel of her old violin long after it had left her. She thought of it as she mimed the Dvořák, imagining the tension of the strings, the feel of the Guarneri under her chin. She would probably never hold a violin like that again, never hear its velvety timbre, feel the thoroughbred shiver of its strings, but there were compensations, she told herself.

Summer had brought with it a kind of peace after the turbulent weeks of late spring. The vegetable patch was flourishing. She had bought a large freezer and put it in the dining room for the excess, and now that the summer holidays had started Kitty had taken on the hens, breeding black cochins, little bantams, huge, petticoated buff Orpingtons. The eggs and chicks brought her a small but steady income. The two doors to the house stood open during the daylight hours, and Isabel would often find an extravagantly feathered cockerel eyeing her beadily from the sofa, or a broody hen nestled in a pile of washing. She found it hard to get too aggrieved; she loved to see Kitty and Thierry bent over the chicks. It was good to see them interested in something, no longer mourning what they had lost.

Thierry spent much of his time in the woods with Byron, bringing back mushrooms, leaves they could use in salads or barrowloads of firewood for the winter. Isabel imagined him shouting for the puppy Byron had now handed over. Her son's expression when he had understood it was really his had made her eyes fill with tears. Say something, Thierry, she had urged silently. Be pleased. Whoop, shout, like the boy you are, but he had walked over to her and put his arms round her waist. She had squeezed him back, afraid to show him how much she had hoped for more.

'He'll have to start training that pup soon,' Byron had remarked, in front of Thierry, and Isabel prayed that the little animal would lead her son back into speech.

That morning, Byron had taught her how to chop firewood.

She had been doing it all wrong, apparently. The axe was blunt. Resting one end of the timber on a log and hacking at the middle was dangerous and could blind her. She should split it, not cut it; he showed her how to remove the axe from the wood by hitting the back with a sledgehammer, his strong hands slicing through it with a clean blow. 'It's good for you, though,' he said, grinning as she raised it again. 'Helps clear your head. Therapeutic.'

'As long as I don't chop off my feet.'

Isabel's own hands, meanwhile, grew roughened and scratched from chopping, braving gooseberry bushes and raspberries. She had nicked them with the blades while she skinned rabbits, and her palms were calloused from painting the inside of the house where it wasn't sheathed in plastic. She was determined to brighten it wherever she could. She thought that Laura McCarthy and her ilk would probably consider it a mess, with its roughly painted woodwork, the primitive colours, the murals that trailed upstairs in ivy shoots of green and yellow. She didn't care: every imprint made it feel more like home, rather than somewhere she, Kitty and Thierry had landed accidentally.

But that was the odd thing about the Spanish House, which she could only admit to herself after Kitty had remarked on it. 'I like this house,' her daughter had said one evening. 'Much more than when we came. Even with all the holes and mess. But it never really feels like home, does it?'

Isabel had made reassuring noises about it being unfinished and impossible to judge until it was entirely theirs. About new bathrooms and replaced windows. But she knew that there was truth in what Kitty had said.

Is it because of you? she asked Laurent silently. Is it impossible for us to make a home without you?

Throughout this period, she had avoided Matt – as far as

it was possible to avoid someone who was in and around her house every day. Sometimes it was easy, such as when she went out to give violin lessons, which she dreaded. She had developed all sorts of strategies to ensure that she was never alone with him – sticking close to Byron or the other men when she brought out cups of tea, asking the children to accompany her while she completed some task, and saving any necessary conversation for when his son was working beside him. Matt played along, a little less cheerful and talkative than he had been, but sometimes she convinced herself that this new distance suited him too.

There seemed to be trouble between him and Anthony. They hardly spoke to each other, and Anthony regarded his father with barely concealed disgust. If the boy had been anything other than charming to Isabel, she might have worried that he had discovered the truth. Just occasionally she felt Matt's eyes burn into her back, but most of the time she could brush it off.

She was in the vegetable patch when he caught her alone. It was late afternoon, Kitty and Thierry were in the woods with the puppy, and she had decided to dig up some of the pink fir apples for their evening meal. Afraid of slicing through them with her spade, she was pulling them up with her fingers, kneeling on an old sack and throwing them into a tin bucket ready to wash. There was something satisfying about pulling potatoes, about feeling the oddly shaped prize beneath the earth, being happily surprised by its size as it emerged. She paused to push back her hair and noticed her fingers. Once white, they were now freckled, the blunt nails black crescents of dirt. Oh, Laurent, what would you make of me now? she thought, smiling. And then realised, with a mixture of relief and regret, that it was the first time she had been able to think of him without an accompanying stab of grief.

She pulled out the last potato, separated it from its string and pushed back the earth where the plant had been. Then she rubbed her palms together to dislodge the soil, and jumped as she heard a voice: 'They're still lovely.'

Matt was behind her, leaning on the spade. 'Your hands are still beautiful.'

She tried to read his expression, then stood up and shook out the sack. 'How's the bathroom?' she asked, carefully neutral. 'You thought you'd be done by this week.'

'I don't want to talk about that,' Matt said. 'For weeks we've been skirting round each other. I want to talk about us.'

'There is no us, Matt,' Isabel said firmly, picking up her bucket.

'You can't say that.'

He moved closer to her and Isabel wondered if the children were close – or anyone else.

'I was there, Isabel,' his voice was low, intimate, 'and I felt how you were – how *we* were. What I said afterwards . . . it was a mistake, a misunderstanding. I haven't stopped thinking about it. About us.'

Isabel set off briskly towards the house. 'Please don't, Matt,' she said.

'I know what I felt, Isabel.'

She spun round. 'Perhaps it would be best if we settled up for the work you've done and left it there.'

'You need me here, Isabel. No one knows this house better than I do.'

'Maybe,' she said, into the wind, 'but I don't think this is doing either of us any good, do you? Let's just get the bathroom done and then . . .' She had reached the kitchen. 'I've got to go,' she said. She closed the door and stood against the other side of it.

'Isabel? What have I done to make you so angry? Why are you being like this?'

She hoped he wouldn't try the door.

'Isabel, I didn't mean what I said that night. It came out wrong.'

'I'm not going to discuss it,' she said.

A moment passed. Then she heard his voice again, close to the door, as if he had laid the side of his face against it. It was low, conspiratorial. 'You can't pretend nothing's changed,' he said.

She waited, hearing the weight of the silence outside, and then, as his footsteps eventually moved away, and finally disappeared, she let out a long sigh. She raised a hand to her face, one dirtied, soil-covered hand, almost unrecognisable even to herself. It was shaking.

Matt drove the short distance home alone. Byron, who had barely spoken to him all day, had disappeared before he'd finished, and Anthony had said that he'd like to stay with Kitty for a bit longer.

'Your mum's expecting you,' Matt said, envying the boy's freedom to stay in the house.

'No, she isn't. I told her I was staying here to watch a film. You don't listen.'

In other circumstances Matt would have slapped down such insubordination, but he was distracted by the sound of Isabel, apparently unconcerned by their exchange, tuning her violin upstairs. Listening to her play was uncomfortable for him now. It flashed images into his mind of that windy night, her gasping beneath him. He didn't understand what had just happened between them: he knew how she felt – why was she denying it?

He skidded into his drive and slammed the cab door

bad-temperedly. Bernie hobbled out to meet him, but he brushed past the old dog, trying to quell his thoughts. *No 'us'*, she had said. *Like it had been a mistake.*

He opened the oven and saw it was empty. 'Where's my dinner?' he yelled up the stairs.

There was no answer so he moved round the kitchen, lifting up plates and pans, trying to work out where she had put it.

'Where's my dinner?' he said again, as Laura appeared in the doorway.

'Hello, darling, had a nice day? Lovely, thanks,' said Laura, flatly.

'Hello, sweetheart,' Matt said, with exaggerated patience. 'I just want to know where my dinner is.'

'Well . . . there are chops in the freezer, a carton of soup or some cold chicken in the fridge. Cheese and biscuits. You choose.'

He stared at her.

'Matt, you've refused for weeks to tell me when or if you were coming home,' she said, 'so I thought it would be easier not to bother. You can sort yourself out from now on.'

He straightened. 'This your idea of a joke?'

She met his unfriendly stare with one of her own. 'No, Matt. I don't think it's funny at all, but I'm not a glorified kitchenmaid. If you can't be bothered to say hello to me when you come in, why should I go to the trouble of making you supper?'

'Don't give me a hard time. I just want something to eat.'

'And I'm telling you where it is. There's plenty of food. All you have to do is put it together.'

She jumped as Matt slammed his hand on the work surface. 'This your revenge, is it? Your petty little revenge? Where do you think I've been all day, Laura? Across the lane, with your son, doing the thing you wanted, which is moving us closer to getting that bloody house. Laying pipes. Installing baths. Replacing windows. And just because you're not getting all my bloody attention, you think you'll make your point by letting me starve.'

'Don't bully me, Matt. You know very well what this is about.'

'I'm going to the pub. I don't need this after a day's work.' He pushed past her towards the door. 'I'll get some supper there. And a bloody welcome.'

'Good!' shouted Laura, as he climbed into his van. 'Perhaps you'll find a bed there too!'

Even the twin comforts of a microwave lasagne and several pints could not raise Matt's spirits. He sat on his bar stool, muttering only the most cursory responses to anyone who tried to talk to him. He was lost in ill-tempered reflection.

He had seen the landlord nudge Theresa several times, mouthing, 'Watch him.' A few regulars who might normally have shared a joke with him had picked up on whatever radiated from him and kept their distance.

'You all right, Matt?' Mike, the estate agent, had stopped next to him. 'Fancy another?'

Matt's glass was empty again. 'Pint. Thanks.'

'Quiet in here tonight.' Mike addressed his comments to the bar at large, perhaps registering Matt's mood.

'Football,' said the landlord. 'Always like this. They'll be in around ten, if there's no penalties.'

'I hate it,' said Theresa. 'It's boring. But I get bored easily.'

'How's the house going, Matt?' Mike pushed him his pint along the bar. 'I hear you've virtually stripped the place out.'

Matt nodded. 'You know what it was like,' he said.

'Certainly do. I'd like to see what you've done with it some time, if you wouldn't mind showing me.'

'It'll be beautiful,' Matt said, lifting his head suddenly. 'It's going to be fantastic. A dream house. Better than you can possibly imagine.'

Mike eyed him. 'Well, I'll look forward to it, mate. I'll give you a ring in the week.'

Theresa waited until Mike had left and the landlord had gone out the back, then headed over to Matt. 'Go steady,' she said. 'You're sinking those a bit fast.'

His blue eyes were belligerent. 'You going to tell me what to do now, are you, Theresa?'

Her face fell. 'I don't want you to get in any trouble. Drink-driving, I mean.'

He looked at her then as if he were seeing her for the first time. 'Care about me, do you?' he slurred.

She laid a hand surreptitiously over his and let her fingers trail across his knuckles. 'You know I do. More than anything.'

He sat up straight, and glanced round the half-empty pub. 'Meet me out the back,' he said quietly. 'I need . . . to talk to you.' He saw trepidation and delight on her face. Then she tottered over to the landlord and muttered in his ear. 'Five minutes,' he heard the man say, as he sent a frown in Matt's direction.

Then, the ground swaying beneath him, Matt was in the fresh air, heading for the car park.

She was in the yard, beside the crates, moths fluttering in the security light above her head. As he approached her, she threw her arms round his neck. 'God, I've missed you,' she said, kissing him. She tasted of breath-freshener, as if she had sprayed her mouth in the few seconds since they had been inside. 'Tell me what you want to say. I thought you'd gone off me.' She ran her hands inside his T-shirt. 'I hate not seeing you. When you don't come in, the nights just drag and drag.'

'You care about me, then?'

Her chest pressed against him. She smelled of vanilla. 'More than anything. Anyone,' she breathed into his ear. Her fingers trailed round the back of his neck.

'Hitch up your skirt,' he said, thickly.

If he saw her falter, he chose to ignore it. His actions had become heavy and clumsy, pulling at her blouse, grabbing at her skirt and pressing her back against the crates.

'Matt, I don't know if I . . . Not here.'

But he took no notice. He hooked her leg round him, his lips buried in her neck, kissing her, fondling her breasts, her buttocks, her hair, until her protests died away. Then he was pushing into her roughly, losing himself in her, eyes shut, trying to recover the sensations he had felt in the darkness of that house, *her* hair falling round him. He was fucking *her*, possessing *her*, hearing *her* music in his ears. It was *her*. *It had to be her.* He lost himself in a dark place, his actions coarse and frenzied. He didn't care who saw or who knew. He was dimly aware that Theresa's gasps were becoming limp and passive, as if he were simply pushing air out of her. Then, with a muffled roar, he came, and collapsed against her. Empty. Ugly.

It was no good. It was worse than no good.

Matt let out a long breath and stepped back, steadying himself with one arm.

He straightened his jeans and saw that Theresa was eyeing him warily, pulling her top back together, her fingers struggling with the stretched fabric. 'Sorry,' he said, when he registered the missing buttons.

He had expected her to put her arms round his neck again, gaze adoringly into his eyes in that soppy way of hers. To tell him it didn't matter. That whatever he did was fine by her. But she seemed bewildered and shrugged off his hand.

'Theresa—'

'I've got to go in,' she said, and hooking her other shoe back on to her foot, she ran back into the pub.

Laura was in bed when he got home. He went into the still house, noting the closed curtains, the landing light on upstairs. It was immaculate, welcoming, peaceful. It was all wrong. He wasn't ready to go upstairs, not even sure where he would lie down when he did.

He kicked off his boots, flicked on the television, poured himself a tumbler of whisky and downed it. It didn't make him feel any better so he drank another, his thoughts racing.

Finally, at a quarter past twelve, he picked up the telephone and dialled. 'It's me,' he said.

Upstairs, Laura lay in the king-size bed, listening to her husband moving around heavily downstairs. He was plainly drunk. She had guessed when he didn't return home at closing time that he would be. In a rare move, wondering whether she should make amends, she had rung the Long Whistle. A girl had answered. 'Has Matt McCarthy been in this evening?' she had said, and almost added, 'It's his wife.' But she couldn't bear to take on the role of rolling-pin-wielding spouse. 'Curfew', he had said. Like she was his gaoler.

There was a pause. She imagined this was a publican's natural diplomacy.

'Yes,' the girl said. 'But he's not here now.'

Ten minutes later she had heard tyres on the gravel. Laura didn't know whether to be relieved that he had simply been to the pub and returned, or disturbed that he had not come upstairs. She didn't know what she would do if he did. She didn't know much any more. She thought of Nicholas holding her hand, telling her that her husband was a fool. She had been embarrassed and had pulled away. She heard her voice revealing the most intimate secrets of her marriage to him, and felt disloyal. There had been intensity in the way Nicholas looked at her. All she had to do, she knew, was give him a signal. She had told him too much, but she hadn't done anything else.

The piece of paper with his scribbled number was upstairs in her gardening trousers. She would throw it away, she told herself. Yet this didn't make her marriage any easier, because Matt didn't know about her self-restraint. He just shouted at her, went to the pub and came home drunk.

Laura sat up in bed, her head in her hands. It was a mess, and she had to do something about it. What had her friend said to her? Do you want to be right or do you want to be happy? She would apologise. She would try to move things on.

She was about to open her bedroom door when she became aware that Matt was on the phone. It must be his mobile, as the phone by her bed had not clicked. Laura opened the door silently and went out on to the landing, her toes curling on the beige carpet.

'It's me.' Matt's voice floated up the stairs. 'I've got to tell you something. Pick up the phone. I've realised something.' He paused, and she strained to hear whether there was another side to the conversation. 'You've got to pick up,' he said. 'Please pick up . . . Look, I've got to tell you how I feel. Everything we said after that night – it's all been a stupid mistake. Because I know what you're so upset about. And it's because of Laura. You're not like . . . You're not one of those women. But I never saw you like that – you see? Not some bit on the side . . . We can be happy together, me and you, in the house. It's you, Isabel. It's you . . .'

Laura's life fell away from her. She thought briefly that she might pass out.

'So call me,' came her husband's voice, slurring heavily. 'I'll wait by the phone all night if I have to. But I know . . .'

Apparently he had fallen asleep. Above him, Laura McCarthy walked, as if in a trance, into her bedroom and shut the door. She took off her dressing-gown, folded it neatly at the end of her bed, went to the window and pulled back the curtain. She could just see the Spanish House outlined through the trees, a single light on in an upstairs window. Laura watched it, heard the faintest sound of music playing. A siren call, she observed, her whole self shot through with pain. A siren call.

Seventeen

It was not something she would have said aloud, but the woods around the Spanish House reminded Isabel of the sea, capable of subtle changes in mood and appearance, a source of threat, thrill or pleasure. Several months in, she had discovered that what she drew from them was a reflection of how she felt. At nights, when she was at her worst, they had been dark and terrifying, full of the unknown, of unseen malice. When her children were whooping and calling, running through the trees with the puppy barking alongside them, they were magical, a haven where innocence and wonder could still prevail. When she thought of Thierry calling, deep within them, she considered it a benign presence, a safe place, a barrier to protect them from the wilder world beyond.

Now, in the hour shortly after dawn, it was a bringer of peace, with birdsong drowning the frenzy in her head. Healing, soothing. A place where she could forget.

'Mind that root.' Beside her, Byron motioned towards a thick outgrowth, curling from the ground.

She adjusted the basket of mushrooms on her hip and slowed as she hoisted the gun to her shoulder. 'I don't understand. My aim is good now – I've done enough practice on the cans. I can hit a half brick at thirty feet. But every time I go out, they vanish before I've even raised the gun.'

Byron thought about it. 'Do you make any noise? You could be alerting them more than you know.'

She trod round some nettles. 'I don't think so. I'm conscious of sound.'

'And you're going out at the right times? I mean, you're seeing plenty of them around?'

'Late at night, like you said. Or early in the morning. There's no shortage of them, Byron. I see them everywhere.'

He held out an arm as they negotiated a ditch. Isabel took it briefly, although she no longer needed it. She had become sure-footed these last few months, her muscles hard and wiry from walking across the uneven ground, from hauling, painting and lifting. As someone who had never been aware of her body except as it related to her violin, she was enjoying this new sensation of fitness.

'And you're not wearing your bright blue coat,' he said.

She grinned. 'No. I am not wearing my bright blue coat.'

'Which way is the breeze blowing?' he said. 'If you're downwind of them they'll scent you long before they see you. Doesn't matter how careful you are.'

'What's this for?' she asked, pointing at the thin green scarf he had made her tie round her neck.

'A scrim,' he said. 'So the rabbit can't see your face when you pull it up.'

She laughed. 'So it doesn't recognise me? Like a hangman's hood?'

'You might laugh, but rabbits are smart. No animal is better equipped to detect predators.'

Isabel followed him towards the edge of the woods. 'I never thought of myself as a predator before,' she said.

He hadn't brought his dogs with him today. Too excitable so early in the morning, he had said when, still half asleep, she came out of the back door. They'd alert every creature within a five-mile radius. He must have been waiting for her, even though she had asked him to meet her shortly after five thirty.

It was the third time he had accompanied her, always early, before he had to start work with Matt. Just after dawn was the best part of the day, he had said. They had seen young deer, badgers, a vixen and her near-grown cubs. He had shown her the pheasants he was rearing for a local farmer, their astonishingly bright plumage at odds with the less vivid browns and greens of the English countryside, strutting Indian rajahs transported into a muted landscape. He had pulled at wood sorrel and hairy bittercress, picked hawthorn leaves from the hedgerows and told her how he had eaten them as a child on his way to school. He did not hold them to her lips, as Matt would have done, but placed them gently into her fingers. She tried not to look at his hands; she would not see him that way. She would not ruin something that had become precious.

He had told her he had trained as a teacher, and smiled at her surprise. 'Didn't think I was the type?' he said.

'No. I hate teaching the violin so much that I'm amazed anyone could *want* to do it.' She glanced up at him. 'But you're good with children,' she mused, 'with Thierry. You would have been a good teacher.'

'Yes.' He paused. 'Well, this suits me.'

He didn't say why he had changed his mind about teaching, and she didn't ask for an explanation. When you could live out here, free of the petty restrictions and frustrations of modern life, it was easy to guess why he might have chosen this. She sensed that Byron liked to be alone with her; his movements became freer, his conversation less stilted. Perhaps because he was less awkward, or because she had so few people to talk to, she had told him the truth about the house. 'It's difficult,' she said, 'because I like living here now. I find it hard to imagine being back in the city. But sometimes I fear that the house will ruin us.'

Byron seemed to bite back whatever he wanted to say. Hardly surprising, she thought. He works for Matt. Then, 'It's a big house,' he said carefully.

'It's a money pit,' she said. 'It literally eats whatever I have. And I'd like Matt to finish. I know you work for him, Byron, but I find his presence . . . a little difficult. I'd be quite happy to sell up, move somewhere more manageable, but he's knocked so much of it about – there isn't a room he's left intact. We still don't have a working bathroom. And I can't sell it as it is – not if I'm to make enough money to buy somewhere half decent.

'The really tricky thing is that I can't afford for him to continue. Even with all this,' she waved at the mushrooms, 'all our cost-cutting, there's barely enough to pay him off for the work he has done.' She thought of the hideous answerphone message she had woken to the previous day. She had deleted it hurriedly, horrified by the idea that the children might have heard it. *We can be happy together,* he had said – as if he knew anything about her.

'Anyway, I'm sure I'll sort it out.' She smiled, hoping he wouldn't see the tears that pricked her eyes. 'Perhaps I'll learn some plumbing skills next and install my own bathroom.'

It was a hollow joke, and Byron didn't laugh. They walked on, saying nothing. Isabel wondered if his silence meant she had embarrassed him. His jaw was tight.

'What a gorgeous morning,' she said eventually, conscious that it had been unfair to confide in him about his employer. 'Sometimes I feel I could stay in the woods for ever.'

He nodded. 'I often think,' he said, 'that when you're out here at daybreak you can pretend you're the only person in the world.'

The woods made her feel like that too, she decided.

Sometimes, on mornings like this, she enjoyed being cut off from civilisation, relished the almost primeval satisfaction of returning with sustenance for her family. When you could harvest food from nothing, living here seemed much less daunting.

Byron held up an arm. 'There,' he said quietly.

She put down her basket quietly and crouched behind the tree with him. Ahead, the woods opened out on to the thirty-acre field, now thick with a crop of wheat.

'Big warren at the edge,' he whispered. He wetted a finger and held it in the air. 'And we're upwind of it. Sit quietly and raise your gun.'

She pulled the scarf over her face, lifted the gun to her shoulder and waited, as still as she could. Byron had told her she was unusually good at this, and she ascribed it to her playing. She was strong, and acutely aware of the movements of her upper body, so she found it easy to ensure that those muscles were motionless.

'There,' he whispered.

Through the sights she could see the rabbits about thirty feet away, three or four, a muted grey on the edge of the bridlepath. They hopped around, then scanned the horizon warily.

'Allow them to clear the burrows by five yards,' Byron whispered. 'Remember you want to kill, not injure. You've got to get the head.' She would have only one chance, he had told her.

The rabbit enclosed in her metallic circle had evidently decided there was little threat. It nibbled some grass, scooted behind a clump of weeds, then popped out again. 'Don't think of it as a fluffy little creature,' he had told her. 'Think of it as a vegetable thief. Think of it as supper for Kitty and Thierry. Rabbit and wild mushroom in a creamy garlic sauce.'

'You do it,' she said, trying to hand him the gun.

He pushed it back to her. 'No.'

'What if I miss?' She was afraid to cause hideous pain.

She felt his presence behind her as she raised the gun again and took aim. He smelled mossy and sweet, like summer earth. He did not touch her. 'You won't miss,' he said quietly.

Isabel closed her eyes, opened them again, and fired.

It had been some time since she had been to London, even more since she had been in a restaurant like this. At home Laura's linen trousers and low court shoes would have been considered smart, but here they declared her provincial status. I look like someone dressed up to go to town, she thought.

'You have a booking?' a bored-looking girl said, from under her precision-cut fringe.

'I'm meeting someone,' Laura replied.

The restaurant was full of dark-suited men, monochrome against the grey granite walls.

'Name?' the girl prompted.

Laura hesitated, as if saying it aloud might be construed as evidence. 'Trent. Nicholas Trent.'

He had been so touchingly pleased to hear from her. So happy to hear about her unscheduled trip to London, so keen to organise his day to fit in lunch.

'Don't you work?' she had said, trying to remember what he had said he did.

'I've just given notice,' he said cheerfully, 'which means I can take as long a lunch break as I choose. What will they do? Sack me?'

The girl set off briskly towards the tables under the atrium, apparently expecting Laura to follow. Everyone in London seemed so young, she thought, so fashionable and groomed. Although she had taken trouble to look smart and do her hair properly, she felt middle-aged and out of place. These days she had no idea how she appeared to anyone. Not old, but no longer young. Loved, unloved. Desired . . . not desired. Laura took a deep breath, then let it stall in her chest as she saw him rising from a table with a smile breaking across his face.

He was handsome in these surroundings, as if they reflected something of himself. More than that, he seemed brighter, less beaten down. Perhaps younger too. Or perhaps that had always been something she only imagined she had seen in him; compared to the unstoppable force that was her husband, all men had seemed less vital.

'You came,' he said, taking her hand.

'Yes,' she said. And that word, she knew, was tantamount to admitting she would sleep with him. That she had crossed a line. The touching thing was that he didn't seem to see it like that. He took nothing about her for granted.

'I wasn't sure you would. I thought perhaps last time . . .' His voice trailed away.

'He doesn't love me any more,' she said, as she sat down. It was a phrase she had rehearsed so often in her head that she could say it now as if it meant nothing. 'I heard him on the telephone. I know who it is. So,' she made her voice bright, 'there's little to stop me doing whatever I want.'

As tears came into her eyes, she picked up the menu. She heard Nicholas ordering her a drink, asking the waiter if he could give them a couple more minutes. By the time her gin and tonic had arrived, she had recovered her composure.

'I'll tell you the bare bones of it, and we won't speak about it again,' she said calmly. 'I'd like us to have a lovely lunch and not think about it.' Her voice was unrecognisable to her, tight and brittle. His hand rested on the table, as if he wanted to take hers but was afraid it might be an imposition.

'It's the woman who owns the big house,' she said. 'The house across the lake, the house you thought beautiful.' She thought she saw him flinch and was moved by his unconscious display of solidarity.

'My husband is doing the renovations there so I suppose they—'

'*Your* husband?' It was odd, the way he said it, but she forged on. If she stopped now she might never get the words out.

'All this time he's told me he was working on the house for *us*. We wanted it, you see. We'd been virtually promised it by the old man who lived there. We had looked after him for a long time. When the widow moved in, Matt offered to do the renovations for her. He said – in private – that she would never be happy there, that she couldn't afford the work that needed doing, that she would be gone by Christmas. He let me believe he was doing it all for us.' She stopped for a sip of her drink.

'Well, I overheard a conversation. And guess what? He's planning to move in with her. So that woman gets not just my house but my husband too.' She laughed, a sharp, unhappy sound. 'He's been using the plans we drew up together. All the little touches I'd thought out. He even wanted me to be friends with her. Can you believe that?'

She had thought Nicholas would take her hand again then, that he would offer words of comfort, tell her again what a fool her husband was. But he was apparently lost in thought.

Oh, God, I've bored him, she panicked. He thought he was getting lunch with a vivacious woman, and I've given him a bitter, betrayed wife.

'I'm sorry—' she began.

'No, Laura. I'm sorry. There's something I must tell you. Something you need to know . . . Please. Don't look so afraid.

I just . . . Oh, for goodness' sake.' He waved away the waiter, who had been hovering beside them.

'No,' said Laura, keen to delay this moment. She called the waiter back. 'Let's order, shall we? I'll have the bream.'

'The same,' said Nicholas.

'And some water,' said Laura. 'Still, please. No ice.' Now she was fearful of what Nicholas would say. He was married, after all. He had changed his mind about her. He had never been interested in her, not in that way. He was dying of a terminal illness.

She turned back to him. His eyes had seemingly not left her face. 'You were saying?' she said politely.

'I don't want there to be any secrets between us, any misunderstandings. It's important to me that we're open with each other.'

Laura took another sip of her drink.

'That day we first met in the lane, I wasn't lost.'

She frowned.

'I wanted to have another look at the Spanish House. I'd come across it by chance a couple of weeks before, had been told its history, and I thought it would make the most superb development.'

'Development?'

'That's what I do. What I used to do. I'm a property developer. I take – well, settings, really, and try to create something wonderful.' He leaned back. 'And, if I'm honest, something that will make a lot of money. I thought that house had potential.'

'But it's not for sale.'

'I know. But I'd heard about the state it was in, and that the owner had little capital, and I thought I might make her an offer.'

Laura folded and unfolded her napkin. It was a beautiful,

heavy thing, starched white. About to be soiled. 'So why haven't you?'

'Timing, I suppose. I wanted to make sure it was right. And I wanted to find out as much about the house as I could. I thought perhaps if I waited until she was in dire straits, she'd accept the lowest price. It sounds ugly, but that's how development works.'

'How handy for you to have met me, then,' said Laura, tightly. 'Someone who knew so much about it.'

'No,' he said emphatically. 'You distracted me from it. Think back – we never talked about that house, Laura. You never said anything about it. I didn't know you had a connection with it. I just thought you were this – this vision in the forest.'

She had become so distrustful, she realised, that she found it hard to believe anyone could have a straightforward interest in her.

Now his hand reached out for hers and she took it. It wasn't such a great leap. His fingers closed round hers, soft, elegant hands with perfect nails. So unlike her husband's.

'All my adult life I'd wanted that house,' she said. 'We've never been a real family, and I thought living there would somehow make it better.'

'I'll make us a fortune. We can build an even better house.'

Her head jerked up.

'I'm sorry,' he said. 'That was probably a little premature. It's just that I haven't felt like this since I met my wife, my ex-wife, and that was a long time ago. I wanted you to know the truth.'

An ex-wife. She tried to digest this. Why should it be a surprise that he had been married? 'I don't know very much about you, do I?' she said.

'Anything,' he said, leaning back in his chair. 'Ask me

anything. I'm a middle-aged man who has spent years in the doldrums, believing himself an utter failure, who suddenly has a sense of great things happening. My career's back on track, I'm feeling better than I have done for some time, I have money in the bank, and I have met this beautiful, un-appreciated woman who doesn't know how utterly wonderful she is.'

It took Laura a beat to grasp that he was referring to her.

'You're amazing, Laura,' he said, lifting her hand to his lips, 'you're smart and kind and you deserve so much more. Of everything.'

Their hands separated as the food was set before them with a dramatic flourish. Laura stared at the fish, roasted, on a bed of vivid green spinach in some endlessly reduced sauce. She realised that the distant sensation of absence she felt was not caused by hunger. She was missing the gentle pressure of Nicholas's hand. She looked at him as he thanked the waiter, taking in his aquiline features, the self-knowledge in his face. And as the man moved away, she stretched out her hand to his.

'What time did you say you had to be back at work?' she asked, as his fingers closed over hers. This time her voice was confident, familiar.

'I didn't. I'm here for as long as you want.'

She looked down at her fish, then back at Nicholas. She let her eyes linger on his. 'I'm not hungry,' she said.

She had been so excited when she hit it. 'Did you see that?' she said. 'Oh, my God! Did you see it?' She had clutched at his arm, then ripped the scarf off her face and scrambled to her feet.

Byron had stood up. 'Clean as a whistle,' he said, walking over to the rabbit. 'Couldn't have done it better myself.

There's your dinner.' He held it up, still warm. 'We should go and pull up some garlic now.' He checked that it was dead, then brought it to her, holding it by the back legs. She reached out to take it from him, then snatched back her hand when she felt the warmth of its fur. Her face fell. 'It's so beautiful,' she said.

'I don't see them like that,' he said.

'But its poor eyes . . .' She tried to close the lids. 'Oh, my goodness, I really killed it.'

Byron frowned.

'I know . . . It's a strange feeling, knowing that it was alive and now it's dead because of me. I've never killed anything before.'

It was indeed a shocking thing to hurt a living creature. To alter the course of a life. Byron sought an explanation that would make her feel better. 'Think of a battery hen,' he said, 'and then think of this rabbit, its whole life spent doing what it was meant to do, experiencing everything it was meant to. Which would you rather be?'

'I know it sounds silly. I just hate the idea of inflicting pain.'

'The end was so fast,' he said, 'that it wouldn't have known a thing.' He saw her flinch. 'You okay?' he asked, when she didn't move. 'Isabel?'

'That was what they said about my husband,' she said, her eyes fixed on the dead rabbit. 'Driving up the motorway, looking forward to seeing his son perform at school. Singing, probably.' She smiled. 'He had a *terrible* voice.'

Around them, the birds had started to sing again. Distantly, Byron was aware of a blackbird, and the insistent rhythmic pronouncements of a wood-pigeon. And Isabel's words, low and soft: 'A lorry crossed the central reservation and hit him head on. That's what they said when they came to tell me. *He wouldn't have known a thing.*'

Byron heard the bleakness in her voice. He wanted to speak, but sometimes he felt he had held things in for so long that he didn't have the words any longer.

She was trying to smile again. 'He had been listening to Fauré's *Requiem*. The ambulance man said nobody could turn off his stereo while they cut him out. It must have been the last thing he heard as he died . . . I don't know why that made me feel better, but it did.'

She gave a deep sigh. 'It was us who felt everything. He knew nothing.'

'I'm sorry,' he said.

She looked at him then, and he couldn't tell if she thought him stupid. Her eyes were almost questioning, as if she was searching for something. She was so strange, one minute laughing, striding, vital, the next like nothing he had seen before. One minute a grieving widow, the next a woman who would let Matt arrive at her house in the dead of night . . .

She seemed to haul herself back into the present. She kicked something off her shoe. 'You know what? I don't think I'm much of a predator. I'm very grateful, Byron, but I might have to stick to executing potatoes.' She handed back the gun, ceremoniously, with both hands. He noticed that her palms were freckled with paint, and studded, at the point where they met each finger, with callouses. He wanted to draw his thumb across them.

'We'd better get back. You've got work.' She touched his sleeve, then moved past him, treading back confidently towards their path. 'Come on. You can have breakfast with us before Matt arrives.'

Keep your head down, Jan had warned him, when he had confessed his suspicions to her. You need every penny and employers don't grow on trees. *Not when you have a prison record*, was the silent addendum. Byron watched Isabel striding ahead of him, humming quietly to herself as she moved carefully through the trees. That was what prison did to you: it reduced your choices, took away your ability long afterwards to behave like a normal human being. He would spend a lifetime suppressing his feelings, having to ignore the behaviour of people like Matt McCarthy, just so that he did not confirm what they suspected to be true.

'You half asleep, Byron?' He had been dozy all morning, his expression closed as if his thoughts were far away. 'I asked you to pass me that pipe. No, not that one, the plastic. And shift that bath to the side of the room. Where's Anthony gone?' For some reason his son wouldn't talk to him. He walked out of any room Matt entered.

Matt shouted his name, remembering Isabel's visit to the jeweller in Long Barton the previous day. He hadn't meant to follow her. When he came out of the bank he had noticed her parking and, curious, changed his route to see where she was going. It was easy to keep track of her: she stood out in the little town, her clothes too vivid, her hair a wild tumble. He watched her walk swiftly across the road, clutching a roll of velvet, and waited, trying to work out what she was doing. He had gone in afterwards. The man had the velvet roll and was inspecting something through an eyeglass. 'That for sale, is it?' he said, trying to sound casual. He could see a pearl necklace and a flash of something red.

'Will be,' said the jeweller. Matt had taken the man's card and gone to sit in his van. She had not sold her jewellery because of his invoice. It was not his fault. It would be to give herself a fresh start, free herself from her husband's memory, he told himself several times, but he had still felt jittery and bad-tempered.

Matt had made sure that Byron spent much of the morning

moving waste from the old drawing room to the skip. The sight of the other man disturbed him at the moment, although he couldn't say why. It was easier to have him working elsewhere. Matt and Anthony had begun in the bathroom. She had harped on about it so much that he had to make it look as if they were doing something. It had taken four of them an hour to get the cast-iron bath upstairs, which Matt had quietly resented. In a few months' time, when he finally owned the house, they would have to move it again. 'When you put the boards back down make sure you hit the nails into the joists, not the pipes, or it'll come out of your wages,' he had warned Anthony, who was wearing his ridiculous woollen hat.

Anthony was straightening up when Matt called him to help move the bath again. 'Over there,' he said, grunting with the effort. 'Where the two feeds are showing through.'

His son began to haul at the cast-iron weight, then stopped. 'Hang on, Dad. You can't put it there.'

'What?'

'The joists. You've fed the pipes underneath. They'll only be a few centimetres thick where the bath sits on them.'

'Well, the bathroom's not going to stay here,' he muttered.

Anthony frowned, puzzled, and Matt realised he had said aloud what was running through his head. 'I don't understand,' his son said.

'You don't have to,' Matt said. 'I don't pay you to understand. Just get on with moving it.'

Anthony pulled at it again, and stopped. 'I'm not being funny, Dad, but if Mrs Delancey really wants the bath here, surely we should be feeding the pipework round the sides?'

'And you've just done a City and Guilds in plumbing, have you?'

'No, but it doesn't take a plumber to see that—'

'Did I ask your opinion? Did you get a promotion I'm not aware of? The last I heard, Anthony, I employed you and Byron for the heavy lifting. Clearing. Brainless stuff.'

Anthony took a long, deep breath. 'I don't think Mrs Delancey would be very happy if she knew you were cutting corners.'

'Oh, you don't, don't you?'

'No.'

Something scalding washed through Matt's veins. Laura had poisoned Anthony against him. All this answering back—

'I don't want to do this any more.'

'You'll do as I bloody tell you.' He stalked into the middle of the room, blocking the exit, and saw uncertainty in the boy's eyes. At least the boy knew who was boss.

'Matt?'

Byron. He was always there when he wasn't wanted. 'What do you want?'

'I belive this is yours.'

Matt had taken the pet-carrier before he knew what he was doing. The words, and their implication, settled heavily in the silence.

'It was in the far skip,' Byron said. 'Second I've found here. Mrs Delancey won't want any more unexpected visitors.'

Matt glanced at his son, and saw that Anthony hadn't yet grasped the significance of what Byron had said. The boy was edging towards the door, apparently planning his escape.

'I'm going home.' Anthony took off his tool-belt and dropped it on the floor.

Matt ignored him. 'Mrs Delancey, Mrs Delancey. Everyone here seems to be a mind-reader when it comes to her. Well, I don't think Mrs Delancey would like it if she knew your history, do you? Plenty of people round here wouldn't give you the chances I have – wouldn't even employ you.'

He met the other man's steady gaze. 'Your problem, Byron, is that you don't know when you're well off.'

'Matt, I don't want to argue with you but I can't just stand here and—'

Isabel had appeared in the doorway. 'I've brought you all some tea,' she said, edging round the door. Her hair was tied back, and she had changed into a pair of shorts, revealing long brown legs. 'Anthony, here's a cold drink. I know you don't like tea. Oh, and Byron, you left your keys on the kitchen table this morning. You'd better have them. I nearly threw them away with the leftovers.'

'Breakfast?' Matt said, his brain reeling with this new information. 'Breakfast with the Delanceys, eh? How cosy.'

Isabel put the tea tray on a crate.

'Got your feet right under the table, haven't you, Byron?' Matt went on.

'He's been helping me. Tea and toast was the least I could provide,' Isabel said.

Had she coloured? Or was that his imagination?

His son shoved past him contemptuously.

Matt felt giddy. 'I don't think you'd have been quite so hospitable if you'd known.'

That got him. Byron's eyes closed briefly and his shoulders slumped.

'Known what?'

'You mean he hasn't told you?'

'It's okay, I quit,' Byron said quietly. 'I can't do this any more.'

'What's going on?' Isabel demanded.

Byron reached for his keys, but Matt was too quick for him. 'Isabel – you know I've always looked out for you? Right?'

'Er, yes,' she said, cautiously.

'I would have told you before, but I wanted to give Byron a chance. But I don't feel it's fair for you to be the only one not to know the truth, especially as you seem to be spending time alone with him. Are you happy at the thought of a convict sitting down for breakfast with your little family or out in the woods alone with your son?'

He saw the flicker of doubt pass over her face. He always knew how to strike at someone's weak point.

'You didn't know Byron's been in prison? I thought he would have told you during one of your cosy little outings. What did you serve in the end, Byron? Nearly eighteen months, was it, for GBH? I seem to remember you did that bloke a fair bit of damage. Put him in a wheelchair, right?'

She didn't ask if it was true. She didn't have to: it was written all over Byron's face. Matt registered the sudden loss of trust, the instant re-evaluation of him, and felt the exultation of victory. 'I thought you'd have told Mrs Delancey . . .'

'It's all right,' Byron said. 'I'm going.' As he picked up his keys, he didn't look at Isabel. His face seemed cast in stone.

'Yes, off you go. And stay away from this house.' There was triumph in Matt's voice. He turned to Isabel in the empty room. Somewhere below them, the front door closed.

'There,' he said, as if that decided something.

Isabel looked at him as if clouds were falling from her eyes. 'It's not your house,' she said.

Eighteen

It was all pretty simple when you thought about it. A near-perfect solution. Matt placed the new pane carefully in its frame and started to work the putty with his thumb and fingers until it was warm and malleable. He pressed it carefully down the side of the glass with a precision born of long practice, the putty smooth, its edge clearly defined. The light bounced off the glass, and the woods were alive with the birds and other creatures. Sometimes you got so close to something you couldn't see the wood for the trees. He couldn't help smiling at his own joke.

While the putty was drying, Matt adjusted his tool-belt and took the specially moulded wood to the other window. This was going to be the most beautiful room he had ever built. He had never put so much of himself into anything. It was dual aspect, so that when they woke, their first view would be of the lake, mist rising from it in the early morning, birds taking flight across the trees. He had ordered the cornicing and plasterwork mouldings from a specialist Italian company, then cut and shaped each piece so that it fitted together like an intricate three-dimensional jigsaw. He had plastered the ceiling so expertly that there wasn't so much as a fingermark on its surface. It had been almost worth bringing the original ceiling down for the pleasure of creating something so beautiful for her. He had relaid the floor, board by board, so that her bare feet would never need to feel an uneven surface. He pictured her, pulling that red silk robe round her as she slid out of their huge, rumpled bed. He could see her so clearly, the dawn lighting her face as she opened the curtains. She would turn to smile at him, the light outlining her body through the silk.

Why hadn't he worked it out sooner? It had solved everything. He would move in with her and continue the work he had started. She wouldn't have to pay for any of it, once they were together. Her money worries would be over. It was plain she couldn't cope by herself. Since he had begun here, she had deferred to his judgement, been reassured by him. The house would be theirs. He would be master of his dream home. Possessor of Isabel Delancey. Laura would be fine in the coach house, with her coffee mornings and complaints. She was as fed up as he was. It was astonishing – he barely thought about her now. It was as if she had become an irrelevance. Isabel had pushed everything else away. She was everything. Everything he had ever worked for, everything he had been told he couldn't have. Everything he had had to leave when his father was cast out of this estate. Sometimes he found it hard to work out where she ended and the house began.

With renewed purpose, Matt tapped in the piece of moulding, moving to some new internal rhythm. It was possible he could have cut part of it away, saved the main bit, but he had learned long ago that sometimes the only way was to cut out the dead wood entirely.

Byron woke to the sound of banging and registered brightness sliding under the door. It took him a second or two to grasp the significance of this, and then he checked his watch. It was half past seven. Matt was already at work.

Beside him, the dogs sat silent and expectant, their eyes trained on him. He pushed himself upright, rubbing at his face, his hair. Outside, the birdsong had lost the boisterous enthusiasm of the dawn chorus and mellowed.

'You could have told me,' he murmured to Meg and Elsie. 'How the hell are we meant to get out now?'

He had barely slept, walking the woods until almost midnight and then, when he returned to the boiler room, lying awake for hours as he tried to work out what to do next. He thought of ringing Jan, but he had seen how things were for them in that little cottage and didn't feel he could intrude. He still didn't have enough money for the deposit on the farm cottage. He had wondered whether he had been too hasty in quitting the job, but he couldn't have continued to go along with that man's deception. He couldn't have guaranteed that under Matt's constant taunts he wouldn't eventually have behaved in a way he would regret.

He thought again of Isabel's face as his past had been revealed to her. Her surprise, followed by uncertainty. *But he seemed so nice, so ordinary.* Byron had seen it many times before.

'Christ.' He scrambled into the corner as the door opened, then closed behind Thierry and the puppy, which ran to Byron and leaped on to him.

'Ssh – ssh!' He was trying desperately to stop it yapping.

When he looked up again, Thierry was balancing on one leg. Byron pushed himself half upright. 'Jesus, Thierry. You gave me . . . How did you know I was here?'

Thierry nodded at Pepper, the puppy, who was sniffing at its mother.

'Did – did you tell anyone?' He got out of his sleeping-bag, peering behind the boy to the door.

Thierry shook his head.

'Christ. I thought it was . . .' He ran a palm over his face, trying to steady his breathing. Thierry appeared oblivious to the fright he had caused. He knelt down with the dogs now, hugging them, letting them lick his face.

'I – I was sleeping here for a couple of nights until my new place is ready. Please don't say anything, okay? It might . . . look odd.'

He wasn't sure that Thierry had heard him. 'I didn't want to leave Meg and Elsie. You understand that, don't you?'

Thierry nodded. A moment later, he reached into the neck of his shirt and brought out a small square parcel, wrapped in a white napkin, which he handed to Byron. Byron opened it and found two pieces of lukewarm toast made into a sandwich. Then Thierry pulled a squashed carton of juice out of his pocket and handed that over too. Then he knelt down again with the dogs to tickle Meg's belly.

Byron hadn't eaten since lunchtime yesterday. He bit into the sandwich, which was filled with jam and butter. Then he laid a hand on the boy's shoulder, moved by the unexpected act of kindness. 'Thanks,' he said, and the boy grinned. 'Thanks, T.'

'Why aren't you here yet? You said you'd be with me at three.' Kitty was lying on a blanket by the edge of the lake, listening to the crickets and staring into the infinite blue above her. Occasionally a bumblebee would hum past her ear, but she didn't flinch even when one landed on her T-shirt. It was too hot to move. Besides, she was trying to get a sun tan. She had read in a magazine that your legs looked better brown. In London their tiny garden had faced north and never got any sun.

'My mum's being really weird,' Anthony said.

She chewed a blade of grass. 'They're all weird. It's their job.'

'No. She's . . . I think there's something weird going on between our folks.'

Kitty dropped the grass and waited, listening to her mother hammering at skirting-boards downstairs. The noise echoed across the water, splintering the peace of the lake. She thought she had probably preferred it when her mother had played music. 'Weird in what way?' she asked.

He sounded uncomfortable. 'Don't say anything, okay? But I think my dad's been overcharging your mum.'

'Overcharging?' She squinted at a cloud, pulling at a strand of her hair. 'He's a builder, Ant. I thought that came with the territory.'

'No, I mean by a lot. Serious amounts.'

Anthony lowered his voice. 'I went into the office this morning and my mum was there, going through all the receipts to do with your house. She looked really odd . . .'

'Are you and Dad still not talking?'

'We don't seem to have much to talk about at the moment,' she had replied calmly. She glanced at the copy invoices, all of which were made out to Mrs Isabel Delancey.' She had picked one up. 'It seems your father and I have very different ideas about the right way to treat people.'

'What do you mean, Mum?'

She looked up, and it was as if she had only just seen him. 'Nothing, darling. Just talking to myself.' She stood up, brushed down her trousers, fixed on that bright smile. 'Tell you what, I'm going to make some iced tea. Would you like some?'

Anthony's voice was low and hurried. 'I think she's worked out Dad's been overcharging. She's quite old-fashioned, my mum. She wouldn't like that kind of thing. When she went downstairs, I had a look at a couple of the invoices. That hot-water tank – I'm pretty sure he charged your mum twice what it cost him.'

'Wouldn't that be the labour cost, though?' Her mother was always going on about that. 'I mean, my mum doesn't seem to think there's much wrong. She says it's costing a fortune, but when you look at what he's done . . .'

'You don't understand.'

'The house is falling apart.'

Anthony was impatient now. 'Look, Kitty, my dad's an arsehole. He does what he wants and he doesn't care. He wanted your house for years, and I reckon that's why he's been overcharging your mum. To try to force her out.'

Kitty sat up. She drew her knees to her chin. She felt suddenly cold, despite the balmy air. 'He wanted our house?'

'Before you came, yes. Him and Mum. Once you'd moved in I thought they'd got over it. It's just a house, right?'

'Right,' said Kitty, uncertainly.

'Besides, I don't usually pay much attention to what my dad does. You learn to keep your head down in this family. But there was that invoice, and Mum, and I don't think the work he's doing is right. And I overheard some weird stuff Asad was saying to him the other day.'

'*Asad?*'

It was as if he guessed he'd said too much. 'Look – don't say anything to your mum. Not yet. I reckon mine might get him to pay some of it back, put it right. He owes her at the moment—' She heard him call a muffled response. 'I've got to go. Listen – do you want to meet me at the pub later on? They're doing an outdoor barbecue tonight and anyone can go.' He added, 'My treat.'

The water was opaque at the edges, a sludgy film leaching on to the shore. 'Okay,' she said.

Isabel was kneeling on the floor, daubing the boards in the hallway with pungent pale grey paint. 'Don't come too close,' she said, as Kitty ran up the steps from the kitchen. 'I haven't accounted for footprints.' She sat up and surveyed what she had done. There was a spot of grey paint on her cheekbone, and her white shirt hung limply from her shoulders. 'What do you think?' she said.

'It's nice,' Kitty told her.

'I wouldn't have painted them, but they were such a horrible mismatch of colours, and so grimy. I thought this would brighten things up a bit.'

'I'm going out,' Kitty said. 'There's a barbecue at the pub and I'm meeting Anthony.'

'That's nice, lovey. Have you seen Thierry?'

'He was in with the chickens.' He had been talking to them, telling off the larger ones for bullying, but when he had seen her he had shut up.

'I'll be stuck here for a while yet,' Isabel said. 'I need this side to dry before I start on the other. Do you think paint dries faster in the heat?'

They heard footsteps on the stairs and Matt appeared, his tool-belt round his waist and his T-shirt sticking to his upper body. He halted at the bottom. 'I'm done. I thought we might go for a drink if— He started when he saw Kitty, then recovered himself. 'If either of you ladies fancied it.'

'No, thanks,' said Isabel. 'I have a few things to do. Is the bathroom working now?'

'I've been doing the master bedroom. You should take a look.'

Her mother looked up at him. 'But I asked you to do the bathroom. We need a bathroom, Matt. We agreed you would focus on that.'

'I'll do it tomorrow,' he said. 'You should take a look at that bedroom.' It was as if he'd not heard her. 'You'll love it. It's beautiful. Go on – go and take a look.'

Kitty watched her mother's jaw tighten. She wanted to say something, but she had told Anthony she wouldn't. 'I'm so sick of that tin bath,' she said instead. 'Shouldn't be that hard to plumb in a bathroom.'

Matt didn't seem to notice. 'You'd never know that ceiling had come down. In fact, I'd say the cornicing in that room is better than when it was originally built. Go on – I want you to see it.'

Her mother sighed and pushed a sweaty strand of hair off her face. She was obviously struggling to contain her frustration. 'Matt, could you go past so that I can finish painting this floor? Kitty darling, I want you home before it gets dark.'

'Okay,' Kitty said, staring at Matt.

'Anthony will walk back with you, will he?'

'Yes.'

'You going to the barbecue, are you? Do you want a lift to the road?' said Matt.

'No.' She glared at him, then added, under her mother's pointed stare, 'Thank you.'

'Suit yourself,' he said. 'You sure I can't tempt you, Isabel?'

Kitty waited until Matt's brake-lights had disappeared, then walked briskly through the woods to the road, the shade offering welcome respite from the heat, which even in the early evening hung low and sticky over the valley. She no longer saw imaginary spooks behind trees, or mad axemen in the distance. She knew now the real threat lay far closer to home. She thought of Matt, his jokes and chat, his bags of croissants, the way he had pretended to be their friend. How they had *all* pretended to be their friends. How many people had known what he was doing?

When she came out of the woods, her head was spinning. She had promised to meet Anthony at six, but the light was on in the shop and she could see people inside. At the last minute, Kitty Delancey changed direction.

'So he says, "How *dare* you?"' said Henry, trying to keep a straight face. '"My name is *Hucker*. Rudolph Hucker."' He slapped his hand on the counter and roared with laughter.

'Don't make me laugh,' gasped Asad, who was bagging up change in the till. 'I'll wheeze.'

'I still don't get it,' said Mrs Linnet. 'Tell me again.'

'Perhaps you should have introduced him to Tansy Hyde.'

Mrs Linnet put down her cup of tea. 'What? Is she one of the Warburton Hydes?'

The door opened and Kitty came in, bringing with her a gust of warm air from outside, and a blast of music from the pub garden across the road.

'Our very favourite teenager,' said Henry. 'Oh, I'd love to be young again.'

'No, you wouldn't,' said Asad. 'You told me it was the unhappiest time of your life.'

'Then I'd love to have my teenage body back. If I'd known then how handsome and unlined I was, instead of fretting over non-existent blemishes, I'd have spent the entire time in a pair of Speedos.'

'When you get to my age,' said Mrs Linnet, 'you're just grateful if it still works.'

'You could wear your Speedos now,' said Asad. 'We could make it a regular theme. Put a sign up: "Thursday is Speedos day."'

Henry wagged a finger. 'I've never thought it classy for a shopkeeper to put his damsons on display.'

'Prunes, surely?' Asad was giggling again.

Henry struggled to keep a straight face. 'I suppose I should be grateful you didn't start with raisins.'

'Mrs Linnet, you're a bad influence,' Asad said. 'Do stop now.'

'Yes, do stop, Mrs Linnet. We have an impressionable young girl in our midst. What can I get you, Kitty? Or have you brought us some more eggs? We're nearly out of the last lot.' Henry leaned over the counter.

'How long have you known that Matt McCarthy is trying to get us out of our home?'

The shop fell silent. Henry shot a glance at Asad.

Kitty intercepted it. 'Shall I take that as "a lot longer than just now"?' she asked bitterly.

'Trying to get you out of your house?' queried Mrs Linnet.

'By overcharging us, apparently,' Kitty said matter-of-factly. 'It seems we were the last to know.'

Asad opened the counter and came into the shop. 'Sit down, Kitty,' he said. 'Let's have a cup of tea and talk.'

'No, thank you.' She folded her arms. 'I've got to meet someone. I just wanted to know how many people have been laughing at us behind our backs. Silly townies, eh, thinking they could do up that big old house?'

'It wasn't like that,' Asad said. 'I had a suspicion that something wasn't right, but I had no proof.'

'Asad wanted to say something,' Henry interrupted, 'but I told him, "You can't just steam in making wild accusations." We had no idea what was going on in your house, what he was doing.'

'But you knew he wanted the house. Before we came.'

They looked helplessly at each other. 'Well, yes. It was common knowledge.'

'Not to us,' said Kitty. 'It would have been helpful if someone could have warned us that the man who was bashing our home to bits and charging us the earth for it was the same man who had wanted it for himself. Still, I guess now we know who our friends are.' She turned to go.

'Kitty!' Asad called her back. 'Does your mother know? Have you talked to her about this?' Henry heard the wheeziness in his voice, signalling his distress.

'I don't know what she knows,' said Kitty. 'I don't want to cause more problems.' Suddenly she became a child out of her depth. 'I don't know what to do. Still, I suppose it doesn't matter now because he's got to stop soon anyway. We've run out of money. We'll just sit in our semi-derelict house, work out how much we've lost and try to get on with our lives.'

There was a hint of drama in her delivery, but Henry couldn't blame her for that. 'Kitty, please wait. Let me explain a little—'

The bell jangled again and the door closed behind her.

'Well!' exclaimed Mrs Linnet, into the silence. And then again, when no one said anything, '*Well.*'

'She'll come round,' said Henry. 'When she thinks about it. God only knows what that man has done to the place. I'm sorry, Asad,' he said, as he walked round the shop, pulling down the blinds. 'You can hit me with the I-told-you-sos. We should have said something, even if it was just a suspicion.'

'You knew he was up to something, then?' Mrs Linnet asked.

'Well, no,' said Henry, wringing his hands. 'That was the problem. We just didn't know. And what can you do? I mean, you don't like to spread unfounded rumours, do you? Especially not when it concerns someone like him.'

'He's in the pub,' said Mrs Linnet. 'I saw him go in not ten minutes ago, like butter wouldn't melt.'

Asad undid his apron.

'Do you know,' she continued, 'I've always thought there was something not quite right about him. When he did Mrs

Barker's extension she said he'd put the handles too close to the door frames. The times she's skinned her knuckles . . .'

'Where are you going?' said Henry. Asad was taking off his apron.

'I have never felt so ashamed. Never.' There was something impassioned, barely restrained, behind his words. 'That child was right, Henry. Everything she said was right. We have all behaved shamefully.'

'But where are you going?'

'To talk to Mr McCarthy,' said Asad, 'before Mrs Delancey hears what's been going on. I'm going to ask him to behave like an honourable human being. And I'm going to tell him exactly what I think of him.'

'Asad, don't,' said Henry, blocking his path to the door. 'Don't get involved. This isn't your business.'

'It *is* our business. It is our duty as friends, as good neighbours.'

'Our duty? Who ever looked out for us, Asad?' Henry was shouting now, oblivious to who might hear. 'Who ever stepped in when we faced those bigots after we first got here? Who helped us when they were throwing things through our windows? Scrawling things on our door?'

'She is alone, Henry.'

'And so were *we*.'

'That was many years ago.' Asad shook his head, uncomprehending. 'What are you so afraid of?' he asked, and then he was gone.

The man behind the barbecue was wearing an apron with fake breasts and a pair of frilly knickers printed on the front. From time to time he clapped his hands over the breasts or held up a sausage, clamped in his tongs, and pursed his lips, as if he was doing something rude. Occasionally he would gyrate suggestively to the music, which rang out from the stereo someone had balanced on a small table by the door. Kitty only half noticed. Her nerves were jangling. The Cousins had been so shocked, so upset by what she had said to them, but they had obviously known. Why had they said nothing?

'There she is,' said Anthony, as a woman moved behind the barbecue to tell the man something. Her hair, scraped up in a deliberately messy confection, had thick blonde and gingery streaks running through it. 'That's the woman my dad's been shagging.'

Kitty's drink stalled at her lips. 'What?' she said, unsure she had heard correctly.

'Theresa Dillon. The barmaid. My dad's been shagging her for months.' He said it so casually, as if it were half to be expected that your father might be sleeping with someone other than your mother.

Kitty lowered her cola. 'Are you sure?'

'Course.' He stared at the woman with contempt. 'And she's not the first.'

Sometimes, this past year, Kitty had felt like the oldest teenager in the world. The only person in her household capable of making sensible decisions, paying bills, organising their household in the face of Mum's chaos. There were still times, though, like today, when she felt she was travelling through a landscape she had not even begun to understand. Matt had sauntered over when she had sat down with Anthony. He had joked that she could have got the drinks in if she'd taken his offer of a lift. Anthony had barely looked at him, she had been muted by fury, and in the end, muttering about teenagers, he had moved to where he now sat with some people.

'If you know that for sure,' she said carefully, 'why don't you tell your mum?'

He looked at her as if she was a complete innocent, and

she remembered telling him how happy her mum and dad had been, how Mum had almost fallen apart after Dad died.

He offered her a crisp. 'You don't know my dad,' he said dismissively. They sat on the bench for a while, the heat of the lowering sun penetrating the fabric of Kitty's dress.

'Want some more crisps? I'll get some more salt-and-vinegar before they run out.' Anthony rummaged in his pockets for change. Then he stopped. 'Uh-oh. What's going on there?'

Asad was standing in front of Matt, who was seated on one of the bench tables at the other side of the garden. She could not hear all of what was being said, but she could tell from Matt's rigid expression and from Asad's bearing that it was not good.

'You don't know what you're talking about, Asad, so I'd keep your nose out before you embarrass yourself.' Matt's voice carried above the music on the still air.

'You are a shameless man. You rely on the fact that people are afraid of you. Well, I am not afraid of you. And I am not afraid to tell the truth.'

The garden had become very quiet, as everyone picked up on the disturbance.

'The truth?' Matt said. 'Village gossip. You sit there in your silly little shop spreading it like old women. The pair of you. You're a joke.' He laughed.

Kitty's heart almost stopped. She glanced at Anthony, who shook his head. 'Oh, no,' he murmured.

Matt stood up, and Kitty moved forward, but Anthony's arm held her where she was.

Henry, who had just come into the beer garden with Mrs Linnet, cast around for Asad, then hurried up to him, muttering something Kitty couldn't hear.

Asad didn't seem to notice. 'I'm asking you to do the right thing,' he said calmly.

'And who are you? Some kind of moral judge and jury?'

'Someone who is not prepared to see a good woman cheated.'

When Matt spoke, his voice was tight. 'Asad, a piece of friendly advice. Go and play with your tinned peas.'

Asad's voice was louder now. 'All that money – and her a widow. Have you no shame?'

'Mrs Delancey is very happy with the work I'm doing on her house,' Matt said. 'You ask her. Okay? Ask her how happy she is.'

'That is because she doesn't know the truth.'

'Asad, leave me alone.' Matt flicked his hand and took a deep swig of his drink. 'You're beginning to bore me.'

'She doesn't know that you have been systematically over-charging her, crippling her—'

Henry pulled at his arm. 'Asad, let's go.'

'Yes, Asad. Go – before you say something you regret.'

'My only regret is not speaking out sooner,' said Asad. 'You know very well what I—'

'What the fuck is that supposed to mean?'

'I am going to tell her,' Asad said, wheezing now. 'I am going to see Mrs Delancey to tell her what you have been doing.'

Suddenly Matt McCarthy's demeanour changed. He leaped to his feet and loomed over the older man. '*Go home*,' he said venomously, his face barely an inch from Asad's. 'You're winding me up.'

'You don't like the idea that someone will tell her the truth?'

Matt was jabbing a finger at him. 'No. I don't like *you*. Why don't you piss off out of my business? Why don't you keep yourself to yourself and stop meddling?'

'Matt—'

Another man laid a hand on his arm, but Matt shook him off. 'No! This idiot's been in my face for weeks, insinuating things, dropping hints. I'm warning you, Asad. Stay out of my business or there'll be trouble.'

Kitty's heart was thumping. Over by the barbecue, a mother grabbed her small child's hand and led him towards the gate.

Henry was pulling at Asad now. 'Please let's go, Asad. Think of your chest.'

Asad refused to move. 'I've known bullies like you all my life,' he said breathlessly. 'And you're all the same. All relying on the fact that people will be too scared to get involved.'

Matt struck Asad's chest with a palm. 'You just won't leave it, will you? You stupid old man – you don't know when to leave well enough alone!' He shoved Asad backwards, causing him to stagger.

'Matt!' the barmaid with the streaky hair was tugging his shirt. 'Don't—'

'You're always sticking your nose in where it's not wanted, making threats. And you know *nothing*, you hear me?' Matt yelled into Asad's face. '*Nothing.*'

Kitty was trembling, and Anthony ran to his father. But Matt no longer seemed to hear anyone's protests.

'You shut your mouth and go away, you hear me?' *Push.* 'Stop spreading your poisonous gossip, you stupid old fool.' *Push.* 'Okay? Shut your mouth and go away.' *Push.*

At this Asad stumbled and was audibly fighting for breath. 'You – do – not – frighten – me,' he said.

The expression in Matt's eyes made Kitty shiver. 'Don't fucking push it, Asad,' he said.

'Matt, stop it. He's an old man.' The barbecue cook was now standing in front of Matt, tongs in hand. 'Henry, get Asad out of here. Matt – I think we should all just calm down.'

But Matt sidestepped him, prodding Asad's chest. 'You say one word to Isabel Delancey and you're fucking dead, you understand?'

'That's it.' Barbecue Man had been joined by several others, all of whom were steering Matt away from Asad. 'Get a grip on yourself, McCarthy. Go home and cool down.'

'Dead, you hear me?' He twisted away from the hands that held him. 'I'm going. Just leave me alone. He's the one you should be chucking out.'

'Oh, Christ!'

Flanked by a semi-circle of bystanders, Asad was sinking to the ground, his long legs crumpling elegantly beneath him, one clenched brown hand raised to his chest.

'Get his puffer!' Henry yelled. 'Someone get his inhaler.' He bent his head. 'Deep breaths, love.'

Asad's eyes were screwed shut. Kitty glimpsed his complexion, peculiarly purple, as the crowd closed round him. Someone muttered about asthma. Mrs Linnet fumbled with a bunch of keys. 'I don't know which one!' she was wailing. 'I don't know which one unlocks the shop door!'

Anthony was talking urgently to his father in the gateway.

On the barbecue something was burning, sending puffs of acrid smoke into the balmy evening. Kitty watched the scene recede from her, as if she were no longer part of it but watching from afar through a glass barrier. The birds, she noticed absently, were still singing.

'Someone hold him. Hold him for me. Oh, please . . . Call an ambulance! Someone call an ambulance!' And then, as Henry bolted past her, towards the shop, she heard him say, as if to himself, '*This*, Asad . . .' He was almost weeping, his face flushed with effort, his own breath coming in gasps. '*This* was what I was afraid of.'

Nineteen

Andreas Stephanides had the most immaculate fingernails Nicholas had ever seen on a man: even, perfectly regular, a well-buffed seashell pink. He must have had a manicure, he thought absently. The thought of asking Andreas Stephanides whether he did in fact have regular manicures made a nervous laugh rise to the back of his throat and Nicholas coughed, trying to cover it.

'You okay?'

'Fine.' Nicholas waved away his concern. 'Aircon. Throat . . .'

The older man sat back in his chair, and gestured at the papers in front of him. 'You know what? You've done me a favour. My wife, she's at that age . . . she needs a project.'

He picked up one of the sheets. 'This is what they're all doing now, right? The kids leave home, it used to be they'd make curtains. Colour schemes for each other's homes. Perhaps some charity work. Now she wants to rebuild whole houses.' He shrugged. 'I don't mind. It keeps her happy. And this house she likes. She likes it a lot.'

'It's got potential.' Nicholas crossed his legs, conscious of his new suit. It had been years since he'd been able to treat himself to one of such quality, but on feeling the fine wool against his skin, he had recalled that bespoke clothing made one feel – appear, even – more of a man. It seemed inconceivable now that he could have arrived in this office wearing anything less. Andreas's first payment had financed it.

Andreas nodded. 'She agrees with you. As I said, she's very happy. And if she's happy . . .'

Nicholas waited. From long experience he knew that it was wise with Andreas never to say too much. The man was a poker player, and he took you more seriously if he thought things had been left unsaid. 'Only a fool reveals all his cards,' he was fond of saying. While he waited, Nicholas gazed at the view of Hyde Park. It was another warm day and office workers were on the grass taking their lunch break early, sleeves rolled up and skirts hitched above knees. The traffic congealed in a thick artery around them, moving in short, ill-tempered bursts, but Nicholas could hear only the faintest hint of horns and engines. In this office, with its panelled walls and thick glass, one was insulated from noise, fumes, the messiness of everyday life. Money could protect you from almost anything.

'You want cash deposit?'

Nicholas smiled at him. 'Five per cent should do it.'

'You think you can get more like this?'

Nicholas returned his attention to the desk. 'Andreas, you know as well as I do that such properties don't grow on trees, especially in that area of London. But I'll keep my ear to the ground.' He had 'turned' them – valuing them low for a quick sale, and accepting a cash kickback from both buyer and seller, acting as an invisible middle man. It was not strictly legal, but so much of what went on with property was in a grey area. The seller, the son of the deceased owner, had been happy enough not to pay an agent's fee.

'And you – you're doing okay out of this?'

'It's petty cash, if you want the truth.'

Andreas was a handsome man, his hair thick and black even in his sixties, his immaculate dress and deceptively laid-back demeanour bringing to mind a 1950s lounge singer. His cufflinks were scattered with tiny diamonds. Everything

about him and his office spoke of big money, ostentatiously
spent.

He reached for his telephone and called his secretary.
'Shoula, bring us in some lunch, please, and drinks.' He raised
an eyebrow at Nicholas. 'You have time?'

Nicholas shrugged, as if time were of no importance.

Andreas replaced the receiver and lit a cigarette. 'So what's
in it for you? This is the second property you have found
me at well below market value. You're not a stupid man,
Nicholas. You're a developer yourself. Why are you doing me
a favour?'

Nicholas had been hoping this question would crop up
after drinks. He took a deep breath, hoping to appear unconcerned. 'Well . . . I thought you might be able to help me
with a little project . . . There is a property,' he said carefully, 'and it's a bit special. I want to develop it myself, but
I need backing.'

'Why did you not develop these two?' Andreas gestured
at the property details on the desk. 'You could have cleared
six figures, even if you just sold them on. A good builder, a
few months, maybe twice that.'

'I didn't want to be distracted. This will take a lot of attention. And I need to move quickly.'

'But you don't want me to develop this "special" property with you? In partnership?'

Nicholas laid his hands on the desk. 'I want a loan. I can
do a percentage return on profit, if that makes it more attractive. This one's personal, Andreas.'

'Personal?'

'There is a woman . . .'

'Hah! There is always a woman.'

The two men broke off as Andreas's secretary entered with
a tray. It contained half a dozen small plates, upon which

were laid out titbits: strips of pitta bread, hummus, tzatziki, olives and halloumi. She poured wine, laid out two napkins, then left the room.

'Please.' Andreas waved at the food. Nicholas was too tense to eat, but he made himself take a couple of olives.

Andreas sipped his wine and swung his chair round to face the window. 'The best view in London,' he pronounced, of the green expanse below.

'It's very fine,' Nicholas agreed, and wondered where to put his olive stone.

'This property. You own it?'

'No.'

'It has planning permission?'

'No.'

'No property, no planning permission,' Andreas remarked, as if he were humouring someone not quite sane.

'I can get both. I know what I'm doing.'

They picked at the food for a few minutes, then Andreas spoke again. 'You know something, Nicholas? I was surprised when you rang me. Very surprised. When your business went down a lot of people said you were finished. You had lost your nerve. They said without your wife's money you were nothing.' When Nicholas remained silent, he continued, 'I am going to be honest with you. There are still people who consider you a bad bet. What should I say to them?'

Nicholas clutched his napkin. The banks wouldn't lend him anywhere near what he needed. Few investors would even give him meeting time. Andreas knew all of this. He thought for a moment. 'Your people are right. On paper, I'm not a good risk.'

The older man pursed his lips.

'I'm not going to waste your time in trying to convince you of something you may already have decided, but you know as well as I do, Andreas, that it's on the longest odds you make most money.'

It seemed several years later that the man smiled, long enough, anyway, for sweat to break out in the small of Nicholas's back despite the air-conditioning.

'Hah!' Andreas said. 'It's good to see that ex-wife of yours didn't take your *arhidia*, as well . . . Okay, Nicholas. I like a good comeback story. You tell me a little more about this project. And then we will talk money.'

It took her several rings to answer. When she did, she sounded hurried, as if she had run to pick it up.

'It's me,' he said, grinning.

'I know.'

'You've put me into your phone?' He was surprised by her audacity.

'Not exactly. You're Sheila.'

He stood in the street, the London traffic roaring past, belching smoke, the aroma of dirt and fast food rising from the shopfronts around him. If he pressed the phone firmly enough to his ear and blocked the other, he could just make out birdsong in the background, could picture her standing in the field by the woods, could smell the honeyed scent of her hair against his skin.

'I had to tell you,' he said. 'I got the money.' He felt as if he had passed some kind of test, as if it had been the final step to his resurrection. He felt like a somebody again. All these things he wanted to tell her, knowing she would under-stand. He wanted to do it for her. She had given him a reason to prove himself.

'Oh.'

'I'll probably come up and meet the woman after the weekend. I was wondering if I could see you at the same time.'

'You're going to make her an offer?'

'Something like that.'

Her silence lasted long enough to make him uneasy. 'Are you okay?' A lorry's brakes let out a screech beside him and he strained to hear her.

'It's strange. The thought of that house being redeveloped.'

'Would you rather they lived there together?'

It was a mean shot, and he was ashamed as soon as he said it. 'I'm sorry,' he shouted, against the traffic. 'I shouldn't have said that.'

He detected a break in her voice as she said, 'No, you're quite right. It would be unbearable. Better it goes to someone else.'

'Listen,' he said, not caring about the curious glances of passers-by, 'we'll find somewhere better. Somewhere with no bad memories.'

He could not hear her response.

'Laura. I love you,' he said. It had been years since he had said those words. He said them again. 'I love you.'

There was a slight pause. 'I love you too,' she said.

Laura turned off her phone and took a few deep breaths before she went indoors to allow the glow in her cheeks to subside. She had found it hard, these last days, to believe that Matt couldn't see what was written on her face, was so visible in her walk. She had always been able to tell with him.

She carried Nicholas's touch on her skin. His words of endearment floated in her mind. They didn't stop the hurt, but they dulled it, reduced the effects of Matt's demolition job on her sense of self. This man loved her. This kind, cultured man loved her. She had not only slept with him, just hours after meeting him, but she had told him she loved him. Laura McCarthy was nearly forty, a boring pillar of the local community whose airing cupboard was organised with military efficiency and who always had enough food in the freezer to knock up a meal for twelve. Suddenly she wondered who she was becoming.

Matt was in his office. 'I'm going to the shops. Are you not working today?' she asked politely. She no longer offered him a mug of tea; even when he said yes these days, he would leave them to go cold. She would find them, untouched and congealing, on sideboards and tables. 'I thought you'd be working across the road.'

'Waiting on materials.'

'You couldn't go to the Dawson job instead?'

'They cancelled.'

'Why? I thought they were happy with the quote.'

'Don't know. They just cancelled.'

'Matt, is this anything to do with what happened at the pub?'

He kept his eyes on the desk, lifting pieces of paper and putting them down again.

'Anthony said a little, but I thought you might tell me what actually happened.' She kept her voice neutral. She didn't want to provoke an argument. She didn't tell him about the neighbours who had refused to meet her eye in the supermarket, or of how Mrs Linnet had muttered darkly that Matt should be ashamed of himself when she had passed her in the car park.

'Gossiping like all the rest,' he said dismissively.

'Asad's in hospital, Matt.'

'It's just asthma. He's fine.'

'It's never "just asthma". He's an old man, Matt, and you could have killed him. What's going on?'

He pushed past her towards the filing cabinet and began to pull out drawers, lifting and replacing files. 'He got on my nerves, okay? We had an argument. He got an asthma attack. No big deal.'

'No big deal? And why are we taking Byron off the payroll? It was only a few weeks ago you wanted him put on the books.'

He seemed to be looking for something. Suddenly she realised that the invoices were in a shambles. All the paperwork relating to the various jobs was muddled and lay in chaotic heaps where it had fallen on the desk. Matt was meticulous with his paperwork. He liked to know exactly where he stood, account for every last penny. She had never seen him before with his papers in such a mess. I don't care, she told herself firmly. Soon this will be someone else's problem. Soon I will be with someone who appreciates me. *Would you rather they lived there together?*

'Matt?' This distant, hostile man was her husband. She couldn't understand how they had fallen apart so comprehensively, so fast. Don't you know where this is headed? she asked him silently. Another man has just told me he loves me. A man who spent several hours last week in a London hotel room worshipping my naked body. A man who says his idea of heaven would be waking up next to me, only me, every morning of his life. A man who says I am everything to him. *Everything.*

But Matt didn't care. He loved Isabel Delancey. Laura cleared her face of emotion. 'Matt? I need to know where he is so that we can get the paperwork straight.'

'I don't want to talk about Byron,' he said, flicking through a ledger. He didn't even look up.

She stood there for a moment longer, then turned away and walked down the stairs.

Another long, hot day eased into evening. In the clearing in the woods, there were new layers of sound: the playing of a violin after the clattering accoutrements of supper were cleared away, the barking of an overexcited puppy, desperate to chase balls, the distant musings of a teenage girl on a telephone, filtering through the open windows of a tired old house, and the occasional piercing whine of a mosquito, followed by a determined slap.

Byron sat in his chair in the boiler room, his eyes trained on nothing. Those sounds had become familiar to him over the past two months, the backdrop to the end of his day. Now he tried to guess what sounds would filter through his future life, and none of them was welcome: the incessant low roar of traffic, the blaring television heard through paper-thin walls, the endless ringing of competing mobile telephones. The sounds of too many people in too little space.

When he had first come here he had been filled with shame. Now he felt oddly at home in what was essentially a dark, dirty outhouse. He was still haunted by the sounds of prison: the endless clang and slide of metal doors, the thumping music from other wings, a voice raised in argument or protest and, underneath it all, the buzz of threat, of fear, anger and regret. Compared with that, these Spartan surroundings spoke not of homelessness but of a strange freedom, something civilised and warm close at hand. A different way of living. It meant being close to Thierry, Isabel and Kitty, hearing Isabel's easy laugh as she strode through the trees at dawn, to hear her, lost in sound, to watch, while trying not to watch, the faint shadows of anxiety that were never far from her face. If his situation and his past were different, he might have offered more than edible weeds and firewood.

Byron forced himself to get up. Reflection was a route to misery. He moved around the room, gathering his few belongings into neat piles, his muscular frame moving easily in the gloom. He heard the door open and Thierry edging in with the puppy at his heels. The boy held out a bowl filled with raspberries and wild strawberries, cream and a homemade biscuit.

'Tell your mum you were eating this outside, did you?'

Thierry grinned.

Byron gazed at him, this good-natured, silent child, and felt suddenly guilty at what he had to tell him. 'Come on,' he said, gesturing towards the door. 'Can't have you going without your pudding. We'll share it.'

She'd got lucky with the weather, this summer, Byron thought, as he and Thierry played cards afterwards, trying to stop the puppy stealing them off the crate he used as a table. The taste of the berries lingered in his mouth. Perhaps she was a natural at growing things. Some people were.

'Snap,' he announced. Thierry still wouldn't say it aloud. He gave a grunt and an emphatic slap. Byron took the cards, smiling at the boy's rueful grin. Thierry had grown taller since he had lived in the house, his sad pallor replaced with freckles, a quick smile and a healthy glow. But with his emergence from grief into the happiness he showed when he was adventuring outside or playing with his dog, why would he still not speak?

Byron coughed quietly and cleared his throat. Then he dealt new cards. He did not look at the boy as he spoke. 'I have to tell you something, Thierry. I'm, ah . . . I'm going to move on.'

The boy's head jerked up.

'There's no work for me here,' Byron explained gently, 'and nowhere proper for me to live, so I have to pack up and go somewhere else.'

Thierry was staring at him.

'I wouldn't go if I didn't have to. But that's the thing about being grown-up. You need a job and a roof over your head.'

Thierry pointed upwards.

'I can't hide out here for ever. I must have a proper home, especially before it starts to get cold.'

The boy was trying hard not to show it, but Byron could see his devastation and knew it mirrored his own. 'I'm sorry, T. I've enjoyed your company.' He had grown accustomed to Thierry, hanging from the branches of trees, racing the dogs, his brow knitting with concentration as he checked the honeycomb of a morel for insects. There was a lump in Byron's throat and he was glad that the little room was still fairly dark. 'Sorry,' he said again.

He reached behind him to stroke Meg's head for an excuse to turn away. Then Thierry moved round the table to sit next to him. He rested his head against Byron's arm. They remained like that for a few minutes. Isabel's music reached a crescendo, then stopped. He could hear the same note played again and again, as if in question.

'I'll let you know where I am,' Byron said quietly. 'Write you a letter if you like. You can come and visit.'

There was no movement.

'You haven't lost me, you know. You've got Pepper, and I've got his mum, so we'll be linked that way. And there's always the phone.'

The telephone. A useless device. Byron looked down at the mop of dark hair. He waited a few moments. 'Why won't you talk, Thierry? I know you can. What is it that's so hard to say?' Byron couldn't see his face, but something about the child's intent stillness made him wonder. His voice caught in his throat as he said, 'Thierry, did something bad happen?'

There was a faint but imperceptible nod. He felt it against his arm.

'Something other than what happened to your dad?'

Another nod.

'You don't want to say.'

The boy shook his head.

Byron waited. Then he spoke quietly. 'You know what I do when something bad happens? I tell Meg or Elsie.' He let this sink into the silence. 'Dogs are very useful things. You tell them something, and they always listen. But they never let on. How about you tell Pepper and I'll sit here and not listen?'

No movement. A bird, disturbed, flapped its wings noisily outside.

'Go on, T. It'll be a weight off. You'll see.'

Byron stared at the wall as he waited in silence, then finally, just as he was about to give up, he heard a faltering whisper. The scrape of the puppy's paws as it wriggled in the boy's arms. And as Thierry's voice tailed off, Byron closed his eyes.

The sun, a fiery red ball, sank behind the trees, sending out vivid streaks that showed only as the faintest glints through the canopy of leaves. Isabel walked beneath them, trying to keep the melody in her head, fingering invisible strings. Once, music had run like a continuum through her mind, barely interrupted by the demands of her children, her conversations with her husband. Now it was frequently interrupted, disjointed by the realities of everyday life.

Today, as with most days, it was money. Matt's latest bill had not come in, but according to her little book, thousands were owing on plant hire and new windows. She had thought the sale of her violin would provide a cushion for her and the children, see them through to the other side of the building work, but it was unfinished, and now Mr Cartwright was talking about capital gains tax. 'Why should I have to pay tax on the sale of something that belongs to me?' she had asked him, appalled, when he brought up the topic on the telephone. 'All I'm trying to do is survive.' He had no answer.

She had sold her jewellery, everything but her wedding ring. And she was still watching her savings shrink with every passing week.

'Brahms,' she said aloud. 'Second movement. Come on, focus.'

It was a vain hope this evening, but she had found that walking through the woods helped. It wasn't just the constant low-level noise of her home: the television, Thierry and the puppy, Kitty's mobile. The real noise was silent, so much more invasive. The house no longer felt like a refuge: it was a series of problems, a reminder of jobs still undone, work still unpaid for.

She hesitated, glancing through the trees at the lake. It was at its most beautiful at this time of day, the sun's last rays a vivid pathway across the water, the birds almost silent as they settled to roost. She could ask to defer payment until she had sold the house. She could try to borrow. She could pay Matt with all the money she had left, and hope they could support themselves until more work came through for her. Isabel sat down heavily on a tree stump. She could curl up here and forget everything.

'Isabel?'

Byron was silhouetted against the sun, his large frame black against the trees. She jumped to her feet, trying not to appear as startled as she felt.

But he had seen it.

'I didn't hear you,' she said. She couldn't see his face.

'I did call.'

'It's fine,' she said, too brightly. He was so broad across the shoulders – his whole body spoke of strength, solidity. Now, though, she couldn't help but think of the damage such strength could inflict, the menace implicit within it. Since he had walked out of the house several days previously, Byron, her gentle, awkward accomplice, had become a stranger to her, the things she had thought she'd known smashed away by Matt's words.

'I was on my way back to the house,' she said, determinedly upbeat. 'Did you want something?' She found herself walking towards the lake, as if being in daylight, out of the shadowy confines of the woods, was safer.

When he turned, he seemed more nervous than she felt. It was then that she saw he was holding out letters. She took them, observing that there was something familiar about the handwriting. Both envelopes had been opened. 'I didn't read them,' Byron said, 'but Thierry did. I should tell you . . . He thinks . . . it's not safe to talk.'

'What?'

Isabel read the first fourteen lines of beautiful, looping handwriting. She stared at the words written by the unknown woman. The woman who had been unaware that Laurent had died, that he was not avoiding her. She reread the note, trying to make sense of it, forcing herself to recognise the truth. This had to be a joke, she told herself, half beginning to laugh. Then she read it again.

It was the letter Kitty had tried to make her read all those months ago when Mr Cartwright had shamed her into looking at the Pile. One of the first letters she had received, barely a week after he had died. She hadn't opened it – she hadn't opened anything for months. Why had Thierry taken it?

It couldn't be right. The second had been forwarded from Laurent's office, and as she read the urgent words her heart, what she had believed remained of it, dropped into an abyss.

No, she said silently. And the music was gone. She was left with the deafening silence of her own wilful ignorance. *No. No. No. No.* Byron was still standing there, watching her. And she realised that he had known what the letters contained.

What was it he had said? *He thinks it's not safe to talk.* Not her husband. Her son. And her sense of betrayal was overwhelmed by another emotion. 'He knew?' she demanded, holding up the letter, her voice quivering. 'Thierry knew about this? He's been carrying it all this time?'

Byron nodded. 'The woman delivered the first by hand. He recognised her. And later he saw the other in a pile of letters.'

'*Recognised* her? Oh, God.' And now it all made sense, and she was engulfed by her husband's betrayal, by her own ignorant betrayal of her son, who dared not speak because he knew too much. And now there was nothing left of the little family who had once lived in a warm house in Maida Vale. Because there were no memories, no innocence, nothing she could salvage from that car crash. Isabel sank back on to the tree-trunk. There was no one who could help, no one who could make this better. And she could no longer even mourn the love of the husband she had lost, because she knew now that she had lost him long before.

'Isabel? Are you okay?' The question sounded so stupid, hanging between them.

Thierry, she thought blindly. She had to go to Thierry.

She stood up a little shakily. 'Thank you,' she said politely, unsure how she had forced her voice into such a semblance of normality. 'Thank you for letting me know.'

She walked briskly towards the house, stumbling on the rough ground now that the light was ebbing. The woods rose and fell around her, blurred at the edges. Byron was beside her. 'I'm sorry,' he said.

She spun round. 'Why? Did you sleep with my husband? Did you drive the lorry that killed him? Did you traumatise my son into silence? No. So don't be ridiculous. It's nothing to do with you.' She was a little out of breath and the words sounded shrill and unforgiving.

'I'm sorry to have brought you bad news,' he said. 'I just thought you should know for Thierry's sake.'

'Well, good for you.' She stumbled over a fallen tree-trunk.

'Isabel, I—'

'Who else knows? Perhaps you could nip down to the Cousins, be the first to tell them. No doubt it'll be all over the village by morning, anyway.'

'No one knows.'

She could see the house. Her son would be inside. Upstairs, perhaps, silently locked into a computer game. *How could I not have seen? How could I have let him suffer like this?*

'Isabel. Slow down. Give yourself a minute before you speak to him.'

He laid a hand on her shoulder but Isabel shook it off.

'Don't touch me!'

He stepped back as if he had been stung. There was a short silence. 'I would have burned them if I could. I was just trying to help Thierry.'

'Well, I don't need you to help him,' she snapped. 'We don't need your help or anyone else's.'

He searched her face, and then, jaw set, he walked away from her.

Isabel watched him go. 'I can protect him myself!' she yelled.

He was about fifty feet away when she added: 'I can protect both of them!'

He didn't slow down.

A great sob escaped her. 'All right,' she said, her voice breaking. 'Byron, tell me why.'

He stopped and turned. She was beside a fallen oak, the lake just visible behind her. Her hands were on her hips, her face flushed.

'Why did he tell you all this and not me? Why couldn't he tell me? I'm his mother, right? I may not always have been a very good one, but I've loved him his whole life. I'm all he's got left. Why did he tell you and not me?'

He registered the hurt on her face, the shock and misery underneath that fierce exterior. A wounded animal would lash out at anyone.

'He was afraid,' he said.

She seemed to crumple a little then. She lifted her eyes to the sky, closed them briefly. If he was anybody else, Byron thought suddenly, anyone else in all the world, he could have walked up to her and put his arms around her. He could have offered this bruised woman the smallest comfort.

'His silence was supposed to protect you.'

He waited, just until she turned away, then he began to walk steadily towards the road.

He was awake when she returned. Even in the half-light of his room she could see his eyes on her. She suspected that he had been waiting for some time. He must have guessed what Byron would say. But now she was here she wasn't sure what to say to him. She wasn't even sure she had taken in the truth of what she had been told. But she knew she had to relieve him of his burden. She laid a hand on his head, feeling the familiar soft hair. 'I know everything,' she whispered, 'and it's all right.' She focused on keeping her voice calm. 'People . . . don't always behave in the way they should, but it doesn't matter. I still love your daddy and I know he loved me.'

A small hand emerged from the covers and took hers and she stroked his fingers.

'What you saw in those letters doesn't matter, Thierry. It doesn't change how much we loved Daddy, or how much he loved us. You mustn't worry about it.'

She closed her eyes now. 'And you have to know something

else, something very important. Nothing is ever so bad that you can't tell me. Do you understand, Thierry? You don't have to keep anything like this to yourself. That's what I'm here for.'

There was a lengthy silence. It was completely dark outside now, and Isabel lay down on the bed beside her son. Out of the window, the stars were illuminated pinpricks in the night sky, hinting at some great brightness beyond.

How inadequate a mother had she been that her younger child had felt unable to lean on her? How fragile, self-absorbed and selfish she must have seemed that they had both felt obliged to protect *her*.

'You can tell me anything,' she said, almost to herself now. She was weary with grief and shock, and wondered briefly whether she might just sleep here. Moving upstairs seemed impossible.

Thierry's voice cut into the silence. 'I told him,' he whispered. 'I told him I hated him.'

Isabel was instantly awake. 'That's okay,' she said, after a beat. 'You're allowed to say what you feel. I'm sure Daddy understood. Really, I—'

'No.'

'Thierry, darling, you can't—'

'The day I saw them. Before the concert. She came to the house and I saw them . . . and Dad tried to pretend it was nothing. But I'm not stupid. And I told him . . . I told him I wished he was *dead*.'

He began to sob into her chest, his small fists clutching her shirt. Isabel screwed her eyes shut against the dark, against the black place where her child had been for months, and swallowing down the cry that rose in her throat, placed her arms tightly around him.

Twenty

That day she had come out of the house twice, once to pick leaves from her vegetable patch, strolling head down along the path, a colander dangling from her hand. She had been wearing a faded T-shirt and cut-off shorts, her hair swept carelessly into a large pin from which it made a tangled bid for escape. Heat made her clothes stick to her skin. It hung over the lake all day, smothering movement and sound, with only a whisper of breeze to bring relief.

In the woods it was a little cooler, but through the trees the house shimmered in the heat. Those roof slates that had been repaired gleamed, free of the moss that coated their neighbours. The weatherboarding that had been replaced contrasted starkly with the older wood. In time, it would be painted one colour, but even now it was clear that quality work had been undertaken. The restoration would transform the building.

When he was working to his own architectural plans, Matt McCarthy cut no corners. He understood the beauty of true workmanship, and had gained enough experience over the years to know that it was always the thing you attempted to save money on – cheaper fittings, bargain flooring – that haunted you in the end. If you wanted something to look beautiful, you did not cut corners. His house would be perfect.

At first, if his good taste and attention to detail had cost Isabel Delancey more than she could afford, he had considered it no bad thing. It simply speeded them towards the time when he could move his family into the Spanish House and she could take hers home to London. The things she had asked him to do, the few requests she had made, he had completed in a slipshod manner, knowing there was little point in paying too much attention to a job he would only have to redo within a few months. When she had been un-deterred by his charges, by the apparent hazards of the house, be it rat or rotten floor, he had invented more jobs. A wall that needed knocking through, joists that had to be replaced. He had been secretly amazed that it had taken her so long to question anything he did.

Matt swatted at a fly that buzzed through the open window. She had come out a second time shortly after lunch, rubbing her eyes as if she had only recently woken. He had thought of walking over to talk to her, but the boy had run out after her, the dog yapping at his heels. She had bent and kissed the child, and he remembered how her lips had yielded to his, her body wrapped round his own.

He might have dozed off for a while, the front seat of his van reclining as he attempted to rest his eyes. It was so diffi-cult to sleep at the moment. His own house had become an unfriendly place: Laura's accusatory stares followed him around, and her questions were bitterly polite. It was easier to avoid the place as far as he could. He suspected she had moved into the spare room: the door had been firmly shut the last time he had made his way upstairs. But then so had the door of their bedroom.

The last weeks had taken on an odd shape. Heat bled through the days, causing him to wake and doze at odd hours, to feel alternately exhausted or almost manic with energy. His son avoided him. Byron had disappeared. He had forgotten sacking him and, on ringing him to find out where he was, had been shocked when Byron had curtly reminded him. It was the heat, Matt had explained, messing with his brain. Byron had not responded. Matt had talked on for some time before it dawned on him that there was no one at the other end of the line.

He had gone to the Long Whistle. He couldn't remember when he had last had a proper meal. Theresa would make him something, give him a friendly smile. Instead she had told him baldly that they had stopped serving food, and when he had begged, she had offered him a dried-out ham roll. She wouldn't talk to him, even when he made some joke about the length of her skirt. She stood, arms folded, near the back of the bar, watching him as one would a dog with a mean eye. He had sat there for some time before it occurred to him that nobody in the pub was talking to him.

'Have I grown another head?' he said irritably, when their scrutiny became too much for him.

'You need to sort out the one you've got, mate. Eat that roll and then leave. I don't want any trouble.' The landlord took his newspaper from the bar and disappeared into the back.

'You should go home, Matt.' Mike Todd had approached him, lowered his voice so that no one else could hear. Patted him on the back. There was something oddly like pity in his eyes. 'Go home and get some rest.'

'When are you coming to see this house of mine, then?' he said, but Mike appeared not to hear.

'Go home, Matt,' he said.

It had been easier just to sit in the van. He was not sure how long he had been there now, but it was a while. He had forgotten to charge his mobile phone, but it didn't matter as there was nobody he wanted to speak to. Matt stared at the façade of the house, seeing not the scaffolding at the back, the overflowing skip, the window with the flapping tarpaulin but his house. The big house, restored to its former glory, with him strolling down the lawn to the lake. He remembered sitting astride his bike in this exact spot, as a boy, vowing his revenge. They had accused his father of stealing two spare wheels from the vintage cars, had been too embarrassed – or lazy – to backtrack when the offending items were discovered at the garage, even though George McCarthy had worked blamelessly for the family for almost fifteen years. By then it had been too late: Matt and his sister had been moved from their estate cottage to the council house at Little Barton, and the family name had been tainted by the Pottisworths' carelessness. Since that day he had known the house must be his. He would wipe the smirk off Pottisworth's face. He would show Laura's family, who had eyed his shoes, the way he held his knife and fork, with polite, blinking distaste.

He would have the house for the McCarthys. He would show everyone round here that what mattered was not where you came from but what you could achieve. He would restore the house and his family's reputation.

It should have been fairly simple to ensure that the widow, the interloper, did not stand in his way for long. But then, on a blustery early-summer night, the widow had become Isabel, breathing, pulsing Isabel who had flooded his head with music and made his life seem drab, grey and silent. Isabel, who floated ethereally through the trees, whose hips swung with music, who had looked at him with slanted, defiant eyes, who had made him realise what he was reaching for, what had been missing all the time he had been preoccupied with practicalities and square footage. The only woman who had ever posed a challenge. He still wanted the house – oh, he still knew it was his. But it was no longer enough.

Matt McCarthy shut his eyes, then opened them, trying

to clear the noise in his head. He fumbled with the CD player in the dashboard until Handel's *Water Music* started. He turned up the volume. Then as the strings soothed him, restored him, he grabbed his notebook from the glove compartment and began methodically to write a list of all the things he had still to do, from sealing pipework to installing that last window. He could remember every last nail, every last piece of plasterwork. No one knew that house better than him. He sat and scribbled, ignoring the darkened pages that fluttered to the footwell, as the sun dropped behind the Spanish House.

For three days and two nights Isabel did not sleep. She lay awake, engaged in a million silent confrontations with her dead husband. She railed at him for his infidelity, berated herself for leaving him alone so much that he had felt the need and taken the opportunity. She replayed family events, holidays, her trips away, inserting this woman into what she had considered their memories. The excessive spending, his more frequent trips away last year: it all made sense, and knitted together into an ugly pattern. Nothing was hers now, nothing solely theirs. His affair had corrupted everything. And she hated herself for having been too self-absorbed to notice what was happening, too complacent to think of checking bank accounts, credit-card statements.

   She had hurled her wedding ring into the lake at midnight, not sure whether to laugh or cry when she did not hear the splash. But mostly she wept for what he had done, by default, to their son. That very morning, at breakfast, she had recalled, Laurent had kissed Thierry's head and made some comment about how grown-up he was. Was that some coded message? Had it been Laurent's way of warning Thierry not to speak? Had hiding his infidelity meant more to him than his son's peace of mind? Or had he said that Thierry was growing up simply because he was?

It corrupted everything, this knowledge. It made her head spin.

Matt had come the morning after she had made the discovery and when she heard his van, and the knock at the back door – she had removed the emergency keys from under the mat – she had opened it and told him it was not convenient.

'You need the bathroom doing,' he had said. 'You've been going on about it for weeks. I've got all the stuff in the van.' He looked awful. He had several days' stubble on his chin and his T-shirt was grubby. Not building-work grubby, but crumpled, greyed, as if he had slept in it.

'No,' she had said. 'Now is not a good time.'

'But you said you wanted—'

'We've been using a tin bath for months. It's hardly going to make any difference now, is it?' And she had closed the door, not caring that she had sounded rude, or that Kitty would wail yet again that they were living in prehistoric conditions. She hated Matt for being a man. For sleeping with her when he, too, was married, and not having the grace to appear as if he had given it a second thought. She winced when she remembered her own unthinking duplicity. Hadn't she done to Laura what she was so distraught at having had done to herself?

No one else came to the house. She ignored the few telephone calls. Outwardly she gave a virtuoso performance. She cooked, admired the new chicks, and listened attentively when Kitty returned with Anthony from the hospital where Asad was recovering well from the asthma attack. She listened, with satisfaction, to her son's voice. He was tentative at first, and self-conscious, but he asked for breakfast instead of helping himself silently to cereal, he called his puppy, and later that afternoon she heard him laughing at it as it raced after a rabbit near the lake.

She was glad that the children no longer wanted to return to London: the house in Maida Vale had morphed overnight from a lost idyll, a comforting home, to a place of deception, of secrets.

At night, when the children were asleep, unable to play the violin, she walked through her unfinished house, accompanied by the mosquitoes that had found their way in through unfixed windows, the scurrying of nocturnal creatures under the floorboards or in the eaves. She no longer saw the naked plasterboard. That it was a shell in places did not make it any more or less a home than the supposed haven in London. It was not about décor or soft furnishings, or the number of floorboards that were missing. It was not about wealth or security.

She was no longer sure what made a home. Any further than it was about two quietly sleeping bodies upstairs.

Jack-by-the-hedge. Hairy bittercress. Wild thyme and chanterelles. Byron walked round the edge of the woods, where the aged trunks segued neatly into pastureland, hemmed by years of successive farmers, and, in the dim light, picked himself a supper from the places he had known since he was a boy. He had lost weight, but suspected it was due less to his having to forage than to his lack of appetite.

He had spent the last few days holed up in the daytime, sleeping in the heat, and wandering the woods at night, trying to work out what to do next.

She was wary of him now. That much was clear. He had seen it in the way she had jumped when she saw him coming through the trees, in the way she fixed on a smile, too broad, too bright. He had heard it in the determined nature of her greeting, as if she wouldn't show him how afraid she was. He knew that reaction: he had seen it in those villagers who knew him by reputation rather than in person.

When Byron thought of Isabel being afraid of him, of her family believing he could do them harm, something heavy fell upon him like a shroud.

There was little point in attempting to remain in the Bartons, he knew. His past, no matter how misreported, would hang around him like a filthy stench as long as people like Matt were there. And with the land shrinking, swallowed by 'unique' new home developments, industrial units or arable farming, there were few people locally who could offer him work. He had seen the new career options for people like him: shelf-stacker, security guard, mini-cab driver. Something in Byron died even when he was reading the advertisements and picturing himself in a concrete car park, being told by a supervisor when to take his fifteen-minute break and paid, begrudgingly, the minimum wage.

I should not have challenged Matt, he told himself, for the hundredth time. I should have kept my mouth shut. But he didn't believe it.

'Hello?'

She had put the first line of her address at the top of the letter: 32 Beaufort House, Witchtree Gardens. An odd thing for a lover to do, Isabel thought. To be so specific. As if he might confuse you with somebody else.

Forty-eight hours after she had received the letters, she had called Directory Enquiries and found there was only one Karen living at such an address. Karen Traynor, destroyer of marriages and memories. Who would have thought that two words could have such an impact on so many people's lives? Isabel pictured her as tall, fair, athletic, perhaps in her late twenties. She would be immaculately made up – women with no children always were: they had time to be self-obsessed. Did she play music? Or had Laurent relished possession of someone whose mind wasn't always drifting elsewhere?

She didn't know what she would say, although she had rehearsed a hundred arguments, a thousand pithy put-downs. She suspected she might shout at her or scream. She would demand to know where all their money had gone. Where had Laurent taken her? How many hotels, Paris breaks, expensive treats had there been when Isabel had assumed he was away on business? She would show the woman what she had done, explain to her that, contrary to what Laurent might have said (what *had* he said?), she had been an intruder in a marriage that was still full of passion, still pulsing, still alive. She would put her straight, this unthinking, selfish girl. She would make her see.

And then the ringing stopped, and a woman's voice – well spoken, unremarkable, probably not that different from her own – said, 'Hello?' And after a pause: 'Hello?'

And Isabel, a woman who considered life empty if her own head was not full of glorious sound, found she could only listen in silence.

On the third evening the heat wave broke. The sky grew dark abruptly, with a rumble of thunder, like timpani warming up for a big finale, and then, following mucky clouds that scudded towards them, in an impatient rush, a torrential storm. It sent the creatures in the grounds scurrying for shelter, and rivulets of water gurgling towards ditches.

Byron sat under the house and listened, first to the exclamations of Isabel and Kitty, who were running to the washing-line, squealing and splashing as they gathered in the laundry; then, with a wry smile, to Thierry, who was singing to himself as he passed the boiler room. 'It's raining! It's pouring! The old man is snoring!' joyfully unselfconscious. The dogs sat alert, their eyes switching from the door to Byron, waiting for a signal, any signal, that they, too, could run outside, but he held up a hand and, with a groan, they settled.

'He went to bed and banged his head and couldn't get up in the morning.'

As the footsteps disappeared inside, Byron stood up slowly. He had packed his belongings neatly into two bags. When the rain slowed a little, he would walk through the woods to where he had left his car and go.

A door banged. Above him, abruptly, the air was flooded with music. A whole orchestra – something dramatic he had heard before. He heard Kitty's voice, pleading, 'Oh, not *this*,' and then the sound was muffled as someone closed a window. He could just hear whirling violins, voices, escalating to a frenzy.

Byron pulled out a pen, and wrote a short note, folded it neatly and placed it on top of the boiler. Then he sat, in the encroaching dark, and waited.

'Nicholas?'

'Did you get them?' He didn't ask who it was.

'They're beautiful,' she said softly. 'Absolutely beautiful. They came just before tea.'

'I was worried. I thought perhaps he'd want to know where they'd come from. But you said—'

'He's not here. I don't know where he goes, but he's rarely here now.' She didn't tell him she had seen her husband's car parked in the woods when she was out walking the dog. Why not park outside the widow's house? she had asked him silently. At least then you'd be honest.

'I wanted to send roses, but I thought they'd be too obvious.'

'Most roses don't have any fragrance now, anyway.'

'And the woman suggested lilies. But aren't they a bit over-powering? And funereal?'

He wanted to show her how much thought he had put into buying the flowers for her. She was touched by this. 'Peonies are my favourite,' she said. 'You're so clever.'

'I suspected they might be. I wanted you to know . . . that I think about you all the time. I'm not pressuring you but—'

'I will decide, Nicholas.'

'I know—'

'It's just that it's all moving terribly quickly. I promise it won't be long.'

She sat on the side of the bed and gazed at her left hand, the diamond-cluster ring her mother had considered vulgar. Was a vulgar ring preferable to an adulterous daughter? 'It's complicated. With my son and everything.'

'As much time as you need.'

She wished he was there. She felt certain of everything when he was with her, when she felt his hands on hers and could see the sincerity in his face. When she was alone, with Matt's absence casting a shadow over her home, and the Spanish House making her imagination run riot, she felt wretched. Was he there now? Laughing at her? Making love to that woman?

She could barely show her face in the village. The Cousins' shop was still closed. Since Matt's fight with Asad people had barely looked her in the eye, as if she were blamed by association. She could not see her girlfriends: she was not ready to tell anyone the truth of what was happening to her marriage. What had happened to her marriage. She had lived there long enough to know that her life would be conversational currency before long.

A tear fell, unexpectedly, leaving a dark stain on her trouser leg, spreading outwards.

'Can I still see you on Tuesday?'

'Oh, Nicholas,' she said, wiping her face. 'Do you really have to ask?'

It was the first time it had rained and nothing had leaked, and Isabel, who no longer took such things for granted, considered that a small miracle. Perhaps Matt had his uses, after all. The storm had lifted something, bringing a different perspective, so that briefly she could forget bills, betrayal, Laurent, and instead relish the shrieking lunacy of the children in the rain, and the rainwater on her skin after days of sticky heat. She had listened to their chatter that evening, not complained when they threw wet socks at each other, causing the puppy to bark. She had slept that afternoon on her unmade bed, and woken calm and cool, as if a fever had passed. They had all been lightened by the storm.

She went to Thierry's room. He was in bed now, the dog on the duvet. She would not scold him: if it made him happy, a few muddy footprints were a fair price to pay. Isabel drew the curtains, hearing a distant thunderclap, seeing the strange blue half-light as the storm moved east. Then, as she bent to kiss him goodnight, he put his arms round her neck. 'I love you, Mum,' he said, and the words sang in her head.

'I love you, Thierry,' she said.

'And I love Pepper,' he said.

'Oh, me too,' she said, firmly.

'I wish Byron wasn't going.'

'Going where?' She was tucking him in now, one eye on the map of the constellations that covered a hole in the plaster. Another job that hadn't been completed.

'He's got nowhere to live,' he said. 'He's got to move away to get another job.'

She remembered, with shame, how she had raged at Byron. She remembered the letters in her hand, the scent of warm mould rising from a rotten tree-trunk. The sick flood of adrenalin that accompanied an unwanted discovery.

She had been so maddened that she couldn't quite remember what she had said to him.

'Can you give him a job? He could look after our land.'

She kissed him again. 'Oh, lovey, if we had the money I would . . .' She would go and apologise, she thought. She didn't want Byron to leave on those terms. All the things he had done for her, for Thierry. '*We don't need your protection*,' she had snapped at him.

'I'll talk to him. Where's he staying?'

Some pauses are weightier than others. He looked at her, as if judging something, and she realised with some shock that her son had been holding more than one secret. 'Anything, Thierry. Remember? You can tell me anything. It's okay.' She reached out a hand for his, trying not to let her voice betray her anxiety.

The briefest hesitation. Light pressure on her hand. 'He's under the house,' he said.

Isabel walked silently down the steps, her bare feet splashing on the York stone paving. She had been so stunned by what Thierry had told her that she had forgotten she wasn't wearing shoes until wet gravel had met the soles of her feet. By which stage it had seemed hardly to matter. The light was failing now, and thin rain continued to fall, long after the storm had passed. She walked round the house, ducking to avoid the scaffolding, treading carefully in the places she knew there might still be shards of glass among the stones. Eventually she came to the stairs that led down to the boiler room. She had never thought to use them.

She saw a faint light, and hesitated briefly. Then she heard a dog growl. The door creaked as she opened it and at first she could make out nothing, but her ears, acutely sensitive to differences in sound, detected movement.

Her heart was thumping. And then the moon came out from behind a cloud, and partially illuminated the man at the back of the room. She let her eyes grow accustomed to the darkness, vaguely aware of his dogs at his feet.

'How long have you been here?' she asked.

'A couple of months,' he said, from the shadows. And as she digested this: 'I'm sorry. I'll be gone at dawn. I've got a couple of possibilities over at . . .' He tailed off, as if he were not even capable of convincing himself.

Outside the rain fell, a faint hissing in the trees, a distant rushing as the run-off from the fields met the ditches. She could smell the drenched earth, the warmth sending its moist scents into the still air.

All this time, she thought, he has been here, beneath us.

'I know it must seem . . . I needed a roof over my head.'

'Why didn't you ask me? Why didn't you tell me you had nowhere to go?'

'What Matt said. I don't want you to think I've been down here and . . .' He stumbled. 'Christ. Look, Isabel, I'm . . . sorry.'

She left the door open and went into the room below her house, conscious not of alarm but an unexpected comfort that over these last lost days she had not been alone.

'No,' she said. 'I shouldn't have listened to Matt. Whatever he said, it's unimportant.' She shook her head.

'I need to talk to you about him.'

'No,' she said firmly. 'I don't want to talk about him.'

'Then I need you to know,' he said. 'I'm not a violent

person. That man – the man Matt talked about – he had been beating up my sister. She didn't tell me, but Lily, my niece, did. And when he found out Lily had told me, he went for her.' His voice hardened. 'She was four.'

She winced. 'Byron, stop. You don't have to—'

'But it was an accident. Really.'

She heard the pain in his voice.

'I lost everything,' he said. 'My home. My future. My reputation.'

She remembered something he had once told her. 'You couldn't be a teacher.'

'I'd never hit anyone before that. Not in my whole life.' His voice dropped to a whisper: 'Nothing is the same after something like that, Isabel. Nothing. It's not just the guilt. It's the shape of things. The shape of yourself.' He paused. 'You start seeing yourself as other people see you.'

She stared at him.

'I don't,' she said.

They stood in the dark, neither quite able to see the other. Two outlines. Two mere shadows of people. For months, she had seen Laurent everywhere, in every man. She had seen the shape of his shoulders in those of strangers and heard his laugh on crowded streets. She had murmured to him in her dreams and wept when she couldn't make him real. In a fit of madness, she had imagined him in Matt. Now, finally, she knew he was gone. There was a sense of absence now, rather than loss. Laurent had ceased to exist.

But who was this man?

'Byron?' she whispered, and lifted a hand, unsure what she was doing. What did these fingers know of anything? The music they had conjured was false, a distraction. She had placed her trust in something she knew now to be an illusion. 'Byron?'

She reached out until she found his hand, which closed on hers. The skin was roughened, warm in the night air. The world swam. Her mind closed on the damp air, the scent of evening primrose, the sulphurous odour of the boiler. A dog whined, and Isabel gazed through the dark until she knew his eyes had lifted to hers.

'You don't have to stay down here,' she whispered. 'Come upstairs. Come and be with us.'

His hand lifted, and slowly, gently, his thumb wiped the damp from her face. Her head inclined towards it as her other hand reached up to press it to her skin. And then, as she took a step closer, a voice whispered, 'Isabel . . . I can't—'

Isabel, flooded with shame at the memory of Matt's hands on her, her own complicity, leaped away from him. 'No,' she said, quickly. 'I'm sorry.' She turned away, slipped back up the stairs and out, too swift even to hear his own stumbling apology.

Twenty-one

Eleven eggs, and one still warm. Kitty pressed it to her cheek, her hand encircling the fragile shell. There would be enough for breakfast, and a half-dozen to take to the Cousins. Asad was returning to work this morning, and over the past days she had prepared four boxes of eggs for him. 'You'll be short of stock,' she had said, sitting by his bed two days ago, the pastel floral curtain against her back.

'Then we will only open for conversation, not food,' said Asad. He still looked tired. His collapse had bruised the areas under his eyes, made his angular face appear cadaverous. It was only over the last couple of days, Henry had grumbled, that he had been eating properly.

She had been afraid that neither man would speak to her, given her part in that terrible afternoon, but when she apologised, Anthony standing awkwardly behind her, Asad had pressed her hand between his long, leathery palms. 'No, forgive me, Kitty. I should have warned you of my suspicions long ago. It has taught me a lesson. I suppose it is good to find I am not too old to learn something.'

'I've learned to carry a big stick. And a spare inhaler.' Henry fussed with Asad's pillow. 'He won't be able to lift anything, you know. That man . . .'

'Is he still working at your house?'

'I haven't seen him.'

'I don't know where he is,' said Anthony. 'Mum saw him the other day but she said he didn't say much.'

'I don't know how he can show his face.' Henry gave the pillow a final, too vigorous pat. 'He's probably steering clear. With a bit of luck your mum won't have to pay any more.'

Asad had glanced at Anthony. 'I'm so sorry you have to hear us talk about your father in this way.'

'Nothing I haven't heard before.' Anthony shrugged, as if it didn't matter. But Kitty knew it did, and later on when they sat on the plastic visiting chairs she had squeezed his hand to tell him she understood.

Thierry walked in through the back door now, and peered over her shoulder as she arranged the eggs in the boxes. 'How many?'

'Eleven. Would have been twelve but I dropped one.'

'I know. On the steps. Pepper ate it. Guess who's in the bedroom?'

She closed the lids carefully. 'Which one?'

'The master bedroom. The one Matt did up.' He grinned. 'Byron.'

'What? Working?'

Thierry shook his head. 'Sleeping.'

'Why is he staying in our house?'

Thierry gave an annoying flick of his head. 'It's just temporary,' he said. 'Until he sorts himself out.'

Kitty's mind leaped forward. Rent! Perhaps they'd have some more money coming in. She thought of her birthday lunch in a few days' time, to which she had invited Asad, Henry and almost half of the village. She had not yet told her mother how many were coming.

It would be useful to have Byron here – he could help set up the heavy stuff, maybe move the furniture outside. As the dining room still had holes everywhere, and the forecast was fair, she and Mum had decided it would be best to hold it on the lawn. She could picture it now, a fluttering white tablecloth laden with the things they had made, their guests admiring the view across the lake. They could swim, if they wanted. She would tell her friends from school to bring their costumes. Kitty hugged herself, suddenly glad to be living in this strange house. Somehow, in the warmth and the sun, the chaos of the building work seemed not to matter any more, the scaffolding and the dusty floorboards. If it wasn't for the lack of a proper bath, she could probably live like this for ever. Her mobile phone rang.

'Kitty?'

'Yes?'

'It's Henry. Sorry to call so early, darling. You wouldn't happen to know where I could find Byron, would you? We've got some bits need doing and we're hardly going to ask You Know Who.'

Kitty heard unfamiliar footsteps making their way across the floor above. 'Funnily enough, yes, I do.'

Byron lay in the soft double bed and stared at the immaculate white ceiling above him. For two months he had woken to the sight of a dirty floor, the hiss and thump of the boiler as it kicked into life. This morning he woke to peace, bright light flooding through restored windows, birdsong – and, somewhere below, the aroma of coffee. He padded barefoot across the sanded wood floor and stretched at the window, admiring the spectacular view of the lake.

His dogs were flat out on the rug, apparently reluctant to rouse themselves. As he stooped to stroke her head, Meg thumped her tail lazily.

Isabel had shown him into this room the previous night,

still awkward with him after their near-encounter in the dark. 'It's finished,' she said. 'I'll make up the bed for you.'

'I can do that.' He accepted the neat pile of bedlinen, flinched as their hands touched.

'Just . . . treat this as your home,' she said. 'Help yourself to what you want. You know where everything is.'

'I'll pay you. Once I find work.'

'Really. Just get back on your feet before we worry about money.' She had a way of blinking hard when she was embarrassed. 'Help out with the food. Look after Thierry when I have to go out teaching. That'll be enough.' She smiled wryly, finally lifting her eyes to his. 'There are enough things that need doing here, after all.'

It was as if she trusted him completely. Byron sat on the bed, marvelling at his luck. Isabel would have been justified in accusing him of trespass or worse. Anyone else would have done.

Instead she had opened her home to him, invited him to sit at her table, entrusted him with her children. He rubbed his hair and stretched again. Then, gazing at Matt's handiwork around him, he wondered briefly what had taken place between the two of them, but forced away the thought. Isabel had freed him of the burden of his history; the least she could expect was that he would do the same for her.

Besides, thinking of them together made something in him tighten uncomfortably. Thinking of Matt exploiting her, like he did everyone else, brought back feelings he had long made sure to smother. How much damage could one man be allowed to do?

Staring at the ceiling, he was struck suddenly not by its beauty, but by the vast gulf that existed between this house, its owner and his own life. She had let him in, yes, but this was a temporary measure. Staying in this house, in this room, was not the same as belonging here.

His darkening thoughts were disrupted by a knock at the door. Thierry's face appeared, a smile breaking across it. He looked, Byron realised with rare pleasure, overjoyed to find him there. 'Mum says there's breakfast downstairs.' He wiped his nose on the back of his sleeve. 'And Kitty says can you call the Cousins? They've got some work for you.'

He hadn't noticed a thing. Laura moved gracefully round her bedroom, sorting clothes – those she would take, and those she would leave behind – and wondered at her husband's ability to return home after nearly three days away, then simply fall asleep. He had let himself in shortly before dawn and, actuely aware of every tiny noise in the house now that she lived virtually alone, she had sat bolt upright. Perhaps he had come because he knew. She had prepared herself for confrontation. But he had walked upstairs, past her bedroom door, and through the wall she had heard him crawl heavily into bed. In a matter of minutes, he was snoring.

He had been asleep ever since. It was now almost midday.

Laura picked up a suit she had worn to a wedding last year, a pale designer two-piece, cut on the bias. Respectable, not too revealing, the way Matt liked her to dress. She had done everything as he liked it, she thought, listening for movement next door. Their food, her clothes, Anthony's education, the décor of the house. And for what? For a man who could disappear for three days, then return home to sleep with no suggestion that there might be anything out of the ordinary in that. For a man who could screw a next-door neighbour, right under her nose, and not consider there to be anything wrong in it.

She was doing the right thing. She had told herself so

many times now, and on those occasions when she lost confidence in her decision, Nicholas had said it for her. Nicholas, who was always at the other end of the phone. Nicholas, who never sounded anything less than delighted to hear her voice. Nicholas, who held her in his arms and spoke her name as if it were a mirage in a desert.

Nicholas would never be unfaithful to her. He wasn't that sort of man. He wore his restored happiness like a badge of honour, hard-won, and was plainly grateful for it. Why could *you* not have been grateful to have me? she asked Matt silently, through the bedroom wall. Why could I not have been enough for you?

She thought of the hundreds of times over the years that Matt's behaviour had caused her to decamp to the spare room, her mute protest at his absence, his unthinking cruelties, his infidelity. He always won her back, of course. He would simply follow her, climb in beside her and make love to her until he had won her over. As if none of it mattered. As if it were of no significance which bed he was in.

She glanced out of the window at the Spanish House, despising it suddenly for what it had done to them. If the widow hadn't moved in . . . if Matt hadn't set his heart on it . . . if Samuel Pottisworth hadn't taken such relish in abusing her care over the years . . . if she had never believed that living in it would somehow be the answer to all their problems . . .

Laura shoved the wedding suit back into the wardrobe. But it was the Spanish House that brought Nicholas to me, she reminded herself. And a house cannot be responsible for anything. People create their destiny.

She wondered when Anthony would be home. He had been the one to suggest she left Matt. Now she had to put his idea to the test.

★　　★　　★

Isabel sat at the far end of the kitchen table and watched Byron and Thierry prepare a rabbit pie, Byron chopping onions and shelling broad beans, Thierry expertly disembowelling the carcass. Outside, the sun gilded the garden, and from the sideboard the radio burbled companionably. Occasionally a soft breeze would lift the white muslin curtains, bringing with it a fly or bee that, after a few moments, found its way out again. Byron's dogs lay beside the Aga, apparently content to soak up the extra heat. The atmosphere was homely, peaceful. Even Kitty was relaxed about meat preparation now, using the kitchen work surface to shape biscuits for her birthday party.

Byron had returned half an hour previously from fitting extra locks for the Cousins. He had walked into the kitchen laden with two heavy bags of food. 'I didn't want to charge them anything, but they said most of this was headed for its sell-by date and we should have it.' He placed his haul on the sideboard with the quiet satisfaction of a hunter-gatherer.

'Chocolate biscuits!' Thierry exclaimed, peering in.

'I bags those for the party. *And* the cheese straws. Olive oil! Risotto rice! Crisps!' Kitty fell upon the bags.

When Isabel checked at the dates on the cans of soup and packets of luxury biscuits she saw that they had still several weeks to go. But she recognised that both the Cousins and Byron had gained from the exchange and, filled with pleasure at the prospect of a full larder, she chose not to mention it.

'Oh . . . do you think there'll be enough? I wish we had more money. Then we could do salmon or a hog roast or something.' Suddenly Kitty had flushed. 'Actually – there's lots. It'll probably go further than we think.' She smiled at Isabel, and Isabel, touched by her daughter's sensitivity, smiled back, wishing she could give her a sixteenth-birthday party untainted by lack of money. Now she watched her daughter rolling out pastry, her hair tucked behind her ears, a pink tinge to her skin because she had spent so much time outside. She had not told Kitty what she knew. Thierry would not mention it. She would protect Kitty's memories of her father. It was a birthday gift of sorts.

At the other end of the scarred pine table Byron's dark head was bent low as he listened to Thierry chat about Pepper's latest exploits. Pepper appeared to have acquired superdog skills when he was in the woods with Thierry – able to climb trees, run faster than hares and scent deer from several miles away. Byron listened to these tall tales with an encouraging murmur.

For a moment, she felt a faint ache, watching her son with Byron when his father should have been beside him. But Thierry had opened out again. He was no longer the hunched little boy he had become. She knew she could only be grateful.

On the few occasions she found herself gazing at Byron, she forced herself to concentrate on the figures in the accounting book. He had gently turned down her impulsive advance. He would leave them within weeks. He was a friend. She cursed herself for her own neediness. It would be simplest for everyone, the children especially, if she chose to see him only in those terms.

The call came after lunch. They had decamped outside, and were collapsed in frayed deck-chairs that had been dug out of one of the outhouses and pulled on to the lawn a few feet from the scaffolding. An old golfing umbrella was tilted against a stepladder, affording some shade. Thierry, stretched out on the grass, read aloud from a children's joke book, prompting occasional groans of dismay while they sipped elderflower cordial. Byron heard the phone through the open window and disappeared inside.

'Isabel?' Byron was standing over her. He looked cautiously pleased. 'I've been offered some work near Brancaster. A wood needs coppicing. A man I worked with a few years ago has just bought it and wants it pulled into shape.' He added, 'It's a good rate.'

'Oh,' said Isabel, oddly discomfited. 'How far away is Brancaster?' She shielded her eyes with a hand, trying to see his face more clearly.

'A couple of hours. He wants me to stay over, though. He thinks it'll take the best part of two, maybe three days. There's a lot of work.'

Isabel forced a smile. 'When are you going?'

'Straight away. He wants me there as soon as possible.' She could see his mind was already on the job. Why on earth should she feel misgivings?

'Can I come?' Thierry stood up, the book splayed at his feet.

'Not this time, T.'

'You've got to help us with the party, Thierry,' said Isabel. 'You'll be back for that, Byron? For Kitty's lunch?' She tried to make the question seem casual.

'I'll try, but it'll depend on the work. Kitty, I'll give you a list of some things you can do for your party. I was thinking you could make elderflower sorbet. It'll be easy with the freezer.' He began to scribble instructions and, despite herself, Isabel felt pleased for him. It would have been hard for him to rely on others. The prospect of employment, of being needed, had changed his demeanour.

'You'll be all right? By yourself?' He handed Kitty the piece of paper and glanced at Isabel.

'Oh, I think we'll manage.'

'I meant to say to you. Call the council. Get the building regulations officer over. It's their job to check stuff. Make sure you're happy with what Matt's done.'

She made a face. 'Do I have to think about the house today?' It always came back to the house. 'It's so lovely out . . .'

'It might give you a bit of leverage when you come to talk money with Matt. Look, I'll ring them for you, on my way.'

'Then I'll make you some sandwiches,' she said, standing and brushing down her shorts. 'And something for tonight.'

Byron was already on his way to the house. 'No need,' he said, his hand raised in a goodbye salute. 'I'll have something there. Enjoy your afternoon.'

'I don't understand why you're so shocked.'

Laura's smile wavered. She had picked her moment so carefully, waited until she'd heard Matt leave the house and Anthony had finished his lunch. She had made him fried chicken and potato salad, his favourite, but had little appetite herself.

She had told him gently, presented it not as a *fait accompli* but as an option. A happy accident. Something that would make life better for them both. She had tried not to let her happiness show too obviously, had fiddled with her hair to disguise her blushes when she had said Nicholas's name.

But Anthony was clearly appalled.

When the length of the silence became uncomfortable, she spoke again, rearranging the salt and pepper on the table. 'It was you, Anthony, who told me I should leave him. You urged me to go, remember?'

'I didn't mean you should leave him for someone else.'

She reached towards him where he sat behind the table.

He moved away from her. 'I don't believe this. I just . . . All this time you've been slagging Dad off, you've been shagging someone else.'

'Don't use that word, Anthony. It's . . . ugly.'

'But what you're doing is beautiful, right?'

'You *said*, Anthony. You were the one who said I should leave him.'

'But I didn't mean for someone else.'

'What are you saying, then? That I should stay by myself for ever after?'

He shrugged.

'So it's fine for him to do as he wants, but when I have the chance of genuine happiness, a real relationship, I'm the bad guy?'

He wouldn't look at her.

'Do you know how long I've been alone, Anthony? Even while your father's been living under this roof? Do you know how many times he's been unfaithful to me? How many times I've had to bite my lip walking around the village, knowing I'm probably talking to someone who's just got out of bed with him?' Her sense of injustice was making her say things she knew she shouldn't. But why should she be the one accused?

Anthony brought his gangly legs up to his chest. 'I don't know,' he said. 'It's just . . . I can't get my head round it.'

The clock in the hall chimed. They sat opposite each other for a few minutes, each looking at the table. It was scarred, she saw, running a finger across its surface. She hadn't noticed before.

Finally Laura reached out again. This time he allowed her to take his hand. His mouth was set in a thin line of unhappiness. 'Just meet him, Anthony,' she pleaded, her voice soft. 'He's a good man. A kind man. Give it a chance. Give *me* a chance. Please.'

'So you want me to meet him, and then live with you both in your new house?'

'Well . . . I suppose you could put it like that . . .'

He looked up at her, and in his expression, in the sudden

coldness of his eyes, she saw, for the first time in years, his father.

'Jesus,' he said. 'You're just as bad as he is.'

She had tried for almost forty-five minutes to play the Bruckner, but now her hand dropped to her side. Neither her heart nor her mind was in it. Kitty had disappeared to the village, having received an urgent summons from Anthony, and Thierry was in the woods, from which she could occasionally hear him calling his puppy. Byron had left more than an hour ago.

He had been in their house for only one night. She wasn't sure why his absence had left her so at odds with herself.

She put her violin under her chin again, and rethreaded the Dampit that would humidify the instrument and keep it from cracking. *The Romantic*, this fourth symphony was called. The second movement had been described by the composer as a 'rustic love scene'. She almost laughed at the irony. 'Come on,' she scolded herself. 'Focus.'

But it was no good. The romanticism eluded her. It was the fault of the new violin, which she could not yet bring herself to love. Perhaps it was lack of practice. Isabel sat at her empty kitchen table and stared out at the lawn.

She wasn't sure how long she had been there when she heard the door knocker. She leaped up to answer it. He had changed his mind.

But when she flung open the door, Matt was there, toolbag in hand.

'Oh.' She was unable to hide her disappointment.

His hair stood up on one side, as if it had been slept on, but he seemed calm, less exhausted than when she had last seen him, more like the old Matt. 'I wasn't expecting you today,' she said, embarrassed by the transparency of her reaction.

'Shall I get on, then? Plastering, dining-room skirting-board and the bathroom, if I remember rightly.' He consulted a scrappy piece of paper.

Isabel did not want him there. She did not want the echoes of their night together radiating from him. She would settle up now, if she had to. She had had enough.

He seemed to sense her hesitation. 'You still want the bath-room pipework connected up, right? For Kitty?'

Kitty, she thought, would think it the greatest birthday present ever. A long, luxurious bath in a proper tub. She could buy her some bubbles, lovely bath oil. 'You're really going to do the bathroom? Today?'

'I could have most of it done by this afternoon. Kitty'd love that, wouldn't she?'

'Those three things,' she said, reluctantly, 'and then we'll settle up. I have the money ready for you.'

'Oh, we can talk about that later,' he said, and made his way towards the dining room, whistling as he went. 'Mine's with two sugars. Remember?'

He could relax now that he was here again. Over the last few days when he had stayed away he had felt uncomfort-able – homesick, even. Now, back in the Spanish House, with Isabel making his tea, he was calm. The turmoil that had churned within him had settled. He had slept and eaten, and now he was back where he should be.

He worked his way along the skirting-board in the dining room, attaching each piece, then filling the gaps along the top. They would look good in pale grey, he thought. Perhaps a chalky blue on the walls. It was a south-facing room and could probably cope with the chilly colour.

Downstairs, Isabel was playing her violin, and he stopped what he was doing to listen. He was remembering that night, the sight of her on the landing, the instrument pressed to her shoulder, lost in her music. He had walked towards her, and she had looked at him, and it had been as though she had known he was coming. They hadn't even needed to speak. It had been a meeting of minds. And then of bodies. That wild hair tousled round his face. Those long, elegant fingers clutching him.

The range kettle whistled and the music stopped. He finished the skirting-board and stood back to admire his handiwork. A room never looked finished without good skirting. In the master bedroom he had used the tallest, most expensive moulded pieces available, reflecting the height of the ceiling, the delicacy of the room's dimensions. She hadn't noticed, but it wasn't her fault. She didn't understand buildings, architecture, in the same way that he didn't understand music. You just knew instinctively when something was right. He heard a faint sound outside the room, went to the door and saw, with disappointment, that she had left his tea in the hallway. He had half hoped she would come in and praise what he had done, perhaps talk to him about it. He would have liked to explain to her how important it was that the key elements of a room should speak to each other. People didn't imagine a builder would know about such things.

But she had to work, he reminded himself. She had her music to attend to. It was probably for the best. He took a deep draught from the steaming mug. And she was too much of a distraction. With Isabel in the house, he didn't know how he'd ever complete the job. In fact, faced with the daily prospect of Isabel in the house, he wasn't sure he'd ever want to work again.

Isabel was in the kitchen, where she could hear Matt hammering. He was doing what he had said he would do for once. He seemed calm. When Kitty saw the working bath her face would be a picture of delight. So why did she feel this knot of anxiety?

It's because you haven't played properly for weeks, she told herself. A break from music had always made her almost physically uncomfortable. And it was easy to let your imagination run riot in a house as isolated as this, without constant traffic, doors slamming and passers-by to bring you down to earth. She would focus on the Scherzo and by the time she had it right Matt would have finished and could leave their lives for good. He would be a neighbour to whom she nodded as they passed in the lane, perhaps called upon if they needed any building work. A distant presence.

Matt had briefly abandoned the bathroom to check on the plasterwork repairs in Thierry's room. He let his fingertips run lightly over the pink surface to ensure there were no bumps. The plaster was as cool as alabaster. Around him, Thierry's clothes and toys lay scattered wildly, as if a tornado had passed through. Bits of Lego stuck in pyjama bottoms. Pants, socks, books tossed into corners.

It reminded him briefly of Anthony's when he was little. Matt had built him a wooden garage, a beautiful thing with a working lift and little bollards to mark out parking spaces. But Anthony had refused to play with it, preferring to make things from clay and Plasticine, which Laura had said was 'educational', then treading minuscule pieces into the beige carpet.

He picked up the poster he had taken down to do the plastering, and laid it on the bed. Then he pulled up an old dust-sheet from the floor and went out on to the landing to shake it out and fold it. As he wielded the rough fabric, he could just see through into the master bedroom. The bed was made up.

Matt gazed at the expanse of white linen. She had finally moved into the room he had created for her – for them. Why had she not told him? It was a momentous thing. She was there, in his room.

Downstairs, her music was going better, stopping and starting less often, more fluid. Some long, dreamy passage was flowing up the stairs, and he wondered if it contained a message for him. Music was her way of expressing herself, after all. Matt dropped the dust-sheet on to the floor and went into the bedroom, moving slowly, as if influenced by the tempo of the music. He registered the sunlight, the gleam of unscuffed varnish on the floorboards, the opalescent blue of the sky through the bay windows. It was as beautiful as he had known it would be.

And then his eyes came to rest on the work boots at the foot of the bed. Two large, dirty boots, faded with dried earth, their soles still bearing the imprint of some recent outing.

Men's boots.

Byron's boots.

Matt stared at them, then lifted his head and saw the bags in the corner. The towel slung across the radiator he had fitted. The toothbrush placed neatly on the windowsill. Something in him shut down, and shrank in on itself, leaving nothing but a great black hole, a vacuum, where feeling had been.

Byron and Isabel in the master bedroom. His bedroom.

His bed.

Matt shook his head, twice, as if attempting to clear it. He stood very still. The loud rushing noise he heard was his own breathing. He walked out and across the landing, then went slowly and deliberately down the stairs. Towards the music.

There were so many things she had loved about playing in an orchestra, Isabel thought, as she entered the last bars of the Finale. She knew some musicians who thought of it as a factory floor, and considered the strings section no more than a musical sausage machine, playing to order, following instructions. But she loved the camaraderie, the excitement of building a wall of sound, the way that even the harmony of tuning in front of a good audience could make you catch your breath. And there were the rare moments of inspirational genius that came from a great conductor. If she could escape to it, even a couple of times a month, it would restore something to her. Remind her of who she was outside this house.

It was as she rosined her bow that she heard something. 'Matt?' she called, thinking perhaps she had heard him on the stairs. But there was no reply.

Isabel lifted the violin to her chin again and checked the strings, making minute adjustments to pitch. This violin, she thought absently, could never sound like the Guarneri. Someone else was probably playing that at this very moment, enjoying the rich notes of the G string, the shimmering brilliance of the A. What do I have? she thought, almost laughing. Twelve square metres of reclaimed clay roof tiles and a new septic tank.

She was about to resume playing when she noticed a low thump, steady and repetitive. She stood very still, mentally calculating what she had asked Matt to do. He had completed the skirting. Plastering wasn't noisy. The bathroom, to her knowledge, only had to be fitted. But it continued, *thump, thump, thump,* until a crash and the whisper of plaster dust from the ceiling brought her to the door.

'Matt?'

Nothing. Then again – *thump, thump, thump.* An ominous sound.

'Matt?'

She put her violin on the kitchen table and began to make her way up the steps to the hallway. He was on the first floor. She went upstairs. The sound was easy to make out now – something heavy meeting something solid.

She walked slowly to the master bedroom – and there he was, sweating slightly with the effort, a huge sledgehammer in his fists, rhythmically hitting the wall. A hole some four feet by five showed through to the unfinished bathroom.

Isabel stared at the concentration on his face, his muscular strength as he swung his hammer backwards and over his head. At the great hole in her wall. 'What are you doing?' she said.

He didn't appear to have heard her. He swung again, knocking out several bricks. Chunks of plaster fell over the white bedlinen.

'Matt!' she yelled. 'What are you doing?'

He stopped. His expression was unreadable. His eyes, a bright blue, seemed to pierce her. 'It's no good,' he said, his voice hideously calm. 'It's no good, this room.'

'But it – it's a beautiful room,' she faltered. 'I don't understand.'

'No,' he said, his mouth set. 'You've ruined it. Got to take this out now.'

'Matt, you've spent—'

'Nothing else I can do.'

At that point Isabel knew she was trying to reason with someone who could no longer see reason. She was in her house, alone, with a man holding a sledgehammer. Her mind raced as she tried to work out how to make him stop, whether he would begin on some other room next. A small part of her was gauging the level of threat. Be firm, she told herself. Don't let him know you're afraid.

She glanced out of the window, and saw Thierry coming

across the lawn towards the house. Her heart began to pound. 'Matt!' she called again. 'Matt! Look – you're right,' she said, her hands fluttering upwards. 'You're absolutely right.'

He stared at her, as if this were something he had not expected.

'I need to rethink the whole thing.'

'It's all wrong,' he said.

'Yes. Yes, it is,' she agreed. 'I've made mistakes. Oh, lots of mistakes.'

'I just wanted it to be beautiful,' he said, looking up at the ceiling, with something in his face that gave her hope. She let her eyes slide to the window. Thierry had vanished. He would be heading for the back door.

'We should have a talk,' she said.

'That's all I wanted. To talk to you.'

'I know. But not now. Let's have a think about things, and we'll talk tomorrow, perhaps.'

'Just you and me?' The hole in the wall was a great gash behind him.

'Just you and me,' she agreed. She laid a hand on his arm, half reassuring, half keeping him at a distance. 'But not now, yes?'

His eyes searched hers for the truth. She kept hers steady, her breath stalled in her chest. 'I've got to go, Matt. I must practise. You know . . .'

It was as if she had woken him from a dream. He tore his gaze away from her, rubbed the back of his head, nodded. 'Okay,' he said. He didn't seem to notice the chaos he had created. 'You practise and we'll talk later. You won't forget, will you?' She shook her head, mute.

Then, finally, he walked to the door, the sledgehammer hanging loosely in his hand.

★   ★   ★

Fourteen times she dialled Byron's number, without making the call. How could she? He had been happier than she had ever seen him, with the prospect of paid employment, a cooked supper with an old friend, in a house where he had earned his keep. What could she say to him? I'm afraid? I feel threatened? To explain that, she would have to tell him a little of what had taken place between her and Matt. And she didn't want Byron to know what she had done all those weeks ago. She remembered how his hand had closed over hers the previous evening, and thought about his gentle refusal, which had told her he wanted her no closer. She had no right to ask him for anything.

Several times she had considered calling Laura, but had not because she didn't know what she would say to her. How could she tell a woman whose husband she had slept with that she now felt terrorised by him, that she suspected he was having some kind of breakdown? She could hardly expect a sympathetic response.

Besides, it was possible that Laura knew already. Perhaps she had thrown him out, and thereby sent him over the edge. Perhaps Matt had told her what had taken place between them. It was impossible to know what was going on outside these walls.

She tried to imagine Byron was still under the house. Come back, she told him silently. And then, almost before she knew what she was saying: *Come home.*

That night, Isabel did not allow the children to stay out until dark. She called them in on a pretext – persuaded Kitty to make more biscuits for the party, and Thierry to do some reading aloud. She was cheerful, attentive. She explained away her compulsive checking of window and door bolts by saying Matt had left expensive equipment upstairs and asked her to be extra careful with it.

Finally, when they had gone reluctantly to bed, Isabel waited an hour, then went into her bedroom. From her near-empty jewellery box, she removed a small brass key, which she tucked into her pocket. He had placed it in the loft, well away from curious children. Now she climbed up and, huffing with the effort – the case was made of solid wood – brought it down the rickety ladder and hauled it into the bedroom.

She did not look at the hole in the wall: its significance, its threat, seemed so much greater at night. She unlocked the case, pulled out the gun and loaded it. Pottisworth's hunting rifle, which Byron had found on top of the kitchen cupboard.

She made sure the safety catch was on and checked the sights. Then she walked round the house, double checking the locks, and letting Pepper out of his normal sleeping place in the kitchen so that he could patrol too.

She checked her phone to make sure Byron hadn't called. Then as the light faded, as the birds outside finally grew silent, she sat at the top of the stairs, where she could see the front door, the rifle resting lightly across her knees.

Isabel listened, and waited.

Twenty-two

She woke to the sound of someone whistling. She opened her eyes and lay still, registering with a glance that it was a quarter to seven and Matt was in the bathroom. She could hear the water running, the sound of a shaver on rough skin. Laura remembered that she hadn't bought him any new blades. Matt hated to use a blunt one.

She pushed herself upright, wondering whether he had been in here while she slept. Whether he had noticed the two suitcases. If he had, he wouldn't be whistling.

Laura slid out of bed, padded out of the bedroom and paused at the bathroom door, taking in the now unfamiliar sight of her husband stripped to the waist.

'Hello,' he said, catching sight of her in the mirror. It was an oddly casual greeting, the kind you might make to a neighbour.

She pulled her robe round her and leaned against the door. It was the closest she had been to Matt for several weeks. His body, semi-naked, seemed as familiar as her own, yet alien, as if it were no longer something she was supposed to observe.

She pushed a frond of hair off her forehead. She had rehearsed this conversation so many times. 'Matt, we need to talk.'

His gaze didn't shift from his reflection. 'Haven't got time. Important meeting.' He lifted his chin, the better to examine the stubble beneath it.

She kept her voice level. 'I'm afraid this is important. I need to tell you something.'

'I can't stop. Got to be out of the house in . . .' he consulted his watch '. . . twenty minutes. Max.'

'Matt we—'

He turned round, shaking his head.

'You never listen, do you, Laura? You never actually listen to what I'm telling you. I can't talk to you now. I've got things to do.'

There was something odd in the way he said this, his voice a little too deliberate. But it was impossible to know what was going on in Matt's head. She chose to say nothing. She let out a long, shaking breath. 'Okay. When will you be back?'

He shrugged, still scraping at his chin with the razor.

Is this how it ends? she asked herself. No proper discussion? No fight? No fireworks? Just me scheduling a time to sort out the basics, watching you shave for someone else? Is this me, handling it in my usual ridiculous, ladylike fashion, politely trying to get you to admit that this is the end of our marriage?

The words emerged uncomfortably, as if her throat were swollen. 'We need to resolve this, Matt. What's happening. With us.'

He said nothing.

'Can we talk tonight? Are you coming back here?'

'Probably not.'

'Can you tell me where you will be? At the Spanish House, perhaps?' She was unable to keep the anguished note from her voice.

He brushed past her and was gone, back down the hallway, as if she were of no more importance than the milkman. Laura listened to him whistling and closed her eyes. When she opened them, she saw that the soft white towel, which he had jammed back on to the rail, was streaked with blood.

'Napkins. You need napkins. Unless you have those lovely damask ones.'

'Do we really if we're going to be sitting outside?'

Henry indicated left and pulled the car into the nearside lane. Kitty sat in the back and scribbled another entry on her lengthening list. She had never held a party before. She hadn't known quite how much organisation it would take.

'We used to have some proper ones,' she said, 'but they disappeared in the move.'

'And my roller skates,' said Thierry, beside her. 'We never found them either.'

'You'll find the napkins in two years' time. Probably just after you've bought new ones. They'll be in a cardboard box somewhere,' Henry said.

'I don't want to wait two years for my skates.' Thierry lifted his foot so that it rested against the back of Henry's seat. 'They'll be too small. Is there going to be breakfast when we get there?'

She hadn't intended to bring Thierry, but when she'd got downstairs, she'd found her mother asleep on the sofa, still wearing the previous day's clothes. She had probably been up all night, practising. It wouldn't be the first time. If she had left Thierry and Pepper behind, she reasoned, Mum would have been awake within five minutes and she'd looked as if she could do with a rest.

'Cola. All the young people drink cola. They have good deals at the cash-and-carry,' Henry mused. 'And fruit juice. You could mix it with sparkling water.'

'I don't think I can stretch to fruit juice. I'm going to make more elderflower.'

Asad was humming along with the car stereo, one hand tapping a rhythm on the dashboard. 'Ice cubes,' he said. 'A big bag. You still have no fridge, so you can borrow our cool box to put them in.'

'And who's going to carry them?' Henry enquired. 'They weigh a ton.'

'We will,' said Thierry. 'I've grown an inch and a half in six weeks. Mum marked it on the door.'

'You need to set yourself a budget,' said Henry. 'You'll find your money will go a lot further here but you're still trying to feed a lot of people. How much have you got?'

'Eighty-two pounds,' she said. It would have been sixty-two but her French grandmother had sent her a birthday cheque that morning.

'Barbecue,' said Henry. 'What do you think, Asad?'

'Too expensive. Just hot dogs,' he said. 'And lots of lovely rice and pasta salads for the vegetarians. I can do those for you. Is your mother still doing berries for pudding?'

It was going to be the best party ever, Kitty thought. Nearly everyone from her class was coming. When she had told them about the lake, they had been really excited. One of Anthony's friends was going to bring a blow-up dinghy, and Anthony had a Lilo. 'We've got some old bunting in the store room,' said Henry. 'We could drape that around, disguise the scaffolding.'

'It's so long since we cleared out that store room it's probably marked "Silver Jubilee",' said Asad.

'And tea lights,' said Henry, 'leading down to the lake for when it gets dark. We could put them in old jam-jars. You can get a hundred for a couple of pounds.'

It had taken a while, but Kitty, sitting in the car with the two men chatting in front, decided she no longer felt homesick. Six months ago, if someone had told her they would still be here, that her idea of fun would be visiting a cash-and-carry with two elderly gay men, she would have cried for a week. Now she thought she probably didn't want to go back to London. She missed Dad still – she didn't think there would ever be a time when she thought about him and didn't get a lump in the back of her throat – but perhaps Mum had been right. Perhaps it really had been better to make a fresh start here, away from all the reminders of him.

'Some kind of syllabub or fool. Strawberry or gooseberry.'

'How do you make a gooseberry fool?' said Asad.

'Put her in a car with two old queens, eejit,' said Henry, and burst out laughing as the children stared blankly from the back seat.

'But what exactly did he say?' He clamped his phone between ear and shoulder. 'Hang on, I'm going to pull over on to the hard shoulder.' He gestured an apology to the driver he had inadvertently cut up, ignoring the bad-tempered blast of a horn.

'What was that noise? Where are you?'

Laura had told him she was at the bottom of the garden. He could picture her there, her hair lifting in the breeze, a hand pressed over her other ear. 'I'm on the motorway, junction twelve.'

'But Matt's here,' she whispered.

'I'm not coming to see you,' he said, glancing into his mirror. God, there was a lot of traffic this morning. 'Much as I'd love to.'

'You're going to speak to her today?'

Nicholas braked to allow someone to change lane, then slid to a halt on the hard shoulder, leaving his engine running. 'I can't wait any longer, Laura. The money's in place . . . Laura?'

'Yes?'

The length of her silence had unnerved him. 'Are you all right?'

'I suppose so. It's just . . . odd. An odd feeling. That it's all finally going to happen.'

His car shook as a lorry roared past. 'Look, change is always . . .'

'I know.'

'I understand, Laura. Really. I've been through it myself.'

She hesitated a little too long.

'You still want that house? Is that it?'

'It's not—'

'I'll scrap the Spanish House development.'

'What?'

It had left his mouth before he realised what he'd said. 'I'll scrap it,' he repeated, 'if you really want that house.'

'But that's your great project. How would you move on without it? You told me—'

'I'll manage.'

'But all those plans. Your backers—'

'Laura! Listen to me!' He was shouting into the phone now, trying to make himself heard above the noise of the motorway. 'If you really want that house, I'll make sure you have it. We can still turn it into the home of your dreams.'

This time her silence was of a different tenor. 'You'd do that for me?'

'Do you need to ask?'

'Oh, Nicholas.' There was gratitude in her voice, but he wasn't sure what she was thanking him for.

They were silent for a few moments.

'He may be there, you know. You won't say anything, will you?'

'About us?'

'I think it should come from me.'

'You mean I'm not allowed to say, "Mr McCarthy, I've been sleeping with your wife. And, incidentally, she has a bottom like a fresh peach."'

She couldn't help laughing. 'Please,' she said. 'Let me tell him later.'

'Your husband, Laura, is a fool, and I'd be delighted to tell him as much. But at a time of your choosing. Look, I've got to go. I'll ring you after I've spoken to the Delancey woman.' He cancelled the call and sat there as the traffic rushed by, hoping she hadn't meant he must make the choice he had promised.

Matt pulled the little leather box from his inside pocket, and opened it, allowing the ruby ring with the seed pearls to glint in the sunlight. It had been so easy to spot what had been hers. 'Nice ring,' the jeweller had said. 'Victorian. Unusual.' It had glowed in the little shop, stood out from other jewels. Like she did.

Matt suspected he had been charged twice what Isabel would have received for it, but he didn't care. He wanted to see her face when she opened the box. He wanted to see her gratitude when she saw what he'd done for her.

What did the money matter now? He and Laura had had money sitting in the bank for years, and what good had it done them? He had not yet managed to convey to Isabel how he felt. The ring would prove to her that he understood what she wanted and what she had lost. He liked the fact that no one else knew about her ring but him. A ruby: the colour of passion, of desire, of sex. Holding it had felt like holding part of her.

He was about to drive his van out of the woods and on to her driveway when he saw another car pull up. A man in a suit got out.

Matt watched him glance up at the house. Some old friend,

perhaps. Or an official. His sense of anticipation evaporated. He had wanted to pick his moment carefully, make sure the children weren't there. It would only work if the two of them were alone.

He put the ring back into his pocket. He was a patient man. He had all the time in the world.

'Yes?'

For a moment he was stumped. He had knocked on the door for nearly ten minutes, then decided that nobody was in so had taken a few steps back to get a comprehensive view of the house that had occupied his thoughts for so many weeks.

There was a large crack running from the upper window diagonally downwards – subsidence or heave, which was perhaps not surprising when the house bordered a lake and woods. A new window had been poorly fitted, daylight visible in the gap between wood and brick where no one had filled it. A piece of pale blue plastic flapped listlessly over the glass. The roof was unfinished, plastic guttering unfixed. The walls were partially clad in scaffolding for which he could see no obvious purpose.

He took another step back. An assortment of mismatched and ramshackle garden furniture stood on the lawn, but even that could not detract from the beauty of the setting. The lake made up for everything. This beautiful, peaceful place had an atmosphere he had rarely encountered, the kind of ambience one expected to find around a Scottish loch or somewhere much further out in the wilds. This part of Norfolk was commutable – Mike Todd had told him so. *Work in London and live in the heart of the countryside.* He could almost see the glossy brochure now. Perhaps he and Laura would take one of the houses – there was something so seductive about the place.

And then he saw her: a tousled woman in a crumpled linen shirt, squinting at him. 'Yes?'

For a moment he forgot what he wanted to say. He had had his opening prepared for so long and her unexpected appearance had wrongfooted him. This was the woman who had caused Laura such unhappiness.

'I'm so sorry to disturb you,' he said, striding forward and extending a hand. She allowed him to shake hers. 'Perhaps I should have rung first. I've come about the house.'

'Oh. Gosh. That was fast,' she said. 'What time is it?'

He pulled back his cuff. 'A quarter to ten.'

This appeared to surprise her. When she spoke it was to herself. 'I don't even remember dropping off . . . Look, I need to make a cup of coffee. Would you like one?'

He followed her in. She walked a couple of paces ahead of him into the kitchen. He tried to suppress his instinctive dislike. He was not sure what he had expected – someone less chaotic-looking perhaps, someone a little more calculated.

'In here,' she muttered. 'Do sit down. This may sound a silly question, but have you seen any children around?'

The kitchen was badly in need of updating. It had not been touched for decades. Nicholas gazed at the cracked linoleum, the faded paintwork, which had been decorated with odd photographs, dried flowers and a piece of painted clay – an attempt to bring domesticity into an environment that, frankly, he would have considered uninhabitable. Around the outside of the house, visible through the windows, fruit and vegetables hung in orange nets in the shade of the eaves, like multicoloured teardrops.

She ran water into the kettle and placed it on the stove, then opened the larder, reached in and sniffed at a carton of milk. Still okay. Just. 'We have no fridge.'

'I'll take mine black, thank you,' Nicholas said stiffly.

'Probably sensible,' she conceded, placing the carton back inside. She handed him the coffee, then picked up on his surprise at their surroundings. 'This is the only room that hasn't been touched. I don't suppose it's any different from when my great-uncle lived here. Do you want to take a look round?'

'You don't mind?'

'I guess you'll need to see everything.'

Who could have told her he was coming? He had thought she might be defensive, suspicious, even, but she seemed to be anticipating whatever he had to say.

She picked up a piece of paper from the table, and studied its scribbled contents for a minute. Then she glanced out of the window at the lake. 'Do go ahead,' she said, taking a swig of coffee. 'I'll follow you up in a minute. I need to pull my head together.' She smiled apologetically and gestured to some steps. 'It's all right. There's no one here to disturb.'

He didn't need telling again. Nicholas took his mug and went to re-examine the house that would be his future.

It was almost twenty minutes before she reappeared. She had changed into different clothes, a fresh T-shirt and loose skirt, and had tied her hair back.

He glanced up from his notes. From the landing, he had been staring in through the door of what must be the master bedroom. 'Are you knocking these rooms through?' he asked. Rubble and plaster dust lay on the bedlinen.

'That,' she said carefully, 'is a long story. But no. We won't be knocking through.'

'You need to repair that hole quickly, or get someone to fit an RSJ. It's a major gap in a load-bearing wall.' He inspected a crack in the corner, but when he turned back to her she was peering out of the window. 'Mrs Delancey?'

'Yes? I'm so sorry. I . . . haven't slept much. Perhaps we should discuss all this later.'

'Do you mind if we go outside? I've seen everything I need inside.'

He had certainly seen enough to clarify his thoughts. Laura's husband was a cowboy. The house was a bizarre mixture of high-quality craftsmanship and demolition job, as if two separate tradesmen had carried out the work, almost in opposition to each other. What was clear, however, was that repairing the house would be a greater challenge than even Laura could have imagined. When he had last come here, it had seemed merely tired, a series of jobs that needed doing. What he had seen today had confirmed his belief that the best thing for this building would be to bring it down and start again. But how to put that to Laura?

He followed her downstairs and out into the sunshine. The sun was hot and he regretted wearing a jacket almost as soon as they set foot outside. He followed her to the scaffolding, swatting vainly at flies.

'That chimney is going to be capped,' she said, pointing. 'At least, I think it's that one. And there's a new drainage pipe under here . . . or it might be there . . .' She listed some other works, most of which were impossible to quantify.

He felt sudden pity for her. Her house was being brought down around her ears, and she was sitting in the midst of it all, apparently unaware of what was going on.

'So, what do you think?' she said, perhaps catching his solemn expression.

'Mrs Delancey,' he began, 'I . . .' He was lost for words.

They stared at the cracked brickwork, the piles of rubble and bags of cement.

She regarded him carefully. 'You think it's awful, don't you?' She didn't wait for him to reply. 'Oh, God, I do know

it's a mess. I suppose . . . I suppose when you live with it
you stop seeing quite what a disaster it all is.'

She looked crushed, and Nicholas fought the urge to
comfort her. He could see in her then what had captivated
Laura's husband. She was a girl-woman, whose air of vulnerability demanded that he protect her. Inadvertently she would
bestow on any man the sheen of a suit of armour.

'So, what should I do?' She had painted on a brave smile.

'I suppose,' he said, 'it might be helpful if I outlined what
I thought was wrong. If you really want me to.'

'Yes,' she said firmly. 'I need to know.'

'Okay. Let's start with the roof . . .'

Matt watched through his windscreen as the man showed
Isabel his notebook, then pointed past the scaffolding at the
back of the house to the point where the ridge tiles met
the chimney stack. At first he had thought he might be a
musician, then perhaps a teacher – there were so few men
round here who wore suits – but now he was apparently
discussing Matt's house, Matt's work. And from the shaking
of his head, and Isabel's tense expression, what he was saying
was not complimentary.

Matt placed the little jewel box in his pocket and climbed
out of the van. He closed the door quietly and walked closer,
taking care to remain partially hidden by the trees. It was no
one from the council. He knew almost everyone in the
building regulations department. This man was well spoken,
unfamiliar. A touch of bookishness about him, like a professor.

'Structurally, something has become weakened here,' the
man was saying, gesturing at the wall. 'We haven't had a particularly dry summer, or a wet winter, and the crack looks fairly
new so I assume that it was caused by the building work.'

'The building work?' Isabel's voice was shocked.

'I'm afraid so. Has there been much knocking around inside? It looks like it's taken a bashing.'

She half laughed, a mirthless sound. 'Well, you've seen it all. So much has gone on inside, and I wasn't always keeping track.'

Matt's heart beat an uncomfortably vigorous tattoo. What the hell was the man trying to do?

'I can't say much about the drainage and sewage, but obviously the bathroom's unfinished. The kitchen is completely unmodernised. But these are cosmetic. The master bedroom is the only room that appears to have been renovated to any kind of standard, but there you have the damaged wall . . . There's evidence of damp, and possibly dry rot in the east wing. I took the liberty of removing a piece of skirting-board and I'm afraid it warrants further investigation. I suspect death-watch beetle under the stairs. And you only seem to have half of a hot-water system – some of the pipework is incomprehensible in its layout.'

'Are you saying all this is because of our builder?'

The man in the suit seemed to consider his response. He tucked his notepad under his arm. 'No. I think the house was in a terrible state to begin with. But it's still in a terrible state, and your builder may, purposely or otherwise, have worsened that.'

Isabel's eyes widened. 'Purposely?' she repeated.

Matt could take no more. He burst out of the woods and strode towards the man. 'What the hell are you telling her? Who the hell are you?' he shouted. 'What lies are you telling her?'

He felt Isabel's hand on his arm. 'Matt, please—' She grimaced at the tall man, who didn't notice.

He was looking at Matt as though he was sizing him up. As though he were superior to him. 'You're Matt McCarthy?'

'Who the fuck are you?'

The man didn't answer, just stared at him, which enraged Matt even more. 'What do you think you're doing coming here and telling Isabel lies? Eh? I heard you! I heard every bloody lie! You don't know anything about this house or what I've done here! Anything!'

The man didn't seem frightened of him. Instead he looked at Matt with unmistakable contempt. 'I've been telling Mrs Delancey the truth about what has been done to this house. And I can tell you, Mr McCarthy, that I heard tales of what you'd done here long before I saw it.'

'Tales of what he'd done here?' Isabel echoed. 'What do you mean?'

A mist descended and Matt was yelling now, roaring. He flailed, preparing to take a swing at the pompous, besuited intruder. 'You think you know, do you? You think you know about this house?'

Isabel was pleading with him to calm down, he could smell her faint perfume as she tried to pull him back – but even that could not stop him.

Laura was in the garden, deadheading roses, when she heard Matt raging, a harsh, ugly sound. Then another man's voice, calmer. And a woman's cry, tinged with fear. Laura's stomach churned. Nicholas had told him.

'Mum?' Anthony's face, still bleary with sleep, appeared at the window. 'What's going on?'

Laura looked blankly at him. Then she dropped her secateurs and, with the dog following her, walked and then began to run towards the Spanish House.

The Delancey woman was standing between them, braced, as if waiting for another blow. Nicholas's handkerchief was pressed to his nose. Blood was trickling down his face and spattering his pale blue shirt. Matt was bellowing at him, his mouth almost frothing, his speech all but incomprehensible. Around them, the bucolic scenery threw the ugliness of their actions, their voices, into sharp relief. Oh, Lord, Laura thought. What have I done?

'You're not wanted here!' Matt howled. 'Now, go away before I really hurt you!'

'Matt?'

He stepped back as Laura approached, turned to face her.

'Oh, God, I'm so sorry,' she said. 'I didn't want you to find out like this.'

Her husband was unrecognisable as the cool, distant figure of this morning: he was wild-eyed and radiated a kind of loose energy. 'What the hell are you talking about?' he said.

'Laura, don't—' Nicholas began.

But Isabel Delancey interrupted. 'Is this true? What he said?' she asked Matt. 'That all this time you wanted the house for yourself? Is that why you've been purposely damaging it?'

It was the first time Laura had ever seen Matt look truly shaken.

'No,' he protested. 'No – it wasn't like that. I wanted the house to be beautiful.'

'Huh! You've knocked it to pieces,' said Nicholas, indignantly. 'You've made a complete dog's dinner of it.'

'I was renovating it!'

'There's virtually nothing left to renovate! I don't know how the ruddy place is still standing!'

'All this time?' Isabel's voice resonated with shock. 'Your jokes and your advice and your help and your bags of croissants . . . and all the time you just wanted us gone?'

Matt had paled. 'No, Isabel.' Laura flinched as her husband stepped towards the woman. 'No . . . it wasn't like that. Not by the end.' He cast around, as if seeking evidence. 'The master bedroom was a labour of love. There is truth, beauty in that room. You saw the effort I put into it.'

'How can you say that? You knocked a great hole in it! Like a madman!' She mimed it for them. 'I couldn't stop you.'

'But that was because of Byron,' he yelled. 'Byron shouldn't be in that room.'

Laura struggled to understand. None of this made any sense.

'Okay,' Nicholas interrupted. 'Let's move this on.' He had recovered his composure. He mopped his lip with the bloodied handkerchief. 'This is obviously an unusual situation. I would suggest, Mrs Delancey, that you work out what you're going to do about the house as a matter of urgency.'

'But we have nothing left. He's taken all our money.'

'It wasn't just me,' Matt pleaded. 'I wasn't straight with you at the beginning, but I did my best to put it right.'

'Mrs Delancey, I suggest—'

'Don't listen to him, Isabel. Everything I've done wrong I'll put right. Haven't I always looked after you?'

There was a long silence. Laura was staring at Isabel, whose expression was of despair.

'You have ruined us,' she said quietly. 'I trusted you and you have ruined this house.'

Almost before she knew what she was doing Laura stepped forward. 'I will sort it out.' Her voice cut into the air. 'I will pay for whatever damage Matt has done. I will personally cover whatever it takes to put it right.' She could not bring herself to apologise to the woman, but she would not be indebted to her either.

'There is an alternative,' Nicholas interrupted. 'You might consider selling it to me. The condition of the house, such as it is, is not an issue for me.'

'Selling it?' Isabel Delancey frowned.

'Yes,' he said. 'I'd be glad of the chance to talk to you about it.'

'But why would the council want to buy this house?' She seemed nonplussed.

'The council?'

Nobody spoke. Then she said, 'You mean Byron didn't ring you?'

'Who is Byron?' Nicholas asked blankly. 'My name is Nicholas Trent. I'm a property developer.'

Isabel Delancey stared at him. 'A property developer? So you came here today because you wanted this house.' Suddenly realisation dawned. 'Oh, my God – you *all* want this house.' She backed away from them, her hands over her mouth. 'All this time . . .' she said, almost laughing now. 'Is there anybody else? Someone in the village, perhaps? The Cousins? The milkman? All this time you all wanted the house!'

'Actually, no,' Laura said slowly, looking at Matt. And then, with certainty, 'I don't want it any more.'

Matt spun round. She saw him take in what she had said, saw his frown of incomprehension as Nicholas smiled at her, a smile filled with history. She saw Matt recall her apology, Nicholas's use of her name. Her husband looked at her and, unable to meet the intensity of his gaze, she turned away. Anthony, behind her, was staring at Nicholas, his face unreadable.

This is it, thought Laura. There is no going back.

'Here is my card,' said Nicholas, urbanely, pulling one from his inside pocket and handing it to Isabel Delancey as he moved closer to Laura. 'I appreciate that this has been an odd morning. But have a think about what I've said, Mrs Delancey. I'm sure we could come to a mutually beneficial arrangement.'

Twenty-three

The slender hazel switches were no more than seven years old – you could use them as hurdles or thatching spars; he would save the older, sturdier ones for walking-sticks or hedge stakes. He had gathered a small pile of sweet chestnut, for cleft rails and stakes, but the returns on hazel coppicing were higher, and Byron had agreed to restore this ancient woodland almost entirely to hazel. He trod carefully, examining young shoots for signs of vermin. People thought all he was doing was cutting things down, destroying them, but native hardwood trees and shrubs that were cut in this way could produce shoots that grew over a foot in a week. A coppiced tree would live many times longer than one that hadn't been cut back. Byron was sure there was a life lesson in that, but he was damned if he could see it.

He moved, surefooted, through the trees with another armful, to where the woodland opened on to the road. People often went back to the old ways, and it was no different with coppicing. Big money in garden furniture, Frank had said earlier that morning, observing Byron working. Or rustic fencing. They loved that in the garden centres now. Any leftovers you could use for charcoal. There were grants available to pay for restoring coppice woodland. All the wildlife trusts were pushing landowners to do it.

Occasionally, he thought of Matt, and tension crept into his neck and shoulders, his jaw clenched, and he would have to breathe deeply. Matt McCarthy had almost driven him away from his home, almost driven Isabel from hers. He had wondered several times whether to tell her about the rat, about Matt's ruthlessness when it came to getting what he wanted. But she had been so happy the previous day, as if she were finally daring to believe in something good. He hadn't wanted to spoil it for her. His mobile rang.

'It's Isabel.'

'Hi,' he said, unable to disguise his pleasure at hearing her voice. And then again, trying to moderate it, 'Hi.'

'I wondered how it was going. Your work, I mean.' She paused. 'Thierry asked me to ring.'

'Doing well.' He glanced at the area of brambles he had cleared. 'Hard work, but . . . good.' His hands were criss-crossed with scratches.

'Yes.'

'It's nice up here. Near the sea. Feels more like a holiday than work.'

'I'm sure.'

'And Frank, the owner, he's been great. He's offered me more work.'

'Oh . . . Wonderful.'

'Yeah. I was pleased. How's it going with you?'

It was then that he realised she sounded strained. He had watched three cars go by before she spoke again.

'I didn't know whether to tell you this but we – we've had a bit of a scene. A man came, some kind of property developer, who wants to buy the house. Matt turned up unexpectedly and picked a fight with him.'

'Are you okay?'

'Yes, we're fine. The developer man took a punch, but then Laura turned up and it cooled down.' Then she added quietly, 'Byron, I think Matt's having some kind of breakdown.'

'Matt *McCarthy*?'

'He – he's not himself.'

Byron said nothing.

'In fact, he seems almost . . . disturbed.'

I bet he does, thought Byron, bitterly. The idea of someone else taking that house from him. 'Don't worry about him,' he said, more harshly than he intended. 'He'll always look after himself.'

She sighed. 'That's pretty well what the man said.'

He began to walk slowly along the edge of the wood, now oblivious to his surroundings. 'What did you say to the developer?'

'I didn't know what to say. I don't know what to think any more. He told me . . . that Matt has been damaging the house, trying to get me out.'

Byron closed his eyes.

'After you'd gone he knocked a big hole in the bedroom wall. The one you've been staying in.'

His chest felt tight. He shouldn't have left them. He should have warned her, made her listen. He should have stopped Matt. He was crushed by guilt, by the weight of things left unsaid.

'Byron, I don't know what to do.'

'Do you have to do anything?' he said. 'You don't have to decide right now.'

'I can't live like this any more.'

It was in her voice. She had made up her mind. 'You're going to sell the house,' he said.

'What do you think I should do?'

He didn't know how to respond. He had stood by while Matt plunged her into this mess. He would always owe her, even if she chose not to see it. And what could he offer? To come back and chop logs? Skin rabbits? Live under her roof?

If he did, he could never be on equal terms with her, could never give her anything but gratitude.

He swallowed hard. 'Well, I suppose it's sensible to get out before winter comes.'

There was a lengthy pause.

'Oh.'

'If that's what you think you should do.'

'I suppose you're right.' She coughed. 'How long do you think you'll be gone?'

'I don't know. Look – I was going to tell you this when I got back, but Frank thinks he might have a job for me.'

'There? A full-time job?'

The grant was enough for a man's wages, Frank had said. And there was other work besides the woodland. Byron had reminded him of his criminal record. 'That stop you wielding a saw, does it?' he said drily.

'There's a decent mobile home I can stay in. He's talking six months at least. It's a good offer.'

'I guess it is. You know . . . you could always stay with us. For as long as you want. Don't feel you have to rush off.'

'I need to support myself, Isabel. Jobs like this don't come every day.' He kicked a pebble. 'And if you're going to be moving anyway . . .'

There was another pause.

'You're definitely going to take it?'

'I think so. I can still pop by and see you all. Take Thierry out at weekends. If you want me to.' He tried to read the silence.

'Well, I'm sure he'd love to see you.'

Byron sat down on a tree stump near the flint wall that ran along the coast road. The air was tinged with salt from the sea; his eyes were suddenly sore with it.

'Will you make it back for Kitty's party?'

'I've got a fair bit to get through but I'll do my best.'

The phone went dead.

Byron took his axe and, with a grunt of fury, hurled it into the middle of the field.

Isabel put down the phone. Downstairs the children had returned from their shopping trip and had been making decorations. Now they ran on to the lawn, trailing lengths of bunting, laughing as Pepper raced off with trails of it in the gold of the setting sun.

They could be happy again, were lighter even than they had been in London. For them, an irresponsible decision had become a good one. But Isabel could not stay so close to Matt and Laura now that she knew every glance they sent towards the house was covetous, that her family's presence there would always be tainted with what the McCarthys believed they had lost.

And Matt's touch had permeated everything. The few bits of the house that the Delanceys had claimed for themselves no longer felt like theirs.

It needn't be so bad, she told herself. They could move somewhere close by so that Kitty and Thierry could remain at their schools. She could downsize to a cottage in one of the villages. It would be nice to live without debt, without having to scrabble in the earth for their food. Sometimes she wanted to laugh when she told people her address, and watched them reassess her, sometimes becoming almost deferential. Status came with living in the big house. Would you still be so nice to me if you watched me sorting weeds for the children's tea? she asked them silently. If you saw my daughter selling eggs so that we can pay the electricity bill? In a new, smaller house, growing vegetables might be a pleasant diversion rather than a necessity. She would never again have to look at a piece of plasterboard.

Isabel watched Thierry scale a tree to tie bunting from a branch. He would find leaving this place hard; the lack of a bathroom had been no great hardship to him, but to lose the freedom of the woods and Byron's friendship would be a different matter.

Perhaps Byron would still visit, although she wasn't sure. He had sounded different, now that he no longer needed them, more confident, distant, as if he had already grown away from them. Please don't hurt my son, she willed him, and ignored the possibility that she might be talking about herself.

She turned and looked at the hole in the master-bedroom wall, an ugly cavity. That great piece of nothing had frightened her more than almost anything else that had happened in the house. Its symbolism overwhelmed her, the prospect of a future with nothing, a gap where her family and security had once been.

'Oh, for God's sake, it's just a house – a bloody house,' Isabel said, into the empty room, hearing her voice bounce off the varnished floorboards. It was time to pull herself together. It was not their house. If she was honest with herself, it never had been.

She hauled a large piece of plasterboard across the gap between the bedroom and the bathroom until it all but covered the hole. She fetched a drill from downstairs and screwed it neatly into place. Then she found an old framed print, a line drawing of José Carreras taken from some Spanish music festival, and propped it against the wall, covering the space. On the bathroom side, she tacked an old white sheet, draping it softly to suggest that there might be something beautiful behind it.

She would ring the developer and ask him his best price, then call on the local agents for second and third opinions. They would live somewhere ordinary, and their time at the Spanish House would have been a strange interlude in their lives. And she would make sure their last weeks here were perfect. Kitty's sixteenth-birthday party would be magical. It was a good decision. A sensible one.

Isabel surveyed her work with something close to satisfaction. Then she walked lightly downstairs to the kitchen, to the DIY books she had borrowed some weeks ago from Long Barton's understocked library. She had a bath to install.

A short distance away, in her garage, Laura was also making decisions about her future. She had come for the large suitcase, but had been diverted by the unexpected chaos of Matt's spare tools and had found herself tidying them. It might have been force of habit. It might have been that some part of her could not leave the house without it being in good order.

She pushed a pressure washer into the corner, and rolled two empty gas canisters out of the way of the desk that Mr Pottisworth had promised them. She gathered up the rubbish and put it into a wheelbarrow, ready for burning. Laura knew that the most effective way to ease mental chaos was with domestic activity. It took her almost two hours to clear up the worst. Then she broke off to appreciate the neatly stacked shelves, the cans of paint labelled with the rooms they had decorated in case anything needed touching up. Matt, of course, wasn't around. He had walked away, ignoring her calls, and even Anthony, angry as he was with her, had been too cautious to follow him.

'Give him time before you speak to him,' Nicholas had

said. His handkerchief was almost completely sodden with blood, even though his nose was barely bruised. 'He's got a lot to take in.'

She had not attempted to call him. She had learned weeks ago that Matt no longer answered his phone.

Nicholas had left an hour earlier. They had sat in the car in the lane, and he had told her how proud he was of her. He told her how their life would be, the happiness that lay ahead. The house would be their fortune.

'Nicholas?' She focused on her hands, folded neatly in her lap. 'You didn't use me, did you, to get the inside on all this?'

He had been horrified. They stared at each other, and in that moment she saw the suspicion, the mutual deceit and mistrust that had landed them where they were. She saw a house of pain.

'You are the one honest thing I've done in my whole life,' he said.

Laura removed her rubber gloves, wiped her hands on a paper towel and walked out of the garage. She was not ready to go into the house. There, she would be reminded of everything she was about to leave, the family she was about to fracture for ever, the vows she was about to break. Silly things preoccupied her: what would she do about her family paintings? The silver that had belonged to her aunt? Would she take the most precious items with her tomorrow, in case Matt damaged them in a fit of temper? What would Nicholas think if she turned up with several cases of family heirlooms? Would removing them be an inflammatory act in itself? Matt had seemed so unlike himself. He had been so cool, so distant, when he had been doing the leaving. Now he knew that she had someone else she could not anticipate his reaction. And what would her family think? She wanted to ask Nicholas where they would live until their new home was supposedly ready, but too many questions about his house would make her sound picky, as if he himself wasn't enough for her. She hadn't even visited his London home. What if she hated it? What if she found she couldn't live in London? And what on earth would she do with Bernie? He was too old to adapt to London life, but Matt couldn't be expected to look after him. He was hardly ever at home. Should she have Bernie put down to satisfy the demands of her love life? What kind of person would that make her? When Nicholas had asked her to come and live with him, she had suspected it had felt, to him, like some grand romantic gesture. It had felt that way to her too. But if you were a nearly-forty-year-old mother with a home, a dog, school runs and a position on the village-hall committee, extricating yourself from your life wasn't just a matter of walking out of the door with a suitcase.

And as she worried over this, she found herself thinking, bitterly, This is why Matt no longer finds me attractive. Because I never could give in to passion. I am always going to be the person who hangs back, worrying about whether someone has fed the poor old dog.

Laura went back into the garage. She sorted the recycling boxes. She swept the garage floor and then her eyes settled on Mr Pottisworth's bureau. It was a tired old piece of furniture, faded walnut, with chipped veneer and handles that appeared to be far from original. She would treat it for worm, polish it and bring it inside. It would enable her to remove her own writing desk – the one her parents had given her on her eighteenth birthday – with less guilt. Matt wasn't interested in furniture anyway, unless it was too soft or not soft enough.

She pulled on her rubber gloves and scanned the shelves. Then, for the best part of an hour, with the thoroughness

for which she was renowned among her friends and neighbours, Laura dismantled the Victorian bureau, carefully
removing one drawer at a time, sponging it clean, then
painting it slowly with woodworm treatment to ensure it was
saturated, reaching far back into it. It was as she pulled out
the last drawer, turning it over and laying it on top of the
desk, that she saw it. Two pieces of paper, folded several
times and taped haphazardly to the bottom.

Laura removed her gloves and closed the anti-woodworm
treatment can, taking care not to let the noxious liquid spill
on to her fingers. She peeled the tape slowly from the edges
and unfolded the documents, squinting to read them in the
dim light of the garage.

Laura read the first once, then again, checking the official
stamp, the unfamiliar solicitor's address. Then she read it
again, in duplicate. She glanced at the bonfire. Lastly she read
the addition, scrawled at some later date in blue ballpoint
pen. Mr Pottisworth's writing – as spiky and unreadable as
he had been.

> *Let's see how much of a lady you really are, Mrs M.*
> *Noblesse oblige, eh?*

Twenty-four

One drill, one workman's bench, one holdall with assorted metal tools that weighed almost too much for one person to lift – a jigsaw, an electric saw, two spirit levels and a tape measure. A pad, its pages indented with scrawled figures, a transistor radio, batteries missing, and one sweatshirt, its faint scent an uncomfortable reminder of something she would have preferred to forget. Isabel moved the last of these items into the hallway and wiped her dusty hands on her shorts. She would have no trace of him in this house. When the party was over she would move the items into one of the outhouses and leave a message with his wife that he could come and collect them from there.

One large ham on a wooden board, eight French sticks, a cheese platter, two silver-foil trays of mixed fruit. A cardboard box containing the ingredients for several salads, two carefully sealed boxes of marinated meat and fish, two large bowls of rice and pasta salad. One crate of assorted fruit juices, two bottles of champagne.

'Oh, my God,' breathed Kitty, as the Cousins unloaded their car. 'Is that all for us?'

'Hang on to your best compliments, sweetheart. You haven't seen the *pièce de résistance*,' said Henry. He reached in and, from the back shelf, carefully brought out a square silver base with a vast cake. A marzipan figure with bobbed hair stood in the centre, distributing silver candy balls to little hens. 'Happy birthday, poppet.' He beamed.

'That,' breathed Kitty, 'is *ace*.'

'Would that be a young person's vernacular lingo?'

'I do believe she likes it,' said Asad.

'I can't believe you've done this for me!'

'Well,' said Henry, walking carefully across the lawn towards the trestle table, 'everyone should have a really good sixteenth birthday party. It's all downhill from here, you know.'

Two smart outfits, two pairs of jeans, a cocktail dress and several sets of brand-new La Perla lingerie, some sensible chain-store knickers for everyday. Boots, shoes, running shoes, a silk nightdress and a new pair of pyjamas. A washbag, a hairdryer with nozzle attachment, a photograph album and four silver frames containing sepia-tinted family pictures. A jewellery roll. A silver teapot. A christening mug and a porcelain pot containing Anthony's first tooth. A folder containing investment documents, bank-account details, share certificates, her passport and driving licence. The deeds to the house, just in case. And then there had been no more room. That was it: her life, in a three-foot-by-four Samsonite suitcase.

Laura sat on it in the hallway, fiddling with her watch strap as she checked the dial for the hundredth time, her jacket across her lap. The dog lay peacefully at the end of his lead at her feet, snoring, unaware of the cataclysmic way in which his life was about to change. She leaned down and stroked his velvety head, blinking away the tears that threatened to drop on to it.

Anthony was not coming. He would be staying at his gran's, he had announced that morning.

'But I thought you were coming with me.'

'No, that's what you thought. Not what I thought.'

'But you'd love London. I told you, it'll be great. You'll have your own room and—'

'And leave my home? All my mates? No, Mum. You're talking about *your* life. I'm old enough to make my own choices. And I've decided to stay put.'

'You can't stay at Granny's for ever. It'll drive you mad.'

'Then I'll stay at Mrs Delancey's. She said I was welcome to her spare room, if I didn't mind a bit of chaos. They've had an unexpected vacancy, apparently.'

Isabel Delancey's house? 'But why would you want to stay there?' The very idea had almost felled her.

'Because she doesn't give everyone a hard time,' her son had replied. He was wearing his woollen hat, even though it was almost twenty-six degrees Celsius outside. 'She just gets on with stuff. Doesn't hassle Kitty. She lives her own life.'

If it was meant to wound, it had worked. And Laura knew now how much she hated that woman. She had effortlessly stolen not just her husband but also her son.

'You do know she's been sleeping with your father?' she had spluttered, when she could not take the unfairness any more.

His derision had been devastating. 'Oh, don't be stupid,' he scoffed. 'You were there. You heard what he's been doing to her house. She hates Dad.' He laughed mirthlessly. 'You could say he's been shafting her, perhaps.'

'Anthony!'

'You know, I always felt bad when Dad said you were paranoid,' he had said. 'Now I think maybe he was right.' He had held up a hand at her protest, squeezed past her and let himself out. 'Ring me when you're next popping up this way. I don't think I'll be headed to London any time soon.'

She had heard his footsteps fade down the gravel drive, and tried to redirect the sob that had risen to her chest.

He would come round, she told herself firmly, straightening the remaining photographs on the hall table. A couple of weeks of living between his grandmother and his father, and he would come round. She couldn't think of him living in the Spanish House. If she had, she would have hurled her suitcase into the woods and run screaming after him.

The dog lifted his head when the bell rang. She opened the door, trying not to let Nicholas see the redness of her eyes. 'Are you ready?' He kissed her, then glanced down at the suitcase. 'That it?'

'For now,' she said. 'And . . . the dog. If you don't mind. I know we haven't discussed him.'

'Bring the horses, if you like,' he said lightly. 'I reckon we can squeeze two on to the patio if we try hard enough.'

She started to laugh, but it turned into a sob. She dropped her head into her hands.

'Hey . . . hey . . . I'm sorry. It's okay.'

'No,' she said, into his chest. 'It's not. My son hates me. He's going to live with that woman. I can't believe he's going to live with that woman.'

Nicholas's arms went round her. 'Well, it won't be for long,' he said, eventually.

'What do you mean?'

'Hopefully, in a very short time, we'll own that house. So in theory he'll still be living under your roof. Our roof.' He proffered a handkerchief. She took it and wiped her eyes. 'Linen . . . the same one?'

'My lucky one.'

She folded it neatly. Tried to keep her voice steady. 'Has she said yes, then?'

'Not exactly . . .' He studied her face. 'But I spoke to her this morning and when I said I was coming here she asked me to go round to talk to her.'

'And you think she wants to sell?'

'I can't imagine any other reason for her wanting to talk, can you?'

'She probably wants to seduce you too.' She sniffed.

Nicholas smoothed her hair away from her face. 'Oh, I think I'm immune to her particular charms. You can come with me, if you like. Make sure I behave myself.'

He lifted her suitcase and put it into the back of the car. Laura closed the door behind her, trying not to think of what it meant. She encouraged Bernie on to the back seat, then climbed into the front. It was a different car from the battered one he used to have, smarter. The doors closed with an expensively muted clunk.

'Actually, I won't,' she said.

'Won't what?'

'Get out of the car. I don't want to see her. I don't want to see them. I don't even want to see the bloody house.' She stared miserably at the dashboard. 'You talk to her. I'll wait in the car.'

Nicholas took her hand. He looked, she thought, as if nothing could discomfit him. 'It will be all right, you know,' he said, kissing her fingers. 'Today was always going to be the worst day. But Anthony will come round.'

Her other hand was in her pocket, closed round the piece of paper that had scorched through her sense of what was right, of who she was.

Laura bit her lip as the car headed down the drive towards the turning to the Spanish House. She was grateful for Nicholas's certainty. But that didn't mean he was right.

Who would have thought there was such simple pleasure to be found in making coffee in your own kitchen? Byron took a mug from the cupboard, then looked around the mobile home with satisfaction; it was far from luxurious, but it was not cramped. It was light and clean and, most importantly, it was his. His clothes in the drawers, his washing things in the bathroom. His newspaper left out to be retrieved from exactly the same place when he returned. It was somewhere he could call his own, if only for a while.

His dogs were lying, exhausted, on their sides. He rubbed his eyes, trying to force away his own tiredness by will-power. He had considered taking a short nap, but knew from experience that waking up could be so arduous that it was almost easier to go without sleep.

Two spoonfuls of coffee should do it. He needed as much caffeine as he could get into himself. He added plenty of sugar for good measure.

As he was about to sit down, there was a bad-tempered rapping at the door. He stood up wearily and opened it. Frank was waving a piece of paper, his ruddy face purple with anger. 'What's this, then?'

'I didn't want to disturb you,' said Byron. 'You said you were doing your accounts.'

'You've only been here five minutes. What the hell do you think you're doing buggering off already?'

'Frank—'

'Don't you Frank me. I gives you a chance, somewhere to live, sits you down at my dinner table and you's already taking advantage. I wasn't born yesterday, Byron Firth.'

'Listen—'

'No, *you* listen. I employed you to coppice that whole wood as fast as possible. You think you's going to muck me about, running backwards and forwards to see girls and whatnot, you can forget it.'

He turned away and shoved his hat back on his head. 'Mebbe I should have listened to what everyone said. "Oh, no," says Muriel. "Give the boy a chance. He was always such a good lad before . . ." Well. Plenty more where you came from,' he muttered, and strode away angrily.

'But I've done it,' Byron said.

'Done what?'

'The wood.'

Frank stopped in his tracks. 'The whole fourteen acres?'

'Yes. The hazel's stacked behind the Dutch barn. As we discussed.'

Frank wore the same duster coat whether it was minus ten or thirty degrees, and now the worn shoulders rose with disbelief. 'But—'

'I worked through the night.' He gestured at the piece of paper. 'You didn't read to the end. I've promised someone I'd be there for their birthday, and the only way I could do it was to work through. I went back out after dinner last night.'

'You done it all last night? What, in the dark?'

Byron grinned.

Frank reread the note, a slow smile spreading across his face. 'Well, blow me. You allus was a rum bugger, Byron Firth. And you ain't changed none. Bloody hell. Worked through the night.' He let out a great 'Hah!'

'So you're all right if I go, then? I'll be back Monday morning, if that's okay. To start on the twenty-three-acre plot.' Byron took a swig of his coffee.

'Your time's your own, son. Long as you ain't expecting me to keep you in torch batteries. Hah! Working through the night, eh? Wait till I tell Muriel. I reckon she must have put something in the Bakewell.'

They turned up early, as Kitty had guessed they would. Her new friends, disgorged from cars that spun in the driveway, or walking in giggling clumps through the trees to emerge at the end of the lane. She waved them in, pleased, finally, to belong. No longer embarrassed by the state of the house now that she knew everyone's focus was on the lake and how quickly they could jump into it. Her mum had told her the previous evening that they would probably be moving again. When she had added that they would stay in the village, that Kitty would not have to change school, Kitty had felt an overwhelming sense of relief. She belonged here now. It was home.

'You all right?' she said to Anthony, who was pushing listlessly at a rubber dinghy, his face hidden.

'I bet she'll be back,' she said, laying an arm across his shoulders. 'She won't be able to leave you.'

'I saw her,' he said. 'She had her bag packed in the hall.'

Kitty knew about losing a parent. But she didn't know how it might feel to have one leave you voluntarily, and Anthony was so miserable she was afraid of saying the wrong thing.

They sat for some minutes, dangling their feet in the water. Around them, cabbage white butterflies fluttered on an invisible breeze, and an iridescent dragonfly hovered just inches from their feet, its bulbous eyes registering every detail of the two people on the bank.

As it darted away, she turned to him. 'It gets better,' she said, and he looked up at her from under his woollen hat. 'Life. Sometimes it can be really, really crap, and just as you think it's going to be like that for ever, it changes.'

'What's this?' he said. '*The Little House on the Prairie?*'

'This time last year,' she said, 'I thought me and Mum and Thierry would never be happy again.'

He glanced in the direction of her eyes – to her mother chatting with the man in the suit, a necklace of daisies wilting round her neck, to her brother, who was throwing sticks into the lake for the puppy to fetch.

Then she put her arms round his waist, feeling his misery lessen at a human touch. She smiled, and eventually he smiled back – as if she was making him do something he didn't want to. She laughed then. She could make him smile. She was sixteen. She could do anything.

'Come on,' she said, breaking away from him and pulling off his hat. 'Let's go swimming.'

It was a little like being with Mr Cartwright all over again, Isabel thought. She was sitting quietly while a man explained things patiently as if he didn't expect her to understand.

'The new development would be very much in keeping with the surroundings. Ideally I'd like to retain the walled garden, have the houses facing the lake. It would be a sympathetic new build.'

'But you would want to buy the house and the land outright. We'd have to leave completely.'

'Not necessarily. If you were interested in one of the houses on the development we could build that into the deal at a preferential rate.' The pad with the figures lay on the old table in front of her as she sat beside Mr Trent, his pale linen suit oddly out of place next to the decrepit deck-chairs and rusting scaffolding. He thrust a hand into a pocket. 'I'm not sure how familiar you are with the local property market, so I looked up some other development sites to give you an idea of the ballpark amounts involved.' He handed her another piece of paper.

'And this is what the land was worth in each case?' she asked.

'In effect, yes. That's what the owners would have been paid for the house and land, and in most instances the buildings that stood there were demolished.'

'But if this place is unique, as you say, then it isn't a good guide.'

'It's hard to provide meaningful comparisons.'

'And you think there would be demand for houses in a place like this? A spot so isolated?'

'The Bartons and the surrounding area are becoming desirable commuter territory. Because of the lake, second-home buyers might be interested too. I consider this a calculated risk.'

Isabel glanced round at the house, which sat benignly behind its scaffolding, the red brick glowing in the mid-morning heat. Around them, a thrush sang a lazy scale and ducks scrabbled for something behind the reeds. On the lawn, teenagers were changing into swimwear or exclaiming over Kitty's presents. It was possible that he saw hesitation, perhaps even regret, in her face because he laid a hand on her elbow and spoke urgently.

'Mrs Delancey, I'll be frank in a way that is not necessarily wise for someone in my position. This place, this setting, is really special to me.' He seemed awkward now, as if honesty were new to him. 'I haven't been able to think of anything else since I saw it. But I don't think it's worth your while to put any more money into this house as it stands.'

'And why should I believe you, Mr Trent, when I seem to have been unwise in believing anyone else?'

He hesitated a beat. 'Because money talks. And if you sell to me, I will guarantee that financially you will be secure and also have the option to continue to live in this setting, if that's what you wish.'

'Mr Trent, you will understand that as a . . . single parent I have to do my best to provide for my children.'

'Of course.' He smiled.

'So I was thinking a figure along these lines.' Isabel scribbled on the pad, then sat back, as Mr Trent stared at it.

'That . . . that's quite a sum.'

'That's my asking price. As you say, Mr Trent, it's a very special setting.'

He was taken aback, but she didn't care.

Thierry appeared at her shoulder. 'Mum?'

'Just a minute, T.'

'Can I set up a den in the house?'

She pulled him to her. Over the last few days he had tried to replicate Byron's presence in the house. He had been 'coppicing', collecting bundles of twigs, had gathered food and firewood, and now, of course, the den. She understood. She felt Byron's absence too. 'You don't want to swim with the others?'

'I will afterwards.'

'Go on, then,' she said. 'But if you're going to make one in the boiler room, don't leave my good cups and plates in there, okay?'

As he ran off, she turned back to Mr Trent. 'That's it, Mr Trent. That's what I need in order to leave. That's the price of uprooting my children again.'

He began to bluster: 'Mrs Delancey, you do realise this house will cost you a fortune to renovate?'

'We've been living comfortably in chaos for several months. It no longer bothers us.' She thought of the bath, which she had finished installing that morning. She had tightened the last nut, turned on the taps, then watched the initially brackish water clear and run gurgling down the plughole. It had given her as much satisfaction as the completion of a complicated symphony.

He stared at the paper. 'That's significantly higher than the market value.'

'As I understand it, market value is simply what someone is prepared to pay.'

She could see he was wrongfooted. But he wanted the house. And she had done her sums. She had worked out the bare minimum she needed to buy a decent place, and to provide her family with a financial cushion.

And then she had added some.

'That's the figure. Now, if you'll excuse me, I've got to help with the party.'

It really was like Mr Cartwright all over again, she thought, except this time she had understood what was going on. Better than anyone could have imagined.

'I'll have one last look round, if that's okay,' Nicholas Trent said, blowing out his cheeks as he gathered up his papers. 'Then I'll come back and let you know.'

Kitty had barely believed it when Mum had told her what she'd done.

'You did it yourself? And it really works?'

Isabel had held up her hands. 'Plumber's hands,' she had said, then hugged her daughter, who, streaked with pondweed, was wrapped in an old towel. She didn't tell her about the hours she had spent swearing at the incomprehensible diagrams, wrenching at too-tight nuts, the frequent sprays of escaping water that had drenched her. 'Happy birthday, darling. I've bought you some nice bubble bath too.'

'Oh, my God. A proper bath. Can I have one now? Have we got hot water and everything?'

'Now?' said Isabel. 'But you've got a party going on.'

Shivering, Kitty jerked her head towards her friends, who were busy pushing each other out of dinghies. 'They won't care if I'm gone for half an hour. And I could wash off all this green gunk. Oh, my God, a bath! A proper bath!' She jumped up and down with glee, her sixteen-year-old self unable to contain childish joy.

'Go on, then,' said Isabel. 'I'll set up lunch for you.'

Kitty tore into the house, taking the steps two at a time. She would have a quick bubble bath, wash her hair, then be scented and gorgeous at lunch when everyone climbed out of the water. She opened the bathroom door, and smiled when she saw what her mother had done. There were brand-new bottles of her favourite expensive shampoo and conditioner on the side of the bath. They had been using supermarket stuff for months. On the floor, wrapped in a red ribbon, was French moisturising bubble bath, and on the side a soft white towel. A bathmat lay neatly on the floor. Kitty picked up the bottle, removed the lid and breathed in, allowing the expensive perfume to fill her nostrils.

Then she put the shiny brass plug in its hole, and turned on the taps. The water came out, in a thunderous rush, prompting an immediate bloom of steam on the mirrored cabinet above it. Kitty bolted the bathroom door, then removed her swimming costume and draped herself in the towel she had brought with her from the garden. She didn't want the new one covered with green slime. While she waited for the bath to fill, she padded to the window.

Outside, her mother was putting plates on the trestle table, chatting to Asad, who was making a salad. Henry was sipping a glass of wine and shouting something to a group of girls in the water, which made them all laugh. He threw in a ball, then murmured something to her mother, who laughed too. A proper head-back laugh, the kind she used to do when Kitty's father was alive.

Kitty felt the familiar prickle of tears and wiped them away. It would be okay. For the first time since her father had died, she sensed they would be okay. Mum took charge, these days, so Kitty could be sixteen. Just sixteen.

She saw Thierry sneaking a plate of food, then walking

towards the boiler room and banged on the windowpane to attract his attention. She made a face to show him she knew what he was doing. He stuck out his tongue and she laughed, the sound just audible above the rush of water.

And then she leaped backwards as she heard a wrenching noise.

Kitty turned in time to see the white sheet behind the bath flutter as a crash sounded behind it. She yelped as Matt McCarthy appeared, pushing the sheet to one side.

'What – what are you *doing*?' she shrieked, pulling the towel tightly round her.

He stooped to clamber through the gap, and then, in the bathroom, rubbed a dusty hand over his head. 'I'm going to fix this hole,' he announced calmly. He was unshaven, his tool-belt skewed round his waist.

Kitty took an involuntary step backwards. 'Matt, you can't stay in here. I'm about to have a bath.'

'I've got to put it right. That room was beautiful. It can't stay like this.'

Her heart was thumping loudly enough to drown the sound of rushing water. She saw her swimming costume on the floor and wished she was wearing something under her towel.

'Please go away, Matt.'

'I won't be long.' He crouched, ran his fingers round the edge of the hole. 'I just have to fill this in. I wouldn't be much of a builder if I left a great hole here, would I?'

Kitty moved towards the door.

He stood up suddenly. 'Don't worry, Kitty. I won't get in your way,' he said. And smiled.

Kitty's bottom lip was trembling. She willed her mother to come up, or Anthony – anyone. Someone must have seen him come in. The walls of the room seemed to close round her, the faint echo of the voices outside a million miles away.

'Matt,' she said quietly, trying to stop the quaver in her voice, 'I'd really like you to go now.'

He seemed not to hear her.

'Matt,' she said again, 'please go.'

'You know,' he said, 'you're so like your mother.'

It was as his hand stretched out to touch her face that Kitty bolted for the door. She pushed past him, wrestled with the lock, and then, with a muffled squeak, she was tumbling down the stairs to the hallway, not knowing if he was behind her. She fumbled with the front-door catch, and then she was outside, sprinting across the lawn, a sob still caught in her throat.

'There's no point asking me,' Henry was saying. 'I'm a musical Philistine. If it doesn't have some tear-jerker as a finale, it's lost on me.'

'He is only the shortest genetic step from Judy Garland,' said Asad, removing clingfilm from another bowl. Some of Kitty's friends had got out of the water, and were towelling themselves dry or hovering hopefully by the food table.

'I don't think I know any Judy Garland songs,' Isabel said. 'There are more towels over there, if anyone needs them.'

'Do you play only classical music?' Asad arranged the serving spoons in the centre of the table, then popped an olive into his mouth.

'Yes. But it doesn't have to be gloomy.'

'I don't think classical music has quite the emotional drama you get with a show tune, though,' Henry said. 'I mean, I don't think it would make me shed a tear.'

'Emotional drama? Mr Ross, you have been ill-informed.'

'What? You think you could make me cry? With your violin?'

Isabel laughed. 'Harder men than you have been known to fall,' she said.

'Go on, then.' Henry picked up a tea-towel. 'I throw down my gauntlet. Do your finest, Mrs D. Wring me out.'

'Oh, I'm out of practice. I haven't played properly for months.'

'We don't care.'

'But my violin's in the kitchen.'

Henry bent down and pulled out the case from under the table.

'Not any more.'

'I get the feeling I've been played,' she said.

The two men chuckled.

'We had to ensure we got our own private performance,' Henry said. 'It's not like you've been selling tickets or anything. Go on. A quick burst. Rude not to, given it's your daughter's birthday and all.'

Isabel adjusted the violin under her chin. Then she drew her bow across the strings, and let the first bars of Elgar's Violin Concerto in B Minor sing out in the midday sunshine.

She glimpsed Asad and Henry's rapt expressions, and then she closed her eyes, trying to concentrate, to remember the music. She played, and suddenly her violin didn't seem so inferior. It sang of her sadness to be leaving the house, of the absence of her husband, the man she had thought he was. It sang of the pain of missing someone you hadn't known you might miss.

She opened her eyes, and found that Kitty's guests had begun to climb out of the water and sit on the grass. They were quiet, listening, apparently mesmerised. She shifted position, and as she ended the first movement she saw him among the trees and wondered if she had imagined it. He lifted a hand, and she was smiling, a huge, unguarded beam.

Henry and Asad turned to see what she was smiling at and nudged each other surreptitiously.

He smiled back at her. He wasn't her husband, but that was okay.

'You came,' she said, lowering the violin. He looked tired, she thought, but at peace. His job had restored something to him.

'Brought Kitty a present,' he said. 'My sister chose it. I can't say I know much about what girls like.'

'She'll love it,' said Isabel. She couldn't stop staring at him. 'I'm so glad you made it. Really.'

All the old awkwardness had disappeared. He stood tall again. 'So am I,' he said. Out of Matt's shadow, he had become, she realised, imposing.

They stood there, facing each other, oblivious to curious glances.

'All right, all right,' said Henry, flapping a hand at Isabel. 'Sit down, Byron. You don't have to make her stop. I was feeling enjoyably mournful.'

Byron grinned. 'Sorry,' he said. 'Where's Thierry?' His eyes had not left Isabel's, and she realised she had flushed.

She lifted her violin to her shoulder. 'The kitchen or the boiler room or somewhere. He's been setting up a . . . den.' He raised an eyebrow. It was a shared joke now, she thought. Not a source of tension.

He lowered himself on to the grass, his long legs stretched out in front of him, and she fixed her eyes on the Cousins and resumed playing, trying to focus on the music, trying not to think about what his return might mean. I don't care who he is, what he did when he was someone else, she thought. I'm just glad he's here. She closed her eyes, immersing herself, afraid that without the notes to hide behind what she felt would be nakedly apparent, all too visible to her audience.

She loved the second movement, its rich ebb and flow, its reflective, songful tone, but it was now, sliding down the heart-wrenching notes of the descent, that she grasped why she had unconsciously picked this piece. That phrase, the impassioned bittersweet notes before the end of the movement, suggested new knowledge, that there was no returning to the past. Elgar himself had said it was 'too emotional', but also that he loved it.

She opened her eyes. And there was Asad, his head tipped back in contemplation, and Henry, beside him, wiping his eyes surreptitiously. She let the last notes linger, wanting to milk the moment.

'There,' she said, as she let her violin fall to her side. 'I told you I—'

She was almost winded by her daughter hurling herself at her, one hand pulling Isabel towards her, the other clutching her towel. She was sobbing so hard she could hardly speak.

'Kitty!' Isabel backed away a little and peered into her face. 'What's the matter?'

'It's him.' Kitty struggled to speak through her sobs. 'It's Matt McCarthy. He's in the house.'

'What?' Byron was on his feet.

Isabel looked at the house. Then, realising her daughter was naked under the towel: 'Did he touch you?'

'No . . .' said Kitty. 'He just . . . He was in the master bedroom . . . He came through that hole . . . He frightened me.'

Isabel's mind raced. Her eyes met Byron's.

'He was acting really weird. I couldn't get him to go . . .' Kitty was still hanging on to her.

'What shall we do?' Asad had stepped up beside her.

'I don't know,' she said.

'What's he playing at?' Something had hardened in Byron's face and his body tensed. Suddenly Isabel was filled with fear, not of his history but of what he might do in her name.

'He said he wanted to fix the house,' said Kitty. 'The hole. But he wasn't normal, Mum. He was—'

'Thierry,' said Byron, and was sprinting across the grass towards the house.

Upstairs in the bathroom, Matt wiped the glass with a finger and peered down at the gathering below. He saw Isabel look up and, for a moment, could have sworn she had caught his eye. Now she would come.

Perhaps now they could talk.

He did not notice the water level in the cast-iron bath, which had continued to climb after Kitty had fled. He did not hear the creaking of the depleted floor joists, subjected to unexpected pressure from the weight of the water.

Matt McCarthy climbed back through the hole, walked slowly into the master bedroom, sat on the edge of the bed and—

Byron walked slowly up the stairs, glancing into every room he passed in case the boy was there. Years of tracking had made his movements near-silent, and few of the stairs creaked now that the wooden boards had been relaid.

He reached the landing, and heard taps running. The bathroom door was ajar, the room apparently empty. He pushed on the door of the master bedroom, and there was Matt, sitting on the bed. He was staring straight in front of him at the hole. Matt looked up and blinked.

He had been expecting someone else, Byron realised. He stood in the doorway. He was no longer frightened of anything Matt McCarthy could do.

'Where's Isabel?' Matt asked. His skin was grey beneath the tan, apart from two spots of colour in his cheeks.

'You need to leave,' said Byron, his voice low and steady.

But the thumping of his blood as it pumped through his body was so loud he was sure it must be audible.

'Where's Isabel?' Matt repeated. 'She's meant to come up and talk to me.'

'You've just scared Kitty half to death,' Byron said. 'Get out. Now.'

'Leave this house? Who are you to tell me to leave it?'

'You bully everyone, don't you?' Byron could feel an old anger now, an anger he had spent years keeping under wraps. 'You'd bully a young girl if it meant you got this house. Well, I'm telling you, it's over, Matt.'

As Byron spoke, Matt had returned to staring through the hole, watching the water as it gushed to the rim of the bath and then brimmed over the edges. It was as if he hadn't heard him.

'Get out,' said Byron, shoulders braced for the force he would require to eject Matt. 'I'm telling you—'

Matt looked at him. 'Or what? You'll make me? One word, Byron.' Matt laughed, as if at some private joke. 'One word. If you can spell it. P-A-R-O-L-E . . .'

The thumping in Byron's ears became unbearable. He saw Matt's mocking smile, the deadness behind his eyes, and discovered he no longer cared about the consequences. All that mattered was stopping this man, showing him he could no longer frighten and cheat people, exploit Isabel. He lifted his fist, drew it back—

And his breath was sucked from him as, with a terrible cracking, wrenching sound, the bathroom floor began to give way—

Byron, thought Isabel, picking up her violin and trying to think of something cheerful and diverting to play. Everything would be okay because he was here. He would make sure nothing happened— At a splintering, tearing noise she dropped the instrument and spun round—

The noise broke into the still air like a gunshot, a terrible noise, filled with dread; it sucked the atmosphere into a vacuum, and then came a low rumble, a groan, a deafening crash of timbers and tiles all undercut by a terrifying timpani of breaking glass. The Spanish House was collapsing from its centre, as if some great crack had opened in the earth between the two wings. The earth trembled, ducks rose shrieking from the reeds, as the two sides crumbled. As Isabel, Kitty and the guests stared, their gasps of shock stalled in their lungs, the whole thing was gone, folded in on itself, a great plume of dust rising to fill the space where a house had once been. And then it cleared, and there, against the sky, were two half-standing ends of a house, its splintered joists rising like broken bones, its floors, its walls so many piles of rubble, a thin stream of water trickling from a broken pipe, like a celebratory fountain, in the centre.

No one said anything. Sound and time had been sucked away. Isabel let out a little 'uh' of shock, her hands clapped to her mouth, and after a brief pause, Kitty began to wail, a high-pitched, unearthly sound. Her body shook violently and her eyes were fixed on the place where her home had been. Then, when she could finally form the words: 'Where is Thierry?'

Laura stared through the windscreen, unable to believe what she had just witnessed. The sheer magnitude, the unlikeliness, had pinned her to the passenger seat. There was no house where, moments earlier, a house had been, just this terrible skeleton, two sides rising up, the innards of the rooms exposed – wallpaper, a picture still hanging, knocked to a jaunty angle. Half a bedroom, posters still pinned to the wall.

Behind her, in the back seat, her old dog whined.

Fingers fumbling, she managed to open the door, and got out. From there, on the drive, teenagers huddled together in shock, still clutching towels. Isabel was staring at the house, her hands pressed to her mouth. Then the Cousins were behind her, Henry's mobile phone pressed to his ear as he shouted instructions. Pottisworth, she thought absently, feeling his malevolent presence in this, hearing his unpleasant wheezy cackle in the splintering of wood, the delayed smash of a pane.

And then Nicholas was striding towards her, his face ashen, his folder still clasped to his chest.

'What the hell?' he was saying. 'I was in the garage. What the hell?'

And all she could do was shake her head. They began to make their way to the garden.

'Thierry!'

They rounded the corner and Laura's heart leaped into her mouth.

'Thierry!' Isabel stood on the grass a few yards away. Her hair was wild and when she tried to move forward her legs gave way and she sank to the ground.

'Oh . . . oh, no,' Laura breathed. 'Not the child . . .'

Nicholas reached for her hand but, suffused with dread, she could not take it.

'It's Matt,' Nicholas was saying. 'He must have weakened the structure. I'd swear it was sound the first time I saw it.'

Laura could not take her eyes off the Delancey woman. She was white with fear, her eyes blank with catastrophe.

Behind her, her daughter was sobbing.

'Mum?' someone called. And again: 'Mum?' Isabel turned,

and Laura thought she would never forget the look on her face. The boy was coming through the trees, his puppy at his heels. 'Mum?'

She was on her feet and running barefoot as fast as she could across the grass, past them all, and then she had him in her arms, and she was sobbing so hard that Laura found she too had begun to cry. Laura watched her, heard her sobs. Saw grief and pain, brought about in part by her own desire.

She felt suddenly like a voyeur and turned to the house, a great splintered hole in the middle of the woods. The frontage was now a red-brick mask, two blank windows for eyes, its doorway an open mouth of despair.

It was through this that she saw her husband stumble out, his head bloodied, one arm hanging awkwardly at his side. He seemed no more troubled than if he had been sizing up a job.

'Jesus Christ,' Nicholas muttered.

She saw suddenly the depth of Matt's insanity.

'Laura?' Matt said, tramping over the bricks, and she realised that, only a few hundred feet from his home, Matt McCarthy was completely lost.

'Thank you,' Isabel was saying, to some unknown deity, unable to let go of her son. 'Oh, thank you. Oh, God, I thought . . . I couldn't bear it. I couldn't bear it.' She breathed in Thierry's scent, refused to let him pull away from her, her tears on his skin.

'We've counted everyone, all the kids,' Henry said. 'They're okay.'

'Keep them back,' Asad said. He broke off to use his inhaler. 'We should make them stand by the lake.'

There was another low rumble. 'What's that?' said Kitty.

As they stared in horror, the back wall of the west wing,

the remaining half of the master bedroom, teetered and then, as if in slow motion, collapsed in a shower of bricks and glass, prompting a shout from the young people on the lawn, some of whom were running towards the lake. Isabel clamped her arms round her two children, trying to shield their faces with her hands. 'It's okay,' she was murmuring. 'It's okay. You're safe.'

'But where's Byron?' Kitty asked.

'Byron?' Thierry said blankly.

'He went to find Thierry,' Kitty said dully, and turned towards where the boiler room had been.

'Oh, sweet Lord,' said Henry.

Isabel was across the grass, then on her knees hurling pieces of brick behind her. 'Not again,' she was murmuring, her voice thick with fear. 'Not again. Not you too.' And then, as word spread, they were all beside her, pulling at timbers, the teenagers' slim limbs red with brick dust, Isabel's hands raw and scraped. 'Byron!' she was yelling. 'Byron!'

The Cousins had Kitty and Thierry, wrapping them in towels despite the warmth of the sun. Thierry was shaking, his face bleached with shock. Henry poured him a sweet drink. 'Is it my fault?' Isabel heard her son ask, and felt her own face crumple in response.

Six of them were hauling at a roof timber and gasped as it finally came free. Kitty's friends were shouting at each other, warning of glass or protruding nails. Two girls were weeping, and one stood a short distance away, talking on a mobile phone.

'They'll be here soon,' Henry was saying, as if to reassure himself. 'The fire brigade and the ambulance. They'll find him.'

Isabel ploughed on, her movements settling into a rhythm. She chucked bricks behind her, one, two, three, try to see if there's a gap below, one, two, three, shout again. Her breath was uneven, heart pounding against her ribcage.

'Don't let them walk over anything,' Asad called. 'If he's underneath it might cause something else to fall on him.' As if to confirm what he had said, two teenagers squealed as a piece of wood gave way beneath them, and they were pulled to safety by their friends.

'Get them away,' Asad shouted. 'Everyone, move away. The other side might still come down.'

It was hopeless, Isabel thought, sitting back. She glanced at her watch and saw it had been almost twenty minutes now but they still had no idea where he was. A sense of chaos had begun to build, of delayed hysteria. Behind her, two people were arguing about the best way to lift a joist. Henry and Asad were telling the teenagers to stop what they were doing and move away. Underlying everything, she could hear her daughter's attempts to reassure Thierry that it would be okay.

But it was not okay. Byron was somewhere in the remains of the house. And every minute that passed might count. Help me, she told him silently, sweat pooling between her shoulder-blades as she dragged at another piece of rubble. Help me find you. I can't bear to lose you too. Then she sat back on her heels, the balls of her hands pressed to her eyes.

She sat like that, completely still, for a minute. Then she looked behind her. 'Be quiet!' she yelled. 'Everyone, be quiet!'

And it was then she heard it: the distant sound of frantic barking. 'Thierry!' she cried. 'Where are Byron's dogs? Get his dogs!'

Briefly his face lit up. As the bemused onlookers watched, Thierry raced round the lake to Byron's car and let out Meg and Elsie. They flew across the lawn, heading straight for the far end of the house.

'Quiet! No one make a sound!' Isabel called, and there was silence, a stillness more portentous than the crash that had preceded it. Kitty, held by Henry, stifled her sobs, as Isabel threw herself down beside the dogs and shouted again: 'Byron!' she cried out, and her voice was imperious, terrible, strange even to herself. 'Byron!'

The silence seemed to last a thousand years, long enough for Isabel's heart to become still with fear, acute enough for her to hear the chatter of her daughter's teeth. Even the birds were quiet, the whisper of the pines absent. In a tiny corner of the countryside, time contracted, and stood still.

And then, as the noise of the siren broke into the far distance, the dogs barked again, at first whimpering, and then with growing hysteria, their paws scraping at a heap of fallen timber, they heard it.

His shout.

Her name.

The sweetest music Isabel had ever heard.

He had got off lightly, all things considered, the paramedics said. A suspected collarbone fracture, a gash in his leg and severe bruising. They would keep him in hospital overnight, check that there were no internal injuries. As he lay on the stretcher, in the midst of the paramedics' discussions, the abrupt hiss and halt of the police radios, Laura McCarthy had watched the Delancey boy walk up to him. Wordlessly, unnoticed by the adults around him, he had laid his head on Byron's hand, his own resting on the man's blanketed torso. Byron had lifted his head at the unexpected weight, and then, blinking, reached out a battered hand to touch the boy's cheek. 'It's okay, Thierry,' he said, so quietly that Laura almost didn't hear him. 'I'm still here.'

It was then, as he was loaded into the ambulance, that she

had stepped forward. She reached into her handbag and pulled out the letter, placing it in Byron's bandaged fingers. 'I'm not sure what this is worth now, but you might as well have it,' she said briskly, then turned away before he could say anything.

'Laura?' Matt said. Heavily bandaged and flanked by policemen, a blanket round his shoulders, he was like a child, helpless, vulnerable. There's nothing left of him, she thought. He's been demolished, like the house.

In the end, it was so simple. She turned to Nicholas and lifted a hand to his cheek, feeling his skin under her finger-tips, the hidden strength of his jawbone. A good man. A man who had rebuilt himself. 'I'm so sorry,' she said softly. Then she took her stunned husband's arm and walked with him to the police car.

Twenty-five

They had spent the first night in Byron's hospital room. Thierry didn't want to leave him, and there was nowhere else for them to go. The nurses, hearing what had happened, had given them a small side-ward to themselves, and while Kitty and Thierry climbed into the two spare beds there and slept, their faces shadowed from the day's events, Isabel sat between them, and tried not to think of what might have been.

Around her, she listened to the timeless sounds of a hospital at night – soft shoes squeaking on linoleum floors, murmured conversations, a sporadic beeping that heralded a cry for help. In the hours when she drifted off, a wrenching, crashing noise echoed through her dreams, with her daughter's thin wail and Thierry's bemused 'Mum?' forcing her into jumpy wakefulness.

Six months ago, when she was still looking for signs, she would have said Laurent had saved them, that somehow he had protected them. But now, staring at the man in the bed opposite, she knew that was not so. There was no reason, no sense in anything. You were lucky or you were not. You died or you did not.

Dawn broke shortly before five, a cold blue light behind the pale grey blinds, slowly illuminating the darkened room. She stretched, feeling the ache of tension in her neck and shoulders. Then, sure that her children were asleep, she went to the chair beside Byron's bed, and sat down. In sleep, he had lost his watchfulness. His expression had softened and his skin bore simply the weathering of his work. No trace of doubt, anger or wariness remained.

She thought of how he had run without hesitation to where he had thought Thierry might be in danger. She thought of his easy, confident smile when he had returned to the house the previous day. His gaze had been so direct, so full of something she suspected even he couldn't hide. And Isabel saw a future, perhaps for the first time since Laurent had died. She saw her son smiling, heard his voice ring out. She saw her daughter, freed again from premature adulthood. She saw, if not happiness, then another chance at it.

He had felt as she had, she was sure. This isn't impulsive, she told herself. This is the most considered thing I've ever done. Slowly, she lowered her head and dropped a kiss on his lips – which were unexpectedly soft, tasting of hospitals, disinfectant, industrial soap and, underneath, something of the forest.

'Byron,' she whispered, and kissed him again, letting his bruised hands find her, letting herself be held against him as he woke, murmuring her name. She let herself sink against him and the tears came, of gratitude that he was there, that once again she might be held, loved and wanted. She was glad that Laurent no longer stood, spectral, between them, that she heard no echoes of reproach or guilt. He was no longer there, as he had been with Matt.

It was Byron. Only Byron.

You could choose to be happy or you could not.

And when, some time later, she raised her head to look at him, she was shocked to find his expression troubled. 'Are you hurting?' she said, letting her finger run down the side of his forehead, revelling in the luxury of touch.

He did not reply. A bruise at his temple had deepened overnight to a rainbow of livid colour.

'I can get you some painkillers.' She tried to remember where the nurse had put them.

'I'm sorry,' he said quietly.

'Sorry?'

He shook his head.

She drew back. 'Sorry for what?'

'I can't do this. I'm sorry.'

There was a long, heavy pause.

'I don't understand.' She sat back on the bed.

It was some moments before he spoke, his voice low and halting. Outside the door a phone rang, urgent and unheard.

'It's not going to work.'

I know what I just felt, she wanted to say. I know what you just felt. But those words echoed Matt's protestations. 'This is silly.' She tried to smile. 'Can't we just . . . see what happens?'

'You could really do that? Just dive in and hope for the best?' He made it sound like carelessness.

'That's not what I meant.'

'Isabel, we're too different. You know we are.'

She stared at him, at the obstinate line of his mouth, at the way he wouldn't meet her eye. And she lowered her voice. 'You know, don't you?'

'Know what?'

The children were still sleeping.

'About Matt.'

He winced, as she had feared he might.

'I knew it. All this is just an excuse. Well, I'll tell you about Matt. It was the night of the powercut and I was drunk and I was lonely and I was the lowest I had been since Laurent died, and if I'm absolutely truthful, some tiny, stupid part of me thought it was something I wanted.'

'You don't have to tell me—'

Her voice was fierce. 'Yes, I do. Because it happened and it was a huge mistake. And not a day has gone by when I haven't regretted it. But what I did then has nothing to do with how I feel about you.'

'I don't need to hear—'

'Yes, you do. Because it's not how I am. I am not careless with my feelings.'

'I didn't—'

'You know something? Before that, I'd never slept with anyone but Laurent! I was thirty-six and I'd only ever slept with one man . . . I used to laugh at myself. Matt—'

'It's nothing to do with Matt!' His voice exploded into the little room. Kitty stirred restlessly, and Byron lowered his voice. 'I *know* he came to you that night. I was there, remember? But I never judged you. I have *never* judged you. Matt and all the business with the house, it just disguised the truth.'

'The truth?'

He gave a deep sigh. 'That it wouldn't work.'

'How can you say that? How do you *know*?'

'Isabel . . .'

'Why won't you even try?'

'I have nothing to offer you. No home. No security.'

'That stuff doesn't matter to me.'

'Because you have it. It's easy to say when you have it.'

He refused to meet her eye.

She waited.

'I don't want you to look at me in a year's time and feel . . . differently. Because of what I don't have.'

They sat in silence for some minutes. Finally Isabel said, 'You know what happened out there yesterday, Byron? The most terrifying thing I've ever seen. You and Thierry could both have died.' She brought her face close to his. 'But you didn't. Everyone lived. *Everyone lived.* And one thing I know, one thing I've learned this last year, is that you should take any chance you have to be happy.'

She heard Thierry murmur on the bed behind her, but she didn't care. 'You kept us going,' she said. 'Thierry, the children . . . You gave them something back.' She was close to tears. 'Something they needed. Something I needed. Don't do this, Byron. Don't push me away. Nothing else matters.'

His jaw tightened. 'Isabel . . . I'm a realist. I can't change the way things are,' he said, into the space away from her. 'This is for the best. Believe me.'

She waited for him to say something else. But nothing came. Finally she stood up, reeling a little, perhaps from lack of sleep, perhaps because shock had made her giddy. 'That really is it? After all this? After everything we've been through? You're going to judge me for owning a *house*?'

He shook his head. And then he shifted painfully on to his side, closing his eyes against her.

The Cousins had offered the rooms above the shop. Friends and neighbours had stepped forward too, but it was only here that they could stay together. Isabel did not want to be anywhere near the Spanish House but, perversely, she did not want to be far from it either. The insurance documents were still inside it, as were all her other important papers.

Asad had handed her the flat keys. 'Stay as long as you need,' he had said. 'It's basic, but at least you'll have food and drink. We've cleared out most of the stock and we've borrowed camp beds, so if you don't mind it being a little cramped you will have somewhere to sleep, and a bathroom.'

Isabel had sat down heavily on the sofa bed, Kitty and Thierry huddled next to her, and laughed, a strange, hiccupping laugh. A bathroom. They finally had a bathroom. Thierry had looked up at her expectantly, as if she could make it all right. She caught herself teetering and pulled herself together, smiling. That was her job.

They had left the hospital that morning with nothing, no overnight bags, no wallet, just a violin. It didn't matter, she had told Asad. 'It's all just stuff, right? And we're the family who can live off weeds and rabbits.' She kept her voice bright.

'You may find you're not as empty-handed as you thought,' Henry said. As the news had spread, the villagers had arrived in a trickle throughout the day, bringing things they thought might help – toothbrushes, saucepans, blankets. He pointed to the bags and boxes in a corner. 'We've had a look. There's enough to keep you going until the insurance comes through.'

Isabel had assumed it was the Cousins' stock. Now she could see that they were household items, clean, some new, all carefully packed and brought over for them.

'But they don't even know us,' Kitty had said, picking up a soft checked blanket.

'You know, I do believe village life gets a bum rap some-times,' said Henry. 'There are good people here, even if you don't always see them. Generous people. They are not all like . . .'

Kitty picked up a bag and brought it to the sofa. She began to pick through it, holding up items as she discovered them. Some were so thoughtful that Isabel suspected she might cry again: a little vanity case with makeup and hand lotion, a variety pack of breakfast cereal, to appeal to all tastes, Tupperware boxes of food. A sponge cake. There were neat piles of laundered clothes, apparently chosen to fit each of them. Thierry held up a skateboarding T-shirt with unexpected pleasure. There were cards offering phone numbers, help, sympathy.

'The police have got your handbag with your purse,' Asad said, 'and your keys – to the car,' he added hastily.

'Then I guess we're well off, after all,' said Isabel. 'We've got each other, right? All the rest of it is stuff. Just stuff.'

When she burst into tears, Asad had laid a hand on her shoulder and muttered something about delayed shock. He had plugged in the kettle, and told the children to find biscuits. She let them fuss around her. Isabel, her face buried in her hands, could not tell him she was crying not for the loss of her belongings, but because a man she had only just realised she loved did not love her enough to be with her.

The car was in the clearing, parked a little haphazardly. It had been hurriedly left beside the lake some thirty-six hours earlier by a man on his way to a birthday party. He had left it unlocked in his haste to join the gathering on the lawn.

He threw his bag on to the passenger seat. A neighbour had left a number under his windscreen wiper, offering help, and he removed the paper carefully, taken aback by the gesture. He had just collected his dogs from a farmer who had minded them for him, and now he stood beside the Land Rover, watching them race round the lake, gratified by this return to their habitual routine.

Across the water police tape was strung between what had been the front and rear of the house, flapping in the breeze, an unhappy echo of the scattered bunting that lay bedraggled on the grass. The journey to the party, sitting on the lawn in the sunshine, listening to the music – it all felt as if it had taken place several lifetimes ago. He found it hard to comprehend how the house, the lives contained within it, could have been so unutterably altered in a matter of seconds. He was also conscious that in some way the collapse had not threatened him, as everyone seemed to assume, but saved him.

From himself.

A great weariness settled upon him and Byron felt daunted by the long drive back to Frank's place. His sister, Jan, who had arrived at the hospital at lunchtime, had pressed him to stay with her and Jason. 'You look awful,' she had said. 'You need looking after.' But Byron did not want to be around people. He did not want to be in someone else's home, to rub up against the casual happiness of their life together. 'I'm going to head back to Brancaster,' he said.

'You,' she said, 'are your own worst enemy sometimes.'

Byron walked slowly towards the ruined house, wanting to take a last look at it before he left. Twenty-four hours he had lived legitimately in it. He could barely remember feeling as light as he had waking up in that room. But he couldn't have stayed. And in refusing to see that she was fooling herself.

Byron stopped at the easternmost point of the house and picked up a small white jug, its handle snapped off. So many things were buried under here. The remnants of Isabel's family life, now consigned to the earth, perhaps to some distant landfill site. He held the little jug, picturing it in the kitchen, and tried to dispel the image of her face. She had looked as devastated as she had when the house had come down. But he had nothing to offer her. To have her and lose her, to watch her affection turn to irritation when another job fell through or he could not put enough money on the table, to see her wariness every time she heard some piece of old gossip in the village, to have her passion ebb away would be infinitely more painful than if he had never had it at all.

He would be alone with his dogs. It was easier that way.

Meg and Elsie probably needed feeding, and his wages were in Brancaster. He reached into his pocket, hoping for loose change with which he could buy dog food, and came up with a folded piece of paper. A duplicated letter. He tried to remember where it had come from, and had a vague recollection of Laura McCarthy thrusting it at him just before he left in the ambulance.

His P45, he thought. Boy, the McCarthys could pick their moments. He unfolded it, glanced at the printed words, then stood very still. He read the lines, the witness signatures, the scrawled note to Laura McCarthy in Pottisworth's own hand. He reread them, unsure whether that really was his name printed there. He wondered if it was a joke, then remembered her expression as she had handed it to him, grim, yet strangely relieved. He thought back to Pottisworth, muttering about the McCarthys, their greed, their presumption. 'They can't wait to get their hands on this place,' he would gripe. 'Their sort always thinks they're entitled.' Byron had paid him hardly any attention. Pottisworth had never shown him the slightest affection, the merest hint of favouritism. But why would he? This will wasn't about giving something to him, it was about thwarting the McCarthys. It was a final, gleeful test of Laura: the old man had given her both copies so she could, if she wanted, destroy the evidence. It was a final two fingers to Matt.

All this time, he mused, as the truth spread warmth in him, I have been apologising for trespassing on land that was mine, squatting in my own boiler room. All this time I have owned it. The absurdity made him laugh, and his dogs' ears pricked. The idea of him owning anything of that size made his head spin. Him, Byron, master of it all.

And then he remembered Isabel. She would lose everything. Not just the house but its contents. Her savings. Everything she owned had gone into those walls. His gain would be her loss.

Byron sat on a fallen timber and held the paper. He stared

across the lake from his vantage-point. A man who was not empty-handed, after all.

She had walked the last hundred yards through the trees and now stood, some distance before the lane emerged into the clearing, staring at the house, her arms crossed tightly over her chest. She had left Kitty and Thierry in the flat with the Cousins, supposedly to get some provisions. But instead of heading towards the bank or the supermarket, she had found herself taking the turn by the piggery and driving down the rutted lane to the sign that still warned her belatedly: '*Cave!*'

She had thought she would never look at the house again. But she had had to come. She had to see it. Twice, as she drove through the woods, she suspected she had made a mistake and wanted to turn round. But that was the thing about the track: once you were heading towards the house there was no turning back.

There was an unexpected brightness as she drew closer to the clearing. Bewildered, she realised, with a jolt, that of course there was now no expanse of red brick to blot out the light. She slowed the car and stopped it in the drive near the mass of rubble and timber that had once been her home.

The sight made her shiver, despite the balmy evening. No matter how often she had told herself it had never been their home, that it was just a temporary place to live, the Spanish House had become an extension of her family, their hopes, aspirations, affections and history tied up in its walls. To see it demolished was like seeing themselves brought down, the damage a personal hurt.

Isabel wept, no longer sure why or for whom she was crying, but she felt a great sadness for the house. For the shock of there being nothing where once there had been something. For an ending and a thwarted beginning.

She was not sure how long she stood there. Whether it was the peace of the lake, or the sounds of the woods, her shock and horror began to dissipate, and resignation took their place. A house was just a house, and nowhere was that more exposed than in its demolition. It meant nothing, had no greater significance. She did not have to read some terrible portent into its destruction. It had been a sad, unloved building, just bricks, mortar, wood and glass. Nothing that could not, ultimately, be replaced.

'You can have it,' she had told Nicholas Trent, when he called that afternoon. He had rung to see how they were after such a terrible shock. And then he had added, 'I meant what I said about the condition of the house not being an issue for me—'

'You can have it at your offering price,' she interrupted. 'As long as we sort it out quickly. I just want to move on.'

It was as she recalled this conversation that a dog thrust its cold nose into her hand.

She spun round, and there he was, on a mound of bricks a few feet away, the bruises on his face and arms deepening to a blue-green hue.

She couldn't think of anything to say. He looked so different, so distant from the man she had left that morning. They had been pulled together by the accident, as if by a magnetic force, then repelled almost immediately afterwards. She wished he had gone before she came. But she was glad, too, that he was there. 'I needed to see it,' she said, when her presence seemed to require explanation.

He nodded.

'It . . . it's not as bad as I'd thought.' The absurdity of what she had said made her laugh unexpectedly. 'I meant – I mean, it's not frightening any more.'

'We were lucky,' he said.

'In some ways.' She was unable to hide the bitterness of those words.

She stooped, and went slowly round the edge of the building, pulling out the odd photograph, a hairbrush, trying not to grieve at the sight of their things crushed among the rubble. The fire brigade had tried to gather up anything of value on the day of the collapse. 'Wouldn't be too worried about looters, though,' one of the men had told her. 'Most people probably don't even know there's a house here.'

It was a thoughtless comment. There was no house. She didn't really care, she told herself. There was nothing much of value that she owned any more. And she wouldn't care about Byron. She knew now that she could survive alone. It was a whole new start. She glanced back, and saw that he was still looking at her. For a moment he seemed about to speak, but said nothing. She picked her way through the remnants of her old life, mute fury building as his eyes burned into her skin.

Byron watched her wander through the objects scattered on the grass, the way the ill-fitting T-shirt moved against her waist. He noticed the scratches on her arms and fingers, the scars not just of the previous day but of the year that had led up to it. He did not know what to say to her, how to apologise for what he had done. He did not know what to tell her of the things that had happened to him, how one small life could be demolished and resurrected at the same time. Finally, clutching a few things to her chest, she glanced at him and coloured when she saw he was still watching her. 'I've got to get back to the children. I'll come back some other time.'

He didn't move.

She stood there, as if waiting for him to say something, and then, with a tight smile, she said, ''Bye, then.' She tucked a strand of hair behind her ear.

It was as if they were near-strangers, meeting in a street.

'Isabel,' he said, his voice unnaturally loud in the still air.

She shielded her eyes with a hand so that she could see him more clearly against the dying rays of the sun.

'I found these,' he said. He held out the crumpled papers.

She walked up to him and stopped a few feet away. Without speaking, she took them from him. 'My scores,' she said.

He couldn't take his eyes off her. 'I know how much they mean to you.'

'You don't know how much *anything* means to me,' she said angrily.

He was shocked now by what he saw in her face, the rawness of what he had done to her. There was nothing casual here, he realised. Nothing hidden. In her misery, her fury, he saw what he had felt, what he had hidden from himself for weeks – months. And in a few moments she might be gone from his life for ever. What do I do? he asked himself. I thought I had days to work this out.

'Good luck in Brancaster,' she said stiffly, and walked away from him towards her car. His body seemed to constrict with pain – like need. It was so intense, so alien to him, that he found it unbearable. And it was then that he made his decision. 'Isabel!' he called. She didn't turn. 'Isabel!'

She stopped.

'Look . . . I was wrong,' he said.

She tilted her head. A question.

'You were right.' He walked towards her, stepping over loose bricks, taking care not to trip on the bunting.

They faced each other. He waited, knowing that what she said now would decide everything. 'I need you to tell me the truth,' he said finally. 'You really believe what you said? That it's not important who owns what?'

Isabel stared at him. You don't get it, do you? she thought. I am the realist. I am the one who has had to learn the hard truth of what is important. I would want you if you had nothing for the rest of your life. His beautiful face was suddenly vulnerable, and she remembered how he had called her name when he was trapped in the rubble. She could detect great subtlety in tone, and she had heard the truth in it, even if he hadn't. *Isabel*, he had said, and the relief in his voice had had nothing to do with where he was.

He lifted his hand, wincing with the effort. She looked at it, then up at him.

'Well?' he said.

'It's just a *house*, Byron.'

His hand was still raised. She lifted her own, and took his, her slim palm against his broad, strong one. Don't say no to me again, she told him silently, her face, her eyes, her hand willing him. If I can take this risk, so can you. 'It's – just – a – *house*.'

His eyes locked on hers, dark and serious, and she felt weak with fear.

Then: 'You know what?' he said, a smile breaking across his features. 'I think so too.'

He pulled her to him and finally, after the briefest pause, he kissed her. Tentatively at first, and then with growing fervour. At last she could breathe in the scent of his skin, give herself up to the pleasure of being in his arms. He kissed her again, the kiss of a man who owned the world. And Isabel put her arms round his neck, laughing even as she kissed him back, and they stood beside the rubble, wrapped round each other, exulting for some unknown length of time, letting the shadows lengthen as the sheets of music fell from her hand and drifted away, carried on stray breezes into the distance.

The sun had dropped behind the trees when they got back to her car. He would return to work tomorrow. Tonight he would stay with the Delanceys in the little flat above the shop. He would sleep on the sofa. Or downstairs, perhaps. He knew that everything in Nature had a time and place.

It was as they approached the car that he remembered. He removed his arm from Isabel's shoulders and reached down to pick up a large stone. He pulled two crumpled pieces of paper from his pocket, wrapped them round it and, after a moment's hesitation, hurled it into the lake.

'What was that?' she said, perplexed, as she heard the splash.

He was watching the ripples spread outwards and disappear. 'Nothing,' he said, as he dusted off his hands. 'Nothing at all.'

Epilogue

Matt McCarthy never came back to the Bartons. He and his wife went to live in a place close to her parents. The first we knew of it was a couple of days after the collapse when Anthony called at the shop to tell us they were moving. A for-sale sign went up next to their house and it sold within a week. I guess it's not surprising: there was never anything wrong with that house.

Anthony is doing a college course, something to do with car mechanics, and I don't see him much. He was really angry with his folks for a while, but a bit later he told me his dad had had a breakdown and his mum had said there was no point in punishing people for being human. A young family from Suffolk lives in their house now. They have two children whose toys Thierry sometimes finds in the woods. He likes to deliver them back in the early morning, placing them on windowsills and on the fence, so that they think there are fairies in the trees.

Nicholas – we call him Nicholas as we ended up seeing him pretty well every day while the development went up – didn't want to buy Anthony's parents' house, even though Mr Todd, the estate agent, told him he could have made a killing. He used to go a bit odd when anyone mentioned the McCarthys, but then loads of people did for a while. He's gone off to do other developments in London. The new neighbours are okay. We don't have much to do with them.

No one was prosecuted for what happened to the Spanish House. The investigators told us it was hard to say what had caused the collapse, given that the house had been neglected for so long. They found traces of woodworm and rot in the timbers, and told us you can't prosecute someone for shoddy building work. Mum didn't push it. She said she wanted to leave the whole sorry episode in the past, where it belonged.

She's doing okay. She goes to London twice a week on the train to play with the orchestra and she no longer grows vegetables. She buys them from the Cousins, and says it gives her great pleasure to do so.

Byron moved out of his mobile home last spring. He lives in a tied cottage that he got with his new job managing an estate a few miles the other side of Long Barton. On Thursdays and Fridays he manages the land round the Spanish House development and he usually stays with us at weekends. I told Mum I didn't mind if he moved in (it's not like me and Thierry hadn't guessed – we're not stupid) and, besides, I'll probably go to college next year, but she said they were happy as they were. Anyway, she said, everyone needs a bit of space, and Byron more than most. When he's not working, he teaches people about trees, how to cut them to make them grow, what plants you can eat, that kind of stuff. He and Thierry are always outside, digging things up or planting.

You can't see anything of the Spanish House any more. For just over a year now we've lived in one of the new houses by the lake, one of eight, all separated by a good stretch of land and a spindly privet hedge that never grew in quite the way the architect's drawings promised. It's not a particularly beautiful house. It has four bedrooms and an okay garden, which Thierry and Pepper have pretty well destroyed with their football, and inside there's nothing much in the way of decoration – no beams, no cornicing. My mum says it's a 'bog-standard, low-maintenance, totally ordinary' kind of house, and when people look at her strangely, wondering why she's so pleased to say that, when everyone else boasts of square footage and period features, she gets that look in her eye, that look she gets before she starts to laugh.

And then she goes off and does something more interesting.

Acknowledgements

Thanks to Karin Leishman and Matthew Souter of the Alberni Quartet, whose musical brilliance and magical home helped inspire this book.

My gratitude as always to my agent Sheila Crowley, as well as Linda Shaughnessy, Teresa Nicholls and Rob Kraitt of APWatt. Thanks to Carolyn Mays for her editing skills and continuing friendship, as well as Lucy Hale, Auriol Bishop, Leni Fostiropolous, Kate Howard, Jamie Hodder-Williams and all the Hodder staff, especially sales.

Thanks for your continuing faith in me. My gratitude also to Hazel Orme – the most meticulous eye in publishing.

Thanks also, in no particular order, to Tony Chapman, Drew Hazell, Barbara Ralph, Fiona Turner, Chris Cheel, Hannah Collins, Jenny Colgan, Cathy Runciman, and all the members of Writersblock.

Grateful acknowledgement to Cambridge University Press for permission to reproduce an extract from *Letter to Lady Cynthia Asquith* by D. H. Lawrence.

Thanks to my family: Lizzie and Brian Sanders, and Jim and Alison Moyes. And most especially to Charles, Saskia, Harry and Lockie, my favourite, favourite people.

Finally, thank you to the staff of the Emmeline Centre, Addenbrookes Hospital Trust, especially Patrick Axon, who, during the writing of this book, changed our lives completely.